"I Want to Father Your Child."

Taylor turned as white as a witness caught lying on cross-examination. She ran her tongue over her lips, lifting her eyes to him, and shook her head. "It's not a good idea."

Taylor paced to the window in the dining area, then back again. "How am I supposed to look my sister in the eye if I sleep with her husband?" she asked softly.

Mason stepped over to her and put both hands on her shoulders. Tenderly, he said, "You know I'm committed to Jillian. But she'll never have children. You and I both want a child. Why shouldn't we have that?"

TWO SISTERS

NANCY WAGNER

AVON BOOKS ◆ NEW YORK

TWO SISTERS is an original publication of Avon Books. This work has never before appeared in book form. This work is a novel. Any similarity to actual persons or events is purely coincidental.

AVON BOOKS
A division of
The Hearst Corporation
1350 Avenue of the Americas
New York, New York 10019

Copyright © 1993 by Nancy Wagner
Inside cover author photo by Debbi De Mont
Published by arrangement with the author
Library of Congress Catalog Card Number: 93-90234
ISBN: 0-380-76456-3

First Avon Books Printing: September 1993

AVON TRADEMARK REG. U.S. PAT. OFF. AND IN OTHER COUNTRIES, MARCA REGISTRADA, HECHO EN U.S.A.

Printed in the U.S.A.

RA   10 9 8 7 6 5 4 3 2 1

For Iris

With Special Thanks

To my sisters-in-writing
Mary Augustyn
Olga Gonzales Bicos
Deborah Harmse
Maryann O'Brien
and
Meryl Sawyer

" . . . Above all things
Truth beareth away the Victory . . . "

—Inscription, The New York Central Public Library,
I Edras 3:12

Chapter 1

TAYLOR DRUMMOND WONDERED, NOT FOR the first time that evening, whether her sister knew her secret.

As she bantered with her co-anchor, and tossed the show to the weatherman, the question continued to nag her. That the thought could disturb her on-air concentration added to Taylor's concern. It also warned her not to underestimate the emotional difficulty of what lay ahead of her that evening.

Burke Washington, her co-anchor, led into the upbeat closing segment, a story of the birth of two white tiger cubs. Burke's smooth face beamed with paternal pride as he spoke. As she watched him, she couldn't help but think what an actor he was. But then, they both were. That was part of their job.

When a viewer turned on "Channel Six News at Ten," he was guaranteed to see and hear a lot of what was wrong with his world. The goal of Channel Six's management was to deliver that news in such a palatable fashion that the next time he felt driven to learn about his world, he'd return to Channel Six. According to their plan, when Taylor Drummond, with her long black hair, deep blue eyes, pale skin, and rosy cheeks, told a viewer his taxes had risen, his air grown more polluted, and his water was almost undrinkable, the viewer wouldn't switch off the television in disgust. Channel Six: style first, substance second.

Unfortunately for Taylor, management hadn't mentioned any of these theories during her interviews. She credited

her record as an attorney-turned-reporter and her seven
years as a reporter/anchor in smaller markets for landing
her the job at Channel Six. After two weeks in L.A., however, she was beginning to learn better.

Taylor realized Burke was wrapping up. She quickly
smiled at him, wished everyone a good weekend, and said
good night to the citizens of Los Angeles.

"That's a wrap," called the stage manager. A flurry of
movement and voices broke out on the news set. Camera
operators, eager to begin Friday night partying, slung covers over their equipment. Taylor lifted the hot weight of
her hair from her neck and watched the bustle for a moment, postponing the inevitable.

With a sheaf of papers, she fanned away the heat of the
lights. She wished her sister had chosen any restaurant in
town other than the one she had picked for their reunion.
Did Jillian suspect? Had she picked the Pacific Dining Car
as a not-so-subtle way of letting Taylor know?

"Sid wants to see ya," said the stage manager.

Taylor let her hair fall back over her shoulders. "Now?"

The woman grimaced and nodded. "Yeah," she said,
managing to convey sympathy in that one syllable.

"Sid?" Leaning over from his seat next to her, Burke
Washington thrust his seamless face and moussed blond
hair uncomfortably close. "On his bad side already, are
we?"

Taylor ignored Burke and nodded at the stage manager.
She paused as the audio guy, a gnome who might have
worked with David Sarnoff in RCA's infancy, collected her
microphone, then she rose.

"Face the music, Drummond," said Burke, easing his
six-foot bulk from the chair. The square-cut diamond he
wore on his right pinky winked once before the lighting
director killed the lights over the anchor desk. "Whatever
it is you've done, you should've known better. Even if you
do look like Snow White, you've turned a few too many
pages on the calendar to be making waves in this business."

"I'll keep your advice in mind." Taylor turned and,

mindful of the wires and cables that lay across the floor, headed for the station manager's office.

She secretly enjoyed the nickname Snow White, a tag that had followed her around for years, prompted by her long black hair, white skin, and an inability to control a blush that painted her face with swatches of bright pink worthy of a Franklin Mint version of the fairy-tale character. But on Burke's lips the name was an insult.

She knew she had to expect age jokes in a business that idolized youth. She was two years and two weeks younger than Burke's forty. Lines on men's faces counted for wisdom. Who would have believed Walter Cronkite if he'd had an eye job?

She wished Sid went home at a normal time. No other station manager she'd ever met or heard of hung around the station the way Sid Pordsky did. Of course, he wasn't your garden-variety manager. If he hadn't muttered, during her interview with him and the other top brass, "She's bumping forty and doesn't have the fucking experience to handle the job," she might have stayed firmly put in Boston. But Taylor never could resist a challenge.

An arm wrapped around her waist and she jumped. The arm tightened. Taylor, five feet six, looked down to Sid Pordsky's bald head and wrinkled face. As usual, he sported a baggy suit that gave him the appearance of a chorus member in *Zoot Suit*.

"Just the chick I want to see," said Sid.

Taylor worked herself free from his clasp as he ushered her into his office, pointed to the sofa, and shut the door. A bank of monitors across one office wall blared late night talk programs and reruns of old police shows and comedies. Sid slapped the mute button on his remote.

Sitting on the ruby leather sofa, she could see the characters moving through their roles, voiceless faces putting America to sleep. She forced her attention back to Sid, focusing on his mustache. If she followed it as it dipped and bobbed, she wouldn't see the visions on the opposite wall.

"Babe," said Sid, moving over to perch on the arm of the sofa, "we need to talk."

Taylor looked at her watch. "Sure, but I'm meeting some friends for a late supper."

"Food. Goddamn food. How can you eat this late at night?" He vaulted from the edge of the couch and paced, two steps left, two steps back. He pulled on the waist of his trousers. Without seeming to notice, he undid his leather belt and notched it more tightly. "A lot of people pushed for you to get this spot." He looked away, and Taylor wondered whether he would have the audacity to include himself in that number. He dropped to the seat beside her. "And you have the potential to be good."

Taylor smiled inwardly. She pushed her hair back over her shoulder. "So what's the problem?"

"Ten days you're here, and sources tell me you're already asking why there's no goddamn day care. You don't even have a squalling brat and you're asking." He peered at her. "Unless there's something I don't know?"

She dropped her gaze from his mustache and crossed her legs. Tell Sid? No way. The leather couch crackled. Shaking her head, she smiled, as if he had made a joke.

"Why, then?"

Why? A bouquet of roses sent by a lover didn't touch her senses the way the fresh smell of an infant dusted in baby powder did. She stretched her neck, first to the right, then to the left, thinking of the best way to answer Sid. Right now wasn't the moment for the truth; she needed time. An image of "Ozzie and Harriet" mocked her from across the room.

"Dorothy showed me her children's pictures when she was doing my makeup. She told me how she misses seeing them grow up." A lame story, but it would have to do.

"From that you get a day-care center?"

She nodded again. So Sid didn't like kids. A minor complication compared to the other hurdles she faced. Not that she'd raise her child in a television studio. One hour around someone with a vocabulary like Sid's and the child would be swearing before she learned to say mommy.

He chewed on one end of his mustache, then snatched the silk handkerchief from his breast pocket and used it to blow his nose. "Don't get all misty-eyed on me. Can't fucking stand it. Snotty-nosed brats. Think of the liability." He tossed the silk square into the trash. "Drop it for now, okay?"

She opened her mouth, then thought better of objecting. "Sure, Sid, no problem."

He leaned toward her. "Babe, don't get me wrong. I don't care what you do, as long as you let those blue eyes of yours reach out and touch every fucking viewer. Let him feel your heart. Let him fall in love with you. Let him think you'll lay your hair—which, by the way, you ought to hack a few inches off—over his fat ass as soon as the news is over. Ratings, babe, come from sex as much as from being the first to show some damn building on fire." Jabbing a short finger for emphasis, Sid continued, "But don't forget about Hutch when you start trying to rock the boat. Remember him? Grady Hutchings, the guy who owns you and me and all this fancy equipment. He didn't funnel his fortune into this station so his new star anchor could futz around with a kindergarten."

"You certainly have a way of painting a picture."

"I wasn't a salesman all those years for nothing." Sid laughed and stood up. "File it away. Now get out of here. Go meet your lover."

"I'm meeting my sister and her husband." She said it stiffly, as if the clarification mattered.

Sid moved back to his desk and picked up a folder of computer printouts. Flipping through the pages, his back to her, he muttered, "Your love life's no business of mine."

The cacophony of Friday night on Hollywood's Sunset Boulevard assailed Taylor as soon as she stepped outside the insulated world of the studio. Horns demanded attention and got none, music screamed its assault from slowly passing cars and pickup trucks loaded with kids with nowhere else to go to celebrate their rowdiness. The night air wafted through her skin and warmed her lungs. Back in Boston, she'd be bundled in a winter coat. Now she strode to her car in a thin silk dress, jacket thrown over her shoulder, inhaling the unmistakable scent of a Hollywood night. Exhaust fumes. Jasmine. Alcohol and urine. She walked by an old man huddled against the street side of the parking lot fence. The city seemed sadder and yet flashier than it had seven years ago. More poor people; twice as many Mercedes-Benzes.

She herself had been wooed back by the promise of riches and fame. No; in her honest moments, she knew it was more than money or the thrill of the evening anchor job. It was time to come home.

After guiding her BMW out of the chain-link-fortified parking lot, Taylor worked her way down Sunset to the Hollywood Freeway, then flowed with the busy late night traffic toward downtown. She headed south on Alvarado. At night, this section of the city seemed to belong to an older world. Not yet discovered by the high-rise builders, the timeworn storefronts hugged the streets; most were dark, put to bed for the night with iron grilles.

She had locked and barred her heart in a similar fashion. The time had come to set herself free from the feelings that had sent her into self-imposed exile. For seven years she had avoided seeing her sister and Mason together, as a couple, as husband and wife. With her schedule at local stations, excuses had been easy to come by. She worked holidays, and rarely took vacations.

Taylor slowed to let another car pull into the restaurant lot in front of her, wishing she had insisted the three of them meet somewhere else, and not after her ten-o'clock newscast. She had last seen her sister two years ago, when Jillian had dropped in on her in Boston, complained about the humidity, pronounced the seafood not quite as good as she'd expected, and departed abruptly. After two years, what was one more day?

Taylor left her car with the valet, and the past seven years slipped away. She headed inside, to meet the only man she had ever loved. A laughing couple came out the door; the woman leaned on the man's arm and smiled into his eyes. Catching hold of the door and watching them pass, Taylor felt the long-damped pain rise and slash through her. Inside the restaurant, it wasn't Mason her lover waiting, but Mason her brother-in-law, with her sister by his side.

Mason Reed unfastened the button on his hand-tailored jacket and glanced around the Wine Room. For some reason, that area of the Pacific Dining Car always seemed more relaxed. Even when the restaurant rang with the laughter and raucous talk of the attorneys and finance-types who frequented the place, the Wine Room kept an air of quietude about it. One of his fellow attorneys had pointed out that if you got the bad table, the one next to the ladies' room, you could compensate for it by picking out a woman to make a move on.

Swirling the Chardonnay Los Carneros in his wineglass, he admired the play of light on the surface of the liquid. He'd suggested champagne, but his wife had wrinkled her delicate nose and asked the waiter for a double Stoli on the rocks. She'd been doing that a lot lately—both the gesture and the drinking.

Jillian pulled a compact from her purse. Mason watched as she fussed over her face. "You look fine," he said, without stopping to consider whether it was true.

Not looking at him, she said, "I do not. I'm all washed-out." She snapped shut the compact. "The lighting in here is terrible. I look ten years older."

Mason tweaked a heavy strand of her white-blond hair away from her face and studied the peach and gold of her complexion. She didn't even look her thirty years. He was about to tell her so when he caught himself. When Jillian wanted to put herself down, words of reassurance from him only increased her self-derision.

She dipped her chin downward, a move she had been making more and more in their increasingly frequent arguments. Her hair closed like a curtain over her face. He dropped his hand. Jillian was walling herself off from him, and he could find no way in.

She put away her compact, swallowed more vodka, and wiggled her glass at a passing waiter.

His peripheral vision was working well tonight. Mason watched a tall redhead pass his booth. She wore a silk suit that flowed with each thrust of her slim hips. For some reason, the motion made him think of Taylor, but he quickly put that thought from his mind. Taylor's return to Los Angeles had nothing to do with him.

"Did I mention Mrs. Simpson gave notice?"

"What?" Mason heard his wife's voice, without catching the meaning of the words.

"She's leaving. Moving to San Diego to take care of her new grandchild."

"Oh."

Jillian plonked her vodka glass down on the tablecloth. "I have to suffer through finding a new housekeeper, and all you can say is 'oh'?"

Forcing his attention back to his wife, he thought with regret of the lost time when his lovely wife had so filled his vision that no other women existed for him. No longer was he captivated by every word she uttered in that throaty voice he'd once found so intriguing.

"I'm sorry, sweetheart. I've been preoccupied." Mason reached for her hand and stroked the smooth top of it with his fingertips. He leaned toward her, so that his head was turned away from any outside distractions.

Taylor found them like that.

They looked for all the world like two lovers shielding themselves from the crass interruptions of those who do not live on the same rosy cloud. She immediately felt embarrassed by her midnight imaginings of finding the two of them at each other's throats, and Jillian ready to release Mason to more deserving and loving arms. In a too bright voice, Taylor said, "Hello, you two lovebirds."

Mason shifted away from Jillian and rose from the booth in one smooth motion. "Taylor, welcome back."

No other man filled space quite the way he did. He was built with the breadth of a linebacker, yet he moved lightly, a quarterback in control of his field. He opened his arms and took her into their shelter for a homecoming embrace. As he touched his lips to her cheek, she noticed new lines radiated from the corners of his eyes. The lines she remembered had been born of laughter, had edged the eyes she had always thought of as maple syrup brown. He didn't look as if he'd been laughing much lately.

She gave him a sisterly peck on the cheek, stepped back, and turned to Jillian, who had scooted to the outer edge of the booth.

As her younger sister stood, Taylor reached for her and drew her into a silent hug. She could feel the bones in her sister's back, little knobs marking the passage of her spine up her body. "It's good to be together again." At arm's length, she studied her. "You're so skinny! Don't you eat?"

Jillian broke free. "No mothering, okay?"

Taylor nodded, but took another long look. Jillian had always had the lithe build of a model, but now, except for her always generous bust, her body seemed unhealthily thin.

They stood, staring at each other in the way people do at reunions and funerals. Too much to say and no skill with which to speak the words. Jillian fractured the silence with a half laugh, shepherding them back into their booth. She also waved over the waiter and ordered a bottle of champagne.

Taylor thought Mason gave Jillian an irritated look after the waiter stepped away. Well, even lovebirds had disagreements. "It's been so long. Tell me everything you've been up to."

"The usual," said Jillian.

The usual? After two years, that's all her sister could say? "Fill me in. At least the highlights."

"Mason works. A lot. I do aerobics and show myself at all the necessary luncheons." Jillian held her cocktail glass with two manicured hands and dipped her head. Her blond pageboy swung forward. When she lifted her head, her shoulders hunched up almost to her ears. In an elaborately casual voice, she concluded, "Like I said, the usual."

Taylor glanced at Mason, but his expression was unreadable.

The waiter, a lanky man who looked as if he'd be more at ease roping steers than serving steaks on a platter, arrived and opened the champagne.

Mason picked up his glass and asked, "Anyone want to propose a toast?"

Taylor looked at him, then at her sister, who had just drained her cocktail glass.

Jillian switched glasses and said, "To Mother, who made us what we are today."

Taylor lowered her glass. "Why should I drink to that?"

"Why not? It's true." Jillian stared at her, her blue eyes open in her perfected look of innocence that Taylor remembered all too well.

She had a point; malevolent, but valid. Her mother, with her countless stories about how much cuter or more coordinated or charming Jillian was, had shaped Taylor's life. Only, Taylor didn't think it a fact worth celebrating. Her successes she owed to her own determination to prove herself worthwhile, capable, and lovable. Some people might say she should thank the rejection that had forged her will to succeed, but she hadn't developed a large enough heart for that level of forgiveness.

"How about a different toast instead of ten rounds in the ring?" asked Mason.

"Are you siding with Taylor?" Jillian turned her challenge to her husband. She seemed to need to spar with someone.

"Jillian." Taylor couldn't help the admonition that came through in her voice. One side of her sister was sweetness and light; but the other, the nasty obverse of her personality, always seemed to sidle out in Taylor's presence. The more it showed, the more Taylor played big sister; the more she mothered and fussed, the more Jillian resented her. Even after a two-year hiatus, Taylor found herself once again feeding the cycle.

"If you have something to say about the way I talk to my husband, keep it to yourself."

"Why don't you both knock it off?" Mason set his glass back on the table. "You've been with each other all of what, ten minutes? I've never understood you two. My brothers and sisters never act like this. Why can't you get along? Away from each other, you're two of the nicest women I've ever known."

Jillian tossed her hair away from her face. "Well, you ought to know about that."

Taylor drew in a sharp breath. She wondered how much Mason had told Jillian. She wished she could just come out and ask them, but a sense of propriety, or simply fear of the consequences, kept her silent. Mason's expression gave her no clue. His jaw jutted, but he said nothing in response.

Jillian shrugged. "There's no need to get upset. The past is past, right?"

Taylor thought the look Jillian directed to her was a bit pointed, but before she could respond, her sister turned her full smile on Mason and said, "It's the way we are, dear. Sisters."

Mason lifted his champagne flute. After a moment, they followed. He cocked his head, looking first at Taylor, then at his wife. "To family."

"To family," they echoed.

Taylor felt a moment of relief when Jillian smiled at her over the rim of her glass.

"How's the—"

"How's it feel—"

Taylor and Mason laughed. He said, "You first."

"How's the firm?"

"Changing a bit. Wallace retired."

"About time." Taylor puckered her lips in distaste. "I wish he'd retired when I was a lowly associate. The hell that man used to put me through! He constantly pestered me to cut my hair. He loved to tell me that no client would take a princess in a tower seriously."

Mason smiled. "I'm glad you didn't."

Jillian said, "You could use a trim."

"If you'd stayed," Mason said, "you might have treated the new flesh exactly the same way. Some of those first-year associates look like teenagers." He grimaced. "They act like it, too."

"Law talk," said Jillian, wrinkling her nose and turning her head.

"Spoken like a man who's grown old and set in his ways." Taylor wanted to lean across the table and smooth his forehead. "Are you still happy there?"

"For the moment." Mason ran his fingers through his hair, lifting the dense black strands away from his high forehead. "Now, what about you?"

The return of the waiter, carrying the brass stanchion listing the specials, interrupted them. Taylor chose the first item on the board, heedless of the food. She was back in L.A., sitting across from Mason, managing to conduct a normal conversation. Maybe she would be okay. She could admire him, respect him, thrill to watching the smile that lit his eyes—and constantly remind herself how very married he was. She could do it. She was strong.

When her steak arrived, Taylor glanced at the green salad placed in front of her sister. "Is that all you're having?"

Jillian shrugged. "It's my usual."

"No wonder you're skin and bones." Taylor sliced into her medium-rare filet mignon. "You're living on rabbit food." She started to offer some of her steak to her sister, but stopped when she saw Jillian's stony look.

"Sorry, sorry. That was rude of me. But you know me and my manners." Taylor laid her fork on the side of her plate. "Speaking of manners, have you talked to Mother recently?"

Jillian smiled faintly. "Very funny, Taylor. The answer is no."

Taylor felt Mason looking back and forth at the two of them. She caught him at it; her stare demanded to know what was going on.

"Your mother came to visit us recently. We, uh, failed to meet her standards," he said, barely concealing a grin.

"Let me guess. You didn't take her to the latest 'in' restaurants, you bought ballet tickets that weren't in the orchestra section, and you didn't have the right color of toilet paper in the guest bath."

Mason laughed.

Jillian dropped her fork. "I don't find it very amusing. I don't like to upset Mother."

Taylor reached across the table and placed one hand on top of her sister's. "Of course not." Withdrawing her hand, she added, "But you know that you and I have never had the same type of relationship with her." *Talk about an understatement.*

"You were always too smart for her, weren't you?"

"Frankly, she never cared whether I lived or died."

"You got to do whatever you wanted, and I had to toe the line every minute of my life. Look at you—you're famous now. Turn on the TV, and who do you see? Mother's favorite renegade." Jillian's chin quivered. She pushed on her husband's elbow, motioning for him to stand to let her out of the booth, then headed in the direction of the ladies' room.

Taylor realized she'd been holding her breath. She looked at Mason, and tried to smile.

"Forgive her," he said, massaging his temples with his fingertips. "She's been under a lot of stress."

"What's wrong?"

He dropped his hands. "I don't know. The last few months she just hasn't been herself. I honestly don't understand her anymore." He took a sip of water. "Hell of a thing for a husband to confess, isn't it?"

Taylor flashed on the image of the two of them as she had found them earlier. That initial picture had fragmented, and the bits and pieces didn't add up to the whole. Jillian certainly seemed more on edge than she had two years ago. Though she and her sister had never gotten along particularly well, tonight's bickering carried greater hostility than Taylor remembered.

Then the thought hit her. "Do you think she's pregnant?" As soon as she said the words, she knew it couldn't be. Jillian was too skinny, all bones and no flesh.

Mason shook his head and scowled. "No. She never misses her pill." He flushed.

Taylor felt like she'd been caught peeking through a keyhole. Some private matters were better left undisclosed. "It was just a thought. You know we've never been the best of pals, but I'll try harder."

He nodded. "Maybe that will help." He fingered the stem of his glass, his gaze fixed on the bubbles rising to the top of the liquid. He started to speak, then pressed his lips together.

Taylor nervously crossed and uncrossed her ankles under the table, wishing desperately to break the silence, worrying over her sister, wondering about the bitterness in Mason's voice, yet wanting even more to know the words Mason wasn't uttering.

When he spoke, he addressed the tablecloth. "It is good to see you again, Taylor."

Taylor joined Mason in his scrutiny of the table linens. Disappointment warred with relief that he'd said nothing more, confirming that to him the past was, as Jillian phrased it, "past." To her, it was more than good to see him again. It was so very painful. Choosing her words carefully and maintaining a polite, neutral tone, she said, "I thought about this job offer for a long time, but I think coming back here was the right choice."

"I think so," he said with a rush of warmth.

Their eyes met then, and the heat suffusing her body caused Taylor to suffer serious doubts as to the wisdom of that decision. She quickly looked away, and with relief, saw Jillian returning. She watched as her sister glided, rather than walked, past the other booths. Several male heads followed her progress, also. Jillian wore her black silk jumpsuit cinched in at the waist, then bloused loosely over the belt. Blond hair grazed an upturned collar. The years of enforced ballet lessons showed in her graceful control. From a distance she looked serene. The image crumbled as she moved jerkily across the seat and retreated into the corner of the booth.

"I've decided," Jillian said, in a bored tone, "to give

both of you a birthday party. A joint one, two weeks from now."

Taylor looked at her sister, then over at Mason.

Jillian turned her blue eyes, too large in her thin face, toward Taylor. "You can meet some men. It will be good for you."

"I don't object to that," said Taylor, thinking her sister was the last person in the world she wanted to set her up with anyone.

"You're going to be thirty-eight, and I think it's time you were married."

"Did you read this on the bathroom wall?" asked Mason.

Jillian emptied her champagne glass and waved one hand over the plate in front of her. "You have to accept inspiration when it strikes you. But lawyers wouldn't know about that stuff. Too technical, too by-the-book." She smiled, and clasped her hands together on the tabletop, a child waiting for dessert. "I operate on impulse."

Chapter 2

"IMPULSE."

Mason threw another punch at the heavy sparring bag. *Impulse. What in the hell did Jillian mean by that crack last night?* Since the day they had returned from their honeymoon seven years ago, his wife had been the most ordered creature he had ever known. Once upon a time, she might have accurately described herself as impulsive, but along with her wedding ring, she donned a cloak of middle-class respectability.

Dancing like an infidel crossing hot coals, he pelted the canvas deadweight with quick jabs. On their first date, Jillian had crowded his Karmann Ghia with a giant kite. At Venice Beach they skipped and laughed as the kite flew high above the sand. She made him forget the nagging ache that plagued him whenever he thought of Taylor and how he had let her go.

Taylor.

He set upon the bag with a flurry of punches, then stopped to wipe the sweat from his face with his forearm. Taylor, whom he hadn't seen in seven years, had grown into her beauty, rather than out of it as some women do. Her hair was as velvety as the fur of a kitten, and long enough for a man to drown in. Where his wife had whittled her body to skeletal angles that drove him away, Taylor maintained a softness that begged to be fitted against another willing body.

Mason jerked to a halt, and considered turning his gloved hands against his own face. He had no business thinking of Taylor in those terms. Jillian had said it last night: The past was past. He had to concentrate on making his marriage work.

For the first few years, marriage had been easy. Jillian did everything for his benefit—gave dinner parties envied by all the other partners of his firm, kept her size-two figure zealously intact, redecorated their house each time they sold and moved up. He had wanted to marry a woman who enjoyed performing those responsibilities, a woman like his mother, so he couldn't complain when that was what he got. Yet, as the years passed, he wanted more. He wanted a soul mate, not a concierge.

As Mason thought about the downhill path his marriage had taken over the last year or so, he lashed out with a left jab, followed by a right hook, then another jab. Sex. Jillian never wanted to do it. She'd been a nympho in their early years together, but now she always had some excuse. A part of him accepted that married life gradually lost the spark of courtship, as it deepened and steadied, preparing for the realities of the three A.M. feeding and walking the floor with a teething child. But they had no babies, and Jillian refused to discuss pregnancy. He might as well be living in a monastery.

"Ease up, Reed," called a voice from across the room.

Mason ceased his onslaught of jabs and punches, and cradled his numbed hands and wrists against his ribs. His vision cleared. With one gloved hand, he swiped at the salty moisture trickling past the cotton sweatband he wore around his forehead. He looked across the wooden floor crowded with boxing equipment, racks of free weights, and benches, to where Fielding Sanderson stood, a jump rope in one black hand. "Sometimes I forget myself."

Fielding grasped one handle of the rope in each hand. "Sometimes that's a bad thing to do." He spun the rope and jumped, his feet barely touching the floor as he lifted them with each rotation, until finally he called, "One hundred," and stopped.

Mason watched for signs of heavy breathing and saw none. "Do you understand women?" He hated to say something so corny, but he couldn't help himself.

Fielding dropped the rope and walked over. "Women, huh? Is that the reason I found you at your office when I called at the crack of dawn on a Saturday morning?"

Mason began removing his gloves. "I had some work to take care of."

"Things bad at home?" Fielding hefted a fifty-pound barbell and worked his left bicep with a concentrated curl.

For such a skinny guy, he had strength. Hidden strength, like a steel center inside a copper wire. Mason fixed his attention on the laces of his left glove. He wanted to express his frustration and confusion. Fielding, though he wasn't in practice, was a psychologist. That was no reason to dump his personal problems in his friend's lap, though. Mason hated being cornered at cocktail parties by people wanting free legal advice, so he didn't want to use Fielding in a similar fashion. But talking to Fielding as a friend wasn't abusing his services as a shrink, he reasoned. "It's just a feeling, nothing I can put my finger on."

Fielding switched the barbell to his right hand. "Feelings usually come from something specific. You may not know what, but the cause is there."

"Maybe I don't want to know."

"But you will. Your wife will let you know. She may not come right out and say it, but she'll drop hints. Women are like that. They worry about not pleasing you, yet they'll cheat on you, and still fix your favorite breakfast the next day. Then burn the toast, burst into tears, and blame it on you."

Mason cocked his head toward his friend. "It sounds to me as if more than the toast got burned."

"We're talking about you, not me." He replaced the weight in the rack. "What do you think the problem is?"

"Jillian's just not herself. And she won't talk about having a baby. Christ, we've been married almost seven years. She's thirty years old. You'd think she'd be worried about waiting too long."

"Thirty's young. Sure you're not the one who's worried?"

Mason, both gloves off, wiped his fingers with a sweaty

towel. He noticed that his hands trembled. He extended the fingers of his right hand, then flexed. It was a satisfying feeling; the shaking proved he was alive.

A slice of late afternoon sun filtering through a dirt-glazed window caught Fielding in its mote-stream. His skin turned golden brown. Fielding was a good-looking man, a successful man by any measure, yet his wife had left him.

"Why'd your wife leave you?"

Fielding jerked his head toward Mason and shrugged.

The pain in his friend's expression embarrassed Mason. "That was none of my business. Forget I asked."

The black man leaned against the canvas bag, arms crossed in front of his bare chest. "It's never just one thing. Keshia left me a couple of times before she made it stick." He moved out of the way of another man who wanted to use the sparring bag. "Let's shower and get out of here."

Mason gathered his discarded T-shirt and towel. His fingers still shaking, he followed Fielding to the cramped locker room. A friend of Fielding's ran the storefront gym wedged in on a side street in the flower district of downtown Los Angeles. Mason was a member of the L.A. Athletic Club, courtesy of his law firm, and had worked out in the club's diligently refined atmosphere until he struck up a friendship with Fielding earlier that year. Fielding had introduced him to Oscar's Place, and now Mason returned to the Athletic Club only when he had to meet the social demands senior partner status placed on him. The bare concrete of the walls, the aged wooden floor, the mildewed shower area where the water always ran cold—these all satisfied Mason more than the pampering provided by the Athletic Club.

Mason jerked open his locker. A metallic echo rattled along the bank of lockers lining the wall at a drunken angle. Graffiti sprawled over most of the surface. Oscar had gotten the lockers cheap from a junior high school about to be razed for redevelopment.

At the open shower stall across from the lockers, a man

with back muscles like cables soaped his head and sang. "Maria, Maria, I just met a girl named Maria—"

"Put a cork in it, Chico," Fielding called. "We don't want to hear about your fantasy life."

The man turned, shampoo suds streaming into his eyes. "Shit! If it ain't the Dominoes." He swabbed water over his eyes with pudgy fingers. "What the hell you suburban types doing here on a Saturday? Shouldn't you be home mowing the lawn?" He laughed at his own humor, and advanced toward them, grabbing a towel from a hook and swiping at the water and soap dripping from his head.

Mason and Fielding exchanged a glance, and said together, "The gardener comes twice a week."

"You dickheads. I'm out there on the streets risking getting my ass shot off every day while you sit behind your fancy desks and talk about justice." He grabbed Mason by the neck and twisted him under one bulging arm.

Mason relaxed into the man's grip, then slipped easily from his hold. He punched Chico on the shoulder. "Better not let your crooks get away so easily." He stripped and stepped into the stream of cold water that Chico had left running.

"This is my neighborhood, but why do you guys hang out here?"

Fielding stepped under the second shower head and turned it on. Only a trickle of water appeared. "I like it. What about you, Mason?"

Mason let water run in his mouth, then blew it out. Stepping from the shower, he shook his hair, scattering the droplets around the room. Padding back to the only bench, he breathed in the stench fermented by male bodies in a closed space. "There aren't any rules here."

Fielding turned off the shower. "I'm used to that, but Mason here, he still thinks it's a novelty."

"Slumming buttheads." Chico slipped into the last of his shabby clothing.

"Talk about slumming," said Mason, pointing at Chico. "What's the costume for?"

Chico looked around. No one else was in the locker

room. "Moved to undercover last week. Get to hang out around the Midnight Mission on Fourth. Tired of rules? Come visit sometime. Really shouldn't have showered." He pulled on a pair of tennis shoes, cut open across the toes and rotted across the heels. "Catch you blue bloods next week."

Mason watched Chico shuffle out. "I kind of like the guy."

"He makes me want to do something useful." Fielding buttoned up his faded Levi's.

He spoke in a straightforward tone, but Mason couldn't tell whether he was joking or serious. "You don't think what you do is important?"

Fielding ran his fingers over the black mat of his hair, then wiped the moisture off on his pant leg. "I started off thinking how great I was. I could teach any lawyer about juries. Who to pick. What to look for to ensure the verdict of his choice. Whether to wear a striped tie with a brown suit or paisley with black."

"You know damn well the mock trial you conducted helped us save Stratiscon from a ten-million-dollar judgment."

"Like I said, real meaningful." Fielding held up a hand. "No, don't start. I realize I provide a legitimate service. God knows it makes me a lot of money, but meaningful? No. I need something else, but I'm not sure what." He propped a knee on the scarred bench and rested an elbow against it. "The first time I opened a branch office, I got a real thrill. Granny's little boy was going to be rich. I've more offices than I can keep track of, and I'm—"

"Bored?"

Fielding nodded, then shrugged into his UCLA Bruins sweatshirt. "I'm even thinking of a new line of work."

"Yeah?"

"Investigation. PI stuff."

Mason paused. "Why that?"

"I would be drawing upon my psych training, which makes sense. You know I gave up my practice before starting my trial consulting service." Fielding looked across the room, as if seeing a far distance. "I got fed up with the problems that never changed. No matter what I did to help people, the problems just kept coming. My Band-Aids didn't hold together shit." He looked back at Mason. "Sometimes I think I should go back into practice, to prove to myself I can face it, but I don't know. I just don't know. So I thought I'd play around with the PI idea."

Mason tucked his red polo shirt into his cords and pitched his gym things into a duffel bag. "Maybe I'll be your first client."

They headed for the door. "Referring to your wife?"

Mason started to nod, then stopped. "Nah, just routine legal matters."

"Sure, I'll give you a card as soon as I set up shop."

They walked through the gym's street door. The bright morning sun threw the litter-strewn doorways into shadow. Four youngsters who looked as if they should have been playing stickball paraded by, their short hair capped with the red emblem of the Guardian Angels.

Fielding leaned an elbow on the gray metal nub of a parking meter. "About Keshia."

"Hey, I said forget it."

He shook his head. "This one's for me, buddy." He paused while he retrieved a pair of mirror-lensed sunglasses from his Polo canvas bag. "She found Jehovah and I found the bottle." He slid the glasses onto his face.

Mason nodded. He didn't know what to say.

Fielding laughed, a short, sad note that betrayed the pain hidden behind the sunglasses. "I was a drunk, so I can't blame her. After she left, I finally saw the light, but it was too late for us."

"I'm sorry." *Sorry for asking, sorry for making you say it.*

Fielding grinned. "Nobody likes to confess to being a shit." He stepped off the curb.

Mason reached out a hand toward his friend. "Jillian's giving a party in two weeks. I'd like you to come."

"A San Marino party? Shit man, you want to get me lynched?"

Mason hated the "poor black man" routine that Fielding sometimes adopted. "I live in Pasadena, not San Marino. Not that it matters. Yes or no?"

Fielding smiled. "Why not?" He waved and headed for his Porsche.

Mason watched him ease the 1971 911T away from the curb. He drove that car like a grandmother navigating the halls of a nursing home in a walker. What a waste of a 2.2-liter, 135-horsepower, six-cylinder dream machine! Mason tossed his gym bag into his Volvo, hunkered into the seat, and barreled toward a stop sign at the end of the block. A Porsche. He'd buy a Porsche. No, he wouldn't. Where would he put a baby seat in a Porsche?

Jillian squatted at the edge of the friable soil she'd spent weeks double-digging and fertilizing. Mason had been gone all day. He worked long hours, usually six days a week. For that reason alone, she couldn't understand his insistence on having a child. *He* would never be around to see it. She forced the disturbing thought of a baby from her mind and concentrated on the creation of her bulb bed. As she toiled, ideas and images flittered across her consciousness like butterflies sampling a field of wildflowers. While she worked the soil, her communion with the earth filled her senses. The dark images that taunted her at other times rarely forced their way to the surface of her mind.

Leaning back, her bottom resting against the heels of her gardening clogs, she breathed in the odor of freshly turned earth, then sneezed. Dragging her doeskin gardening glove across her face, she smiled. She didn't care whether the gesture smeared her face with a trail of grime. To stop for a tissue would break her rhythm. She wanted to get the rest of the bulbs into the bed before quitting for the day, but the failing light nagged at her. She had to hurry. Was she going somewhere with Mason tonight? Was she supposed to be dressed to go by the time he came home?

Bending forward again, she dropped a corm into its waiting pocket, filled the hole, and tamped the earth to

seal the flower's winter bed. As she paused to open another sack of bonemeal, a mental picture of a naked man,
fat and aroused and laughing at her with shaking jowls,
played to the unwilling audience of her mind. She shook
her head and blinked her eyelids before reaching for the
next bulb. That man was in the past; she mustn't think of
him now.

"Jill, we're due at the Hempels' in thirty minutes!"

She dropped the dirt-covered bulb planter and rocked
back on her heels. "I'll be ready. I'm just finishing." She
hadn't even heard Mason arrive.

"I'm going to change. You want a drink before we go?"

Nodding, she jumped up, brushing dirt off her khaki
pants. "I'm sorry I didn't realize how late it was."

"Get ready right away, and we'll be fine." He headed
into the house.

Jillian stared after him, willing him to look back at her
and smile. She hadn't meant to be late. She piled her tools
and remaining bulbs into the garden cart and pushed it into
the potting shed. Abandoning her tools without cleaning
them bothered her, but they'd have to wait until tomorrow.
She didn't like to keep Mason waiting.

"Feeling better today?" he asked when she came into
their bedroom.

Had she not felt well yesterday? Rather than ask him
what he meant, she nodded.

"Good." He stood in front of the cheval glass, adjusting
the knot on his tie. The Hempels believed in the type of
dinner parties that required men to wear ties. "I thought
maybe seeing Taylor again had upset you."

Jillian paused, one leg out of her gardening pants. "Why
would seeing Taylor upset me?" She stripped the pants
from her other leg. "Where did you put my drink?"

"It's on your dressing table."

Helping herself to a swallow of vodka, she padded
across the gray Berber carpet to the bathroom. If her sister upset her, it was only because Taylor tried to play
mother. Do this. Don't do that. Do it my way. Be famous
like me. True, when she first learned about Taylor moving

back, she had suffered a few qualms of uneasiness, as she
pictured Mason renewing his old friendship with her sister.
That fear had dissipated when Jillian carefully analyzed
the situation and concluded that Taylor never had been,
and never would be, Mason's type. After all, her career always came first, and what Mason wanted was a wife in the
most old-fashioned sense of the word.

Wife and wet nurse, she reminded herself. Tipping the
glass to her mouth, she drained the contents. Capturing an
ice cube with her teeth, she concentrated on the searing
cold and the faint echo of Absolut. At one time she had
enjoyed the bracing flavor of good vodka, but lately it
tasted more like medicine.

Mason finished perfecting the knot of his tie. He was relieved that Jillian seemed more herself tonight. Maybe last
night's outburst stemmed from her sister reminding her of
their mother. Jillian had a schizoid attitude toward her
mother; she praised her one day and excoriated her the
next.

Whistling, he followed his wife into the cool interior of
the master bath. He found Jillian in her underwear, the
grime still on her face. He stopped whistling. Dirt-rimmed
fingers gripping the marble counter, she leaned forward,
her face inches from the mirror. An ice cube, sticking from
between clenched teeth, knocked against the mirror, punishing the image of her face. Moisture from the diminish-
ing ice dribbled down the mirror, like saliva from the
mouth of a rabid dog.

"Jillian!"

The ice cube fell to the porcelain sink, skidded around
the circular basin, and clinked against the metal of the
pop-up stopper.

She jumped away from the counter. "You surprised me.
I-I'm almost ready."

"What are you doing?"

She turned on the water and started washing her hands
and face. "Doing? I'm getting ready for the Hempels'."

Mason stared at his wife. Soil streaked her face and
hands. The heavy strands of her blonde hair were tied in

a queue. She had such lovely hair, hair that used to hang halfway down her back. She used to fold it over him, a golden blanket shutting out the rest of the world. He found himself reminded of the evening a year ago when he'd come home from the office late on Friday to find his Rapunzel transformed into a bad imitation of Twiggy. Thank God it had grown back to a normal length.

"The ice cube, Jillian. What were you doing with that ice cube?" He heard his voice rising.

She smiled at him, as if he'd asked her the time. "Exercises."

He thought he'd heard wrong.

"For my face," she said. "Scram, you're making me late."

Blank blue eyes watched him from only a few feet away. He could tell by her look that he was supposed to accept her explanation and drop the subject. If he pursued it, they'd be late for the Hempels'. He nodded and left the bathroom. He'd go along with her for now, but something was definitely wrong with his wife. Thank God he'd invited Fielding to the party Jillian was planning. That was only two weeks away. Maybe he could make some sense out of her.

From the moment Jillian stepped into the marble entry of the Hempels' elegant Library District estate, she smiled and chatted as if she had nothing heavier than her next charity luncheon on her mind. Her shoulders sleek and glimmering above her strapless cocktail dress, she laughed and talked with her dinner partners. Watching her from across and down the table set for twelve, Mason admired his wife. This composed and gracious woman was his wife; not the distraught shadow tapping her face against the bathroom mirror. He forgot his complaints and forgave her the behavior that had been bothering him. Despite their differences of late, he desired and loved his wife.

As they left the party, he hugged her to him before he handed her into their car. She smiled, but didn't return his gesture.

"Did I ever tell you," he said, sliding under the wheel

and believing the words as they left his lips, "how happy you make me?"

Tipping her head to one side, with one thin finger supporting her chin, she studied him in silence, then gifted him with her slow smile, the one he loved to see lighting her face.

The few blocks to their house were obstacles to his burning desire to possess his wife. He skidded through the last right turn, one hand on the wheel as he slipped loose the knot in his black tie. Tonight she wouldn't turn him away. As soon as they stepped inside the passageway from the garage to the main part of the house, he put his arms around her, pulling her to him.

"I love you." He kissed her, softly, as an accompaniment to his words, then more deeply, as he felt her respond. The entry passage opened into a laundry area, and they swayed against the dryer as he pushed aside her silk duster to caress her bare shoulders and back.

"I love you, too." As she breathed the declaration into his kiss, her whispered words tickled his mouth. They reassured him, too.

"Let's go upstairs." Arm in arm, they moved out of the laundry room.

"You go on up. I have to feed the fish."

"The fish?" How could she think of fish at a moment like this?

"Well, Mrs. Simpson isn't here anymore, and there's no point in the fish starving just because I haven't found a new housekeeper yet." She smiled at him, and stroked the side of his jaw. "Go get comfy. I'll be right up."

"Right." He took the narrow back stairs off the kitchen two at a time, anxious to shed his clothing.

Jillian straightened her evening coat and smoothed her hair. She'd tried; she'd really tried hard all night to please him. Mason was easy to please. As long as she performed the role of the picture-perfect wife, he buzzed around, happy, never questioning. Such a strain, though, to smile at all those people who bored her so. Mrs. Hempel needed to lose a good twenty pounds, and her husband, the lech, couldn't keep his knee to himself under the cover of the tablecloth. So many polished faces, gabbling like Lhasa apsos at a Kennel Club show.

Taking the fish flakes, she headed for the den. Except for the light from the wall-length aquarium, the room sat in darkness. She'd insisted, over Mason's objections, on installing the large tank. She couldn't handle a cat or dog, but fish she wanted. The fish, silent onlookers of her life, never demanded anything of her. Even when she forgot to feed them, they kept swimming without complaint.

Before she fed her quiet allies, she moved to the bar built into one of the bookshelves. The solarium contained their entertaining bar, but she kept a small one stocked in the den. From the tiny refrigerator, covered in walnut to match the bookcases, she pulled a bottle of vodka. Unscrewing the lid, she swigged several mouthfuls. She'd been so good all night.

Satisfied for the moment, she sprinkled food into the dispenser, and watched as the fish swam gracefully to nab the particles.

"Are you coming to bed?"

Hearing Mason's voice in the distance, she took one more swallow and replaced the bottle. She said good night to the fish. Before she turned off the lights in the kitchen, she found a spare bottle of sleeping pills and swallowed two.

By the time she finished brushing her teeth and rinsing her face with black soap the number of times prescribed by Laszlo, her head felt disconnected from her body. Satisfactorily so.

Mason was waiting for her. He wore the silk paisley dressing gown she gave him for Christmas two years ago—the one he called pansy-assed. He wore it to please her. He looked so expectant, she couldn't say no. Not the word, anyway.

Her lips felt the touch of his mouth. No other body part conveyed quite the same sensation. Lips against lips. Nice. Better than the twang of vodka. Superior to the cool thrill of ice cream gliding over her tongue.

She almost said yes. To please him, she blocked her mind to the mocking images that played against her eyelids when she let them droop shut. She tried to keep her head from drifting too far away. If she didn't watch, if she didn't know what was going on, she could say yes. But then his lips parted and he tried to breach the barrier of her teeth with his tongue.

Mason wanted her to kiss him, a full-bodied, loving kiss that drew him into a storm of passion—the way she used to kiss him. A sculptor working a chunk of marble with a chisel got more response. Nevertheless, he shrugged off the ridiculous dressing gown and slipped the lace straps of Jillian's negligee from her shoulders, then followed the descent of the fabric with kisses. He'd bent to her navel when she stirred against him.

And yawned.

Straightening, he looked at his wife's sleepy expression.

"Sorry," she said, one hand smothering another yawn. "If I'd known you wanted to make love, I wouldn't have taken a sleeping pill."

He took a step back and said, "You couldn't tell?" Grabbing her hand, he closed it around his erect penis. "I've been like this since the Hempels' served the soup." He held her limp hand against him. She mustered a few languid pats.

He tightened his hold around her hand. "Don't zone out on me tonight, Jillian."

She freed her hand and covered another yawn.

He bit back his annoyance and gathered her in his arms and carried her the two steps to their bed. She wasn't going to put him off again. Especially not tonight, after she had made him want her, reminded him of the way things used to be between them. She watched him, her supine body swaying with the rhythm of the water bed, as he settled next to her.

Pulling her close, he kissed the hollow that shadowed each shoulder bone. She stirred and offered her lips for a kiss. Mason smiled. His wife—his beautiful, desirable wife—wasn't going to turn him out into the cold tonight.

Her kiss held nothing back. She drew him into a frenzy of desire, her open mouth and seeking tongue promising, offering all. When Mason broke away, he kissed Jillian on her eyelids, which had closed, then lowered his mouth to explore the potential of that kiss.

He kissed her breasts, then shifted lower on the bed. For a woman who had once participated so actively in their lovemaking, she had grown strangely reticent and silent. The infrequent times she made love with him, she never spoke. Pushing away those thoughts, he stroked her blond pubic hair and leaned to taste her. He paused and shifted his glance to her face, wanting that exchange of glances that would signal her desire, and afterward, confirm her pleasure—pleasure that was not to be.

His beautiful, desirable wife was sound asleep.

Chapter 3

TAYLOR KNEW THAT GRADY HUTCHINGS, A Texas machine-parts wizard and self-styled takeover king, purchased Channel Six from Tribune Broadcasting for five hundred million dollars. Two of his right-hand men had been present at her interview in Los Angeles. She also knew, from studying news clippings on him, that he prided himself on his rags-to-riches story. What she didn't know was why a man as reputedly savvy as Grady Hutchings had put Sid Pordsky at the helm of his latest enterprise.

Backed against the edge of her chair at the evening news pod, Taylor folded her arms and looked at Sid as if he had just related a joke. Sid simply returned her look, so she said, "You really want me to read a recipe of the week? On the air? During the *news?*"

Sid nodded.

"I don't see it, Sid. Maybe following the commodities report at noon in some two-horse town, but not in Los Angeles. Not me."

Sid grinned at her, his brown eyes almost twinkling. She realized he was enjoying himself. She wondered whether he used the same grin when he tried to persuade a woman to follow him home. Or did he ever try to charm anyone?

He settled a hip onto her desk, then reached under himself to pull a stack of papers free. After tossing them to the other side of Taylor's work area, he said, "Babe, I know you just blew into town a few weeks ago. You're forgetting that L.A. is a small town. It's not the same sort of cosmopolitan, grown-up, son-of-a-bitch kind of town that San Francisco is, or New York. Or, Lord spare us, even

Atlanta, Jawjuh. Everyone here is from somewhere else. And missing it. Peoria. Des Moines. Jonesboro. Those goddamn yuppies spooning down sorbet all have soil from somewhere else under their fingernails."

"What does that have to do with recipes?" She hated to ask, wanting to end their one-on-one. She sensed the newsroom filling up. Activity sounded all around her, but no one approached. The pod where she sat, a large clover-leaf table with space for five people, would usually be occupied at this time of day with the evening news producer and at least one writer. Obviously everyone else knew the signs of Sid on the warpath.

Sid pulled at one side of his drooping mustache, stretching it even farther down the side of his wrinkle-carved face. "You know damn well the closing segment on the newscast is always a fluff piece. It's a sop to the viewers to send them off to bed with a warm fuzzy after we've shown them how fucked up the world is. So why not, once a week, give them something useful? Recipes are useful, especially to women. It's hard to find a man, and once you do, you gotta keep him. How? Classic wisdom—through his stomach." Patting his own cinched-in beltline, he frowned for a moment. Grief and frustration showed in his eyes, then vanished so abruptly, Taylor thought she had imagined the emotions.

Scooting off the desk, Sid said, "Hell, nowadays some of the men want recipes, too."

"Have you conducted any demographic studies on this plan?"

Sid stared, as if she had offered him a plate of dog crap. "Demographics? You educated types are all alike. Always getting offended at blunt words about feeding the audience milksop, yet if the verdict comes couched in fancy terms and charts, you'll shovel the shit out quick enough."

Taylor stiffened, fighting a rush of anger. Working with this man was going to be impossible.

Sid hitched his pleated trousers higher on his skinny hips. "I'm a seat-of-the-pants manager. I learned about life from experience, not from books. Let me tell you about your average Joe out there, Drummond. He doesn't give a flying fuck about who's running Nicaragua or what tight-ass is trying to wedge himself into the governor's mansion." Sid extracted a monogrammed silk handkerchief from his breast pocket. Taylor averted her eyes; she'd seen this move before. "No, your average dick wants to know whether the Dodgers beat the Astros. He wants to see grisly pictures of murdered prostitutes so he can sit on his sagging sofa and tsk-tsk over how fucked up the world is. At the same time, he'll take a good long peek, to make sure he gets an eyeful of the stiff's tits." Into the trash went the handkerchief.

"I'm surprised you didn't share this philosophy with me during my job interview." She had heard rumors that Sid had campaigned for, and practically promised, her anchor job to a female weathercaster from Nashville. Her qualifications: top-heavy with southern charm, the sources said.

He laughed. "Believe me, I would have if I had known how set Grady Hutchings was on hiring you."

In a dry tone, she said, "It's so nice to be wanted." Her life had prepared her for rejection and taught her how to face tougher challenges than Sid Pordsky. She would simply have to outsmart Sid to deliver the type of news she believed in.

Sid was staring at her. "So come on, whaddaya say Channel Six gives the viewers what they really want?"

"Assuming this is what viewers want, why me, Sid?" She knew her answer had to come soon, but she hated his recipe idea. He had picked on her as the female anchor to read the "woman's story." She wasn't about to walk backward in time to the days when females were consigned to society news, garden parties, and weddings of social import.

Sid worked on stretching the other side of his mustache. Taylor figured he was too smart to actually say, "Because you're a woman." He knew the game and walked just under the fraying edges of the rope. "Babe, I could have simply passed the word to the news director, and presto, there would have been your copy to read. But did I do that?" He opened his arms in a wide shrug. "No. And why not? Because you and me, Taylor, we're part of a team."

Some team. Right now he was the goalie and she was the puck. But no rule said she had to be asked her opinion on a weekly feature. From the corner of her eye, she saw Burke Washington stroll into the newsroom, shedding his Burberry coat as he advanced like a king surveying his subjects. "Sid, I appreciate what you said about us being a team." Feeling like a hypocrite, she gave him one of her biggest smiles. "The recipe concept has potential, and I think I have an idea for making it even better."

"Hit me with it."

Stifling a grin, she said, "Let's assume the recipes are really for the female viewers. Watching me telling them how to crack an egg for an omelet can't be too thrilling. But what about watching Burke describe in loving detail the intricate steps of—of—" Taylor floundered, having no idea how to prepare anything more complicated than a tuna sandwich "—cherries jubilee."

Sid actually put both ends of his mustache into his mouth. Then he grinned. "I like it." Bouncing away like a child with a new ball, he moved across the newsroom, patting a few fannies en route.

Taylor turned back to her keyboard and monitor and tried to focus on the lead-in to a story for that night's newscast. Sid had gone away happy—for the moment—but she wondered whether staying at the station was the right thing to do. It wasn't in her nature to back down from a challenge, but maybe fate was offering her a hint. Scram. Leave L.A. now. Closing her eyes briefly, she pictured Mason as she had seen him the other evening, his easy grace, his dark brown eyes that had turned even darker after he had agreed she'd made the right choice in returning to L.A. Touching her cheek, she felt again the brush of his lips. "Welcome home," he had said.

Taylor drew her mind away from thoughts of Mason and looked at the words before her on the monitor. "In Sacramento today the governor announced a cutback in . . ." Sid was wrong. The average Joe did care about what happened in his world. She wouldn't back down from Sid. Mason, though, was another matter. Avoiding him completely was the only sensible path.

Ten minutes before airtime, Burke barreled into Makeup just as Taylor squirmed in the elevated barber chair, repressing a sneeze while Dorothy darkened her eyebrows. For once, Taylor welcomed the presence of the makeup woman, since it gave her an excuse not to look at Burke. If Sid had told him she had foisted the recipes off on him, he would surely be gunning for her. Eyelids downcast and fluttering with each stroke of the mascara wand, Taylor wondered why Channel Six, a relatively small, independent station, supported a full-time makeup person. Her guess was that Burke demanded the service. She opened her eyes, thanked Dorothy, and nodded at Burke. He still wore a tissue-paper shield around his neck to protect his shirt from the thick foundation. The sight of a grown man sporting what looked like a toilet seat cover always made her want to giggle.

"Taylor, I'd like to speak to you after we've finished tonight. You don't mind sticking around for a few minutes, do you?"

So he was saving the fight over the recipe deal until after the newscast. She had less than four minutes before the cameras rolled. "No problem, Burke. You know I never rush right out." *Unlike you,* she didn't add.

He ignored, or didn't understand, her jab. Beckoning to Dorothy, she said, "I don't like having all the under-eye shadow hidden. I think it takes the edge off my authority."

"Image is everything," Taylor heard him continue as she left the room and headed for the stairs that led to the set one floor below at a fast clip. Before she pushed open the door, she stopped for a moment and drew in a deep breath. Rushing when no one could see her was one thing; in front of the crew, she maintained a calm control. Burke was right about one thing: In television, image exercised a reign of terror.

Taylor stepped carefully across the masses of cables cluttering the floor. She had learned early in her career to pay strict attention while crossing any set. Cables, wires, ladders, long poles used for adjusting the angle of overhead lights, cameras set up for light tests that had to be restarted if some foolish novice wandered in front of the test—the hazards were everywhere.

On television, a news show always looked so pristine. Smiling, well-dressed men and women sharing the latest in knifings, rapes, and murders. The reality—heavy, glaring lights, bulky cameras wielded by burly operators, cigarette butts sizzling in half-emptied coffee cups, crew members exchanging off-color cracks up to the minute the cameras rolled—was oh-so-different.

This was what she loved.

Waving at Red, the operator of camera one, she paused as Vincent, the wizened audio man, attached a mike to the lapel of her copen blue suit. As she took her seat, she saw Burke enter from the opposite side; he had taken the elevator. She would deal with him after the show.

Lucky Perez, the sportscaster, standing just off-camera, blew her a kiss, which she returned, and the weatherman, August Rivers, smiled a greeting at her. She liked them; they were good at their jobs, and their quiet support made Burke's insufferable superiority much more bearable.

"Good evening," said Burke, as he took his seat. The stage manager called, "One minute to air." Taylor straightened her script and checked her TelePrompTer. Burke had the first lead, as usual. She smoothed her long hair back. Her heart quickened as Patty counted five-four-three-two, then silently pointed her index finger to indicate the cameras were rolling.

On cue, Burke flashed his Nielsen-winning smile. "Good evening. I'm Burke Washington."

"And I'm Taylor Drummond."

"Tonight we bring you the inside story on budget slashes in Sacramento—and how they will affect you."

Burke read the top story, then the red light on camera one beckoned to Taylor. She forgot everything else—Sid, recipes, what a jerk Burke was, what she was going to do about loving Mason, what was bothering her sister. Here, in front of that all-seeing glass eye, she was Taylor Drummond, sharing the stories that made Los Angeles both a frightening and redeeming home for millions.

During the stop-down for a commercial, she remembered the time in her life when she had thought law the most stimulating pursuit possible: taking facts, people, tangled business affairs, then burrowing into the complexities of past decisions, seeking precedents the same way explorers search for underwater treasures. While still an attorney, she had begun a stint as a legal-affairs commentator for an L.A. station. The experience had changed her life. She knew, without having to analyze the subject, what made her a good anchor. She loved what she did, and because of that joy, she sparkled. All of her sense of caring came across to the viewer, like a gift, asking to be accepted and loved in return. While the cameras rolled, she had no doubts.

"Good night from all of us at 'Channel Six News at Ten,' " finished Burke, giving his I-could-be-your-father-but-I'd-rather-be-your-lover glance to the camera.

After the wrap, Taylor sat back, drained yet exhilarated. On an intellectual level, she had enjoyed her years as a reporter, and as a lawyer before that, more, but nothing beat the thrill of controlling the tone and essence of the entire newscast. As a reporter, she would have maybe two, three minutes on camera, bits and bites of being the center of attention, nothing at all compared to the central role of the anchor.

"I'll walk back upstairs with you," said Burke.

She nodded, rose, and headed toward the exit, with him at her side. Inside the stairwell, she stopped. "Would you rather take the elevator?"

Burke looked at her with his contact-enhanced green eyes and smoothed his spray-starched hair. He glanced around and said, "No, the stairs are perfect." Before she could move to the steps, he turned, his body brushing against hers, wedging her against the closed door leading back to the set.

"Burke—"

"Relax, Snow White." Burke looked down at her, and stroked her cheek. "I've been wanting to kiss you since our first night together." He reached for a strand of her hair.

She almost laughed. He was so obvious, so transparent. But she knew his ego would never survive her breaking out into a healthy guffaw. And like it or not, she had to work with the man. Easing his hand from her hair, she said, "Under different circumstances, I might be flattered. But you're married, and I have a rule about married men."

"How about making an exception?" He caught her hand. "I think it's time for you and me to get to know each other. Intimately."

"That's not the way I work."

Burke actually gave her a look of surprise. "We're a team, Taylor. We have to move together, think together. You've got to be able to catch any verbal pass I throw to you on air. What better way to get to know one another than to spend some time between the sheets?"

In silence Taylor studied his smooth, tanned face, the hair showing just enough silver-gray to lend him the credibility male anchors thrived on. His body was firm, though a bit on the beefy side. She wondered how many other females had taken him up on his orientation offer.

Extracting her hand from his, she said, "Let's do the best job possible on the air, and off, let's keep it at friends, okay?" She added a smile to buffer the rejection.

He blinked, then nodded, an irritated jerk that betrayed a slight double chin. Reaching for the door that led back into the studio, he said, "It's your loss. I don't make this offer to just anyone."

Somehow, she doubted that.

Taylor pushed away the dessert plate with half the pumpkin cheesecake still beckoning. Eating with Jillian ruined her appetite. Only her sister would suggest meeting for lunch at the Cheesecake Factory, then, after driving to

Beverly Hills from Pasadena, nibble on a green salad and forgo dessert.

"How does it feel?" Jillian asked.

"How does what feel?"

"Fame. Don't look now, but you are about to be accosted by two babushkas." Jillian smiled over the rim of her wineglass. "For an autograph, I'd say."

Two Beverly Hills grandmothers, molded into jumpsuits better left to a younger generation, limbs twinkling with tennis bracelets and coy ankle jewelry, approached the table. One woman, her tucked eyes and incised chin resplendent under hair the color of bottlebrush, pushed an Aprica stroller.

"Dear," said the redhead, "aren't you Taylor Drummond, from Channel Six?"

Taylor nodded, then glanced at the occupant of the stroller. A baby in a white Dior dress, ensconced in a nest of eyelet-bordered cotton, gurgled at her. Her few wisps of blond hair were tied, Pebbles-style, on top of her head with a satin bow. "What a lovely baby."

The woman acknowledged the compliment with a faint smile. "So you get to work with Burke Washington?"

"Yes, I do. We team up for the ten-o'clock news." Sid would be proud of her for using the "T" word.

"Oh, do tell me what he's like. He must be the most wonderful man, and imagine, you get to spend all that time with him." The redhead laughed, a liquid sound, as if the thought actually caused her to salivate.

Taylor marveled at Burke's ability to attract women. This woman, though she had a good twenty years on Burke, wouldn't have said no in the stairwell. "He's a charming man." Taylor offered her hand to the baby, who grasped her thumb with four miniature fingers. She smiled in delight.

The redhead pronounced, "Burke Washington is just what I look for in a newsman."

The other woman edged forward. She was a brown shadow of the redhead, from her hair, eyes, and poolside tan, down to her Joan and David thongs and mocha toenail polish. She spoke softly. "I enjoy your newscast."

Lifting her head but letting the baby keep hold of her hand, Taylor smiled at the shier woman. "Thank you," she said, wondering whether the two women were sisters.

Jillian tried to catch Taylor's eye. She wished her sister wasn't making such a fuss over the baby. Taylor had advanced to gootchi-gooing the creature under its double chin, which glistened with saliva. Jillian checked the crowded restaurant to see whether other diners were watching them. Curiously, despite Taylor's carrying-on, they all seemed to be intent on lunch. In her sweep of the nearby tables, she noticed a gray-suited man, her age, eating alone and reading. His tan spoke of sailing and tennis. Of all the diners, only that man glanced over. And he looked at her, not at Taylor.

"So you will have him send a signed photo?" With a brown-spotted hand, the redhead held out a card.

"We'll both send one," said Taylor, taking the card. "Thank you for stopping." She waved bye-bye to the baby.

The redhead ta-ta'd, backed the stroller between the tables, and headed for the street, her shadow one step behind her.

"Wasn't she adorable?"

Jillian knew perfectly well Taylor was referring to the baby, but she refused to acknowledge the fact. "I don't know. She could have shed a few, if you want my honest opinion. And picked a more subtle shade of red."

"I was talking about the baby."

"Babies all look the same. Especially white babies. They all look like Winston Churchill."

Taylor swallowed some coffee. "What have you got against babies?"

"Nothing. I was simply embarrassed watching you waste a public relations opportunity. You had two fans trying to talk to you, and you were drooling over the baby instead of paying attention to them."

"Did you see the same scene I just took part in? Of

course I paid attention to the women. My image is part of my job, and I do take that seriously."

"Maybe you should be a little more serious, then. All that woman talked about was Burke this and Burke that. She didn't even ask for your autograph. Do you like being upstaged?" Taylor needed to learn a few lessons about pleasing people, something Jillian knew all about, much more than she had ever wanted to know.

"We're hardly in a popularity contest. What I care about is good journalism. Besides, Burke's a ..." She leaned closer to Jillian and whispered, "A jerk. And that's just between you and me."

"He may be a jerk, but he has a tremendous following. Surely you've noticed how sexy he is."

"He's married, has two point five children, and has a reputation, which I can tell you is well earned, for chasing every female in the newsroom."

Jillian shrugged, as if to say, *See what I mean?* "That redhead was old enough to be his mother, and she'd unzip that jumpsuit for him if he crooked a finger." For a moment she wondered how her sister knew his reputation was well earned, but she dismissed the possibility that it was based on personal experience. Her sister was too self-contained to find herself being chased around the anchor desk by even the smoothest lech.

"Is there a point to this?"

"The point, dear sister, is that I'm worried about your image. What happened to the strong Taylor Drummond? Somehow all that chin chucking doesn't seem like you." Jillian had never really understood her sister, but she had settled into the idea of Taylor as the hard-bitten professional—the woman who didn't need a man. Watching her drool over a baby made Jillian nervous.

"I don't take my image to lunch with my sister." Taylor crushed the vestiges of the cheesecake crust under the tines of her fork. "When I left the law firm and decided to make a go of it in news, I threw myself into the challenge. All I did was work. I'm doing okay now, but suddenly I want more than twenty-three hours a day spent trying to get ahead." Should she tell her sister or not? Tossing and turning the previous night, she had wrestled with the question. Taking Jillian into her confidence might help form a bond between them. She also wanted to share her plan. All these months she'd kept her dream bottled up.

"Are you telling me you're finally going to try some serious dating?"

"Dating. Dating. Dating." Taylor threw her arms wide, almost knocking a passing waiter in the ribs. "You've been married for a long time. You don't know about dating. I've gone out with them all. Ad execs who want a house in the burbs. Brokers who only want your money. Producers who want to be told how clever they are. Writers. Ugh, writers, who'll send you the most poetic love letters and screw someone else at the same time. No, I've dated."

Jillian was laughing.

"What's so funny?"

"You. You sum it up so well."

"Ah, finally, a sense of appreciation for my finer talents." Taylor smiled, happy to see her sister looking relaxed. *I will tell her.* "There's something I want to share with you. I've decided . . ." Suddenly she felt silly.

"Yes?"

Taylor felt her cheeks growing warm. Why did she always blush at moments like this? "I've decided to have a baby."

"How nice."

"Nice? That's all you can say?"

"Well, you know the old rhyme: First comes love, then comes marriage, then comes so and so with the baby carriage. Who's the lucky guy?"

"No guy. I'm planning to have the baby on my own."

Jillian laughed aloud. The couple at the table beside them turned to look. She spoke more softly. "Did you flunk biology, or what?"

In a low voice, controlling her hurt, Taylor said, "I'm going to use artificial insemination, then raise the child by myself."

Her sister's blue eyes widened and she shook her head. "You can't be serious."

Taylor nodded. It wasn't her first choice, but it was better than never knowing what it felt like to have life stir within her womb. Better than living without the thrill of raising a child who looked up at you as if you knew who took over the helm when God went to bed at night.

"Well, if you are, you'll still need a man at some point." "True."

"Where do you go for that sort of thing?" Jillian wrinkled her nose, as if even asking the question was distasteful.

"I'll be using a sperm bank, but women sometimes ask a very good friend. In a way, I'd rather the baby know who its father was. A sperm bank will give you the genetic profile of a donor, so a child can know about any inherited diseases. But what the child loses is the family tree, cultural traditions. But when the donor is someone you know, people have ended up in court, arguing over custody, even after agreements that the father will donate and then disappear from the scene."

"You've been studying this."

"Once a lawyer, always a lawyer. I'm nothing if not thorough. Besides, this decision is the most important one of my life." She waited for further response from her sister, but Jillian made a production of swirling the remaining wine in her glass. Her eyes almost closed, she drank it in three long swallows. Her sudden silence reminded Taylor of the calm that precedes a tornado.

Swinging the glass down on the table, Jillian said, "Why would you go to that much trouble just to have a baby?"

"I want a child, a family of my own. I don't want to look back on my life and realize I've missed out on one of the most incredible experiences a woman can have."

Jillian stared into her empty glass. "You'll ruin your body, your life will never be the same again, and for what? Some kid who grows up hating your guts and runs away from home at eighteen."

"How did you get to be so jaded?"

"Look around you. I know what I'm talking about."

"That won't happen to me." She felt so sad, watching the distaste blend with fear and darken her sister's face. "I'll love my baby."

"If I hear that word one more time, I'm going to be sick. You and Mason. All you talk about are babies, babies, babies. You two ought to grow one together."

If it weren't for you, that's exactly what I would have done years ago. Taylor resisted the impulse to scream the words at her sister. It wasn't Jillian's fault. She could have lost Mason to any other woman. He had happened to choose her sister. "You really don't plan on children at all?"

"I've been married seven years. If I'd wanted a baby, I could have had one by now."

Relief weakened her anger. She'd been thankful with every passing year that her sister hadn't borne Mason's child. Somehow that would have been the final loss. Yet why hadn't they had any children? She would be willing to bet Mason hadn't changed his mind about wanting a family. "Did you and Mason talk about kids before you were married?"

"Why?"

"Just curious." Because he'd told her he wanted six kids, an English sheepdog, and two tabby cats.

"I can't remember. That was a long time ago. Probably. Probably not. You whisper such silly things when you're in love. Not many of them connect to real life."

"That's not my idea of love."

"No?" Jillian gave her a thin-lipped smile. "Well, when you fall in love and get married, you can do it the right way."

"Ouch." Watching the distant look in her sister's eyes, Taylor decided not to respond to the jab. What was wrong between Jillian and Mason? Her sister's words weren't the speech of a happily married woman. For the tiniest instant, Taylor pictured Mason free—free from his marriage to Jillian. Free to love her, to begin again. Then she squelched the image. Jillian and Mason would work out their differences. Taylor would stay single, but soon she would have her own family to love.

Breaking their silence, she gave in to the question she knew better to leave unasked. "Are you and Mason unhappy?"

"Unhappy?" Her sister dabbed her lips with her napkin and laughed. "No. Why would you ask that? We're fine. Just fine. Have your baby. Then maybe Mother will stop asking me when she's going to get a grandchild."

Taylor didn't say what they both knew—her baby, especially born outside of marriage, wouldn't satisfy her mother. She'd probably not even acknowledge it.

The smog outside seemed to have drifted in, weighting her lungs and stinging her eyes. The lunchtime sounds had died down in the restaurant. She regretted fooling herself into thinking it a good idea to share her plan with her sister. Right now, Taylor wanted to be anywhere other than where she was.

"It's gotten awfully late." Taylor reached for the check. "I'll see you at the party on Saturday."

Jillian stopped her hand. "Until then. Leave the check, though. I'm going to have an espresso."

Taylor rose, wanting some gesture of affection from her sister before she left. Pausing, she watched her sister withdraw cash from her Gucci wallet. "Jillian?"

She looked up, her eyes not quite focusing. She appeared to have passed back into the nervous inner world she inhabited. Taylor didn't know how to ask her sister for comfort, especially not when Jillian seemed more in need. "Thanks for meeting me for lunch."

"Anytime. I like going out for lunch." She smiled a crooked, almost bitter smile. "It gives me something to do."

Jillian waved her sister off, and looked around for the waitress. One cup of coffee and she'd retrieve her BMW from Geary's parking lot and drive home before the traffic grew too congested. As she signaled the waitress, she saw the gray-suited man she'd noticed earlier. Watching her.

For only a moment, she let herself think of the motels strung along the sidewalks farther south on La Cienega. A few minutes past the chrome and gold splendor of Beverly Hills, the street changed its character. The currency stayed the same, though. Once the cash appeared, the desk clerks never asked questions.

As Jillian sipped her coffee, she wondered whether Taylor was serious about the baby thing. If her sister had a kid, Mason would never let up on her. Pregnancy. She found it difficult to form the word in her mind, let alone consider its consequences.

"Hello."

Before she lifted her face toward the voice, Jillian knew it belonged to the man in the gray suit. He hadn't invested time watching her for nothing.

A chair scraped back and she heard sounds of a body settling in. No. She had told herself only last week she had quit. Quit for good. She'd finish her coffee and go home.

Home to her empty house. Her empty life.

Just once more. Her pulse quickened and she breathed twice, slowly, to control the anticipation beginning to race through her body and cloud her mind. Raising her face toward the man, she smiled and thought, abstractedly, that he would be pleased at the perfect white teeth of her smile. Men like this craved perfection.

"I've been watching you," he said, settling into the chair Taylor had vacated. "I'm Ross McAllister, West Coast Talent. I could use someone like you." He opened a platinum business card case and handed her a card.

She accepted it and conducted an inventory of the man, taking in the polished face, slicked-back hair, gray wool suit, burgundy tie with blue and gray squares in the Italian silk, and the gold wedding band. The physical details actually mattered little. Once a fish had been hooked, she cared little for the weighing in, and the gloating over the catch. The thrill came with the seduction, peaked at the very instant she knew she had her man, then plummeted as rapidly as the elevator in Arthur Hailey's *Hotel*. The act that remained to be done was only that. An act.

"So, didn't I see you on 'A.M. Los Angeles' last week?"

She shook her head; her hair swung gently. She had expected better from this one. Rubbing her thighs one against the other, she summoned and listened to her own body. Yes, she felt a thrum, an awakening in her vagina. He was pretty. And she'd been so good.

"You're not an actress?"

She smiled again, a quirk to her lips, as if she found the idea amusing. She had him. Picturing how he would gaze at her when she slipped the black silk off her shoulders and revealed her swollen nipples, she forgave him his awkward pickup line. He would serve her purpose. He'd want her, admire her, use her, and discard her.

She fished a pen from her purse and glanced around the restaurant. Then, bending over the card, she began to write.

"Let's discuss it over dinner," he said. "Say Friday night at Morton's?"

She held out his card.

Leaning toward her, he claimed the space between their bodies and took the card.

On the back, she had written:

I'M NOT AN ACTRESS. I'M A HOUSEWIFE. DO YOU WANT TO GO SOMEWHERE AND FUCK?

Chapter 4

SOMEWHERE TURNED OUT TO BE A TOP-FLOOR room at the Rodeo Hotel. It was convenient; neither one of them needed to repark a car, both of them were panting to fulfill their purpose.

"You're one slick piece of goods." McAllister leered at her as he yanked his shirt out of his pants. He'd unknotted his tie and undone his cuff links before Jillian had finished carefully locking the door to the room.

With an arch look, Jillian advanced on him. "If I'm slick," she said with an exaggerated wink, "it's because you make me so hot, baby." She guided his hand to her crotch and rubbed against him. He palmed her quickly— too quickly, she thought with a familiar rush of disappointment—and returning to his undressing, moved into the bathroom.

Jillian opened the top two buttons of her black jumpsuit. She liked the way men reacted when she first revealed the lush globes of her breasts, nipples swollen and pouting, crying out to be suckled. Her breath came faster and she wanted to cry out. With a smile, she unfastened the rest of the buttons, the last one exposing the blond tuft of her pubic hair. Waiting for McAllister to emerge from the bathroom, she shrugged the silk off one shoulder and glided a dampened finger over the hard knots of her aching nipples.

When McAllister popped through the door, she'd inch her way out of the jumpsuit, offering him first one nipple, then her other breast, then the rest of her, wild, wet, and writhing.

The door opened and Jillian arranged her lips in her best pout. She half turned, then stopped still.

McAllister, naked, paraded in front of her, a canary-swallowing grin splitting his face. Her mother always said staring was impolite, but this time Jillian couldn't help herself. She was staring at the biggest cock she'd ever seen.

"Go ahead, say it." McAllister laughed and rubbed his hands over his chest hair.

"I—"

"Say it, bitch."

He laughed again, nastily, and Jillian felt prickles running along her forearms. A cock that big was practically a weapon. And she doubted the condoms she always carried would take care of things.

"What's the matter? Cat got your tongue?" He tweaked her breast, hard, and yanked her jumpsuit toward her ankles.

Trying not to watch his prancing cock, she obediently stepped free of her clothing. She stood naked, afraid to confirm that in her state of confusion, her nipples were losing their peaks. He whistled and walked around her, studying her like a prize mare.

"Yeah, you're one slick piece of goods," he repeated.

Trying to regain control, Jillian held out a hand, indicating the bed. All her excitement, the tingling moment of awareness and the firing of sexual neurons, all that had faded, and the longer he watched her, preening over his own body, a look of near-animosity in his eyes, the more she wanted to leave.

But she couldn't leave. He hadn't dismissed her.

Suddenly he lunged, thrusting her to her knees with a sharp jolt. "Quit staring, bitch, and suck it."

Pride kept her from gagging as he jammed himself into her mouth and down her throat. Closing her eyes, she forced herself to relax, to call upon the skill she knew she possessed.

Within moments, she knew he wasn't going to last long at all. Without breaking her rhythm, she nudged him onto the bed, onto his back. With relief, she brought him to a climax, all thoughts of her own sexual satisfaction an empty memory.

He said nothing, just rolled off the bed and began dressing swiftly. Jillian lay facedown on the bedspread, too disgusted with herself to even raise her head. She had serviced him, and for herself had gotten nothing.

Something fluttered to the bed, brushing her leg. In another moment, McAllister's voice came from across the room. "Catch you later, baby."

Three times Mason called his home number from his car phone. No response. Where in the hell was Jillian? What did she do with all her time, anyway? She should be home raising babies. His babies. But no, she was always off someplace. Charity work, she said.

He wondered whether Jillian had forgotten their anniversary, too. Not until his secretary had asked him if he and Jillian were celebrating in any special way had he remembered today was their seventh anniversary. Hiding his chagrin, he had asked her to make a reservation at Jillian's favorite restaurant, then left the office early to surprise his wife. He usually came home late, avoiding the slugfest of the Pasadena Freeway in rush hour. Today every red brake light heightened his frustration. Every time his foot tapped the brake pedal of his car, his mood swayed. What better time than their anniversary to discuss starting a family? Yes, he'd do it; no, he'd wait. Over dessert and coffee, he'd bring up the topic. Casually. Gently. This time he wouldn't force it.

The blue jays outside Jillian's window jeered her. She ran her tongue over her teeth, wondering how many more times she'd have to brush with Crest to rid her mouth of the taste and smell of McAllister. He was a creep, pure and simple, and to top it off, he'd tossed a hundred-dollar bill on the hotel bed before strutting out the door. She usually wanted to laugh at the guys who left cash, but this time she was left feeling perilously close to a whore. She obviously didn't fuck them to bolster her financial liquidity; but so many of them paid anyway. This guy had left his business card, too; only, the real one didn't read West Coast Talent. What a phony. Another stockbroker. Oh, well, if the market stayed open later, she'd have no men at all to pick up.

Glancing at her bedside clock, she saw it was almost six o'clock; that put her an hour behind schedule. She slipped downstairs, splashed vodka over ice, and returned to her bedroom. As a rule, she tried to be back home by five, on the off chance that Mason would call about dinner plans. Today, though, she had needed time to recover from Taylor's baby talk. Mr. Talent Scout had helped her forget, even if he had left her feeling sexually frustrated and unfulfilled. She didn't know what was wrong with the men she met. They all seemed to want her to do all the work and give all the pleasure. She'd read in a novel that vampires could go for a longer period between feedings if a victim had been particularly satisfying. No wonder she had been feeling the need to prey more and more frequently.

It wasn't like it had been at the beginning, two years ago. She had just finished an extensive remodeling job that had required her attention for a year and given her an outlet for the frantic bursts of nervous energy that often threatened to overwhelm her. The day the last piece of hand-painted tile had been grouted and the last Richard Pettit fish portrait hung, she had showered, dressed, and driven to a local bar. There she flirted with the men sitting around her, though she found none of them particularly attractive. She drove home tingling. The next time she went there, a week later, she didn't leave alone.

Stepping out of her black jumpsuit, she stood naked for the second time that afternoon, gazing out the French doors that opened onto a spacious balcony. Her nipples rose to attention as she thought of the thrills of those early conquests. Oh, how exciting her secret life had been in the beginning. Now she only met men like McAllister who, like all the rest, was obsessed with achieving his own satisfaction. Not all men, she corrected. Mason always thought of her first. Maybe that was one of the reasons she avoided sex with him. She didn't deserve a man who made her feel good.

With the icy mouth of her vodka glass, she traced circles around first her left nipple, then her right. With sorrow gripping her heart, but losing out to her desperate need for sexual release, she dropped to her knees, one hand sliding down to caress the soft fur of her pubic hair. Even as the frosty glass puckered her nipples, her own liquid warmth seared her fingertips. With the rising tempo of her fingers, she began to pant. Eyes closed against the beauty of the afternoon, head flung back, she cried out as she finally came.

Blinking her eyelids, she regarded the glass in her hand as if she had no memory of putting it there. One blue jay sidled closer to the window and jabbered at her. Slowly she withdrew her hand from between her thighs and shooed the bird away.

Jillian rose, knowing she needed to hurry. But first she pulled McAllister's money out of her purse. From her bureau drawer, she selected an envelope from a stack rubber-banded together. Yes, Planned Parenthood. That had been one of her favorite charities since they had ministered to her needs at the age of fifteen. After sticking the money inside the envelope, she licked it shut and placed it in her purse.

When Mason reached his home, he walked through room after room, calling her name. Their house was too big for two people. What good were five bedrooms and four bathrooms without children to fill them? Bounding up the stairs, he realized he needed a decision, and he needed one now. Tonight, either his wife would agree to start a family—or else.

When he found Jillian toweling herself dry in their bathroom, he felt like a fool. Especially when she gave him one of her brightest smiles. His anger waning, he stood staring at his naked wife. Her smile faltered, and she wrapped the thick, candy apple red towel around her body.

Setting his briefcase on the tile floor, he moved into the room.

He intercepted her fingers as she started to fasten the ends of the towel over her breasts. "Don't hide from me, Jillian." When she didn't answer, he tugged the terry cloth free. Alert pink nipples greeted him. He felt his blood speeding, rushing through his body, engorging him. Bending over, he rubbed his cheek against one breast, then kissed its peak.

Jesus, how long had it been? Judging by his erection, it must have been longer than he remembered. She always seemed to have some excuse. Not tonight. No excuses.

"It's been too long." He nuzzled her ear.

She said nothing, but remained within his embrace. He kissed her lips; she tasted of Colgate and Listerine. Her hair smelled faintly of coconut; he took a few strands into his mouth and smiled. He never tired of tasting her, of pleasuring her.

He kissed her earlobe, then whispered, "I want to nibble on you before dinner."

She stood before him, not moving, except for the swift retrieval she'd made of the towel. Hooked inside her elbows, it covered her backside. Breaking from his hold, she pulled the towel around her. "I've just showered."

"So?"

"I'll have to shower again."

"I'll soap your back." He stripped off his Brooks Brothers coat, and worked the buttons of his long-sleeved dress shirt with impatient fingers.

"Mason?"

"Hmmm?" Shedding the rest of his clothing, he held out his arms to his wife.

"Not now."

For the first time since he'd walked into the room, Mason stopped and actually looked at her face. A tiny furrow showed in the fine skin between her eyebrows. Her mouth had strained into one taut line.

"Why not?" Damn it, he needed her.

She shook her head and shrugged her shoulders.

"What kind of answer is that?"

"I don't feel very sexy."

"Jillian, look at you!" Pulling the red cotton shield off her, he turned her to face the mirror. The mirror returned an image of firm, full breasts, outlines of ribs, a stomach so flat, it curved inward, a froth of dark blond pubic hair. And two eyes firmly shut against the sight.

Standing behind her, Mason pulled her backward, fitting her against him. He'd been so patient—more so than most men would have managed. "You can open your eyes, beautiful." Flesh against flesh, he considered taking her right there, in front of the mirror, but the fantasy evaporated when he realized she was sniffling.

She pulled free. Without looking at him, she began to dress. After a moment, she said, "I told you I don't feel like it right now."

"You could have said so sooner." Stepping back, he reached for his shorts and pulled them on. "I might as well have been living on a desert island lately, for all the sex we've had." He gathered the rest of the clothes he had discarded so eagerly. The pounding of his blood slowed, and with the decrease, he surrendered his erection. "Just don't forget how, or we'll have trouble having a baby. That is, if we ever get around to that."

She stopped combing out her damp hair. "Baby?"

"Yes, you know, a man and a woman, and nine months later, a baby." With the suffocation of his desire, his anger returned full force. "If you weren't so goddamn afraid of gaining a few lousy pounds, and not half so self-centered, we'd already have a family!"

The comb clattered to the marble counter. Reaching for a tissue, she wiped her eyes. "Don't criticize me."

Holding his clothes, Mason expelled a frustrated sigh. He watched in silence as she blew her nose.

"I come home early to take you out, just you and me. We're both awake and home at the same time, but no, you don't want to have sex. What about me? What about what I want? My needs?" Mason knew he was shouting again, but he didn't care. The faint vee between her eyes, the slight flaw he'd first seen only moments before, creased more deeply. Let her worry. He left her standing there.

He shrugged into his jogging sweats and was searching for his running shoes when he sensed her walk up behind him.

"I'm sorry," she said, and he could tell she was crying. "You just don't know how impossible it is for me. There's no way you could ever understand."

Standing, he turned to face her. A few tears, just enough to make him feel guilty, slipped down her cheeks. No heat of desire stirred within him now. "I've heard all about your crappy childhood a thousand times. That's no reason not to have a baby. And you won't even deal with the question. You could at least see a shrink and work out your feelings."

"You don't understand," she whispered.

"You're right." He bent to put on and lace his shoes. "I'm jogging to Tops for pastrami. You can call the Chronicle and cancel the dinner reservation I made for us." Grabbing his keys from his suit pocket, he added, "By the way, happy anniversary."

He left her standing there, too furious, both with her and with his own lousy handling of the situation, to consider going back to smooth things over.

When he returned, after walking the many miles it took to vent his frustration, she was asleep. No wonder. As usual, a plastic container of Halcion tablets and a glass of water decorated her bedside table.

Disgusted, Mason picked up the latest Robert Ludlum novel and climbed into their California king water bed. Jillian, leaden under the influence of the sleeping pill, lay supine, her mouth slightly open.

What had he done wrong?

As he lay next to her, his book unopened, he replayed their shouting match in his head. He wondered about the "or else." Divorce? Marriage counseling? He groaned when he realized he had that order strangely in reverse. Divorce. He believed marriage meant forever. He didn't approve of the attitude of trading in spouses like out-of-

date automobiles. Only last January, his parents had cele-
brated their forty-second wedding anniversary. If Jillian really loved him, though, why wouldn't she have his baby?
Before they had married, she said she wanted children.
She had said not right away, since she was so young, but
she certainly hadn't revealed any psychopathic fear of
childbearing.

Thirty-eight next week, and no kids. What difference
did his success make when he was a shell devoid of what
really mattered to him? His life felt as gray as the carpet
Jillian had insisted on despite his preference for blue. He
had drifted, deluding himself that Jillian would change her
mind tomorrow. He looked across the bed at her silent
form and saw too many tomorrows come and gone.

He didn't want any more of his life slipping past him.
He wanted a child, children, a family. He had watched
some of his friends enter parenthood as if it were an opportunity to model the picture-perfect child in a designer
stroller or as a mannequin to display the latest in Bellini
baby furniture. Mason always ached a little inside when he
saw them. For him, the desire to have children came from
a much deeper yearning. What he felt was a stirring that
he had always associated with women—with the biologi-
cal urge to reproduce, to create and carry a new life. It
wasn't just a "female thing." He wanted to give life, to
sacrifice, to love, to see himself replicated and achieve, in
that small way, a smattering of immortality.

Jillian stirred and turned over, facing away from him.
With a sigh, Mason pressed the remote control to turn on
the television. He usually watched the news at eleven, but
his disastrous evening had put him to bed earlier. He
flipped to Channel Six.

Taylor chatted with the smug-looking guy sitting next to
her as if they shared some intimate secret. Irritation
pricked at Mason. The two of them smiled, then disappeared as a commercial blared onto the screen. Ignoring
the voluptuous woman inviting him to sculpt a new body
at the Sports Expression Gym, he registered his reaction to

Taylor's co-anchor, then dismissed it as merely protective, in a brotherly sort of way.

As soon as the newscast returned, he studied Taylor. She looked softer than she had in her attorney days. She'd always been Ms. Business First, consistently billing more hours than any other associate. When the screen switched to a close-up of her, the look in her blue eyes seemed so intense, so personal, he thought she must be trying to reach out to him.

Mason shifted his position. Damn if he wasn't getting aroused. Suddenly he felt embarrassed and self-conscious, as if she could see him. What had been between them was long passed. In seven years, Taylor had never once made an effort to see him. What would she think of him now, lusting after her, while his wife—her sister—slept beside him?

Another string of commercials zipped across the screen. Mason looked down at his book, but left the television on. Before he had read more than the words "Chapter One," her image commanded the television again. Memories, long bolted down in a corner of his mind, fought their way free. Taylor, warm and giving, snuggled against him, her black hair wildly tangled from a night of lovemaking. The book fell to the floor.

The thud did it. Mason lassoed those stray memories, herding them back where they belonged. He jerked the bedclothes up to his chest, like a teenager whose mother walked in the room at the wrong moment, and hit the Off button on the remote control.

After a glance at Jillian, he got up and began pacing the bedroom, weaving a path past the bed and around the chaise to the French doors overlooking the pool. What was he doing mooning over Taylor? He had to think about Jillian. About their family, their future. Looking around the bedroom, he marveled again at the contrast of his elegant home to the cramped farmhouse that had been home until his eighteenth birthday. He'd worked hard for this, and he shared it all with Jillian. He gave her everything any woman could ask for. A big house, no pressure, lots of free time, clothes, jewelry, vacations. Not to mention his love. So what in the hell was wrong with her that she couldn't grant him the one thing he wanted more than anything else?

Turning toward the bed, he watched his sleeping wife. He tried to picture her abdomen extended, big with child, or her lying next to him, suckling their baby. As he stared, concentrating on her perfectly toned and aerobicized body, another vision crowded in.

Taylor.

Taylor asking him to rub cocoa butter on her swollen belly, laughing as the baby kicked against the massaging motions. Taylor—

With a groan, Mason thrust open the French doors and stepped outside. He needed to cool down. Damn, he needed a cold shower. Maybe his mid-life crisis had come early. He had to be out of his mind thinking of Taylor as earth-mother material. She was the most career-first woman he knew. But somehow, she had a softness, a yielding ability to gather in others and love them, that Jillian lacked.

As he rested his elbows on the cool balcony rail and inhaled the jasmine-scented night air, he knew he and Jillian would have to resolve their impasse. They had to talk about her fears about having a baby. No more blanket statements about how he couldn't possibly understand, followed by tears and no further explanation. She must delve into it. Once she shared that with him, she'd be free from whatever held her back. If that didn't work, she would *have* to see a shrink.

Or else.

The shrink Mason had in mind was lying on a lumpy bed in an Inglewood motel room, avoiding the eyes of the slender black woman glaring at him from the end of the bed.

Tapping the toe of her high-heeled shoe, the woman looked around the room. She glanced at her watch and swallowed a yawn. "Take my advice, Sandy, and get yourself a girlfriend. You've been moping around ever since Keshia left you."

Rolling over, Fielding grunted. "Girlfriends are trouble."

She rose from where she sat at the foot of the bed. Smoothing her short leather skirt, she walked toward him, punctuating each accusation with a jab of a finger spiked by a purple Press-On nail. "Some big hotshot you are. You and your fancy cars and your big house in Hancock Park. But underneath, you're afraid of life. You've been running away from life for years."

Fielding raised his hands over his face in a weary gesture. "Don't, Treena."

"When's the last time you came to visit? When's the last time you came to see your granny? She raised you, and what kind of thanks do you give her?"

He sat up against the headboard, crossing his legs covered in his favorite worn jeans. "I don't deserve that one. That stubborn old woman wouldn't move out of that shack if a wrecking ball was coming at it."

"You only called me today because you wanted someone to feel sorry for you. 'Oh, Treenie, I can't decide what to do with my life.' Well, I know what I do with mine. I could be using this bed right now. Making money. But no, I'm listening to you whine about the meaning of life."

"Treena—"

"Don't 'Treena' me. Get yourself a girlfriend who'll listen to you. Face up to your own mistakes, or cut the crap. You and me, we used to be friends." She glowered at him. "But look at you now: all wound up, moaning about something missing in your life. You need a good screw, and you won't even use my professional services."

He caught her wrist. "If I wanted to have sex with you, it wouldn't be for money." He released her arm. "Girl, we go back a long time. You can change your life, too. I'll help you."

Backing away from him, she shook her head. The beads in her cornrow-braided hair rattled. "No, thanks, Sandy. You've gone your way and I've gone mine. I don't want your money . . . unless I earn it." When she reached the door, she paused. "You've got ten minutes to clear out. Us working girls don't have time to stew over the meaning of life." She shut the door quietly behind her.

Fielding lay back on the pillows and stared at his face in the mirrored ceiling. He, Dr. Fielding Sanderson, graduate of Brandeis University, had just been taken to task by a twenty-five-year-old prostitute. And rightly so. Not that she should talk. Fielding's grandmother had raised her, too, but his granny didn't count her as one of her successes.

Despite Fielding's achievements, he wasn't sure his granny was proud of him either. He continued to drift back and forth between the world of his business success and the grittier world of his childhood in South Central L.A. His friends outside in the bar, the Motel Quality's finest asset next to the rooms available by the hour, called him an Oreo man. Not to his face, of course, but he'd heard about it from Orville.

Orville the peacemaker. The bartender stood a good six foot seven. When he leaned over the bar toward you, you didn't need a sappy TV commercial to tell you to listen. Orville had told him, many months ago, to leave his success-in-the-white-man's-world stories in the parking lot. "Park 'em with your Kraut car," he'd said. Fielding had started to explain the Jag wasn't a German make, that was his other car, but the look in Orville's rheumy brown eyes shut him up. Since then, he'd counted Orville as a friend.

Especially since Orville served him mineral water with lime without smirking. Most of the other recovering alcoholics Fielding met avoided bars, but not him. After he'd dried out, it had been a test of will to open the doors to the darkened interior of a bar in the middle of the afternoon. The voices of the TV, the murmurs of the fellow tipplers, the universal language of "What'll it be?"—those familiar sights and sounds wrapped their tentacles around him and pulled him in. He knew himself helpless against those desires. Acknowledging that had been his first step toward saving himself.

He still loved his favorite haunts; they were even more of a home after Keshia left him. Being home alone was the worst. The aching need to drown himself in alcohol actually decreased within the comfort of the bar.

So, eight years sober, he continued to frequent one of his two favorite bars: The Huntsman, at the Motel Quality, just off Century Boulevard in the armpit of LAX. The ceaseless jets, flying, landing, taking off, landing, taking off, at Los Angeles International Airport, provided background noise if no one slipped a quarter into the jukebox. Boisterous men, rough laborers, but laborers who owned their own businesses, hung out at The Huntsman. An ex-football player with the unlikely name of Seymour could be found there every evening from nine P.M. to closing. He held court in the corner opposite the big-screen TV, telling stories about life in the pros. Newcomers ordered a Budweiser for him, and paid homage through two or three rounds a night. If you didn't do this for at least your first few visits, Seymour'd run you out of the bar.

A wise man didn't challenge tradition at The Huntsman.

Still staring into the mirrored ceiling, Fielding scratched himself and stretched. He had money. He had a nice house in Hancock Park. Why did he feel this restlessness? Ah, yes, Dr. Fielding, why? What, we're out of time for this session? Too bad. Fielding laughed at himself and bounded off the sagging bed.

Time to say hello to Orville, then return to his other life. He was due at Mason Reed's birthday party in three hours. He liked Mason, but he knew why he'd been invited to the party. Free consultation. Psychological workup on the mysteriously ailing Jillian Reed. Another socialite wife with no purpose in life. Precisely the reason he abandoned his private practice in the first place—well, not the real reason, but his favorite excuse. Mason was his friend, so he would go to the party. But he'd be damned if he'd take on another sick chicken.

A few hours later, after changing both his clothing and

his car, Fielding maneuvered his Porsche up a tree-lined avenue. San Pasqual. Nice name. Nice houses. He bet every one of their occupants voted Republican and sent their kids to private schools.

As he coasted to a halt in front of number 2102, an imposing Mediterranean on a corner lot, a red-jacketed Hispanic youth reached for his car door.

"Take your car, sir?"

Fielding considered the offer. Glancing into his rearview mirror, he spotted a Mercedes sedan. The car idled raucously, as only a diesel engine could. "I'll park it myself." He jerked a thumb toward the Mercedes. "Go put that guy out of his misery."

Grinning, the boy saluted Fielding and jogged to the other car.

After sheltering his Porsche around the corner, he approached the canopy-covered sidewalk. Tiny white lights glittered in the archway and among the hedges. All the place needed were a few dolls and he'd start whistling "It's a Small, Small World."

He knocked on the carved mahogany door, realizing he felt awkward coming to a birthday party empty-handed, even though the invitation had specified "no presents." When no one responded, he pushed open the door and stepped inside. Standing on the terra-cotta entry floor, he looked around. To his left, in a step-down living room, a crowd huddled around a long table. Dance music filtered from the back of the house. The buzzing of party talk swept over him. Spotting two of Mason's law partners in the crowd, he headed over to check out the action.

Craps. Exactly like Las Vegas. Table, dice, dealer, and all the drinks you could guzzle.

"Fielding. Good to see you." Richard Jackson extended his hand, then turned back to the craps table to watch a slim-hipped number in a sequined bustier and miniskirt raking in the chips with her stick.

Fielding smiled at Jackson, took a closer look at the croupier, and walked over to the other partner, Rosemary Carmichael. Rosemary came from the old school; she'd graduated from Stanford in Sandra Day O'Connor's class. Watching the elegant lady in her long-sleeved, high-necked blue silk dress, calling, "Don't come," made Fielding chuckle.

"Mrs. Carmichael, I never pictured you a gaming sort."

She grinned, sparking a light in her gray eyes. "Never judge a book by its cover, Dr. Sanderson. What's your game? If it's not craps, there's a roulette wheel in the den, and poker out back."

He smiled, but she'd already returned to the play in progress. Whatever Mrs. Mason Reed's problems might be, she certainly knew how to throw a party. A passing waiter offered him champagne, and Fielding had to stop himself as he automatically reached for a glass. He asked the man for mineral water and set out to explore the rest of the party. He was, after all, a man on a mission.

The band swung into "Lady in Red," and someone rendered a fair Stevie Wonder imitation. He found himself in a book-lined den. As Rosemary had described, the large room held a roulette table. He looked over the laughing gamblers to the far end of the room. A vivacious blonde, with a pageboy smooth as steel, held court. Without staring, Fielding observed the swell of her breasts above the holly berry red dress. Did she call that a neckline or a waistline? Smiling and chatting with three men, she managed to exude innocence along with a stark dose of sexuality.

"Fielding." A firm hand clapped him on the shoulder, turning him around.

"Mason. Happy birthday." They shook hands, then Fielding gestured around him. "Quite a bash."

"Thanks. When Jillian decides to do something, she goes all out."

The waiter paused on the far side of the room, then headed toward Fielding with his mineral water.

"Speaking of which, I want you to meet my wife, then I'll set you up with some chips."

He nodded, thinking he far preferred staring at the blonde to a hand of poker. He'd ask Mason who she was.

Before he could, the woman broke away from her ad-
mirers and started across the room. She stopped once, at
the roulette table, and the dealer let her spin the ball.

"Honey," called Mason, "I want you to meet a friend of
mine."

The woman he'd been admiring stopped beside Mason,
who put his arm around her waist. A proprietary gesture.
"Jillian, Fielding Sanderson. Fielding, my wife, Jillian."

Fielding swallowed. He extended a hand to her. Her
skin was softer than he could have imagined. A square
ruby sparkled on her right hand, looking far too heavy for
her delicate finger. He released her hand. Closer up, she
looked much thinner, hollowed out along her cheeks,
shoulders, and arms. Whatever diet she was on hadn't
whittled down her breasts, though. "Mason is a very lucky
guy, Mrs. Reed."

She smiled back. "Call me Jillian." Placing her hand on
Mason's arm, she said, "Darling, I have to check on the
caterers, so if you'll excuse me." She graced them with
another brilliant smile, then moved off.

Fielding had to force himself not to stare at her as she
crossed the room. She had Lauren Bacall's voice—his all-
time favorite sexy voice—and his friend got to hear that
voice every day. He noticed Mason watched her as she
glided from the crowded room, smiling and greeting people. A mixed look of pain and pride flickered on his face.

"She's beautiful," said Fielding.

"Ah, yes, she is."

"Sounds like a sigh to me."

"Well, hey, it's my birthday."

"Doesn't sound like a party noise."

Mason glanced around, the host surveying his guests to
make sure all were properly satiated with food and drink.
Then he took Fielding by the elbow, and guided him away
from the center of the room.

Without looking him in the eye, Mason said, "I don't
really know how to say this. When we talked at the gym,
I wasn't completely open with you. Jillian hasn't been herself lately."

Fielding nodded. People rarely opened up when they first discussed a personal problem; often they reported a few vague symptoms, unaware of the underlying causes.

"I want her to go for counseling, but so help me, bringing up the subject with her is impossible."

So now we get to the reason behind my invitation. He could make it easy on his friend. After all, how many times had Mason helped him out with referrals for his trial consulting service? "Any specific reason you think there's a problem?"

Mason hooked a finger inside the collar of his shirt and pulled, as if it were suddenly two sizes too small.

Fielding had seen that look before. "She's turned off the taps on you?"

He laughed. "That's one way of putting it, yes."

No more nooky. Fielding thought of her curves, waiting to be explored like a winding backcountry road. The three men hanging on her every word. That voice, that come-hither melody. Mason didn't strike him as your typical cuckold, but if someone wasn't getting some from Jillian, he'd turn in his diploma. "Anything else?"

"She fades in and out. I don't know how to describe it, but it's as if she's not really present. She can't seem to sleep without sleeping pills. And she has some irrational fear of having a baby."

Fielding nodded, letting the sounds of the party overtake him. Laughter, carefree shouts, the whir of the roulette wheel—who in this room had any problems? He knew from long experience that looking into a person's life was like picking up a heavy rock. On the bottom squirmed hordes of bugs and worms that thrived in the damp darkness of the underside. He sighed and looked at his friend. "You want me to get to know her? Meet for lunch and talk? Something casual like that?"

"Yes." Mason lifted his shoulders. "I'll tell Jillian you'll be calling. I don't think she'll refuse to see you, because she would view that as social rudeness, a sin she would never commit."

"I'll meet with her if that's what you really want, but

you should be aware that people pushed into seeking help often refuse to respond. They don't take kindly to others thinking there's something wrong with them."

"I'm prepared to take that chance. Send the bill to my office."

"Whoa." Fielding shook his head. "No fee."

"Why not?"

"This isn't business." If it were, he'd be out the door, running in the opposite direction. How in the hell was he going to explain to his friend, once he'd verified his hypothesis, that his wife was having an affair?

"All right. I won't argue it for now. There's one more thing I have to say. I feel like an idiot saying it, but if I don't, you'll just think I'm a fool blinded by love."

"What's that?" He sipped his water.

"You'll probably consider whether she's seeing someone else." Mason paused and looked at him.

He didn't touch that one. Not yet.

"Of course, it isn't true. I'd know if she were. A husband knows that sort of thing."

Chapter 5

TAYLOR TOLD HERSELF THIS WAS JUST ANother party, another occasion where she mingled with those she had once known and others she might come to know. The house was just another house, a two-story Mediterranean that ruled the corner of a well-tended street. Best not to think of this house for what it truly was—the home where Mason and Jillian made love, drank coffee, read the paper, curled up together by a winter's fire.

She rang the doorbell and repeated, "Just another house."

Jillian appeared, dressed in a fire engine red dress that made Taylor's strapless black cocktail dress look like a nun's habit. "There you are. It's very naughty of you to be late."

No greeting, no *happy birthday*. "Sorry." The word sounded lame, but she couldn't exactly tell her sister the truth: I'm late because I've never gotten over loving your husband and I thought I could handle it but now I'm not so sure, thanks for the party. Gotta go.

"Never mind, the party's swinging along nicely." She linked her arm through Taylor's. "You look lovely in black."

"Thanks." Taylor regarded her sister's bright eyes, the half-empty champagne flute, and wondered at her sister's friendliness.

"Of course, I wouldn't wear gold with that shade. Try silver next time."

Taylor had managed to forget how well Jillian had learned the technique of delivering compliments from their mother. The formula: For every nice word said, add one poison barb.

Taylor shrugged this one off and let herself be pulled into the crowd. This was her party. As she walked with Jillian through the first floor of the house, she admired the evidence of her sister's decorating skills. Terra-cotta tiles, whitewashed walls, and burnished hardwood floors all stayed true to the simplicity of the Mediterranean/Spanish-style house. Rather than cluttering, Jillian had streamlined. Yet Taylor wondered about the lack of the personal touches—no family pictures, no skid marks from romping dogs, no favorite record albums left lying about for easy access to play over and over again. What was missing, to Taylor's curious eye, was Mason's imprint. It was as if he had agreed to write the checks and keep his personality to himself in return for the honor of living in a first-class hotel.

Where was he now? Playing host, listening to a guest with that intense look that communicated how much he cared about what was being said, laughing as he egged on a group of partiers at the roulette table? Once she saw him, she'd be okay, but the tension of knowing he was around and she hadn't yet sighted him and made his presence okay within herself would tug at her, fire an edge to her laughter, cause her to smile and try just a bit too hard.

Taylor forced herself to pay attention to Jillian's chatter about who was at the party. Her sister soon steered her to a group of Mason's partners at Harper, Cravens, several of whom had been associates during Taylor's tenure there. They clustered around her, welcoming her back to Los Angeles, with offers of friendship that had been withheld when she had worked with them, another success-hungry associate competing with them for the limited partners' slots. Without bitterness over the past, she accepted their openness now. She knew she had been fairly insufferable at Harper, Cravens. She'd been far too busy climbing up, up, up, to bother making friends. Until Mason had entered her life.

Joining the group at the craps table, she threw herself

into enjoying the party Jillian had engineered, laughing and joking with the others. Every so often, she'd glance around.

"That's quite a pile of chips you've got."

Taylor started when she heard Mason's voice. He stood behind and to her right. If she turned, her arms would fit naturally around his waist, her face press against his chest. With a reckless thrust of her hand, she pushed her stack of chips onto "pass" and turned, managing not to brush against him. "I'm winning and loving it."

"Good. Everyone should win on her birthday."

He wore a white dinner jacket and black trousers. The jacket contrasted with his dark hair and showed the soft gold of his November tan to advantage. He looked wonderful—and just as forbidden—as a hot fudge sundae to a woman on a grapefruit diet. With what she thought was the right amount of casualness, she said, "Happy birthday to you, too, Mason."

"Thank you." He kissed her lightly on the cheek. "Happy birthday to you. Shall I take your wrap?"

She had kept the silk shawl earlier when Jillian had asked the same question. Now she dropped it from her shoulders and let it fall into his hands. He passed a look over her bare shoulders, a look that traveled the line of her throat, down to the swell of her breasts where skin disappeared into black lace and satin. She tilted her chin upward and touched the corner of her lip with her tongue. As crazy as it was she wanted him to admire her.

A slender black man approached, then hesitated. Mason looked from her back to the silk shawl and waved the man over. "Fielding, I'd like you to meet Taylor Dummond, Jillian's sister."

He extended his hand. "Fielding Sanderson."

His grip was firm and confident, the direct look in his dark brown eyes warm and appraising. Taylor liked him immediately. She also appreciated the interruption. Playing with fire was playing the fool.

"Dr. Sanderson," Mason added.

Fielding raised his eyebrows.

"Fielding's a very modest man. He heads Jural Relations, the trial consulting service we've been using at the firm."

"Trial consulting." Taylor made a mental note, shifting into her businesswoman persona. "I think I sense a feature report here. Stop me now, Dr. Sanderson, or I'll start the interview while you're still enjoying the party."

He produced a card. "Give me a call and I'll be happy to show you through our setup. Although you may disillusion your public when they realize how we actually serve up justice on a silver platter."

Taylor smiled, her reporter's instincts kicking in. "I'll definitely call you."

"Taylor was an associate at Harper, Cravens, well on her way to partner, when she gave it up for television news," said Mason.

"That's an unusual career change," said Fielding.

"Is it?" asked Taylor, unwilling to comment.

"Forgive me. I didn't mean to tread on sensitive ground."

"It's not sensitive," Mason answered before Taylor could. "Taylor was a damn good lawyer, and she's a damn good news anchor."

Taylor sensed Fielding knew he had hit a sore point and was tactful enough to back away. Before she could steer the conversation in a different direction, Jillian wove into view, champagne flute in one hand, Burke Washington attached to the other. Mason slid an arm around her and pulled her to his side, planting a kiss on her smooth blond hair. A fist twisted in Taylor's gut. Round and round went the eddies of pain, radiating out, warning and reminding her of the facts of life. At that moment, standing and chatting so urbanely, the difference between intellectually acknowledging a fact and truly *knowing* it hit her with a body slam.

Jillian introduced Burke to the others. Managing the proper show of enthusiasm blended with ennui, controlling the feelings roiling inside her, Taylor offered her cheek to Burke. He took the opportunity to smack her solidly on the lips. "Happy birthday, Snow White," he whispered, with a quick up-and-down of one eyelid.

"Thanks, Dopey," she replied, for his ears only, grateful for the distraction. Mason still had his arm around Jillian, who wasn't exactly relaxing into the embrace, but she seemed to accept the offer of affection as her due—along with the homage of Burke and Fielding. Taylor knew she was pretty, she knew she was attractive, yet she could never get over the feeling that, in Jillian's presence, she would always and forever be the wallflower. Men *wanted* her sister; Taylor, they respected.

She let Mason, Fielding, Burke, and Jillian carry the party chitchat, and switched her thoughts to the safer topic of the irony of having to appear friendly with a man she'd otherwise never speak to. Viewers had to believe that anchors were the best of friends. In the 1970s, television consultants had devised the "happy talk" format that had lit upon local newscasts like lawyers upon the relatives of air-accident victims. The cheerful chatter among anchor team members would fall flat on its masked face if viewers didn't believe all that camaraderie was 100 percent genuine.

Always working, aren't you, Taylor? She laughed inwardly at her own insistent striving toward career perfection while she smiled at two women turning from the craps table to gaze at Burke. Taylor never ceased to be amazed at how "the public" fawned over any television personality. News, sports, weather, game show host or model, talk show maven—you name it, once you were on, about, or connected to television, you became someone special. Years ago, she had linked the phenomenon to a loss of religion and community among Americans. Humans had a need for idols—that had been true for centuries. When gods no longer walked the earth and talked to man, men and women created their own—in full color, living, breathing, graven video images.

When the two women, who turned out to be paralegals at Harper, Cravens, joined their circle, Taylor dutifully signed an autograph and chatted with Burke as if camera

number one had its red light switched on. When she got
Jillian alone, she would cream her for inviting Burke. Of
all the nerve; she must have called him at the station and
talked her way through to him. And naturally Burke had
left his wife at home. Rumor had it she was about to deliver their third child, but Taylor didn't consider that ade-
quate reason to leave her abandoned at home, in a medical
variation on purdah.

Taylor noticed Jillian nodding at one of the tuxedoed
waiters. As soon as a polite pause occurred in the conversation, she asked the guests to gather outside by the band
for the cake cutting. Mason grinned at Taylor, a friendly
I-told-you-so look. Excusing herself, Jillian moved off,
grabbing another glass of champagne from a passing water. Burke offered his arm to Taylor, and she accepted,
walking outside with him to the terrazoed area by the pool.
With Jillian's usual flair, she had lit the large backyard
with flickering torches. The flames reflected in the swimming pool. As people gathered, the band cut its volume to
an echo of its earlier blast.

Taylor stood between Burke and Fielding, hoping Jillian
wouldn't make too great a fuss over the birthday cake.
Thirty-eight was thirty-eight, and she didn't want to dwell
on her age. Not in her career and not in her motherless
state. Jillian, of course, outdid herself. Out came two towering cakes, wheeled by a caterer. On top of one stood a
scale of justice; on the other, a miniature television. The
guests buzzed their appreciation at the twin cakes as waiters circulated, refilling glasses.

Jillian and Mason followed the cakes, arm in arm. In
her bright red dress, snuggled against Mason's white dinner jacket, Jillian reminded Taylor of a cherry atop
whipped cream on a sundae. Her sister—forever irresist-
ible.

Burke must have had similar thoughts, because he said,
as he accepted a glass from a waiter, "Now, that's a
woman I could appreciate."

"She's very married."

Burke raised an eyebrow. "Of course she is. A man can admire a work of art, though."

She had heard that corny line before, usually before some married man asked to buy her a drink. If only she could align her wayward feelings for Mason with her beliefs about fidelity and marriage, her soul would rest a lot more easily.

"Smile," called Jillian, snapping an Instamatic camera.

Taylor felt Burke straighten beside her and sensed him flashing his best on-camera look. She did the same, out of habit, though she hated having her picture taken. Television, she loved; still photographs, she despised. Those slices out of time always seemed to catch her at her worst, with a stray hair across her nose, or her bra strap peeking out. That never happened to her on-air. But then, her personal life had never been as neatly packaged as her professional.

With a hostess's sleight of hand, Jillian caused Mason and Burke to change places and the cakes to end up beside Taylor. Jillian raised the camera again, and Mason draped his arm across Taylor's shoulders. They stood so close that the warmth of his breath tickled the flesh above her strapless dress. When she chanced a glance upward at his face, she saw with disappointment that he looked as involved as if he were reading a law review article on Rule 10-b. As she registered the nonchalance with which he posed and the distant look in his eyes, she felt like the fool she was. Mason hadn't cared enough to beg her to stay seven years ago, and he certainly didn't care now.

Jillian's camera flashed, the band broke into a Muzaked version of "Happy Birthday," and someone called, "Make a wish." Mason nodded toward the wavering candles oozing wax onto the gleaming white frosting. "Shall we do the honors?"

As soon as the last candle flickered and guttered, Taylor eased away from Mason. Burke insisted on proposing a toast—to his and Taylor's long and profitable association with Channel Six. She found his casual commercial plug amusing. In his own way, Burke was always working, too.

The waiters began dispensing cake, and the guests drifted off to their preferred party stations.

Taylor heard a hiccup and turned to find Jillian beside her. She watched in surprise as Jillian giggled. Her sister was not one to take a breach of social etiquette lightly. Thanks to dear old Mom, of course. She realized Jillian must have been swilling the champagne—and it was very good champagne—for hours.

Jillian handed her untouched plate to Burke and placed a hand on Taylor's arm and her other on Mason's shoulder. The resulting stretch showed off her décolletage to advantage, which Taylor was positive Burke wasn't missing despite searching about for a spot to dump the cake plates.

"So, did you both make a wish?" Jillian hiccuped again, then dropped her hand from Taylor's arm and propped her hand over her mouth like a naughty child.

Taylor could have sworn she saw Mason grimace. She nodded in answer to her sister. "You know you can't tell a wish or it won't come true." Burke wasn't the only one dishing out corny lines.

"Well, sister, I know what my husband wished for. So I guess that means it won't come true."

She heard her own intake of breath, accompanied by Mason's short, "Let's drop it. Okay, Jillian?"

Jillian pouted. "But I want to know if Taylor wished for an artificial inseminator."

"A what?" asked Burke.

Taylor glared at her sister, then looked around to see who else was within earshot. Not that anyone else mattered, when Burke, all ears and eyes, stood not two feet away. When Burke got hold of a good story, it made its way all over town.

"She said she couldn't have a baby without one, so I just want to know if that's what she wished for," said Jillian.

"I told you that in confidence," said Taylor, struggling to control the anger in her voice, fighting to hide her outrage from Burke.

"Oh," said Jillian, with an innocent lift of her shoulders.

Taylor gripped her cake saucer. She wanted to slap the perfect skin of her sister's cheek. "Don't you understand what a secret means? Don't you have any respect for my feelings, or at least my privacy?" she demanded quietly, her voice trembling with rage.

"Sorry." Jillian covered a tiny yawn, as if the matter concerned her not at all.

"Why don't we dance?" Burke took Jillian by the hand and led her to the far side of the pool.

Mason watched them move away. "Do you mind telling me what that was all about?"

Setting down her untouched piece of birthday cake, Taylor said, "I don't think I can talk about it right now. You can tell Jillian tomorrow, after she sobers up, what a memorable party this was." Turning, she headed for the interior of the house. She hated the sarcasm in her voice. Jillian always knew exactly how to get to her. Blurting out her baby plans in front of Burke could easily cost Taylor her job. Once she was established, and the ratings improved as she believed they would, management would have a much harder time dumping her because they thought a single, pregnant anchor would offend viewers. With less than a month invested in her, they might decide to pull the plug on her now. What luck that Burke had been standing right there when Jillian exposed Taylor's plan. She knew darn well that he hadn't dragged Jillian off to dance to smooth over an uncomfortable scene; he'd done it so he could pump her for information.

Taylor reached the front entry and opened the coat closet. In frustration she shoved hangers from side to side, trying to locate her wrap. A few people might notice her early departure and speculate. Let them wonder; she wasn't staying under her sister's roof one more minute.

"Let's take a walk."

She swung around to find Mason behind her. Without giving her a chance to object, he steered her out the front door. Before they cleared the porch, he shed his dinner jacket and slipped it around her shoulders. "I find myself apologizing for Jillian again."

"She can apologize for herself." Taylor stalked down the sidewalk, still fuming at what her sister had done. She had known, too, that she was in the wrong. All their lives, Jillian had transmitted exactly that sneaky, innocent look whenever she did something she knew damn well was wrong. She had done it at age five, when she flushed Taylor's sanitary napkins down the toilet, ruining the plumbing, then told their mother Taylor had done it. She had done it at age fourteen, when Taylor came home from college for her father's funeral and Jillian gave her the wrong time, so that she ended up missing all but the final pieces of sod being laid by blank-faced cemetery workers.

"I don't think she knows what she does sometimes."

"Then you don't know her very well." Taylor swept through the front gate, held open by the valet. Kind, forgiving, generous, loving Mason had married the wrong woman. That he continued to make excuses for Jillian convinced her even more of this fact. He'd been deceived into thinking she was the consummate wife. But she was poison, antithetical to every value Mason stood for. No matter how many of their friends thought they had the model marriage, no matter how much like lovebirds they had looked the other evening at dinner, Taylor knew the truth. Mason had made a mistake. That she could do absolutely nothing about that situation only made her frustration worse.

Taylor strode on, despite the abuse her pace caused her feet, shod as they were in party slippers with four-inch heels. Her fury commanded her; her fury and her desire to increase the distance between herself and her sister. Mason matched her pace, not speaking, letting her have her lead. Within a few blocks, the silence of the darkened street began to soothe her mood. Trees on either side, grown together to form a canopy, blacked out the starlight.

When she slowed, Mason asked, "It's true, isn't it? What Jillian said?"

She nodded, then remembering the darkness, added a low "Yes."

"Why?"

"Why not?"

"Please, just answer the question."

"The witness has been instructed—"

A car passed by, slowing to ease over the speed bumps. The headlights illuminated Mason's profile. His brows drawn together, lips pursed, he looked more serious than she'd ever seen him. Touching his arm, she said, "You want to know why I want a child or why I am willing to go about it in this stubborn, independent fashion?"

"Both."

"I want a child." *Your child—but that can never be.* "It's a drive within me, something I simply must do. When I tried to explain this to Jillian, she seemed absolutely horrified and refused to even try to understand. But becoming a single parent isn't something I'm doing with no thought. I want it more than I want almost anything else."

"I don't understand it." He sounded puzzled, almost angry. "Oh, not the having-the-child part of it. That, I understand, because I feel exactly the same way. But you always wanted success, independence, to be the best in your field. I never thought of you as even wanting to be a mother, let alone willing to deal with the hassles you're talking about facing. Why a baby now?"

"You just watched me blow out thirty-eight candles. People change."

"You never once talked about wanting a child—"

"At Harper, Cravens?" She interrupted so he wouldn't finish the sentence with a more personal reference. "Because I wanted to make partner didn't mean I didn't have other desires and goals in my life. I wanted a family then, only it wasn't the right time."

"I wish I had known that a long time ago." He stopped. They had reached the end of the long block. Turning to her, he said, "If you want a family, why haven't you married?"

She stepped off the curb. She felt a pebble tear at her stockings and pinch between her toes, chafing at her the way his question did. "The right man never came along," she said, proud that she managed to say the words in such a light voice. "What about you—why haven't you and Jillian had any children?"

"Don't ask," he said, covering what sounded like a groan with a forced laugh. "I'd rather hear about you and your plans. Who's the lucky father?"

Taylor hesitated. She felt awkward explaining her choice to him, but she'd weighed this decision for months, and her mind was made up. "I'll be using a local sperm bank. There's one in Century City."

He raised his brows. Even in the pale light she registered his surprise.

"Well, why not? It's simply medical science at work. They'll give me descriptions of donors, I pick a few, they give me a medical history and several questions and answers designed to supply an idea of the donor's personality—"

"From that . . . that shopping list, you pick the father of your child?"

"It's not ideal, but at least I'll know the genetic and medical history." She didn't add that the sperm bank, for an additional charge, would send the sperm by overnight delivery. Mason wouldn't appreciate the detail.

"As much as they've disclosed about it. But what about the man, the person? What kind of guy jerks off, deposits his semen, and walks away without a second thought? That's the possibility of creation, left in a lab for what, twenty bucks?" Mason dragged his fingers through his hair. "Doesn't that bother you?"

"What am I supposed to do? Sleep with some guy I don't care about and leave my diaphragm out without telling him? At least these men realize what they're doing." She had raised her voice. Mason had hit upon a point that sorely bothered her about the sperm bank process. She could almost accept her child not knowing its father, but she wanted to think the man had at least been someone she could respect and care for. The detachment—or the ego—the donors must have worried her.

Mason touched her arm. "I've no right to be yelling

about it. You didn't have to share this with me. It's just that I want, more than anything else, to be a father. I want all that implies—the diaper changing, the endless hours of baby care, watching my children grow and learn and discover." He kicked at a stone, and it skidded over the edge of the curb onto the blacktopped road. They crossed another deserted side street. "I couldn't walk away not knowing what became of any child of mine."

He would make such a good father. Wrapping her arms around her chest, she suppressed a shiver as she longed for what might have been between them. Rather than let her mind wander down that dead end, Taylor focused on the quiet of the nighttime street. As they walked, she realized the hush was illusory. Birds sang to one another, crickets chirped, and from the distance came the muffled snore of the freeway. Compared to the racket of West Hollywood and the din of Boston's Back Bay, this Pasadena street lay in tranquillity. This was her sister's world, and for all its surface calm, tension oozed out, as the nighttime sounds had made themselves heard when she concentrated on trying to absorb what she thought was total silence.

Thinking of her sister reminded her of something that had puzzled her. "I told Jillian my baby plans at least a week ago. I'm surprised she didn't tell you."

"Babies aren't her favorite topic of conversation."

She heard the regret and bitterness in his voice. "It's difficult, isn't it? You wanting a child, and Jillian not."

"'Difficult' hardly begins to describe it." He stopped, and Taylor realized only inches separated her from his broad chest and his troubled face she longed to gentle. He raised his hands, then jammed them into the pockets of his trousers. "Listening to you describe how much you want a child reminds me what a wonderfully loving woman you are."

His statement caught her off guard. She should step away and return to the party. She'd done or said nothing wrong, and neither had he, but still she heard the echo of her mother's voice, standing behind her, tapping her on the shoulder, telling her to give Jillian back her toy—the toy that her younger sister had ripped from Taylor's hands.

He touched her then, ever so lightly lifting her chin so that their eyes met. "Any child of yours will be a very lucky one."

Taylor swallowed, suddenly certain he was about to kiss her. "We shouldn't be here, Mason."

Abruptly he dropped his hold and took a step back, but continued to stare at her as if he were willing away a desire too reckless to consider. "I've been a fool, Taylor. A fool."

Taylor couldn't bear watching the look in his eyes or suffering the feel of his touch again. This was not the time for him to come to a belated awakening that she—not Jillian—wanted all the same things from life he wanted. She couldn't deal with the conclusion—a conclusion that could lead them nowhere. In an even tone she said, "I think we'd better head back."

From the circle of Burke's arms, Jillian watched her husband follow her sister across the patio and into the house. She sniffed, and smiled at Burke. Let Mason go dry her sister's tears. He'd still come running back to his little Jilly. Then she remembered why Taylor was mad at her. The baby thing. And Mason wanted a baby, too. She had to blink her eyes several times to bring Burke's face back into focus.

"Let's go upstairs." He whispered the words into her ear.

"Excuse me?" She widened her eyes, but knew she had heard correctly.

He drew her closer, so the fabric of his dinner jacket rubbed against the peaks of her nipples. With a wink, he said, "I don't think I need to ask twice."

Jillian considered his words. She could pretend, quite politely, to misunderstand his intentions, and walk away as soon as the music ended.

Spinning around in his arms, she thought of the harsh look on Mason's face after she had embarrassed Taylor.

No, he wasn't happy with her, and why should he be? She was bad; she'd always been bad. The motion of circling within Burke's embrace blended with the champagne dancing inside her head. She felt the tingling excitement of the chase and the conquest. Taylor had said Burke was a jerk; maybe he was, maybe he wasn't. She licked her lips and decided to find out for herself.

The song ended. Stepping back, she smiled and thanked him for the dance. In a lower voice, she said, "Take the kitchen stairs; open the first door to your right." Waving over a waiter, she handed a glass of champagne to Burke and took another one for herself.

As she wound her way into the house, she spread a few hostess smiles and made sure the waiters were continuing to shuttle birthday cake to anyone who wanted it. Moving into the kitchen, she checked with the caterer on champagne supplies and tucked a fresh bottle under her arm. The icy bottle cooled her skin, which had started to flush with heat as she thought of having Burke. The chill served as a momentary check on her behavior. Sipping from her glass, she looked around the kitchen.

She had designed this culinary heaven herself, selecting and placing the Sub-Zero, the convection oven, the antique pine cupboards and sideboards, to suit her whims. It was a beautiful room, a flawless room, but as she glanced around it now, she felt, aside from the bustle of the catering staff, that the room was sterile in its perfection. That idea troubled her, so she smoothed her hair, shook away the niggling thought, and headed up the back stairs. She would drink some champagne and tease Burke. That would at least take her mind off her other problems. Just because she was going upstairs with him didn't mean she planned to let him have her.

She stepped into the first guest bedroom off the hall and kicked off the red heels she had bought to match her dress. "Burke?"

He popped his head around the corner from the connecting bathroom. "In here. You took so long, I started the party without you." His head disappeared, and she padded into the bathroom, still carrying the bottle of Tattingers. Burke was just straightening from the marble counter, his tie astray, one finger held against his nose, a scattering of white powder beneath him on the counter.

"Help yourself, doll."

Jillian placed the champagne on the counter and shook her head. "This house is full of judges, attorneys, and a few deputy DA's, and you're snorting coke? You must be crazy."

He caught her between the cheeks of her derriere and pulled her to him. "I'm not crazy, but I do know what I like."

She thrust her pelvis against him. Her heart had started its own familiar *vroom-vroom,* the rapid beating the sure sign that she would soon enter a state of utter disregard for time, place, setting, and circumstance. Covering his mouth with hers, she moved in with her tongue. Burke worked her dress up, and probed her with two fingers. She was already wet.

"Ah, I love a woman who wears a garter belt," he said, as he lowered her to the carpeted floor.

Fielding helped himself to another mineral water garnished with lime. The patio had turned into a remake of Ten Little Indians. First Taylor disappeared, then Mason, then Burke, then Jillian. Who was following whom? he wondered. Well, his job, since it didn't look as if Mason was going to let him off the hook, was Jillian.

Taking his time, he located the kitchen. Every hostess had to check on the caterers occasionally. He found the hangar-sized kitchen chock-full of aproned cooks and tuxedoed serving people—but no lady of the manor. He nabbed a shrimp from a tray, noted what looked like a back staircase, then wound his way through the downstairs. Searching for a breathy blonde in a knockout red dress should be simple, even in a crowd.

He wished Mrs. Mason Reed weren't quite so alluring. The prospect of getting too close to a spiderweb was never a healthy one for a susceptible insect. And ever since

Fielding had first seen Jillian, holding court across the room, he had sensed his own vulnerability. He sighed, remembering the hurt and anger in Keshia's eyes when she'd confronted him with the evidence of his own infidelity. It didn't get him off the hook that his lost weekend had been due to a love affair with the bottle, not with whatever woman he had incorporated into the spree. Keshia only knew how she felt. He'd vowed never to cause such pain again, no matter what it cost him in self-abnegation.

Fielding wished he hadn't promised to help Mason. Infidelity was so painful for everyone concerned. He completed his tour of the first floor. No Jillian. He then drifted toward the kitchen and up the service staircase. Upstairs, he opened the first door he came to. If anyone was in there, it would be better if he didn't act like he was sneaking around. Fielding almost tripped over a high-heeled shoe lying on the floor. He picked it up, and walked to the window. Holding it up to catch the light, he recognized the shade of red, the exact hue of Jillian's dress.

Giggles and moans, the kind that only came from humans in heat, drifted across the darkened room. A crack of light shone from an interior door. He'd come this far. Feeling worse than a voyeur, who, after all, practices his perversion for pleasure, Fielding approached.

"Oh, God." The oath drifted from a room Fielding reckoned must be a bath. The voice, deep and authoritative even in the midst of passion, sounded familiar, but he couldn't quite place it. It wasn't Mason, though. He detected a low-pitched female murmur. Jillian. Closing his eyes, he found himself wishing he were wrong. He glanced at the shoe he held in his hand and heard Mason's words again. *Whatever it is, it's not that. Right, buddy.*

He walked back to the entrance of the bedroom, cleared his throat, and fumbled noisily for the light switch. "Excuse me. All the bathrooms are full . . ."

He heard a "What the hell," followed by muffled sounds from behind the bathroom door. Then silence. During that moment, he placed the male voice. The news guy.

"Sorry to bother you, but—"

"Just a moment." He heard Jillian's voice and dropped the shoe. What was he waiting for? He'd broken up their little party, so why not hightail it? But something bound him to the spot on the floor where he stood, an almost sick curiosity to see how she would handle the situation.

After a moment, the door opened.

"Excuse me," said Fielding. "The bathrooms downstairs were occupied, and you know how it is."

"Oh, Dr. Sanderson," said Jillian, turning her face away from his view and closing the bathroom door behind her. "I'll just show you the one down the hall."

As rude as it was, he bullied onward. "Is there something wrong with the plumbing in this one?"

She bent to retrieve her shoes. Without a hint of fluster, she said, "I'm just freshening up in there."

"I hope I wasn't intruding," he offered. He'd accomplished coitus interruptus, or whatever hell party game those two were playing. As fast as she had recovered, she must have kept her clothes on. Her lipstick had been eaten off, and her breath came a bit too rapidly, but she didn't look nearly as rattled as he thought she should.

She smiled, the result a bit tremulous. She led him down the hall and pointed to a bathroom. Standing in the doorway, he watched as she continued along the hallway and descended the front staircase. What made the woman tick? Screwing another man while throwing her husband a birthday party, yet floating around with that angelic smile on her face, didn't equate.

The professional in him considered a few behavioral diagnostics. But it was the male in him that kept him where he stood until he could no longer see her.

Chapter 6

TAYLOR LAY IN BED THE MONDAY MORNING after her birthday party, a basal thermometer jammed under her armpit, the forbidden litany playing in her mind.

She wanted a baby.

Mason wanted a baby.

Her sister refused to get pregnant.

She wanted— "Stop right now." The solution might have worked were it merely a mathematical formula. But she, Taylor Drummond, could not get pregnant by her sister's husband, not even through a medical intermediary. It simply wasn't right. And even if Taylor could find a way to justify it, Jillian would never, ever understand. She wasn't one to share her sweaters, let alone her husband. With a kick, Taylor knocked the rest of the rumpled bed-covers to the floor and squelched the thought.

After reading the thermometer, she freed her clipboard from the pile of books, magazines, and browning apple cores on her bedside table. For eight months she had been charting her monthly cycles, planning the most efficacious time for artificial insemination. Luckily for her, her body behaved like a fastidious clock. According to her records, this month her three most fertile days would occur just prior to Christmas.

So wipe all thoughts of Mason from your mind and call that sperm bank. Removing her favorite Celtics T-shirt, Taylor sprang from bed and headed for the shower. This morning was no time to dwell on what could never be. She had to get to the station early today, thanks to Sid. He had set up a meeting for her with an image consultant without asking her opinion in advance.

She knew why he hadn't asked her. He knew she despised the idea of being refashioned according to some statistical idea of what appealed to viewers. After her shower, she stood among the shoe boxes, plastic dry-cleaning wrappers, and discarded hangers, surveying her wardrobe. Each jacket nestled on a padded hanger, every pair of pumps lay swaddled in a flannel drawstring bag. Coordinating blouses and accessories hung next to each suit.

As she selected one in midnight blue with an ivory silk blouse, she fumed over Sid. He probably wanted her to wear a cotton shirtdress and cardigan. That image went along with reading recipes, as far as she was concerned. The only good thing she could say about Sid was that his latest stunt took her mind off Mason.

Later that morning, Taylor was discussing ideas for featured series with Reggie Hyatt, the news director, when Sid's secretary summoned her to his office. She told the secretary she'd be there in a few minutes. To Reggie she said, "Are you attending this image meeting?"

Reggie, tall, thin, and graying, had an ascetic appearance that belied his warmhearted nature. "No, Taylor." He patted her on the shoulder. "Your image suits me just fine. But around here it's a good idea to try to make Sid a happy guy."

Taylor smiled, thankful for his vote of confidence. She stopped to brush her hair before going to the meeting.

When Sid introduced Annie Fleischer, specialist from MediaImage, Taylor thought she looked normal enough. Taylor had half expected this unknown media consultant to look like a southerner dressed for Sunday school. Instead, she wore a calf-length black duster over wide-legged black pants and turtleneck. Red hair frizzed out around her face.

Annie held out her hand and shook vigorously. "Pleased to meet you," she said, retaining Taylor's hand and turning it to scrutinize the palm, then the fingernails. As soon as she let go, she walked in a circle around Taylor. "Well, Sidney, you've got yourself a fine one here."

Sid shifted in his desk chair and swung his feet onto the paper-littered top. Then he chuckled.

Taylor experienced a stab of empathy for animals on display at the fair. Annie continued her appraisal. After another uncomfortable moment, Taylor seated herself on Sid's couch.

"Ah, good. Let's get down to business." Annie reached into a large black bag and pulled out a videocassette. She inserted it in Sid's half-inch machine. "Before we start, let's review our goals." She wrestled a cigarette from the deep pocket of her duster and leaned to accept a light from Sid. After a deep drag, she said, "Sid has a plan for Channel Six. He's hired MediaImage to help him make that plan, that dream—" she punched the air with her cigarette "—a reality. That plan calls for Channel Six to become the People's Station, the station that reminds Los Angeles that it's really a hometown, a small town."

Sid was grinning. Nodding and grinning. Taylor felt like losing her breakfast.

"You know, doll," Annie said to Sid, "the brilliance of what you're talking about is just beginning to sink into this ol' brain of mine. I mean, look what Springsteen did with that concept, and Mellencamp. Maybe you could use one of their songs for theme music." She ground out her cigarette and reached for a notebook.

Still scribbling, she said, "Now, this is where you, Taylor, and Burke come in. But especially you, Taylor."

Sitting straighter, Taylor thought about Boston, about the great news team she'd worked with, of how they had told her she could always come back. But going back was out of the question. After the community uproar that occurred when Liz Walker, one of Boston's most popular newspeople, had become a single parent, Taylor had decided that city was not the place to launch into solo motherhood. She wanted to have her baby quietly and without fanfare. "I'm listening," she said.

Annie started the videotape. "These are clips from stations around the country, primarily from the smaller markets. We know what people *think* works in L.A., but what we're striving for is that small-town magic." The head and shoulders of a young blond woman filled the screen as a promo for a Missouri station began. Annie hit the pause button. "Now, look at this child and tell me what's different between the two of you."

Taylor blinked. "Child" was right. The woman looked all of eighteen. "I could be her mother?"

Sid laughed. "Love your sense of humor, babe. We're not talking about age here, so don't get hot under the discrimination collar. It's more subtle than that. You tell her, Annie."

"This is a woman you could borrow a cup of sugar from. This is a woman who smiles and you suddenly know, you just know, that she loves kittens. Notice the blue of her eye shadow. Most people will tell you not to wear blue eye shadow. It's too outdated, the experts say. But millions of women wear blue eye shadow, and you know something? They trust another woman who does."

Annie moved the tape forward, stopping every so often to comment on one anchor's soft clothing, another's womanliness, and the way one played off against the male co-anchor in a supportive way. Before she reached the end, a knock sounded and Burke sauntered in.

"Don't mind me." He settled onto the leather couch next to Taylor and stretched an arm out across the back.

Annie stopped the tape and asked what stood out about that particular anchor. "Nice knockers," Burke said. Leaning closer to Taylor, he added under his breath, "Like your sister."

Annie said, "Absolutely right. Not every breast comes across as attractive on television, but this woman has exactly the right thrust and angle."

Taylor couldn't help but sneak a look downward. She'd sort out Burke's reference to her sister later.

"I see you're curious about your own image, Taylor," said Annie, obviously catching her motion. "We'll play your tape next." She pulled another tape from her bag, then switched the two.

As a child, listening over and over again to her mother

carp on Jillian's talents and Taylor's shortcomings, Taylor had learned to assume the proper expression of attention, then free her mind to roam. She could be anywhere, rafting down the Mississippi, exploring the Amazon, dancing at Twenty-One. Slipping into this state once more, she nodded politely at Annie Fleischer. Let this woman have her say, then she'd pack her bag of tricks and disappear.

The second tape started and Taylor saw herself sitting in front of a view of the Boston skyline towering above the Charles River. Faced with her own image, her mind refused to release its attention. On-screen, she wore a suit almost identical to the dark blue one she had chosen earlier that morning.

Annie hit the pause. "Now, what do we see here?"

"Authority. Intelligence." Burke, to Taylor's surprise, provided those answers. "But not enough cleavage, right?"

Annie nodded. "What we see is a contradiction that confuses the viewer. We have a mature woman with baby-soft skin and long, dark hair. Opposing images. We have a certain sexiness, but that's negated by the stern cut of the suit and the high collar of the blouse."

She reached for another cigarette, practically *tsk-tsk*ing. Inhaling as Sid lit it for her, she said, "And worse than all that, you still look like a lawyer. So you not only turn off the viewer by confusing him, you offend him by projecting the image of one of the most despised professions." She advanced the tape, and Taylor saw more and more images of herself, clad in what she knew were high-quality designer suits with prices to match. She thought she looked sharp, capable, and intelligent.

Annie stopped the tape. "What Sid and I have agreed upon is a new look for you that will draw the viewer in. Your look would work fine for CNN, and the people on the East Coast might not have noticed the contradictions, but for the new Channel Six, the station of the people, you'll need to make these changes." She shuffled through her bag again and handed a three-ring binder to Taylor.

Taylor left it closed. Burke said, "Do you mind?" and reached for the notebook, opening it so that it spread from his lap to hers. "Look at this, Taylor. They've made you into a paper doll and dressed you up."

Taylor glanced at the first page. An artist had drawn what reminded her of a police sketch. The woman in the picture had her coloring, and her hair, although the hair was drawn back in a loose chignon. Instead of a suit, the woman wore a long-sleeved blouse with a high collar and puffed sleeves. She turned the page, and the artist's sketch showed her with her hair flowing over a dress with a low-cut, squared-off neckline and a fitted waist.

"None of these even look like something I'd wear," she said when she looked up again.

Annie blinked. "That's exactly the point."

Taylor started to stare her down and decided not to waste her energy. The woman would soon be gone to Atlanta or Dallas or wherever it was she had flown in from. "What about Burke? Does he have a tape, too?"

Burke stopped flipping through the notebook. Sid said, "Burke's not the problem here."

"Problem?" asked Taylor.

"What he means, hon," said Annie, "is that MediaImage has studied Burke's style and concluded that there's nothing in his delivery that works against Sid's plan. Women love authority in a man, and men respond to it." She tweaked her frizzy hair and smiled at Burke. Taylor thought she could feel heat from Burke's pants as he smiled back.

Taylor considered her priorities. Becoming a single mother would be tough enough; doing so unemployed would be highly undesirable. She swallowed her impulse to toss the notebook of wardrobe sketches back into Annie Fleischer's black bag and stalk out of Sid's office.

"So, babe, study the pictures. Don't worry about sinking your own money into the clothes. When you know what you want, I have a buddy who will work out a wardrobe deal for the station." Sid yanked his feet off his desk and looked at his watch. "Let's go, Annie. We're late for our lunch at City."

Requesting a moment with Sid, Burke rose and walked

him from the room, one arm around the shoulder of the shorter man, his head bent in earnest, whispered conversation.

Taylor watched Burke, wondering what he had actually pieced together from Jillian at the birthday party. His reference to her had been sexual; he'd made no cracks about baby plans. Perhaps he hadn't overheard. One thing was for sure: If she asked him about it, that would only pique his curiosity. She stuck to the problem at hand, asking Annie, "Do you enjoy your job?"

Annie turned from the tape machine, where she was extracting Taylor's demo tape. "It's a job, like any job."

"It doesn't bother you, as a woman, to try to push women like me into slots, into stereotypes?"

"When you're on the air, you're not a woman. You're a product. It's my job to sell that product, and I'm damn good at what I do."

Sid poked his head back in the office. "What's keeping you, woman?"

Hefting her bag, Annie waltzed over to Sid, who put his arm around her and gave her a sloppy kiss. From over Sid's shoulder, Annie shot her a hard look.

Taylor remained on the sofa after they left, the binder open on her lap. She hadn't struggled to rise through the ranks so she could model frosted nail polish and sparkling blue eye shadow. She belonged in a market where solid skills were nurtured and appreciated—not these circus tricks. Two thoughts held her to her seat: one, the possibility that she could make a difference at Channel Six, and two, L.A. was the best place for her to have her baby.

Thrusting aside the picture book, she crossed to Sid's desk, unearthed his phone book, and jotted down the listing for City Cryo-Bank. Sitting on his desk, her feet propped on his leather chair, she dialed their number.

That morning, Mason rose early and left the house before Jillian's Dalmane-battened eyelids fluttered open. Guilt drove him out into the crisp early morning air. After Saturday night, when in a moment of emotional confusion, he had spoken to Taylor so intimately, he had trouble looking his wife in the face. Thankfully, Jillian had been asleep when he left to play golf with friends yesterday, and claiming a migraine, had retired early that night. In their one conversation, he had asked her to speak to Fielding when he called her. To his surprise, she had agreed without protest.

This morning he feared Jillian waking and reading his treachery in the way his fingers stumbled over their routine of fastening his tie in exactly the right knot, in the way he'd explain at length about a breakfast meeting with some important client, in the way he'd only peck her cheek good-bye.

He, who believed in fidelity and scorned couples who simply gave up and moved on whenever a relationship became too difficult, had thought of nothing but Taylor since Saturday night.

He had to stop. He would make it up to Jillian. Next weekend he'd take her to Palm Springs, or fly to San Francisco. They would finally make love again, and that would chase all thoughts of Taylor from his mind.

Jillian wanted to rush the stage and drag Mrs. Manningwell, recipient of the Pasadena Red Cross Volunteer of the Year Award, into the wings. To control her tension, Jillian swung one leg over her knee, twisting her ankle in alphabet circles, as she waited for the blue-haired grandmother to finish thanking her husband for his support. She formed a broad *a*, stroked a *b* with her toe, then moved on down the alphabet. The linen tablecloth at the luncheon table concealed her antics from the rest of the well-bred crowd.

Throughout the endless luncheon, she'd been watching their young blond waiter. When he'd filled her wineglass, she'd observed the strength in his large hands. From his build, she could tell the strength ran up his arms, across his shoulders, and on down his torso. He moved lightly. Tennis? Soccer? What was he doing waiting tables at a Red Cross luncheon? Of course, he was probably a student working his way through school. Judging by his polished looks, he was enrolled at USC.

When he'd served the silver-haired woman sitting directly across the table from her, Jillian had caught his eye. She didn't smile, or simper; she simply held his gaze. Wide green eyes looked back at her from his surf-bronzed face. As he offered *au jus* to Mrs. Walter Rockingham, he nodded, ever so slightly, to Jillian.

That acknowledgment had carried her through the rest of the endless luncheon. She needed the boy to get through the day. She'd felt hung over since Saturday night, Mason had been cold and distant, her sister probably wasn't speaking to her, and she couldn't forgive herself for making it with that jerk in her own house. To top things off, Mason had asked her to meet with his friend the shrink. Out of guilt and her need to figure out what he'd seen and heard at the party, she had agreed. Everybody hated her. She was beyond redemption.

The sound of beating wings caught her attention. She realized the women were applauding. It must be over. Thank God.

Promising to call the woman sitting next to her soon, very soon, she excused herself from the table. She slipped between the other diners, all women, and headed for the back of the banquet room. The polite world of charity luncheons fell away. With every step she took toward the kitchen, her pulse quickened. She might despise herself later, but right now that didn't matter. The boy was waiting.

The blond stud caught her hand as soon as she stepped into the corridor leading off the main dining room. "In here," he said, pushing open a door and pulling her after him.

She found standing room only in what appeared to be a storage closet for linens. Before she could put her purse down, he shoved her against a wall lined with folded tablecloths. She spread her legs and flung her arms wide, nuzzling the soft cotton of the tablecloths. Her four-hundred-dollar purse slipped from her grasp. She was no longer Mrs. Mason Reed, the woman who had purchased the handbag during an idle afternoon of shopping on Rodeo. Licking her lips, she watched him watching her, smiling at the bulge in his pants. "Come and get me," she whispered.

"You're some bitch in heat." Grabbing her breast roughly, he bit her lip and rammed his tongue in her mouth.

She wished he'd brushed his teeth. Then he shoved her dress up and unzipped his pants, and she tried not to think about his breath. He was, after all, giving her what she craved.

"You do this a lot?" he asked, accepting the condom she slipped out of her pocket. He worked the rubber on.

She started to shake her head.

"No, huh?" He thrust into her. He laughed, and still inside her, slid her weight up his legs. "You just happened to forget your underwear this morning?"

Her legs gripped around his firm buttocks, she rode him. "Shut up and fuck me," she said coldly.

"You are one weird lady," he said, then turned his attention to his own pleasure.

Fielding dreaded his morning appointment with Jillian Reed. He had agreed to Mason's request to meet with her and had been surprised when Jillian called him soon after the party. "Come over for coffee," she'd said, in a voice that hinted at nothing more, nothing less.

As he parked his Jag across the street from their house, he registered his reluctance to approach the door. Jillian exuded a dangerous magnetism, like a modern-day Siren. He'd felt it that first night, watching her across the room, not yet aware she was Mason's wife. If he had any sense, he'd stuff wax in his ears and lash himself to the mast, like old Ulysses.

Instead, he abandoned his four-wheeled refuge and crossed the street. The house looked different in the lemon light of the December morning. Gone were the firefly lamps of last Saturday's birthday party. The front yard was dressed in a simple collage of color, from flowers that Fielding guessed bloomed in a commercial hothouse and found themselves transplanted at the command of the lady of the manor.

Lady of the manor, he decided, was an image that suited Jillian. He couldn't picture her lugging a briefcase and rubbing padded shoulders in the business world. Or clicking the keys of a typewriter in some exec's front office. Perhaps she couldn't either; maybe an inability to see herself in any other role was part of her problem.

He passed through her Disneyland of flowers. As soon as he finished partaking of her coffee, which would no doubt be some gourmet variety, he'd tell Mason he was off the case. Life was too short and sweet to be embroiled in the confusion that dealing with Jillian stirred in him. Even though he'd witnessed her unfaithfulness, he still wanted to believe the best in her. And believing the best, he then found himself wanting it.

He was definitely old enough to know better.

Jillian opened the door before he could lift the knocker, her face echoing the brightness of the day. He thought, with a feeling as sweet and fleeting as the first strong pull on a double whiskey, that she looked happy to see him. She wore a print corduroy jumper, drop-waisted, with a crisp white blouse underneath. She looked about seventeen.

"Please come in," she said, offering him a cool hand tipped by pale pink nails.

He took her hand, for a moment, then followed her inside. Studying her face for any sign of embarrassment, for recognition of the compromising position in which he'd last seen her, he found none. Anxiety knew no place on her features as she led him into the den, chatting about what lovely weather they were having.

Fielding was a trained observer, experienced in intercepting and interpreting body language and the difference between words spoken and thoughts not expressed. From Jillian, he garnered nothing other than a polite welcome to a guest. He wondered whether his own wayward feelings about her were clouding his ability to study his subject, then shrugged off that thought. The lady was an expert at hiding her emotions.

When she'd settled him in a bookshelf-lined room, she invited him to watch the fish in an enormous built-in aquarium, and excused herself. Fielding glanced briefly at the fish puttering around, but they disturbed him. They were like prisoners in a cell, pacing off the distance. Twelve strokes left, turn, twelve strokes right. On a hunch, he figured the books belonged to Mason; the fish, to Jillian.

The coffee service was silver. Very old, very expensive. Fielding accepted a delicate china cup and saucer from her, wondering if the coffee would taste any different served in this kind of getup. When he sat down, he carefully placed his back to the aquarium. Jillian perched on the edge of a leather chair opposite the coffee table. She left her cup, untouched, on the table.

"So," she said, wrapping her tapered fingers around her crossed knees and pinning him with her blue eyes, "Mason asked me to talk to you."

Instead of answering, he drank from his cup and nodded.

"He probably asked you to get to know me."

He nodded again.

"Therefore, you're here because you want—" she rose and transplanted herself onto the love seat beside him "—to get to know me better."

He nodded again, thinking he must look like one of those toy dogs with movable heads old ladies propped in the back windows of their Cadillacs.

"So," she said, leaning back against the sofa, and not moving closer, much to his relief, "what would you like to know?"

He almost said, *Whatever you'd like to tell me.* Then he caught himself. No shrink talk. "What do you like to do in your spare time?"

"Spare time?" She sat up, swinging one knee back and forth. "I hardly have any spare time. Running a house like this is a lot of work. And I have obligations." She faced him and smiled. "More coffee?" As she poured, she continued, "Many obligations. Luncheons, fund-raisers, business dinners. I don't know what I would do if we ever had children. There just isn't time."

He thought of his grandmother, working two jobs and raising not only her kids, but her grandchildren and several others off the streets. "I didn't mean to imply you had a lot of spare time. I was just curious about hobbies, that sort of thing."

"Oh, hobbies." She clasped her hands over her crossed knees and stared across the room. After a few minutes she said, "I've always hated that word. What does it really mean? That your life is so empty, you have to invent ways to pass the time between sunup and sundown? That's what 'hobby' means. No, I don't have any hobbies."

Before he could stop her, she refilled his cup again. When she handed him back the saucer, he thought she rested her fingers against his for a moment longer than necessary. Maybe he should leave. Go before he confirmed what he suspected she really did with her spare time.

"Do you have any hobbies?" she asked.

He nodded.

"Well?"

"Cars. Boxing. Kite flying."

"I love kites. But I haven't flown a kite in years. Not since . . ."

"Not since?"

"Oh, before I got married, I guess. Marriage changes you, you know. Are you married?"

"Not anymore."

"Divorced?"

"Yes."

"It happens, doesn't it? One day you wake up and realize the other person isn't the one you married, or thought you married." She looked away. "I'd die if that happened to me. If Mason ever decided he didn't love me anymore, I know I wouldn't live through it."

"He certainly seems to love you." What was he supposed to say? *He loves you, but even though he denies it, he thinks you're screwing around on him, and that's why I'm here, and do you realize that?* Or did she know it, and that explained her protestations of affection? He couldn't help but notice, though, that she hadn't said *she* loved Mason.

"I have to be loved." Her eyes, so blue and serene earlier, had grown paler. A hint of a crease showed between her eyes. She reached out a hand toward Fielding's cup. He surrendered it, thinking he'd burst if she gave him another refill. But she settled it on the table and turned toward him. Capturing his hands, she repeated, "I have to be loved." This time she crooned the words, like a mother whispering nighttime secrets to her baby. Stroking the back of his hand, she said, "I'm so happy you came to see me. I knew you would, from the first moment we met. I knew you'd come."

He sensed the increase in her breathing. He saw the distant, glazed look now in her eye, and doubted whether she even knew who he was at that moment. Leaving his hands within hers, he said, "Jillian, you are loved. Mason loves you. You're a special person."

She licked her lips. "To you, too?"

He nodded.

She moved up against him, and undid the top button on her blouse. "Show me you love me."

"Don't do that."

Reaching under the bib of her jumper, she undid the next few buttons.

"Jillian, stop."

"No, no, you love me; you said you love me. If you don't show me, how can I ever believe you?" She grabbed for his crotch. He winced as she found the hard bulge beneath his pants, and she looked at him in triumph. "I knew you wanted me."

When she fiddled with his zipper, he gripped her hand in his and shook her. "Listen to me. Because I do care about you, I'm leaving. Right now." She seemed not to focus on him. He shifted away from her, and she started to sniffle.

"You said you wanted to get to know me better. Why won't you stay?"

He had to get out of there. If he stayed to comfort her, she'd keep up with her tricks. Before he knew it, she'd be out of that little-girl dress, parading naked in front of him and her fish. She'd already discovered his physical reaction to her, but he'd be damned if he'd betray Mason. Doing so would be exactly like falling off the wagon—a few minutes, even a few hours, of physical pleasure or senseless oblivion just wasn't worth it.

He grabbed her wrist and forced her back to her side of the couch. "Does this come-on have anything to do with what I interrupted at the party?"

She gasped. "Why would you say that? I want you."

"Like you wanted that man?" He took her face in his hands. "Jillian, look at me. Me, Fielding Sanderson. I'm a person. Treating me like an object makes me less than human. Don't throw yourself at me unless you want *me.*"

A tear worked its way down one side of her cheek.

He rose from the couch and looked down at her. "You didn't have to offer yourself to me in hopes that I wouldn't mention to Mason I interrupted you and your lover in your own home." He straightened his pants. "Nice try, though." He hated the harshness he heard in his voice, but he couldn't help himself. She didn't care who he was; she didn't think of him as a man unlike any other, and that hurt.

What hurt even more was that he wanted to take her up on her advances. He felt the hardening of his own flesh and the weakening of his resolve. Turning, he headed for the front door, reminded of his granny's Bible story of Lot fleeing Sodom and Gomorrah. Poor Mason. Jesus, did the woman come on to everyone? He realized he wanted to think she had wanted him, but he knew he was no one special. To her, he was an object, a thing, a dildo.

When he reached the sidewalk, he spit. Jillian left a bad taste in his throat, which made him even more disgusted at

himself for being so intrigued with her. Opening the door
of his car, he started to step in when he heard her garage
door swing open and saw Jillian backing recklessly out of
their driveway. What the hell? Reaching for his ignition
key, he swore under his breath, then swung his car around
to follow her.

She drove heedlessly, zipping around cars that slowed
her headlong rush. He stuck with her, navigating the
change from one freeway to the next, wondering where
in the hell she was headed. When they reached Beverly
Hills, he groaned, assuming she would work off his rejection of her through an expensive shopping splurge.
Nonetheless, he remained on her trail. She pulled her car
into a city parking lot close to the Beverly Rodeo Hotel.
Fielding did the same, then kept behind her on foot. She
entered the hotel and approached the registration desk.
The clerk handed her a key, and Jillian headed for the elevator. Fielding paused at the edge of the tiny lobby,
from where he could watch both the shadowed hallway
and the street door. Jillian was here to meet someone,
but who? She must have made an assignation immediately after he'd exited her house. Who had hustled over
on such short notice?

The street door swooshed open and Fielding saw a tall
blond man with a distinctive face—the type men would
win awards for if they held beauty contests—sweep in.
Not a face easily forgotten, especially when that face
graced the "Channel Six News at Ten" five nights a week.
Burke Washington walked past him, heading for the telephone. Fielding yanked his Dodgers cap from his jacket
pocket, pulled it down over his face, and strolled with him
to the phones. Picking up a house phone, the man asked
for Jill Smith's room, waited for the connection, then said,
"It's Burke. Give me your room number." With a satisfied
smile on his photogenic face, he replaced the receiver and
sauntered to the elevator.

Of course. He and Jillian were about to finish what
Fielding had interrupted at the party. How could she do it?
How could she say she'd die if Mason didn't love her,

then put the move on two men the same morning? Walking back to his car, Fielding grimaced as he remembered how Keshia used to ask him similar questions.

How could you get drunk when you know we're expected at my parents' anniversary party? How could you disappear on a binge the weekend we were supposed to celebrate my birthday? If you loved me, you wouldn't drink.

He had loved her. He'd loved alcohol more.

Jillian's behavior echoed his own, as if she were driven by some obsessive need to claim love in the arms of whatever man would have her. But Mason loved her, and according to Mason, she'd practically dried up the supply on him.

Guilt.

Fielding had suffered, returning home from a drunken binge, begging understanding from Keshia, and on not getting it, blaming her for the whole thing. All the time, he'd been racked with guilt for being such a shithead. Probably Jillian felt the same way, and as a result, felt unworthy of Mason. It was crazy, though, because she kept crying out for love, and by her own actions, denying the open-armed acceptance offered by her husband.

She needed help, as he had needed help. He acknowledged the bond between them. At first he had ascribed it to animal attraction. But it was far greater than that; he heard and experienced the pain that she herself denied. He had denied his own pain, too, and had only been set free when he'd begun to allow it out, a little at a time. At first he'd been afraid, and angry at the possibility that inside he was a miserable, bleeding mess. After all, his life was solid, successful. By God, he was a shrink. If he felt pain, he'd be in touch with it. But no, he'd drowned all feeling. Through his own prior psychoanalysis, he had upheld the intellectual bullshit level, had been able to discuss supposedly deep and complex feelings about his childhood on cue. And all along, he'd kept burying himself deeper and deeper, in the liquid death of the bottle. Using a different substance, Jillian was digging the same death-in-life for herself, and he wanted to help her.

Did that mean he didn't tell Mason what he had discovered? What man, what husband, would understand his wife was acting out from fear and pain? No, he would most likely think his wife was screwing around because she was a bitch and didn't love him anymore. And for that, Fielding wouldn't blame him.

He retrieved his Jag and crept up Rodeo toward Wilshire, deciding that he would wait to tell Mason about Jillian's problem. Maybe he could aid her, and Mason wouldn't have to know.

Jillian hated to be told to relax. Especially during sex. What was relaxing about two writhing, sweating, contorting, slobbering bodies trying to simultaneously gratify themselves and provide some pastiche of pleasure to the other? But when Burke kept muttering over and over again, "Relax, baby, relax," she only smiled and continued to pant. She didn't want to relax and she didn't want the tongue job. As she stared through slitted eyelids at the ceiling, she wondered what she did want.

Burke lifted his head. "You're not into this, are you?"

She opened her eyes and tickled his chin with a toe. "Why do you say that?"

He lunged forward and grabbed her chin. "Don't fuck with me. You're here because you want to be with me, or you and I have nothing to say to each other. Who do you think I am? Some street-sleeping gigolo? I can get better ass from some starry-eyed novice reporter than what's in front of me right now."

As his tirade continued, his breathing grew fast and harsh. Jillian lifted his hand from her chin and smiled up into his eyes. She wasn't about to lose this port in a storm. He'd been willing to come when she called, and that was worth a little bit of effort on her part.

"Of course I'm here for you." Running a hand over his smooth hair, unmussed despite his physical exertion, she pulled him down for a kiss. She worked his lips and mouth as if her life depended on it. And perhaps it did. After a very long moment, she said, "I'm just not used to such pampering. Why don't we begin again?"

"You look like the cat that swallowed the canary. Where the hell have you been?" Taylor landed on Burke the minute he showed his face in the newsroom. "People are looking for you. I had to do the live promo spot solo."

He merely smiled and started humming under his breath.

Taylor tried her best to ignore him. Thanksgiving was tomorrow, and she had a longtime habit, sentimental though it might be, of remembering and commemorating the good things in life on Thanksgiving Day. The holiday had been born out of a celebration of survival, and she related to that. But her day had been going less than well. Upon arriving at work and checking her mail, she had found an envelope marked "Personal." It contained a sheet of Harper, Cravens stationery bearing the words "Please forgive me."

She had sat, staring at Mason's handwriting, hearing over and over again, both pain and desire in his voice as he had said, *I've been a fool.* Her reverie had been broken by a staccato phone call from Annie, in which the woman announced Taylor had to cut her hair.

Burke turned up the volume on his humming. The man was impossible. If Taylor had failed to show for a live cut-in to promo the evening news, she would have been embarrassed sick by such unprofessional behavior. He didn't seem to realize what he had done was wrong. Judging by the grin on his plastic face, he'd been with some floozy all afternoon. "Burke, what are you humming? It's starting to get to me."

He grinned. "An old classic. It's called 'If You Knew Jilly Like I Know Jilly.' " Moving over to her desk, he grabbed a chair and rolled closer to her. "At least one member of your family has some taste." He winked and rose from the chair.

He was only trying to get her goat. "I assure you my

sister has too much taste and good sense to take you up on any proposition."

"Of course," said Burke. "Of course she does." He turned to take a phone call. After he hung up, he shrugged into his suit coat. "The wife's in labor, so I've got to pop over to Cedars."

"How exciting!" For a moment Taylor forgot she couldn't stand the man.

He straightened his tie. "Third time around, it's not too exciting. More bills, more sagging breasts." He leaned over to Taylor, and hummed a few more bars of the same tune.

She pushed him away with her hands. "Give my best to your wife." Reaching for a pen, she made a note to send flowers. God knew Burke's wife deserved them.

Through the rest of her evening routine, Burke's refrain reverberated in her brain. At least he didn't pick it up again when he slipped in before the ten o'clock news. As they practiced their lead-ins aloud, he stuck to his script and didn't pester her once. He mumbled something about the baby taking a long time, and rushed out right after the newscast ended.

By the time she reached her apartment, Taylor had stopped wondering about Burke and Jillian. Despite the fact that his wife was in labor, Burke might be cheating on her. She wouldn't put it past him. But he couldn't possibly be sleeping with her sister. No woman in her right mind would cheat on Mason.

Chapter 7

FIELDING PARKED HIS PORSCHE ON A PASA-
dena side street and pulled his blue Dodgers cap lower
over his forehead. Four yards away, Jillian stepped out of
her car. He told himself he should call out to her, ask to
speak to her. Instead, he studied her every move, struck
once again by how magnificent she was, marveling at how
such a perfect creature could hate herself so much. God,
but she was beautiful. That lean body, tucked into what
looked like black silk, and partially hidden by a coat
draped over her shoulders, flowed toward the back entrance of the pub. Her hair shone pale blond in the December sun. Large dark glasses hid her eyes, but her full lips
conveyed a sensuality that spoke directly to his body. As
he felt himself stir in response, he ducked his head and
pulled the cap even lower over his face, as if he were
afraid his primal urge would signal his presence to her.

Like the fool he was proving himself to be, he had
missed his moment. Now he could sit here and wait, or
march into the pub after her—or go sensibly back to work.

On impulse, he'd followed her that morning. He'd been
pulling up to her house, having decided after a running
battle with himself to confront her about her compulsive
behavior.

He had driven there thinking to offer himself as a friend
if she needed someone to unburden herself on. Such an action was definitely not that of a professional psychologist,
but in this territory, he acted as Mason's friend, fellow suf-
ferer of addictive behavior, and as a man. In what order he
was serving those interests, he purposely did not examine.

Wanting to move beyond his male hormonal reaction to Jillian, he'd hired out the job of confirming his suspicions about her habitual practice of sex with strangers. The investigator had phoned that morning and reported three encounters within the last week and a half. Fielding had thanked him, and without thinking through his actions, he'd headed for his Porsche.

With a sigh, Fielding settled into his seat. He'd wait a little while longer. So far, Jillian had lunched at the Chronicle with two women, then driven up and down Lake Avenue, one of Pasadena's "shopping" streets, before turning in to the parking lot of a restaurant/bar. Fielding didn't think she was looking for a second meal.

On the sidewalk next to his car, a grizzled woman bundled in a scarf and sweater slowed her pace. She walked a poodle that looked as if it had been left in the dryer too long. She beetled her gray eyebrows at Fielding, then let the shriveled pooch close in on his new Pirelli wheels. Fielding groaned as he pictured the dog whizzing on his tire. Only the thought that Jillian might change her mind, return to her car, and spot him kept him from bounding from the car and making mincemeat out of the mutt. Dog and woman moved on, and he was left watching cars speed by, most traveling well over the posted 35-mph speed. He wished he could pump life into his engine and roar off with them.

Fielding felt like a Peeping Tom.

What did he expect, slumped behind the steering wheel of his Porsche, waiting for Jillian to emerge from the pub? When he had played with the idea of becoming a private eye, he really hadn't been realistic. Following a man's wife to see whether she was getting some on the side— that was no way to spend the day. Besides, it reminded him of the time he stumbled across the facts of life.

He had been a scrawny kid at five years, all ribs, no flesh, his grin a tunnel of missing teeth through which he tried to whistle. His father had "gone away." He had been gone a long time when one night his mother put him to bed, then crept out of the apartment. Later, hearing a man's voice, Fielding woke and hurtled out of bed. His dad was back! But the voice he heard through the door didn't belong to his father.

Barefoot and starting to shiver, Fielding squatted outside the door and listened. At first he thought the man must be hurting his mother, but then she laughed and laughed. Fielding finally grew sleepy and went back to bed.

Somehow, after that night, he knew his father was never coming back. When he mentioned what he heard to his grandmother, he thought she was going to puff up like one of the fish in his animal books and explode. She and his mother had a screaming match. From then on, Fielding lived with his granny. He understood now how his mother, only nineteen at the time, had been unable to cope. As a kid of five, he only wondered what he had done wrong to cause his mother to leave him.

As he grew up, he became convinced that sex, and most other things that went on behind closed doors, were better off left private. One of the aspects of his psychology practice he had hated was the tendency of his married clients to zoom into the office screaming each other's faults, particularly their sexual and personal inadequacies, at top volume. He never favored the crude descriptions bandied about in locker rooms and bars either. The guys who talked the loudest probably got the least action. When Fielding discussed sex, it was with a partner he cared for, someone who meant enough to him that it mattered to him whether he pleased her.

His revulsion at reporting to Mason on his wife's activities reminded him of one early attempt to get sober. He had taken an alcohol-aversion drug, given to inhibit drinking. He got sick, all right, but that hadn't stopped him from tossing back a few more beers. He didn't quit until he passed out.

Fingering the gearshift knob, Fielding laughed. At himself. He thought he had learned to listen to the voice inside himself that said, *This doesn't feel good. Stop now and ask yourself why not?* He didn't want to be a PI. He wanted to help people get all they could out of life. Though he was

reluctant to face the link he still harbored in his brain between his days as a shrink and as a drunk, he now knew
he wanted to go back to private practice. The obstacle he
had to face was his fear—fear of himself and of the power
of the bottle.

Jillian knew she needed to work fast. She shifted closer
to the man seated on the barstool to her right, engineering
her move so that her thigh nudged his like a boat along-
side a dock. For the last half hour, he'd been regaling her
with tales of clients who thought they knew more about
the stock market than he did. He'd bought her last glass of
wine. It was time to set sail.

"So . . ." she said, and hit him with what she knew was
one of her most beguiling, and effective, smiles.

He lifted his glass in a salute and stood.

"Ready to go?" she asked.

He nodded. "Business to attend to."

"You're leaving . . . alone?" She reached for his hand.

He jerked it back. "Alone." He looked her in the eye.
"Don't think I'm not tempted, honey. But the day of the
casual fuck is over." He tilted her chin up. "Not that
you're not a great piece of goods, but you just can't be too
careful." Turning abruptly, he shouldered his way through
the afternoon crowd.

Jillian didn't dare look to her left or right. Who had
overheard him? She was going to die, right there, on the
barstool, from humiliation. What a prick! Who did he
think he was, rejecting her like that? She reached for her
wineglass.

Thick fingers closed around hers. In her ear, she heard
a gruff voice whisper, "I don't mind a game of Russian
Roulette." The fingers squeezed their way up her arm,
closing on her shoulder and managing to scrape the top of
her breasts. "Especially not with odds like you're offering."

She swiveled her head around to see who her savior
was. A massive cowboy hat, brim tilted downward, covered most of his face. When she smiled, he lifted his hat

in greeting, then set it back farther on his head. Registering a fiftyish face, with reddened jowls and broad neck, and deciding he would do, she nodded at him. Ignoring her usual cautious concern that an acquaintance might spot her, she walked out of the pub with the stranger, but insisted on driving her own car, agreeing to follow the man to his apartment. She tried to avoid going to a stranger's house, but her needs of the moment overpowered her sense of caution. She was having a rotten day. She had gained two pounds. Her mother had called and invited herself out for Christmas. And one of the women she lunched with just found out she was pregnant. The conversation had consisted of the pros and cons of breast-feeding and which obstetricians at Huntington Hospital were the absolute best.

She followed the aging cowboy to a bungalow apartment building centering around a small courtyard. Noting the paint hanging in shreds from the walls of the front cottage, she wrinkled her nose and reminded herself that beggars couldn't be choosers.

He led her to the back unit. Inside the bungalow, the shades were lowered. He made no attempt to turn on the lights. It was just as well, because she preferred the shadowed gloom of the afternoon as protection from the mess she'd probably see.

Gathering her in an embrace, he massaged her buttocks through her coat. She reached for his zipper.

"You're a spirited filly, aren't you?" he said, smothering her mouth with his.

The taste of whiskey choked her. Pulling away, she tried to smile in apology. Maybe she shouldn't have come. He really wasn't her type.

He grabbed for her breast. She looked down at his hand, and caught a slight movement across her Bally pump. Shifting her head so she could see around his beefy hand, she peered down, afraid of what she might see. A black bug, shiny and as large as her thumb, sat on the toe of her shoe.

She screamed.

His hands flew around her throat, choking her, cutting off the sound. "What the fuck are you yelling about?"

Pointing down with one hand, she tried to remove his hands with her other. He loosened his grasp.

"Bug. There's a bug on my shoe."

"Well, it's sure as hell gone now." He tossed his hat onto a pair of rabbit ears atop a television perched on a rickety stand. All three swayed as the hat settled to rest. "Don't scream again, though, or I'll have to gag you."

"I'm sorry, but I think I'd better go." Jillian pulled her coat around her. "I'm not really in the mood anymore."

He hitched up his pants. His face darkened. "I don't think I much care whether a spoiled bitch like you is in the mood. I can enjoy myself just fine either way." Before Jillian knew what was happening, he reached into his boot, and with a swift click, pointed a knife at her throat.

She swallowed. The knife looked very shiny, very sharp, and very, very close to her delicate skin. Moving slowly, she opened the front of her coat. With a bat of her eyelashes, she said, "Maybe I am in the mood." She had to calm him down and get him to drop the knife. Then she had to get the hell out of that place. How, she didn't know.

"That's more like it." He lowered the knife but didn't put it down.

She unfastened the string tie around his neck and the buttons of his shirt. If all he wanted was sex, she could give him that. He would be no different from any other man. She could feel her heart pounding in her chest, but she knew not to show any fear. But the knife frightened her. And the way he had reflexively grabbed to choke her when she screamed. Later, later, after she had rescued herself from this mess, she would break down. And please God, if she did get out alive, she would never be bad again.

When she pushed his shirt open, she spotted the tattoo—a woman, spread-eagle and staked, done in four colors, right over his navel. She shivered. She had to get out of there.

He was turning the knife over and over in his hand,

watching her undress him. She paused and slipped out of her coat, repressing the thought of those awful bugs crawling into the sleeves and pockets.

"I thought you were a spirited filly, and you turn out to be just as fussy as a Baptist minister's wife."

Jillian pushed him onto the couch and grabbed his balls through his pants. "By the time we're finished, you won't mistake me for a preacher's wife."

He smiled and dropped the knife. It fell a few inches from his hand. If she ran for the door, he could easily stop her. "Do you mind if I use your bathroom before we start the party?"

He pointed and said, "Help yourself. Don't mind the water bugs." Laughing, he rose from the couch, but didn't follow her.

Jillian picked up her purse and crossed the small living room. Her earlier lust, full-blown and demanding satisfaction, had fled. She wanted to cry when she thought of that creep touching her. Why hadn't she gone home after lunch? If she could just have another chance, she'd do it all so differently.

The bathroom was the latest in nouveau filth. Water stood in the tub, the linoleum on the floor shifted as she stepped on a broken piece, and the tap dripped steadily. But there was a lock on the door. And a window.

She had seen it done in movies, and she did it now. Flicking the lock shut, turning the taps on full, lifting the window wide, flushing the toilet, removing the screen. She had to sacrifice a cashmere coat, but she could never have worn it again anyway. Not with the memory of that voracious black bug.

Sprinting down the driveway toward the street, she didn't look back. She flung herself into the safety of her BMW, pressed the power locks, and roared down the street.

Within a block, the reality of what she had just escaped hit her. She drove, swiping at her flowing tears and crying harder as her eye makeup running into her eyes increased her pain.

"Oh, my God. Oh, my God. I'll stop. I'll stop. I'll never do it again." Jillian chattered her begging attempt at a prayer over and over again as she tried to calm herself. What if he had cut her? What if he had killed her? What if there had been no window in that bathroom? It was too terrible to contemplate. Even if he had only cut her superficially, he would have ruined her skin, and she'd never have been able to go home and explain it. Mason would find out her worst secrets. And he'd hate her. He'd divorce her. Of that, she was certain.

No, she had to stop.

Stop.

Through her scrambled thinking, she finally registered the red brake lights in front of her. She slammed on her brakes and missed hitting the car in front of her by a few inches. Looking ahead, she saw a field of red brake lights. This time of day, all the traffic was supposed to be backed up heading *out* of downtown. Why, oh, why did she have to run into a traffic jam when she had to see Mason so urgently?

Mason. Without realizing what she was doing, she had headed her car toward downtown and Mason's office.

She knew what she had to do. It was the only thing that would stop her from getting into trouble again, from running into another weirdo with a knife, or worse. She had tried to stop before, but she always found herself out on the prowl again. But a baby would put an end to that. No one wanted to have sex with a pregnant woman. She had to go to Mason and say the words. Now, before she calmed down and changed her mind.

The traffic crept ahead, like honey oozing from a jar. She switched on a classical music station and took a few deep breaths. The cars in the oncoming lanes zipped by, a few with their headlights turned on as the December afternoon darkened to an early dusk. The cars on her side of the road started shifting, in a one-step, two-step rhythm, toward the far right lane. As she edged her BMW to the right to pass by the crash obstructing the road, Jillian caught a glimpse of flashing lights and tangled metal, and a human form, covered with a sheet, lying smack in the middle of the center lane of the Pasadena Freeway.

She stopped her car in the only open lane and gawked at the body. Why had they left it in the middle of the road? A van was parked next to it, with the back doors open. Jillian read CORONER on the side of the van. The driver behind her honked, and she forced herself to move past.

It was a sign from God. Shivering, she looked into her rearview mirror. She had to stop what she was doing. Did she want to end up diseased, divorced, or dead?

Mason sensed the other side beginning to give. He restrained himself from glancing across the conference table to where his partner Rosemary sat. They and their clients, officers of a major bank, plus the attorneys for the plantiffs, employees who had been fired from the bank after consulting the employee assistance program for alcohol abuse counseling, had been locked in this conference room for three hours. Neither side wanted to go to trial; the difference between the two sides was that Mason, and the bank he represented, could afford the cost. The plaintiffs were running out of funds. They were represented by an overbearing, self-proclaimed savior of the people, who refused to consider that the employees had been fired because they consistently showed up at the bank's central cash facility too drunk to work—not because they had given confidential information to an in-house counseling service. One more round of insistent hammering of the facts, the law, and reality, and he could reach a settlement that would scarcely touch the coffers of the bank. The case involved a relatively small amount of money; if the bank hadn't been an important client, Mason never would have taken over the matter personally.

The intercom buzzed.

A paralegal, there to sort records and take notes, answered. He said, "For you, Mr. Reed."

Mason crossed the conference room and picked up the phone, controlling his irritation. Hildy knew never to interrupt him during a settlement conference. Timing was everything.

"It's your wife, Mason, or I never would have buzzed you," his secretary said before he could ask who was on the phone.

"What does she want?"

"She's here, in your office, to see you. She says it's an emergency."

Jillian? He couldn't remember the last time she had come to Harper, Cravens. Possibly she had never been there. "I'll be right out." Mason turned to the people seated around the conference table. "I hope you can excuse me for a few minutes. My wife is here to see me."

"I suppose that's more important than my clients?" The plaintiff's lead counsel scowled at Mason. "I hope she needs something more important than more cash for shopping, because my clients are sick of being stalled and ramrodded into taking far less than their claims are worth." He slammed shut his portfolio. "As a matter of fact, I'm thankful for this interruption. We will see you in court. I don't see why the people I represent, poor workers, counting your cash day after day in some dungeon of a bank, should suffer because they sought help for their problems." He yanked his chin at the other attorney working with him. "Come on, we're out of here."

"We can settle now, or we can settle in the mandatory," Mason said. "I apologized for the interruption, but I can assure you my wife would not drive to my office if the situation were not an emergency."

The two men sat back down, grumbling. As Mason left the room, he heard Rosemary taking over to soothe the opposition. He agreed with the other side on one point: Jillian's visit had better be important.

When he first opened his office door, he didn't see her. Then his leather desk chair swiveled around and Jillian came into view.

"What a nice chair," she said, stroking the leather arms. "I trust you didn't drag me out of a settlement conference to talk about furniture." He moved toward her, studying her, and saw she had been crying.

"No." She folded her hands on top of his desk.

She looked so serious. His mind flashed to the "D" word, then leapfrogged to Taylor and the crazy idea that had first entered his thoughts after their birthday party.

Jillian would never give him a child, but he could offer to father Taylor's.

As he had since the idea first occurred to him, Mason damped that fantastical thought and waited for Jillian to speak. He couldn't walk away from his marriage, but what if Jillian offered him a way out? She'd been so unhappy lately, so hard to reach. He knew, without having to consider the question, that though he would not abandon his marriage, if Jillian wanted out, he would not argue. And that knowledge shamed him. How could divorce have been the first thought to cross his mind?

Taking a seat across from her, he said, "Are you all right? Have you been in an accident?"

She nodded. She seemed to have difficulty speaking. He could swear he saw tears on the surface of her eyes.

"What is it, Jillian?" He kept his voice low and gentle, still ashamed of his wayward thoughts.

"I'm sorry if I seem a bit off," she said, "but I saw the most horrible accident on the freeway. A body lying in the road." She shuddered, then produced a smile. "But I've come to tell you—" she swallowed "—I'm-ready-to-have-a-baby."

"You're what?" he asked, surprised.

She looked offended. "A baby. I've thought seriously about your request to start a family, and I've decided I'm ready." She spoke like a child reciting words given to her by her parent to use to thank an adult. Words that didn't convey a meaning or feeling on behalf of the speaker; rather, they carried a message that had to be delivered.

"Are you sure?" Had she actually asked him for a divorce, he would have been far less surprised. And where was the gratitude, the excitement, he should feel? Of course his wife didn't want a divorce; she wanted a family.

She nodded.

He moved around the desk and bent to kiss her. "That's wonderful, Jillian." He struggled against asking her why she had driven downtown and interrupted his meeting with her decision; after so many years, she could have waited another few hours. But his guilt at having thought the "D" word prevented him from speaking the words.

She kissed him back, her eyes closed, then rose abruptly. "I'm so sorry I bothered you. You're probably very busy, but I wanted to tell you. It was important for me to share this now." Her words skipped one over the other. "I'll make a special dinner and we can talk when you get home."

She kissed him, dry-lipped, and walked to the door. She looked more like a French countess en route to the guillotine than a woman about to decorate a nursery. "'Bye, Mason," she said, slipping out the door.

He stole another moment away from the settlement conference. Massaging his temples, he wondered what had changed Jillian's mind. He hadn't pressed the issue since their fight on their anniversary. Maybe Fielding had helped her talk it out. He'd have to give him a call and thank him, if that was the case. But right now he didn't feel thankful; he felt empty and confused when he should be nothing but happy—and thinking of no woman other than his wife.

Thankful the settlement conference was as simple as it was, Mason carried his troubled self back to the meeting room. It took two more hours, but both sides agreed to a settlement of three thousand dollars for each of the ten terminated employees. After the plaintiff's attorneys left, the bank officers grumbled about blackmail, but their overriding concern had been settling the matter with no negative publicity. While offering the bankers a drink in his office, Mason couldn't help but think about the employees' disappointment when they realized their share, after the attorney's contingency fee was subtracted, would be slightly over half of that. They had no doubt been told by the lawyers to expect riches beyond their dreams of avarice. He hoped they hadn't run up debts in expectation of a larger settlement.

After their drinks, the bankers invited Mason to dinner. He wanted to get home to Jillian, to celebrate properly her good news, but he knew his duty lay in dining with the men. When he called to tell her he wouldn't be home until later, the answering machine took the call. He hoped he had caught her before she began preparing a special dinner. He left the office with the bankers at six o'clock. In between courses, he excused himself. He connected with the answering machine again and assured himself that Jillian would understand. She was used to him dining with clients on short notice.

When he finally arrived home at nine o'clock, the house was dark. Television noises floated from the direction of the maid's room, but otherwise the house was silent. Figuring Jillian had gone to bed early, he headed upstairs by the back way. The narrow stairwell seemed to close around him, and he noticed how each step creaked with the weight of his feet. He caught himself listening; for what, he wasn't sure. Jillian had told him she would have a child; he should be happy, but he felt more like a burglar slipping through a stranger's house, waiting for the right moment to take what didn't belong to him.

She wasn't in the bedroom. Circling down the front staircase, he called, "Jillian?"

No response.

He finally found her in the den, sitting in the dark save for the light from the wall aquarium.

"Jillian?" Perhaps she had fallen asleep on the couch. The fish darted about, every so often spreading their lips against the glass. Turning his back to the sight, he bent to his wife.

He smoothed her hair, and she jerked her head away. "I'm sorry I'm home so late," he said. "I hope you checked the answering machine."

Drawing her knees to her chin, she said, "Please don't touch me."

She hadn't gotten his message and she was mad at him.

That much was clear. Maybe he should have let Rosemary take the guys out for dinner; if he had pled special circumstances, they would have understood. His life didn't belong to the firm. But rushing home to hold his wife's hand wasn't what had made him senior partner. "I said I was sorry. After your visit this afternoon, I wanted to tear home. But you know work comes first." Sitting beside her, he put an arm around her.

She kept her arms firmly around her knees. Speaking into the valley between her knees and chest, she said, "If you're never going to be home, I'm not having a baby."

He withdrew his arm. "So that's what this is about."

"This isn't about anything. I've simply changed my mind."

"Because I missed dinner, you're not going to get pregnant? That's hardly what I call logical."

"Logic." She jumped from the couch. She stumbled and swayed.

He caught and steadied her. "Have you been drinking?"

"What you mean is, have I been drinking alone. Yes, I've been eating my dinner all by myself, and yes, I think I had a drink with dinner. You would, too, if you had to spend the night by yourself, wondering why your husband, who supposedly wants nothing more than to impregnate his wife, doesn't come home to do so." She pulled her dressing gown around her, then sank to the couch.

"Jillian, I told you I was sorry. How many times do I have to tell you that? Once you're carrying our child, there will be times I won't be home; the same goes for when we have a family. But you knew the job wasn't all roses when you signed on."

She was back to hugging her knees. He reached for her hand. As soon as she calmed down, she would say she was sorry, she was only mad at him for staying late at work—and of course, she'd get pregnant. Hadn't she been excited enough to drive to his office to tell him so?

Jillian studied her husband's hand as his warm, strong fingers closed over hers. It appeared to be bobbing like a sailboat off Catalina. For a moment she saw ten fingers, not five, and two hands, not just one, holding hers. But his other hand was moving up to smooth her hair, so she must be seeing double. Double. Yes, she'd had far too much to drink. Yet no matter how drunk she was, she knew two things: From now on, she had to be good, and she just could not bear a child.

She grasped Mason's hand, holding tight to her anchor. She couldn't leave him angry with her. Squeezing his hand, she whispered, "I'm sorry, Mason. Please forgive me." She raised her eyes, blinking her damp lashes, then added, "But you said you'd be home, and I waited, and waited—" She smothered a hiccup and allowed him to pull her to her feet. The sash of her silk robe slipped loose, the parting fabric exposing her breasts.

She heard his inrush of breath and knew she would get what she wanted.

Tenderly he brushed the tops of her breasts. "I'm sorry I came home so late. I should have put you—us—ahead of work. Tonight of all nights."

Her smile trembled and she swayed against him. He took her in his arms, swiftly moving his hands to free her from the folds of silk. "God, you're so beautiful," he said, then bent his head to cover her mouth with his.

She closed her eyes and let her clouded mind go, her thoughts hop-skipping like a pebble flung across a lake. It wasn't so bad, her husband making love to her. He eased her back onto the couch where she'd been sitting and drinking for hours. How many hours, she wasn't sure.

At least she felt safe. A vision of that horrible bug, black and scary, crouched on the toe of her pump, leapt to the forefront of her mind, and she squirmed.

Mason pulled back. Forcing the ghastly image to fade, she puckered up and kissed him, dancing tongue to tongue, crushing him to her breasts, rubbing her nipples against his shirt in a way she hadn't in months.

He broke for air, and Jillian let her mind skip away. He was reaching for his buttons, his fly, his shoes, all at the same time. She wanted to giggle, but instead concentrated on willing herself wet for him. He was too skillful a lover to take her till she was ready, no matter how many weeks it had been since she'd said yes.

Free of his clothing at last, Mason loomed over her. He kissed the tip of her nose, then her lips, then the hollow of her throat as he knelt beside her again and leaned to taste her, to drink from the honey she'd summoned for him. She needed to please him. A satisfied man didn't ask questions. Lifting her hips to urge on his questing lips and tongue, she clenched her eyes tight and reached to cradle his erection.

After a few firm strokes from her sure hand, he broke free with his mouth. "Jilly, Jilly," he whispered in a strangled voice. Opening her eyes, she watched him climb on the sofa and straddle her. In one swift, almost desperate motion, he entered her. As she felt him pump his sperm into her, she stroked his hair and smiled. Thank God for the Pill.

Right after they made love, Jillian disappeared into the bathroom, smiling and claiming she simply had to catch up on some beauty routines. Physically sated for the first time in what seemed like forever, Mason didn't object, though he wished she'd simply come to bed with him. He had just drifted to the borders of sleep when she slipped into bed. At first he thought he was suffering a nightmare, one of those half-awake, half-asleep states in which real life acts in a way totally contrary to the laws of physics.

"I can't do it, you know."

Mason rubbed his cheek against his pillow. He tried to concentrate on what that voice, the voice so much like his wife's, was saying. Foggily he asked, "Can't do what?"

"Have a baby."

Then he wished he were only having a nightmare. Slowly he rolled to his side and, coming completely awake, studied her stiff posture, the stubborn set to her fine jawline. "What are you saying?"

"I just can't have a baby. Not yet."

"Jesus." He jerked upright, threw back the covers, and burst out of bed. Not only was she snatching away the promise of the family he wanted so badly, she was denying him even the simple bliss of postcoital sleep. Grabbing his bathrobe, he yelled, "Living with you is enough to drive a man crazy. Of course you're having a baby. You said so this afternoon, and you can damn well stick to your promise."

"Well, I'm not."

"Either you're having a baby or you're seeing a shrink."

Her chin trembled. "I'll talk to that friend of yours again, if you insist, but right now I'm staying on the Pill."

"Tell me when you make up your mind for good this time." He snatched his pillow and walked toward the door. "And I'll come back to bed."

Jillian watched him go, relieved that he'd left her alone. She moved her legs back and forth, stimulating the rhythms of the water bed. It was a mistake to have told him the truth. She could have let him think she wasn't taking the Pill anymore, and simply wasn't getting pregnant. But she couldn't have borne the questioning look in his eye, the concern with which he'd trundle her off to the doctor to find out why they weren't conceiving. No, for once she had told the truth. If sleeping alone was the price to pay, she didn't mind. She'd enjoy it while it lasted, because Mason, true to form, wouldn't give up. He'd be back, begging for a child. One of these days she would give in, just not yet. She worked so hard to achieve a body every man desired, every woman envied. No matter how scared she had been this afternoon, she was far more scared of having a baby. Who would want her when she was fat and ugly?

Chapter 8

RESTIVE IN HIS SELF-EXILE ON THE HARD MAT-
tress of the guest bed, Mason gave up trying to sleep. He'd
spent two hours staring bleakly at the ceiling, cursing
Jillian, then himself, then Jillian again. He crept downstairs, still too furious to face another encounter with her,
and filled a brandy snifter from the first bottle he picked
up at their solarium bar. He returned to bed, knowing he
was seeking a temporary escape from a situation that offered no reprieve.

With the clarity of the doomed, he foresaw his future,
the years stretching ahead, full of professional and mone-
tary success, Jillian as always so well groomed, her perfect
figure intact. Whatever flight of fancy had driven her to
his office, he knew she spoke the truth only when denying
him a child.

He swallowed a mouthful of the liquor, then gagged, as
the cloying taste of peppermint filled his throat. With disgust, he abandoned his snifter on the bedside table. Drinking wouldn't help him anyway.

He didn't know what would at this point. Jillian was
paranoid about pregnancy. It was no wonder she never
wanted to do it anymore. She probably feared she'd end
up one of the statistical few who became pregnant while
on the Pill. She'd probably only had sex with him tonight
to placate him, knowing full well she intended to renege
on her offer of parenthood. No, she would never change.
And he had married her—for better or for worse. That was
his vow.

Troubled sleep finally brought troubled dreams. In one,

he stood next to Jillian, dressed in his favorite navy blue suit, waiting in the vault of their bank to gain access to their joint safe-deposit box. When requested to, he produced his key, then the clerk turned toward him, the bank's necessary second key in her hand. Only, instead of the clerk, Taylor had taken her place, framed by a wall of locked pink and blue boxes. She held forth the key. He moved to block Jillian from seeing her sister, then realized Jillian had, in the way of dreams, become the clerk, and Taylor had disappeared, taking with her the pastel colors of the boxes. Only cold steel remained.

Mason flung the pillow from his face and wiped the sweat off his chest with the sheet, squinting against the bright morning light.

He could not father Taylor's child.

Not even through donor insemination.

During his long night of tossing and turning, he had purposely refused to think about the idea. Now, with sunshine streaming in the window, warning him he'd probably overslept, he admitted he wanted to at least consider the possibility. "Such is the stuff only dreams are made of," he muttered, then drove his weary body from the bed.

An hour later found him loitering outside the public library, waiting for them to open their doors. The only other person was an old man draped across the courtyard fountain. His stench rose strong and clear, much hardier than the voice in which the man begged for spare change. Mason pulled a dollar from his sterling silver and eighteen-karat money clip, a Christmas present from Jillian a year ago. The man pocketed the money and pointed upward.

Mason caught the inscription over the library entrance. It read: THE ASSEMBLED SOULS OF ALL THAT MEN HOLD WISE.

That stopped him. What was wisdom in this situation? Taylor had already decided to use donor insemination. Why shouldn't he be that donor? Climbing the steps to the library, he laughed at himself for even asking that question. Getting involved with Taylor was not wise, Mason, not wise at all.

But he entered the building.

He had always loved the feel of a library. He'd spent much of his life in book-lined rooms, surrounded by the smell of polished wood and aging paper, comforted by the whispered conversations, the mutual respect for knowledge. It was natural for him to turn to books for information on what he was considering. Another man might have called a doctor; Mason sought do-it-yourself information.

At the catalog terminal, he keyed in a subject search for artificial insemination. As he watched the cursor blinking, he heard the voice in his head telling him to go home, warning him he was crossing a threshold that would alter his life and the lives of others he loved. Rubbing his bleary eyes, he squelched the voice and considered instead what he already knew about donor insemination.

He had first heard of a do-it-yourself home method when one of his associates told him of a case he was taking up on appeal. At the time, Mason had enjoyed a good laugh at the idea of a gay male using a turkey baster to inseminate his lesbian friend. A turkey baster. As if making a baby were as simple as following a recipe in the *Joy of Cooking*. Simple? Nothing about this process could possibly be simple. Especially not how Jillian would react. He'd know he had made a decision to press forward with this crazy idea when he faced telling Jillian. Because he would have to do that. Unless . . . No, he couldn't see himself asking Jillian for a divorce. He had chosen to marry her, and now that she was unhappy and troubled, he had to remember it was his duty to help her get better.

Having found the listings he sought, he headed upstairs for the 600s. He could, he knew, use the services of a commercial sperm bank and inform Taylor. If she chose to accept, fine. But he didn't want to chance the result of lots of little Masons running around—children he had no knowledge of.

Three books covered the topic. He hesitated as he eyed them on the shelf. He could leave the books untouched, call Jillian, and arrange to go for marriage counseling. He could try once more. But he'd seen the truth last night. He knew now she would never give him a family, no matter how long he waited, no matter how careful he was of her feelings, no matter how much he pampered her, no matter how much money they had to hire nurses and nannies. Picturing the stubborn set to her face as she reneged on her offer the evening before, he took down the first book.

He wanted a child.

Fielding stopped by Mason's office first thing in the morning. He had his speech prepared and wanted to deliver it before he changed his mind and told his friend the truth. His guilty rush to discharge his message resulted in him cooling his heels for nearly an hour; for once, Mason's faithful secretary had no idea where her boss was or when he would be in. When he finally showed up, his silk tie had been pulled loose from its usually sober knot. Dark circles showed under his eyes. Wherever Mason had been—and he didn't say—he didn't look as if he'd slept all night.

Fielding followed Mason into his office.

As soon as the door shut behind them, Mason wheeled around. "What's the word on Jillian?"

"She's unhappy, struggling with a lack of identity and low self-esteem."

Mason hit one fist against the palm of the other hand. "Don't turn shrink on me, Fielding. Is she seeing someone else?"

"No." Fielding folded his arms across his chest, surprised by Mason's question. Only a few weeks ago, Mason had insisted his wife wasn't having an affair.

Mason crossed to the floor-to-ceiling windows behind his desk. After a few moments, he turned around. "What did she say when you talked to her? Did you figure out any specific thing that's bothering her?"

"You mean other than poor self-esteem and lack of identity?" Fielding couldn't keep sarcasm from tingeing his voice. "You mean something concrete?"

"Yes. For instance, why she doesn't want children."

Fielding wished he could tell his friend the truth. But he wouldn't understand. No husband would. Avoiding his friend's eye, he said, "She doesn't seem to feel she has time for a child in her life."

"Time!" Mason jerked his hands into the air. What did Jillian know of demands on her time? He thought of the lunch meeting he had scheduled with the CEO of a major oil company. In fifteen minutes he had to clear his mind of his personal troubles and be ready to discuss plans to float a new issue of stock for financing increased domestic drilling, plus the CEO's favorite hobby—horse racing. Following lunch, he had a trial-strategy meeting for defending a nationwide department store in a class-action suit brought by its employees. And after the day died down, they had a partners' meeting scheduled. "Time! What does she do with her day?"

"I told you, she lunches and—"

"Is she having an affair?"

"For some reason, I sense that's the answer you now want from me."

"Maybe it is."

"When you asked me to get to know Jillian, that wasn't the answer you wanted. Something's changed, hasn't it?"

Mason slumped into his chair. "Yesterday Jillian drove here, to my office, something she never does, to tell me she wanted to have a baby. By the time I arrived home last night, she informed me she had changed her mind." He picked up his silver letter opener and jabbed the rounded end against his palm. "As much as I acknowledge my duty, I don't know whether I have it in me to do what it takes to stay in this marriage."

Fielding sat down opposite him. Steepling his fingers, he said, "I don't think Jillian could handle a separation or divorce right now."

"What makes you say that? Did she mention it to you?"

"No. She did say she could never live without you."

"What's that supposed to mean?"

"I think it means she's emotionally fragile and would suffer emotional—or even physical—damage if you ask her for a divorce right now."

"I don't want a divorce. I want my wife back." He

jabbed at his palm again, then glanced at his briefcase and thought of his trip to the library. He wanted Jillian to get better, but he also wanted what he had been so long denied. "I only hope she shows the same regard for me."

Fielding didn't answer.

Mason looked at his watch and rose. "Thanks for dropping by. Jillian did say last night she would talk to you again, so I'd appreciate it if you would do that."

"As a shrink, not as a PI?"

"Whatever it takes."

As soon as his office door shut behind Fielding, Mason picked up his phone and punched in 411. In response to the operator's question, he answered, "Hollywood, Channel Six."

Taylor sat at her desk in the crowded newsroom. She had been at KANG just over a month, and already it seemed like home. She grinned wryly at her thought; considering how poorly she and her mother had gotten along, life with Sid Pordsky at Channel Six *was* a lot like home.

All around her rang the shouts and clatter endemic to journalism, noises she'd grown to love over the last seven years.

"Who's on the Griffith Park fire?"

"Jones, line three is Yaroslavsky's office with a statement."

Trying to concentrate, she tapped out the lead-in to a report on an ongoing investigation into the mayor's financial featherbedding. She wished she had done the actual reporting job. Being an anchor wasn't all it was cracked up to be. In Boston, and before that, Raleigh-Durham, she'd been out on the streets, gathering stories, filing reports, working at the pulse of the news-making process. Sid had woven tales of exciting stories waiting to fall into her lap in L.A., but so far he'd urged her to spend more time making sure her necklines conveyed exactly the right flavor of sex appeal. Between Sid and Annie, Taylor was surprised she managed to accomplish any work.

Taylor glanced at the calendar pegged to the wall above

her desk. She could only put Annie off so long; sooner or later the woman would start to work in earnest on changing her look. After the image consultant's first visit, Taylor had been spurred on to call the cryonics lab and ask for their general information. They had told her she would need a statement from her doctor before using their services. She had squeezed in an appointment with a doctor recommended by one of the reporters.

She had liked the doctor until she picked up on the disapprobation she sensed as he gingerly tried to determine whether she was a lesbian. If she had known his intent in advance, she might have walked out in protest. However, her feet were wedged firmly in his sheepskin-covered stirrups, and she found it difficult to stand on principle right at that moment.

After she re-dressed and joined the doctor in his office for a consultation, she told him that it shouldn't make any difference to him whether she wanted the child to raise with another woman, or by herself, or with a man. Thousands of women far less capable than she gave birth to babies every day. Being married didn't automatically make them better mothers. The doctor had huffily conceded her personal circumstances were none of his business and agreed to sign the consent form. She wondered whether medical schools taught doctors that they took on a little piece of God along with their stethoscopes and diplomas, then made a note to find another doctor. She just hadn't done it yet.

"You always get so involved when you're staring at that computer screen?" Sid, coffee mug in hand, had planted himself beside her desk.

Taylor realized she hadn't written a word. She hadn't gotten to the number two market in the country by daydreaming. What was wrong with her? "Sid, good morning."

He snorted and chewed on his mustache. " 'Morning,' she says. It's fucking afternoon."

"Some of us work nights."

"Not commenting on you. Nothing personal at all.

Look, there's something I need you to do." He slurped from the mug and added, "For me, for Sid baby."

Her trouble sensors went on alert. She crossed one leg over the other. "And what would that be?"

"Annie has worked out a deal with a supplier friend of mine to fix you up with the wardrobe you'll need for your new look. I want you to wear his stuff." He paused. "Exclusively."

"And just casually mention to people where I get my clothes?"

He nodded.

"In between discussions of Cold War thaw and the fight against drugs, just slip it in?"

"You got it, babe."

"No way."

"Look, babe, it's not so bad. Most chicks would scream for this sort of deal."

"Sid," Taylor said as she rose, "most chicks are out on the farm hatching eggs, not anchoring your evening news."

"Okay, okay. Wrong choice of words. You know me, I can always admit when I'm wrong." He grinned. "Part of my charm, you know." He took another slurp. "How about you look at the stuff, then decide? Call it a compromise."

Taylor controlled her desire to tell him off. How did this guy get to her? Of course, "this guy" happened to be the general manager, and if there was one person she needed on her side, he was the one. Nodding, she said, "Okay, Sid, I'll take a look, whenever I can fit it into my schedule, but I'm not making any promises."

He smiled. "I'll tell Annie to call you and schedule the appointment."

She watched him cross the newsroom. He patted two fannies and kissed a cheek or two, then left. The women laughed at him and waved him on his way. Most men would have been slapped with a sex discrimination suit years ago, but not Sid. The women treated him like a wide-eyed four-year-old peeking under a stall in the women's room.

Turning back to her computer screen, she watched the

blinking cursor. Call the sperm bank, find a doctor, it seemed to say. Call now. She reached for the telephone, and as she did, it rang. The switchboard operator put through a call from a Mr. Reed.

Mason?

Calling her?

"Is everything okay? Is Jillian all right?"

"Everything's fine." His voice came through the maze of cables pure and deep, with a resonance that made him feel close enough to touch. "I'm calling because there's something I'd like to discuss with you. A . . . um . . . business matter."

"Business?" *Of course, you idiot, what else would it be?*

"Could I stop by your place tomorrow on my way in to the office?"

West Hollywood was definitely not on his way to work in downtown L.A. Not from Pasadena.

"Taylor?"

"I'm still here. Nine o'clock?"

"That's great. Thanks. Thanks for seeing me."

Not knowing what to say to that, she rattled off her address. He said good-bye and hung up. Taylor held the receiver for a few moments, as if his voice echoed in the earpiece, still connecting her to him. *Business.* He'd said it was business. Sighing, she turned her attention to writing the neglected lines, but not before wondering yet again why he had married her sister.

That evening, Jillian greeted him at the door, a smile on her lips. Relieving him of his briefcase and pouting prettily, she said, "No homework for you tonight. I've made your favorite—ribs, especially the way you like them. And I rented *Casablanca.*" She dropped his briefcase onto a kitchen chair. "Remember the first time we saw it together?"

Silently observing his wife, Mason nodded, though he connected no special experience to the movie. Her cheeks were pinker than usual, from the heat of the grill, he supposed. She was gay and smiling, and trying so hard to be nice. The least he could do was set aside his anger of last night and accept her olive branch.

"Mason?" She tugged at his sleeve.

"Thank you, sweetheart." Noting the relief in her eyes at his response, he was glad he'd made the effort to meet her halfway. If she gave him any sign at all that she would change her mind about the baby, he promised himself he'd cancel his meeting with Taylor.

She plied him with food and drink, asking him about his day at the office, until he found himself relaxing with her, remembering the days when their time together had been fun and enjoyable. After dinner, he headed toward the den, assuming they'd watch the movie there. She caught his hand and gave him a naughty smile.

"I thought we would watch *Casablanca* on the VCR in the bedroom." She ran a fingernail down his shirtfront, hooking her hand under his beltline.

His heart leaped. Placing his hands over hers, he said, "Does this mean you've changed your mind about having our baby?"

Jillian jerked her hand free. All signs of the pleasant, attentive woman who had so lovingly served him dinner disappeared in a flash of temper. "Baby! Baby! Baby!" She stamped her foot. "Fuck the baby question!"

Mason stared in shock. Not once in seven years had Jillian ever said "fuck." "What is wrong with you? You're sweet as pie, we actually spend a pleasant evening together, and now look at you."

She clapped her hand over her mouth. Her eyes had narrowed to slits, her breath came in ragged waves, thrusting her breasts upward with every intake to her lungs. Slowly she lowered her hand.

"It was all an act, wasn't it?" Mason advanced on her. "You were giving a performance, and a damn good one, too, to woo me back into your good graces."

"You were the one who stormed out of our bedroom last night. I was only trying to be nice and smooth things over. If you don't want to kiss and make up—fine!" She stamped her foot again. "Go sleep in the guest room and never come back to bed. That way I'll never have to hear you bugging me about getting pregnant!" She whirled, ran into the den, and slammed the door.

Mason's shoulders sagged. He moved, slow of foot and heavy of heart, back to the dining room and pulled out a chair. Dropping into it, he cradled his head in his hands. To his surprise and dismay, he felt a tear form in his eye. He hadn't cried since he was eight years old and his dog Brandy had been struck by a car. His father had wrapped the collie in a blanket and carried him to the vet. But Brandy hadn't come home.

Mason wiped his face with the back of his hand and sighed. This time his tears were for his dying marriage.

The next morning, after another restless night in the guest room, Mason arrived in Taylor's West Hollywood neighborhood ahead of schedule. He squeezed his Volvo into an on-street parking spot and decided to walk around the block. The area seemed a curious mix of the old and the new. Small apartment buildings from the twenties, decorated with the porticoes and columns of a more graceful age, nestled cheek to cheek with slapped-up stucco boxes. A wizened grandmother, draped in a black shawl, shuffled up the sidewalk, pulling an empty wire grocery hauler. Mason nodded at her, and she ducked her head further into her shawl and hurried across the street. Two young men came out of an apartment. They walked hand in hand, led by a feisty Irish setter out for his morning romp.

The old and the new. It fit Taylor. And it seemed appropriate to his improbable mission. He realized Taylor might well be shocked, enraged, embarrassed—or possibly all three. He checked his watch, anxious to deliver his offer before his customary common sense returned. Finally, nine o'clock. Mason took the steps to the building entrance two at a time, lifted the intercom phone, and dialed the code indicated for Taylor's apartment. He wanted her to understand the spirit in which he made his offer, understand that he regretted his impulsive comments during their nighttime walk from the party and that he in no way intended to dishonor either her or Jillian.

The intercom buzzed to life. "Yes?" came Taylor's voice.

"It's Mason. Down here. At the door."

"Walk on the right of the pool, then take the last stairway. I'm on the second floor."

"Sure." He replaced the receiver. His heart pounded so strongly against the smooth cotton of his undershirt, Mason had a wild vision of it breaking through his shirt. He could see it, *lub-dub*bing down the street, crying, "Look at me, I'm Mason's heart and he's afraid." And his heart was right; he was terrified. What if she thought he was crazy? What if she resented his intrusion on her independence? Willing his pulse to slow, he took a deep breath and crossed the entry. Maybe he could tell Taylor he'd come to get some information for a client on something to do with television news. Anything. He'd make something up.

No. Through the archway on the far right, and up one set of stairs, Taylor waited. She'd understand, be happy with his offer. Her reluctance to use an unknown donor had been unmistakable. She wanted a baby, and so did he. Well, he was here to make it possible. Pushing open the door, he crossed the pebblestone surface separating him from his sister-in-law.

He knocked. When she didn't answer, he knocked again. He wished she'd hurry up, before he changed his mind. Just as he wondered whether her delay was a sign from the gods for him to leave, the door opened. He heard himself say hello, and thought he sounded like a first-grader introduced to a new teacher.

"Hello, Mason." The look she gave him clearly asked what he wanted of her, but she stood aside and motioned him in. "Can I get you some coffee? I made some. It's probably not as good as you're used to, I mean Jillian's, but if you're desperate, the way I usually am?" Abruptly she stopped talking and folded her arms across her chest.

He nodded and wondered why she was running on in such an un-Taylor-like fashion. *He* was the one with a reason to be nervous.

"How do you take it? In the old days it was always with

too much of that white powder poison, but didn't you cure yourself of that right before I left Harper, Cravens? So, milk? Sugar? Black?" She smiled, too brightly.

"Milk, please." Glancing around the entry, he said, "May I come in the rest of the way?"

"You'd think I never entertained." Blushing, she led him into a living room crammed with furniture, books, and audio equipment.

He had always loved the way she blushed. She used to try to control it in front of heavy-hitter clients and in view of the stuffiest senior partners.

"Make yourself at home. I'll get the coffee."

She disappeared around the corner. Left behind in the living room, Mason wondered again why Taylor was so fidgety. Perhaps she was embarrassed after his behavior during their walk the night of the party, and anxious he might repeat himself. His brief note had been a poor apology for his ill-timed revival of old feelings. He would have to make sure Taylor understood his offer was motivated solely by his desire to father a child.

Looking around the cluttered room, he reflected on how much more comfortable her apartment was than his beautiful and sterile home. It amused him that this woman who looked so sharp, serene, and impeccably dressed on the evening news was a closet slob. Her office at the firm had usually worn the look of a cyclone-disaster area. She'd always claimed a clean desk was the sign of a sterile brain.

Magazines, many specked with yellow sticky notes, lay three-deep on the pine coffee table. Chinese takeout cartons, a package of panty hose, and a stack of real estate ads competed for space on an end table. He smiled, thinking if he were a child, he'd choose the freedom of Taylor's home over the stern order of his own house.

The only area of the room off limits to clutter appeared to be the stereo equipment. The cabinets lined with electronic boxes and the speakers that claimed one end of the room indicated an avid interest on Taylor's part. He noticed the digital clock on the VCR, and frowned.

Moving across the room, he called out, "Need some help in there?" He heard only a muffled, unintelligible response, so he decided to find the kitchen and ask again.

Peering around the corner, he spotted her leaning against the kitchen counter, one sock-covered foot slid up the calf of the other leg, her head tipped to one side. Following the direction of her gaze, he saw, opposite her, a collection of coffee mugs strewn across the top of the stove. Something about the artlessness of her pose, the simplicity of her dark blue cotton pants and long-sleeved top, and the sweet touch of pink on her cheeks made him think of a little girl planning a doll's tea party. Every decision crucial.

When he walked into the kitchen, she started. "I was deciding which cups to use." Waving a hand, she said, "Why don't you go sit down, and I'll bring everything into the living room." She gathered a handful of mugs, most of which carried names of various fast-food outlets, and took them to the sink. "These were dirty, cobwebby, you know, from the move. I don't eat at home often."

He leaned against the refrigerator and watched her. Her fretting tugged at his heart. For all her capability and success, she needed hugs just like everyone else. Right at that moment, he wished he could have been the first in line to offer one.

"I hope you don't think I'm silly for pondering over which cup to drink from." Looking at him, she said, "Because it is important, you know, when you have the choice, to choose correctly." She picked up a red one emblazoned in white with THE WINDY CITY. Taylor couldn't believe how she was babbling.

He reached for her wrist and guided her hand back to the stove. "Uh-uh. Not that one. The plain blue ones. We should start with a clean slate."

She drew a sharp breath and looked away, across the kitchen, then back at him. "There is no 'we,' and you and I will be much better off if that is never forgotten," she said sharply, slipping her hand out of his grasp. The skin on her wrist sizzled from his touch, igniting a firestorm that threatened to spread up her chest, and consume her heart.

He nodded briskly. She was right, of course. And he should be thankful Taylor had long since gotten over any feelings she had for him. Given his own wayward fantasizing of late, he would have been in real trouble if she felt at all the same way.

Mason watched her over the rim of the blue mug she filled for him. This seemed somehow all too comfortable, both of them drinking coffee, him ready to buzz off to work, Taylor looking so warm and so damn approachable. No, not approachable. Admit it. Kissable. He'd better get on with this offer and get out of her place while he still had his sanity. And before he stepped over a border he'd vowed never to cross.

"What—"

"The reason—"

He laughed. "Why did I ask to see you?" Rubbing his chin, he said, "Good question." He felt the vertical handle of the refrigerator boring into his back. *Get out of here, Reed. No one's ever going to understand this. Go home, flush Jillian's birth control pills down the toilet, and do it the old-fashioned way—with your wife.*

"Mason?" She looked from him to her coffee cup and back to him, then settled against the edge of the sink. Placing her cup on the counter, and folding her arms across her chest, she said, "Well?"

Suddenly she didn't look quite so kissable. He imagined she could be a tough cookie in an interview. But once she knew, and if she accepted, that softness would bloom again. Motherhood would only add to her womanliness. Not that that should matter to him. This was strictly business, after all. *Dangerous business with your sister-in-law, you fool.*

"I want to father your child." He said it all in one breath, without meeting her eyes. It came out more like "I-wnt-fath-child."

"What did you say?"

She looked puzzled, but perhaps not for the right reason.

Raising his gaze above the level of her chin this time, he repeated his statement.

No answer. No answer at all. Simply a blank, slightly questioning look.

He fiddled with his mug, then set it down on the stove. When he looked back at her, he saw she had turned as white as a witness caught lying on cross-exam. "Taylor?"

She ran her tongue over her lips, lifted her eyes to him, and shook her head. "It's not a good idea."

"But it's your idea. You said you were going to find a sperm donor. Why not me?"

Taylor pivoted and spilled her coffee into the sink. Swinging back around, she parted her lips, then closed them. She paced to the window in the dining area, then back again. Softly she asked, "How am I supposed to look my sister in the eye if I sleep with her husband?"

He stepped over to her side. "I'm in no way suggesting an affair. It's nothing like that. I read up on artificial insemination after you mentioned it at the party. We can go to a doctor or do it ourselves." He swallowed, and added, "We can use a turkey baster." Mason put both hands on her shoulders. Keeping her at arms' length, he said seriously, "You know I'm committed to Jillian. But she'll never have children. You and I both want a child. Why shouldn't we have that?"

With a violent shrug, she jerked free. "You've really considered this from all angles, haven't you?"

He nodded.

"Except for one very important one."

He knitted his brow. "What's that?"

"How—I'd—feel!" She flung her arms outward, then brought them tight around her chest. "You just don't understand how impossible this is for me." She spun away. "Get out and forget you ever mentioned it."

"But—"

"Go."

"Taylor, please." He grabbed her hands in his. "I don't understand. What did I say wrong?" This wasn't turning out at all as he'd hoped. With one hand, he smoothed her hair away from her face. "I didn't mean to upset you."

She yanked back her captured hands and covered her face. "Please just go."

He knew when to retreat. He'd learned that from seven years of marriage to Jillian. "All right. I'm sorry I sprang this on you so suddenly," he said, feeling flustered. "Please—" he touched the backs of her shielding hands "—think about it."

He backed from her place, hating to leave her so upset, but she'd clearly wanted him out. And he needed some time to assess his own feelings. What in the hell had happened to him in there? He'd touched her hands, her hair, and held her in a near embrace. She was his wife's sister. This was supposed to be about his desire for a child, not a child and its mother.

Which it was, he argued during his retreat to his car. He and Taylor shared an important goal. Discussing bearing a child was naturally an emotional topic, and therefore his gut-level male reaction—to hold, protect, and comfort her—was perfectly normal under the circumstances.

Zipping down the street toward the Hollywood Freeway, he kept repeating this rationale to himself. But as he heard over and over in his head the distress in her voice when she'd begged him to go, he beat his hand against the steering wheel in frustration. The last thing he wanted to do was cause Taylor pain. Or Jillian, he echoed. He merged into the heavy inbound traffic. If he weren't so set on creating his own flesh and blood, he'd do well to apologize to Taylor, go home, and persuade Jillian to adopt. The last thing he needed to be doing was dwelling on the vivid image that danced in his imagination and threatened to overtake all others in his mind—that of Taylor leaning into his embrace and turning her soft and willing lips to his.

From her dining room window overlooking the courtyard, Taylor watched Mason walk away from her. She had to stop herself from calling after him. Whenever she saw him, the same feelings stole over her, a rush that started in her toes and swept to the very tips of her hair, leaving her slightly breathless. She didn't understand it, and if any other sane and intelligent woman had confessed to that reaction, Taylor would have considered her somehow suspect.

When she'd opened the door to his knock, he'd looked so good, standing there in his Mr. Attorney suit, his dark hair brushed back from his forehead and trailing over the top of his collar. A breeze had skittered open one side of the unbuttoned jacket. She had wished it were her right to push back the rest of the fabric, peel it from his strong shoulders, and let it fall to the ground. They could have settled the baby question then and there.

Taylor forced herself away from the window and went to dress for work. Such thoughts would get her nowhere. Because she loved him, she couldn't accept his offer. The irony of her predicament wasn't wasted on her. Because she was still in love with her brother-in-law, she had no choice but to turn to an anonymous donor. She wouldn't marry anyone else, and accepting Mason as a donor would press her emotional control beyond the breaking point.

Yet she couldn't stop thinking about his offer.

Mason had seemed different today. When he had first arrived, she'd searched his face for some sign that he cared about her. About *her.* In the look he'd given her, with those serious brown eyes, in the hint of a smile, in the way his body gravitated toward her in the brief space between them in the kitchen when he had made his comment about starting with a clean slate, she had thought, for an alarmed moment, that she'd found it. That frightened her. And pleased her. She'd felt a blush start to work its way across her chest and up her throat, threatening to betray her. That's why she snapped at him. Her reaction also told her what she had to do.

She was an adult who had long ago learned to accept *no.* Halfway through dressing, she stopped to search her purse for the number of City Cryo-Bank. Before she could waver, she called them.

Yes, they would be happy to put a contract and a list of donors in the mail that very day.

Chapter 9

JILLIAN WATCHED THE RAIN DRIZZLE PAST the French doors of her bedroom, and sighed. Another day to face. At least Mason had forgiven her for changing her mind about having a baby. The night before, he had abandoned the guest room. She had been sleepy, lulled by the bottle of wine from dinner, when he had returned to their bed, pillow in hand, making a long speech about how they needed to redouble their commitment to their relationship. He had been so earnest and loving that, had he been any other man, she would have checked his collar for another woman's lipstick. But Mason would never cheat on her.

Pleased that nowhere in his speech did he push the issue of having a baby, she initiated sex, something she hadn't done with him for longer than she could remember. He obliged, but in her alcohol-fogged brain, she registered a definite lack of his usual enthusiasm.

Making a face at the dreary weather, Jillian reached for the bedside telephone. Christmas was less than three weeks away, and she had yet to invite Taylor. Mason had made a fuss over Jillian not including her sister on Thanksgiving, so she didn't want to make the mistake twice. Of course, once Taylor found out their mother was coming, she would probably remember she had other plans. Jillian wrinkled her nose. No wonder she had never wanted children. If Mason had grown up in her family, he would have checked himself in for a vasectomy long ago.

She called Taylor. After ten rings, her sister answered, her voice muffled and sleep-thickened. "Taylor? I woke you? I thought you career women were early risers."

Taylor regarded the receiver through narrowed eyes. Good old Jillian. She hadn't heard from her since the birthday party; she must be asleep and dreaming if she thought for a moment her sister might begin a conversation with an apology. "Some of us work nights."

"Whatever. I'm calling to invite you over for Christmas. We'll be doing dinner midday, to accommodate your schedule."

Taylor pushed the hair out of her eyes and wondered what fluke of genetics had landed her in the same family as Jillian. "Thanks for thinking of me."

"So you'll come?"

"As long as work permits." She wanted to leave herself an escape route.

"I'll take that as a yes. By the way, Mother will be here for a visit."

Taylor clenched the phone. "You waited until I said yes to tell me that so you could trap me, didn't you? Why do you have to do things like that?" If Jillian had caught her when she was fully awake, she might not have spoken her mind so freely, but now she wanted to have it out with her. "First you spill my private plans in front of strangers, then neglect to apologize, then you trap me into Christmas. Why does it always have to be like this? Why can't we just be friends, like normal sisters?"

She heard Jillian yawn, a long, protracted taking in of air that made Taylor want to scream. Jillian finally said, "I don't have any friends."

"Burke Washington seems to think he's your friend." The minute the words were out, she regretted them.

"Back off, Taylor. Quit playing big sister. If you want someone to boss around, have that baby."

The line went dead. Taylor drew the covers over her head. She and her sister had never been friends. She had never belonged in her own family. When she had her own child, she would do things right. Her baby would always be loved.

* * *

Taylor turned the fat envelope from City Cryo-Bank over and over in her hands before settling onto her sofa to open it. The letter must have come yesterday; she had been so tired last night, she had gone straight to bed upon arriving home from work.

She glanced through the pages: doctor's consent, indemnification, donor-matching questionnaire, credit information, screening required of semen donors, fertility parameters, price list. Then she found the donor catalog. She read the category headings: race/ethnic origin, blood type, hair, eyes, skin, height, weight, years of college, occupation, special skills and interests. Three and a half pages of listings followed. Skimming the list, she saw law student, motion picture student, cinema student, graduate student, biology student. Feeling queasy, she stopped reading. At thirty-eight, she could almost be the mother of some of these donors. She had known most donors were students, but looking at this list, knowing she was supposed to pick six choices from which to receive a complete donor profile, the idea unsettled her. Should she pick a six-foot-four Welsh/Polish poli-sci major who liked computers and sailing? Or a green-eyed Russian who dabbled in bridge and cinema?

Taylor fanned her face with the papers. She pictured a six-foot-two English/Irish, black-haired, brown-eyed man who loved law and fast cars. And children.

None of these faceless men listed children as one of their special interests. She tossed the papers onto the overflowing coffee table. She had promised herself to do this right. Up to this point, the idea of donor insemination had at least seemed practical and efficient. Looking at this list, it still seemed practical and efficient. And cold and detached, unnatural and contrary to the very needs that were driving her to have a child. Promising herself she'd look at the list more carefully tomorrow, she went into the kitchen to make herself a cup of tea.

Just where did the Marines find their few good men? Jillian thought crossly, jerking her BMW to a halt in front of a sign that said, RESERVED PARKING FOR THE MANAGER. As far as she could tell, Pasadena was devoid of any sexually potent males. The two shoe salesmen down the street had been more interested in each other than in her. In irritation, she'd walked out without buying a pair of Kenneth Cole shoes she actually wanted.

Now she was hoping a pilgrimage to Jacob Maarse, Pasadena's preeminent florist and one of the most soothing places Jillian frequented, would calm her down.

The shop smelled of Christmas. She inhaled the kiss of evergreen and the tingly fragrance of simmering apple cider. The frown vanished from her face as she smiled in delight at the ceiling-high trees bedecked with bows and baubles.

She detoured to the soap-and-scent aisle to pick out Christmas soaps for the guest bath. Her mother would arrive soon, and Jillian wanted always to be prepared for her.

Studying the display, she became aware, more through her sexual radar than any noise or movement, that a dark-suited, well-groomed man had entered the aisle and stood watching her. Selecting a box of Christmas-tree-shaped soaps, she read the label. The man approached her, pausing only when the sleeve of his suit brushed her arm. Jillian's skin tingled and she suppressed a triumphant smile.

"My wife prefers the goat's-milk soap," he said, his voice deep and scratchy and very close to her ear. "I myself prefer—" he reached across her body, brushing her breasts, and her nipples rose hungrily "—this. Sandalwood. It's much sexier."

Drawing in a long breath, Jillian regarded the stranger. There was a tinge of silver in his smoothly trimmed beard; his eyes were dark and piercing behind horn-rimmed glasses. She checked his shoes. Lizard. Very nice.

Yet one thing bothered her. He seemed familiar, but she couldn't identify him as someone she knew, anyone she had met at a social function. Accepting the bar of sandalwood soap from him, she asked with a look of wide-eyed innocence, "Is your wife shopping with you today?"

He chuckled. Pushing back his sleeve, he glanced at his watch. A Patek Philippe. Jillian smiled inwardly. She was finished with creeps. From now on she would only play with nice men.

"I could ask you to join me for coffee, or perhaps a drink. But I'm a busy man, and you strike me as a woman who has—" head tipped to one side, he regarded her for a long moment "—many responsibilities. So let's say Day and Nite Inn, Colorado Boulevard, just before Rosemead, in twenty minutes?"

She returned his look, unwilling to acknowledge that she knew the motel. He placed the sandalwood soap in the palm of her hand, and with a smile, turned and left the shop.

The strains of "Silent Night" followed Jillian as she left the haven of greenery and growth behind for the other escape she sought, yet despised.

The Day and Nite Inn subsisted on income from nooners, nighters, and out-of-town tourists who didn't know any better or had fallen into the clutches of unscrupulous travel agents. Just off Colorado Boulevard, a street that in its heyday had been known as Route 66, the motel had eighteen units, shaded by a few straggly palm trees badly in need of a good trim. The pothole reached out for Jillian's car, and she swerved to avoid it. One of the virtues of the Day and Nite was that the parking spaces were all in the back, away from the view of the street. She pulled to a stop and waited for a sign of the man.

Within minutes, he strolled from Room 18, coatless, his tie off and shirt sleeves rolled back. He padded past her car, approaching a battered Coke machine. Nodding appreciatively, Jillian slipped from her car and through the open door of the room.

Mr. Smooth had some experience in these matters.

He locked the door behind him and set two Cokes, one diet, one regular, on the fake mahogany dresser.

Jillian turned, twisting one hand around her long strand

of pearls. She hated these moments of beginning. Of ending.

The blow came so quickly, she had no time to react. She fell to the bed, holding her cheek. The man began stripping off his clothing.

"What was that for?" she asked.

He shrugged. "You should have been ready for me." Grabbing her by the front of her dress, he lifted her off the bed, spun her around, and yanked down her zipper.

He smiled.

Under that proper black sheath, she was naked.

"Now, that's more like it," he said, tossing the dress to the floor and shoving her onto the bed.

Jillian's chest rose and fell, causing her breasts to dance. Her pearl necklace pooled in her cleavage. The man knelt over her, watching her with a gleam to his eye she didn't quite trust, yet which excited her. She could feel her cheek swelling. She should be afraid, but all that registered in her brain was the wetness building between her thighs and the tightness in her nipples. She licked her lips and wriggled her pelvis.

The man laughed.

He snatched the pearl necklace over her head, and grabbing her wrists, yanked them over her head and bound them with the best of Van Cleef & Arpels. He jerked her legs apart and lowered his head to torment her with his tongue.

She almost came before he touched her. To find a man who read her so well was orgasmic in and of itself. He probed her with his tongue, then sensing her gathering onrush, lifted his head. He laughed wickedly, then struck her on the other cheek. She lay dazed and panting as he leaned over the bed and fished in his clothing. Working on the condom he'd retrieved, he continued to grin. "You're gonna like this." Then, her hands still bound by the necklace, he flipped her over onto her stomach.

Taylor glanced up from her computer, surprised to hear Burke's voice so early in the day. She'd come in to do some extra work, or so she told herself, knowing she was only avoiding her endless mental wrestling over the sperm bank decision.

She heard what sounded like baby-talk noises and took a swift second look. Burke Washington, ladies' man with a vengeance, was cooing at the blue-blanketed bundle he held. A black-haired, smartly dressed woman, with a diaper bag slung over her shoulder, stood beside him.

"Taylor, come meet the new little one," Burke called.

She rose and approached, amazed, after his callous comments about bills and breasts, that he was showing off his new baby as he would an Emmy. Burke introduced Emily, his wife, but the baby was clearly the focus. Taylor smiled at the red-faced infant, his eyes beneath a shock of jet black hair squeezed shut against the world. Lips like rosebuds sucked the air, seeking its mother's breast for sustenance.

"Oh, he's so precious," she said, aching to hold him in her arms.

Burke beamed and his wife smiled.

"Would you like to hold him?" Burke asked.

"Me?" Taylor's eyes widened. As much as she wanted a child, she realized with a shock that she knew almost nothing about mothering.

"Nothing to it. Crook your arm and cradle his head against your, uh, chest." Burke placed the baby in Taylor's nervous arms and went whistling off.

She was afraid to move, afraid she'd wake him or fail to support his delicate head.

"You're doing fine," said Emily. "Babies are resilient creatures." Her gaze drifted toward Burke. "It's a good thing, too."

Taylor couldn't miss the undertone. Her heart, once again, went out to Burke's wife. "What's his name?"

"Todd." Emily brushed the top of the baby's head. "Burke and I must have been three months discussing names. But as soon as he was born, we took one look at him and knew we had to name him after my twin brother. He looks just like him."

Taylor's breath caught in her throat. For all their problems, Burke and his wife had come together to create this new life. The baby stirred and waved a tiny fist. She thought of the nameless, faceless donors and fought back a shudder.

"Thank you, Emily." With the greatest care, she handed the baby back to his mother. "You don't know how much holding this baby has meant to me." Hurrying to her work station, she gathered her purse and coat, knowing now, with absolute certainty, what she must do.

The offices of Harper, Cravens occupied the fifty-first and fifty-second floors of one of downtown L.A.'s older skyscrapers. As Taylor rode the express elevator, the past seven years rolled away as the numbers ticked off on the elevator counter. All she needed was a briefcase and a prim bow on her green silk blouse, and she could be on her way to work again. She'd be a partner by now, able to delegate the sludge work to other eager, up-and-coming young legal stars.

Taylor noted how the other occupants of the elevator carefully avoided looking at one another. Some things never changed. Glancing down at the conservative suit she wore, she realized her years at Harper, Cravens had shaped her life to a tremendous extent. She still dressed a lot like a lawyer, and as long as she could put off Annie, she would continue to maintain her crisp, businesslike style.

Surveying the reception area, Taylor wondered whether she'd stepped off on the wrong floor. Gone was the massive Impressionist piece that had welcomed clients and employees, gently ushering them into the soothing room of rosewood and tapestry.

In its place hung a fireball of green and red, something like a mushroom cloud done up as a Christmas ornament. Ugly didn't begin to do it justice. Clive Harper must have traded in wife number three, the one with the passion for the Impressionists. By the looks of the art, Mrs. Harper number four was probably even younger than her predecessor.

The receptionist announced Taylor to Hildy, Mason's secretary, and Taylor prepared herself for the onslaught of the older woman's affections. As a green associate, Taylor had been saved from the disgrace of filing the wrong form or missing a court deadline more than once by Hildy's knowledgeable intervention.

"So you've come to show your face again?" Hildy opened her arms, and Taylor returned her embrace. "I don't know why you had to stay away for so many years." She held her out and studied her. "Hmm, it looks as if the East Coast was kind to you. Maybe all that snow and ice are good for something." Linking arms, she led her into the inner corridor of offices.

"When you called and told me you wanted to drop by, but you wanted it to be a surprise, I made sure you-know-who would be well occupied." Winking, she said, "Told him Mr. H. said he'd be by sometime between ten and noon and he was to stay put. No matter how important somebody becomes, they still have a boss to answer to." She stopped at her work area, which was discreetly placed so its occupant could guard the door to a corner office.

Mason's office. He'd moved up in a world measured by the location and number of windows of one's office and by the proximity of the assigned parking space to the building elevators.

"I'm glad you came to see him. You two always seemed to have such a good time together." Hildy gestured toward Mason's office door.

Taylor smiled at her, wondering what the woman really thought of her, popping in after seven years to see her brother-in-law. Wouldn't she wonder why Taylor didn't go to his home? She and Mason had been Hildy's favorite associates, and obviously she'd been rewarded with promotions along with Mason's rise to partnership. Her loyalty to Mason probably overrode any questions she might have about this visit.

Taylor turned the knob and slipped into Mason's office. He sat with his back to the door, his feet propped on an ornately carved mahogany credenza. The Impressionist work she'd missed in the lobby crowned one wall of his office. Thank goodness the modern art invasion hadn't overtaken his private domain.

As she shut the door behind her, she said, "Hello, Mason."

His feet hit the floor. Taylor wondered whether the tenants on the floor below would think the ceiling was coming down. Squelching the inane thought, she trapped a giggle in her throat. Today was not a day for blithering like a fifteen-year-old with a crush on the captain of the basketball team. She'd done that the other day when Mason had swooped in on her to change the course of her life. Today she would be calm.

Practical.

Businesslike.

Swiveling around in his chair, he looked at her. From across the distance of the gleaming partner's desk, across the expanse of carpet, she watched the realization dawn on him. His eyes lit up, like a reflection of sunrise on a pond. The smile traveled from there to his cheeks, to the fine skin around his mouth. He rose and leaned forward on his desk, bracing himself with his shirt-sleeve-covered arms.

"Taylor."

She heard the expectation in his voice. He understood; he knew only one reason would bring her to his office.

She walked to his desk. She didn't want to dwell too long on the look of anticipation on his face. She didn't dare. She had to keep her feelings for him tucked away in the corner of her heart where she'd consigned them in order to allow herself to take this step.

Rising, he indicated one of the chairs in front of his desk, then reclaimed his seat. In that moment he seemed to gain control of himself and his emotions, slamming them in a vault as far from his heart as he could get them. "What can I do for you?" he asked in a businesslike tone. The smile had gone from his face; he spoke as if she were a client, not the woman whose child he had proposed to father.

Folding her hands in her lap, Taylor said briskly, "I've

been thinking over your offer of the other day, and I've decided to accept." She pulled her Day-Planner from her purse.

"There's nothing I'd like more, but I'm not so sure the offer's still open," he said, meeting her gaze in the frank and forthright manner he used in negotiation.

"What do you mean? You told me to think it over." Taylor felt trapped. He couldn't change his mind now.

"Taylor, after you turned me down, I did some thinking of my own. Not all of it was pleasant. I hadn't even thought of what we would tell the child. Then there's Jillian." He glanced downward briefly. "Then there's how you and I will feel. Creating a child together is a very emotional experience, and as you reminded me the other day, there is no 'we' where you and I are concerned."

Taylor felt the calm feeling of control seep back into her body. She had made up her mind; she wanted Mason as the donor and wasn't going to be swayed from her course. If he was going to make this a matter of logic, she could match him point for point. She drew a deep breath and studied her fingernails, wondering which argument to tackle first. "I've considered each of those aspects, and I still think this is the best way to proceed, considering our mutual interests and the options open to us."

"What changed your mind?" he asked.

"Reading the information from the sperm bank in sterile black-and-white print. It was so impersonal. I realized I simply can't accept a faceless, nameless blob of cells as father to my child." She straightened her shoulders. "You were right about that, by the way."

He nodded.

"What changed yours?" she asked in a carefully neutral tone.

Mason paced to the window and back. He felt all his logic unraveling when faced with possibilities he had discarded. "You said it best the other day when you said, 'It's just not a good idea.' "

Taylor searched his face for a clue to his feelings. She had answered that way because she loved him and feared the entanglement. But he didn't love her; he loved his wife. She said carefully, "I had my own reasons. What are yours?"

He moved around the desk, took her hands, tugged her upward, and led her to the sofa under the Impressionist painting. She tried to pull free.

"Don't." Looking her in the eyes, he said, "If we do this thing, make a baby together, we're going to become close—very close." Turning her hands over, he studied her palms, lying within his hands. "Think about it. I'll be the father of your child. I'll be spending time—a lot of time—at your place. I'm not some faceless jock content to jerk off into a jar and disappear from the scene."

There was a rushing sound in her head that seemed to block out all noise except the sound of Mason speaking to her. She kept her eyes fixed on his, mesmerized by what she detected in his voice.

"Do you think we can handle that? Do you think we can be good parents? Do you think we can do these things and remember there is no 'we'?" He was speaking louder, and his grip on her hands had tightened.

She knew what it was she heard in his tone: the agony of repressed desire threatening to break through his control. He had changed his mind for the same reason she initially rejected his offer. Whether or not he was aware of his feelings, he cared for her. But she could scarcely ask him to tell her whether she was right. How he felt about her and how she felt about him didn't matter. It couldn't matter. He was married to her sister.

"Taylor?"

She wrenched her hands free and tucked them into the pockets of her suit jacket. "What I want, Mason, more than anything, is a child. I want my own family even if it's just the two of us, me and my baby. I'm prepared to do whatever is necessary to achieve that. I'd like you to help me, but if this is going to be too much to handle, for either one of us, I'll be forced to reconsider the sperm bank."

Mason paced to the window and stood with his back to Taylor. He massaged the back of his neck and studied the mountains in the distance, thankful that Taylor was waiting in silence, allowing him time to struggle with this choice. He wanted so badly to say yes.

Still with his back to her, he said, "I made my offer because I wanted to. But dammit . . ." He swung around and closed the distance between them. "We could both regret this." His voice falling to a whisper, he added, "For many, many reasons."

Stirred by the emotion she felt in him, Taylor whispered, "Is that a yes?"

Mason gave a swift nod, then moved behind his desk and took his seat. Picking up a pen, he said, "I made an offer. You accepted, and I'm prepared to follow through."

"You make this sound like a real estate contract."

"I think you know I want a child as badly as you do," he said.

She hesitated. "About that, Mason. I think it's best if you donate, then leave the rest to me."

"What do you mean?"

"I think everyone concerned will be a lot better off if you're represented as the uncle, rather than the father." She spoke much more calmly than she felt; the truth of the matter was, she didn't think she could endure Mason constantly underfoot. She didn't want to deprive the child of a father, but her constantly being tormented by Mason's presence would create an even worse situation for the child.

"Forget it." He rose from his chair and leaned over his desk toward her. "If I'm in this, I'm in all the way. If all you want is a donor, call the sperm bank." He paused. "What you're really saying is, you can't handle the situation."

"That's not true." She retrieved her Day-Planner.

"So you agree we tell the child I'm the father?"

She thought of Burke and his wife, united in their adoration of their infant son. She pictured her child old enough to go to preschool and come home asking, "Who's my Daddy?" She remembered how bereft she'd felt as a child, ignored by her own father as he doted on her younger sister. Taylor closed her eyes for a moment, then answered, "Yes."

He sat back down. "I'll speak with Jillian."

"Please make sure she understands this is an um . . ."

"Arm's-length transaction?"

She nodded. "I've already told her about the artificial insemination plan, as you well know. I'll be happy to talk to her with you."

"No. I'll do it myself. Jillian knows I want a child, and she knows I've never been unfaithful to her. I'll explain it as it is, a simple medical procedure done to help out a friend."

"Like donating blood?" Taylor asked dryly.

"The analogy will do."

"She's not going to like it. Maybe I'd better—"

"No. I'll do it."

Dropping the argument, she looked at her December calendar. If she had been closer to her sister, she would have insisted. Or gone to her first and asked her what she thought of the idea. But Jillian was likely to take the news more easily from Mason. If Taylor were there, Jillian might object just to spite her. Thinking that made her sad, but she was becoming more of a realist where her sister was concerned. She studied her calendar, flipping to the prior month, then back to the days she had circled in green ink. "I'll need to see you on the twenty-third and twenty-fourth," she said, then blushed at the awkwardness of the situation. Here she was telling her brother-in-law what days to zip over to her place and squirt sperm into a mustard jar.

"Hey, that's okay." He worked the knot on his tie, as if he wanted to share her blush. "We can't very well make a baby without the facts, you know."

"Call me at the station on the twentieth and I'll confirm the dates. You'll also need to have these blood tests." She withdrew a piece of paper from her calendar. She had written the list that morning, after considering the implications of Jillian's possible infidelity with Burke.

"Blood tests?" He read the list.

"It's routine." She wasn't going to tell him why she wanted them. Whatever went on in his marriage with Jillian was his own business. "I've had them done and I want you to, also. It's for the baby's sake."

"You always were thorough."

Thankful he didn't press the question of why she wanted him, a man married for seven years, to have AIDS and VD tests, she smiled at him and stood up.

He rose and walked her toward the door. Before opening it, he said, "Wait. Don't go yet."

"Is there something else?"

"No. Maybe it's silly, but I feel a need to commemorate this moment." He looked at his hand, then extended it to her.

Taylor gazed at his proffered hand. Somehow a handshake simply wasn't enough to conclude this bargain; they had just agreed that she was going to carry his child. Reaching up, she pulled his face toward hers and kissed him. She meant for it to be a butterfly of a kiss, a light brushing of lips to seal their contract. But he responded, drawing her against him, claiming her mouth, offering her promises neither one of them could fulfill.

He broke away the same moment she pulled back. With a nervous laugh, she said, "We'd better stick to a handshake from now on."

"Or there won't be a next time," Mason said, as much to himself as to her, hustling her out the door.

The scene that greeted Mason at home that evening was of the variety he hated the most.

Silence.

Not that he deserved a happy wife running to the door to greet him. He had reviewed the events of the morning countless times. He definitely should not have returned Taylor's kiss. He should have accepted it as no big deal, patted her on the shoulder, and sent her out of his office. The kiss had shaken him. They would definitely be wise to keep this transaction as businesslike as possible. Taylor obviously didn't regard him as a brotherly sort who would do in a pinch. He now knew how he felt, and suspected what she felt; but did she know, and did she suspect him?

Enough. He had steeled himself, during the drive home late that evening, following the dinner he'd had with his law partners, for what he must do. His problem was, he had no idea how to bring up the subject.

When he drove up to his house, he thought she must be out. No lights shone. In the kitchen, he saw the microwave clock glowed 10:00 P.M. Where would she be? He flicked on the dining room light and stood still when he sighted the table set for one with Jillian's most cherished china and crystal. A note was propped against the water goblet. He read: *I made your favorite dinner and waited for you. Again.*

"Damn." Surely he had told her about the evening meeting. Yes, he knew he had. After writing that note, she'd probably gone upstairs and downed a sleeping pill, which explained the darkened house. He switched off the light and headed up the back stairs. When he entered the bedroom, he found her as he'd expected—sound asleep.

He watched her as he shrugged off his suit coat. She lay curled on her right side, facing away from his side of the bed. That, at least, seemed symbolic. She'd been turning away from him for so long, he couldn't remember when the process had begun. What had started their distancing? They had been backing off from each other, like children sneaking silently away during a game of hide-and-go-seek. He had loved her. She'd been everything he wanted: beautiful, spirited, a woman who wanted to be a wife and mother.

Or so she said. As he undressed, he wondered about that. Had she said those things only to please him? One shoe off, he stopped, frowning. Had they actually talked about children before they'd married? Maybe he had simply assumed she wanted what he wanted. He was trained to get the facts, to marshal them for whatever argument needed to be made. Perhaps, though, Jillian had swept him off his feet, and he had forgotten about getting the facts.

She had been so different from most of the other women he had met.

He'd respected the women he worked with, and dated a few of them, but they seemed so intent on putting their careers first, he'd not been encouraged to pursue any long-term relationships, even with Taylor, whom he had been dating when Jillian came from Chicago to visit her. But as he now realized, he'd suffered from tunnel vision; no wonder Taylor had never spoken of wanting a family. Of course women didn't talk about babies at work; maybe to one another, but not to the men. That was no way to get ahead at Harper, Cravens. They would have been shunted so far from partnership track, they'd have jumped ship in despair at ever advancing. Despite affirmative action and equal opportunity, the legal profession was still a jealous mistress. When you were putting the law first, it helped to have a wife.

Jillian had been the perfect partner's wife. Only, he wanted more than a symbol. He wanted the give and take of a growing, loving relationship. And he wanted a family. Thinking of Taylor, wanting her, and realizing the obstacles separating them, he felt like Robert Louis Stevenson's little boy put to bed early on a summer evening. So much of life was passing him by.

He started to undress and reminded himself that the only thing he should think of as passing him by was the opportunity to tell Jillian about his offer to Taylor. He considered waking Jillian, to get it over with. He wasn't naive enough to think she would simply give him her blessing. *You want to give my sister a baby? No problem; just don't give her an orgasm in the process.* She stirred slightly. Glancing at her, he noticed a bottle of wine on her bedside table. An empty bottle. He walked around the bed. A wineglass lay on the floor. Frowning, he wondered whether she had taken a sleeping pill along with the alcohol. He would never wake her, and even if he did, she'd be incoherent.

He glanced at the television, then at the remote control on the bedside table. Picturing Taylor's intent blue-eyed image, the quirk to her lips when she related an amusing news item, and the rounding of her breasts under the soft blouses she wore, he reached for the remote. Then he tossed the controller to the foot of the bed. He had no right to dream about reaching through the screen to take Taylor in his arms.

Jillian turned over, her mouth sagging open. No matter how much he wanted Taylor, he had to remember he was a married man. And tomorrow he'd have to tell his wife about the baby plans.

But when morning came, he didn't tell her. After he went to the doctor and let the lab tech bleed four vials of blood out of him, he didn't face her. When the results came back clean, he kept quiet. She seemed so on edge, so ready for a fight. Christmas was just around the corner. He wouldn't spoil it by upsetting Jillian. She was antsy enough with her mother due for a visit. As he understood it, there was only a slim chance of Taylor getting pregnant on the first pass. After the holidays, he would tell Jillian.

Chapter 10

ARMORED FOR THE OCCASION IN A STRUC-
tured black wool suit, Taylor crossed the entry at Mason's
first knock. She'd been awake most of the night, her emotions ranging from nervous excitement at the thought of
becoming pregnant to despair that she had been denied the
joy of creating a family with Mason the old-fashioned
way, the way she craved. As she opened the door to him
in the bright light of day, she had to remind herself sharply
of her goal to keep this interaction as businesslike as possible, a goal her heart betrayed with a flutter as she beckoned him in. She could think of no transaction more
personal, more intimate, more designed to forge a bond,
than the one she and Mason were about to undertake.

He, too, wore a suit. In the dark wool, marked with the
faintest of pinstripes, he could easily travel from the
boardroom to the courtroom. She glanced up to the crisp
knot of his tie, the immaculate white collar, and the sturdy
set of his chin. Thank goodness he'd decided to approach
this whole matter in a sensibly serious fashion. Then she
looked at his face and caught him smiling.

"What's so funny?"

He pointed to their suits. "We could play the extras in
a *Harold and Maude* funeral scene."

Stifling a giggle, she said, "Yes, well, I'm on my way
to work. I have a lot to do today, so let's get started." Taylor led him into the living room, speaking over her shoulder. "I've left some supplies for you in my bathroom, the
one that opens off my bedroom. The instructions are there,
too. After you've finished—"

"Taylor." Awkwardly Mason reached his hand to her shoulder. "This isn't a deposition we're taking here."

His hand felt so warm. For a moment she let herself relax within his grasp. If he only knew how badly she wanted to reveal her true emotions. She didn't want to come across as a martinet, but if she wasn't careful, all her control, all her practiced nonchalance, would crumble. Trying to shrug free of his touch, she said, "Let's get started, shall we?"

"I cleared my calendar during the middle of the day because this is important. To both of us," Mason said seriously. "Let's not rush."

Taylor clasped her hands together in front of her, as if she were afraid what mischief they might get into if unleashed. "I'm not rushing. I simply want to do what's necessary."

With a gentle finger, Mason traced the blush spreading across her cheeks. "Are you embarrassed?" he asked quietly.

"No." She pulled away. The intense way he watched her made her nervous enough, without him touching her, too. Agony was closer to what she felt than simple embarrassment. Agony at not being able to lie spent and glowing after making love, hoping they had created life, but feeling so much love for each other that even if they hadn't succeeded that time, there was always tomorrow. Shaking her head to clear the image from her mind, she said, "Can we just get on with it? I'm fine."

"Liar." He wanted her to share her feelings—to admit she was as scared and anxious and yet strangely excited as he was. They were here to make a baby—a child the two of them, no matter how unusual the circumstances, would love and cherish.

Turning her back on him, she stared out the window, wondering whether, now that the moment had arrived, she had the courage to carry through.

Mason walked up behind her. "Taylor, look at me. Please."

When she didn't respond, he gently swiveled her to face

him. "You think I'm not nervous? I woke up this morning and thought about this whole thing and started to throw the covers back over my face. Not to mention all the other complications, having a date with a jelly jar is, frankly, unsettling."

Taylor blushed. Of course, this physical procedure had to be incredibly awkward for him. She started to smile, but resisted being drawn into his mood of caring and sensitivity. To protect her own emotions, she simply had to keep this whole procedure on a detached level. "You're right. I'm nervous. So now can we get this over with?"

"Okay, we'll do it your way." For a moment, Taylor thought he meant to object again, but he pivoted on his heel and headed across the room. At the door to the hall, he paused. "Show me the way and I'll get down to business."

In silence, Taylor led him to her bedroom. "The bathroom is through the walk-in closet." At his puzzled look, she said, "It's the old-fashioned kind, with shelves and cabinets on either side. Go straight through and ignore the clutter." She shut the bedroom door behind him and paced back to the living room to wait.

Mason let her close the door, mulling over her hurry to get this whole thing behind them. She didn't fool him for a minute with her tough-girl act. Taylor was even more apprehensive than he was.

And he was plenty scared. What he was here to do affected so many lives. Taylor. Jillian. The child born to their union of science and nature. Himself. Their extended families, too.

He'd wrestled over and over again with this choice, yet here he stood once more, fixed to one spot of the floor of Taylor's bedroom, staring inward, examining the question again.

With a shake of his head, Mason halted the parade of arguments pro and con. This was the only way he, given Jillian's nature, would ever give life to a child. He moved forward into the bedroom, ready to follow the course he had chosen.

At the sight of Taylor's unmade bed, he smiled. A purple comforter pooled on the floor near its foot, as if she had kicked it off during the night. The midday sun streamed through the curtainless windows, casting warmth and creating a feeling of cheer that seemed at marked contrast to both his and Taylor's moods. Mason crossed the room to the low-lying futon bed and smoothed the indentation on her pillow. He felt his body respond to the image his touch conjured: Taylor, lying warm, supple, and naked, smiling as she awakened to the day. Drawing on a bank of memories long suppressed, he added himself to the scene and pictured them joined together body and soul. Making a child. Their child.

Shaking his head, Mason recalled wondering earlier how he would be able to perform, knowing he'd been superseded by a turkey baster. He had his answer. Simply thinking of Taylor lying with him in her bed had done it. He was aroused, all right. Backing away from the bed, he headed for the bathroom, entering the walk-through closet as Taylor had directed. He noticed that, by her standards, the small room was a model of order. Pausing, he fingered the silk on several of the blouses. An aroma, faint but pleasing, filled his nostrils. As he thought about the sweetness of spring flowers the scent brought to mind, he recognized Taylor's perfume. He jerked his hand away, like a boy caught filching from the cookie jar. He had no right to stop there, absorbing Taylor's secret, personal self. All the same, he took another deep breath before stepping into the bathroom.

The room had been designed to match the twenties feel of the building. A pedestal sink, a claw-foot bathtub with an add-on shower, and a toilet with a pull-chain took up most of the space. An antique washstand stood opposite the sink. Mason expected the clutter of jewelry and makeup. Somehow, it wouldn't be Taylor's bathroom without that. But what surprised him was the *Playboy* propped on a cleared space of the washstand. Next to the magazine sat a glass jar and, as promised, "instructions."

Well, she'd certainly thought of everything. But when

Mason looked at the cover of the magazine, he felt less like going through with his end of the bargain than ever. What aroused him was the woman on the other side of the wall, who was probably at that very moment pacing the floor and wondering if she'd covered all contingencies. Picturing her, one finger to her chin, a severe look on her beautiful, rosy-cheeked face, he frowned. This was no way to make a baby. He knew what he wanted, and it wasn't Miss January.

Mason caught hold of the rim of the sink. A box of hair clips clattered onto the floor. The image of Taylor the first time he met her rose in his mind. She had been standing in the managing partner's office, a luscious mass of black hair tamed conservatively in a heavy French braid falling over the lapel of her perfectly tailored attorney suit. Her demeanor and expression were serious as she was introduced as the new associate joining Mason on a complicated antitrust case, yet not so serious that her expression hid the zest for life shining in her eyes.

Their working relationship had developed an easy, natural rhythm, founded on mutual respect for each other's legal savvy, sheer intelligence, and a lively sense of humor that helped get them through long weeks and months of grueling hours. They practically lived together, often going out for dinner, then returning to the office. The first night they went to his place after dinner, rather than returning to the office, where the carpets were being cleaned, sleeping with Taylor seemed as natural and as right as lawyering together.

Blinded by the blueprint of the "model wife" he carried in his head, he never once considered asking her to marry him. He had always expected to marry a woman like his mother, a woman who lived for her husband, home, and children. Taylor lived for her career; and she never once said anything about being in love with him.

After she had gone from his life, though, he suffered an emptiness that surprised him. But Jillian had been there, eager to fill the void, so ready to soothe him, to please, to offer him promises of the marriage and family he'd always imagined. Within two months after Taylor moved to North Carolina, he married Jillian.

One thing was for sure.

He was a fool.

Mason stared into the mirror over the sink, thinking of their recent birthday party, his outburst during their walk, his desire to reach out and hold her, his reaction to her every time he clicked across Channel Six news, his offer to father her child—no matter what the complications, these facts, these feelings, pointed to only one conclusion.

He was in love with Taylor.

And he had no right to be.

Taylor stopped pacing when she heard the bedroom door open. Was he through? She blushed at the thought of him getting aroused from pictures of naked women. The idea also annoyed her, even though she had been pleased at her thoroughness when she'd stopped at the local market and purchased the *Playboy*. The clerk hadn't even looked at her. Working near the intersection of Sunset and Fountain in West Hollywood, he'd seen it all. *Another dame wants to look at women's bodies. Here's your change.*

Watching Mason walk from her bedroom, his coat tossed over his shoulder, his tie askew, she was seized by a longing so intense, it frightened her. How she wished his presence here with her was an everyday occurrence, the natural result of two people in love, living together. She wanted to forget herself, forget their obligations, forget her sister, and throw her arms around him. She only wanted to share her love with the man she loved. She tore her gaze from him, reminding herself bleakly that Mason no more belonged in her home than a stolen jewel.

"Taylor."

He walked toward her, unsmiling, but with a quickness to his step that caused Taylor to wonder how a man could look so happy and yet so serious. Less than a foot away from her, he stopped.

Struggling with her defenses, she avoided his eyes and asked, "Finished?"

"Taylor . . ." he said. His voice had a strained quality.

"Taylor . . ." His power of speech having deserted him, he could only repeat her name. He dropped his coat onto a chair and yanked at his tie, drawing it even more off-center. Impeccable Mason was a mess.

"What is it?"

"I-I can't do it."

"Oh." Her eyes widened. No wonder he looked so uncharacteristically out of control. For a man, that had to be embarrassing. "Well, uh . . ." She glanced around, unsure what to say. Offer him coffee? A drink? Another magazine. No, not when all she wanted to offer him was herself.

Her conclusion suddenly dawning on him, he gave a strangled laugh. "It's not that, not what you're thinking." He captured one of her hands. "Taylor, forgive me. I've no right to say this, and please feel free to slap my face when I'm done." Falling silent for a moment, he begged her with his eyes to listen to his heart.

Taylor tensed, her hand lost in his. How could she think straight while he kept up that pressure? He shouldn't be doing it; it wasn't right. Each time she had seen him, he'd acted more and more familiar, touched her in more personal and intimate ways. She could only wait for him to speak.

Looking directly into her precious blue eyes, now so dark and serious, he said, "Taylor, I want you. Need you." His grip tightened on her fingers. In a hoarse whisper he said, "I love you." He stopped, stricken at what he'd confessed, at the line he'd crossed, yet relieved and joyous, too.

Taylor's pulse thudded in her throat. The rush of blood to her head made her feel faint. "Oh, Mason . . ." she murmured, unable to believe what she had just heard.

Surrendering her hand, he grabbed for his coat. Gruffly he said, "Under the circumstances, I'd better go."

She held out her arms to him, a smile lighting her eyes. "Mason, it's okay."

He had half turned away. "Forgive me. I shouldn't have

said anything, only I couldn't walk out on our arrangement without giving you the real reason."

"Shhh." Taylor placed a finger to her lips.

Slowly he turned back to face her, finally registering the acceptance and desire in her voice, the forgiveness of her outstretched arms, and the breathtaking smile of love on her face. His jacket fell to the floor. For the first time since he had walked back into the room, he smiled. Gathering her in his embrace, he crushed her to his chest. A groan escaped his mouth as he moved his hands up and down her back, touching, clasping her to him, as if to reassure himself she was really there. Lowering his head, he brushed a kiss on her forehead, then touched his lips to each trembling eyelid.

Taylor sensed him pause, and in answer to his silent question, she parted her lips. He joined his mouth to hers with furious intensity. She matched each demanding kiss, offering herself to him, giving and taking, reveling at his touch after so many years of denial.

Slowly, unwilling to break free of her touch, he pulled back. "Let me love you," he whispered, his heart certain of her answer, but his mind needing her acceptance and permission.

She felt so right in his arms, loved, sheltered, and protected, her body tingling with the fires of desire he'd ignited. "Yes, Mason," she answered. He loved her and she loved him—and this moment belonged to them.

Mason swept her up in his arms and retraced his earlier path to the bedroom, gazing tenderly at Taylor.

She slipped her hands around his neck, pulling him into another kiss. She was vaguely aware of her proper black pumps slipping off her feet and landing with a clunk. All that mattered was that Mason held her in his arms. He wanted her. After years of longing for him and damping her love, she could run her fingers through his hair, draw him to her, kiss his lips. Grant him freely the love she'd kept locked away.

Mason stopped next to where the purple comforter lay on the floor. On impulse, he lowered her, brushing her stocking-covered feet against the silky surface of the fabric before setting her down. She smiled in appreciation of the sensuous feel, and kicking off his shoes, he joined her there.

Almost trembling with desire and anticipation, he nudged her wool jacket off her shoulders. It slipped to the floor.

Taylor unfastened the top button of her white silk blouse, with her smile inviting him to undo the others. Under his reverent gaze, she felt completely beautiful and priceless, like a masterpiece about to be unveiled. Any hesitant thoughts of the few extra pounds her hips and waist had garnered over the past seven years evaporated. Her blouse joined her jacket, followed by the stern black skirt and her lace-trimmed half-slip.

Mason caught his breath. He gazed at her body, wanting her to know how precious and invaluable the gift of her love was to him. She reached on tiptoe to kiss him, then tugged at his shirt.

He stripped free of his own clothing, unreservedly giving his body and the sure evidence of his physical desire to Taylor. Holding out his arms, he drew her to him, kissing her mouth, so warm and responsive, then capturing her nipple through the lace of her bra.

Lifting his head, he whispered, "Thank you for letting me love you." He unclasped her bra and slipped the matching scrap of lace panties down her legs, marveling at how Taylor gifted her body to him, basking in the open, willing, and generous present she made of loving him.

He drew her down to the bed and took her in his arms. After one very long kiss, a kiss that threatened to stop Taylor's heart, Mason propped himself up by one arm and said, "I want to savor the sight of you."

Taylor smiled slightly, knowing that her body was no longer that of the young woman Mason had once known. She lay sideways across the bed, her feet tangled with Mason's, her long hair scattered over the bedclothes and around her shoulders. Returning his look, she offered her body for his hungry and appreciative inspection. And for once, Taylor didn't blush.

He skimmed with a gentle finger the mounds of her breasts, then moved to the gentle swell of her belly. Her body was that of a woman, ripened and lush. "You're even more beautiful than you were seven years ago," he said, slipping back beside her.

Reaching out a finger, she brushed the dark hair that matted his chest. She followed the dark trail down his abdomen and stopped. He was magnificently aroused.

Mason caught her hand and guided it to close around him. "Oh, yes. I want you," he whispered. "I'm amazed at how badly I want you." He lifted her hand and kissed her fingertips before pulling her to him. "But there's something I have to say."

Taylor waited for him to speak.

"Give me the word, and I'll force myself out of this bed and proceed by Plan A." Smoothing away a strand of hair from her forehead, he said, "But I don't want to."

She closed her eyes. The decision was hers. They could still back away from this, this moment that seemed the fulfillment of all her long-held dreams, dreams of union and family with the man she'd never stopped loving, dreams that seemed so natural and true. He felt so right next to her on the bed. His erection nudged against her, and she opened her eyes. "Threaten to withdraw again, Counselor, and I'll make a motion for sanctions."

Mason grinned. Lifting the end of a strand of her hair, he tickled her nipple.

She laughed, and thought she would explode from sheer happiness. He spread her hair on the pillow and took her nipple in his mouth. Then, suddenly serious, he kissed a path downward till his kiss met the hot warmth between her thighs. After only a few eagerly seeking caresses, she cried out from pleasure and delight, bestowing upon him the gift of the waves of heat and honey he'd created.

Mason kissed his way back up her neck and whispered to her, "Our child. We're going to create our child."

Our child. The baby she had planned and prayed for, fathered by the lover for whom she'd waited seven years. She almost started to cry. For joy, for all the years of eating her heart out wanting him. And out of sheer sorrow, knowing their time together had to be brief. Blinking away the moisture that appeared in her eyes at his words, she whispered, "Mason, love me."

In response, Mason lowered his lips to hers. He was a man spared from wandering a lifetime in a desert. He kissed and tasted Taylor, savoring the perfume that clung to her skin and the open gift she made of her body. Tomorrow would bring judgment and a price to be paid for the joy of loving Taylor. He would pay. Without complaint.

When he could hold out no longer, he lifted himself over her. She lay in a tangle of black hair and rumpled sheets, perspiration gleaming on her white skin. "You're so beautiful," he breathed, meaning every word. Fitting himself inside her, fusing them as one, he watched the light that shone in her dark eyes. He filled her, and began to move, at first slowly, and then with increasing rapidity as his senses and blood heated and drove him. He watched her face, stirred by her expressions of excitement and need, and her open display of sensual pleasure.

Greeting his body as he joined and traveled with hers, she welcomed him in, sheathing him in the heat of her love, drawing him upward. Her breath came in shallow gasps and she fixed her eyes on his, murmuring his name between cries of pleasure, savoring every heart-spiraling sensation, every precious moment of union.

When Mason sensed the gathering waves of orgasm overtake her body, he rushed to join with her. As they merged spirit and flesh, totally at one, Taylor cried out, "I love you."

Taylor came back to the present very, very slowly. Mason had shifted slightly to her side, to spare her his weight. She wanted to hold him there with her forever. His black hair swirled into peaks where she had run her fingers through it. He certainly did not look like a serious attorney who had left the office for a lunch meeting.

A lunch meeting. Taylor sat up. The sun had long since faded from the bedroom. "What time is it?"

Mason tugged her back down and rolled her on top of him. "That's not very romantic pillow talk." He blew gently between her breasts. "Don't worry about the time. Not today."

"You're a romantic at heart, aren't you?"

He nodded.

"No wonder I missed you so much." She lay her head against his chest for a moment. So much time had passed. Lifting her head, she said, "Mason, why did you let me go?"

"I thought it was what you wanted."

"More than I wanted you?" The question was unfair; she had been afraid to reveal how much in love with him she was.

"I thought the job meant more to you than I did. Besides—"

"It doesn't matter now." She cut him off, not wanting to sorrow over the past. She kissed him, a generous and thorough kiss. And forgot about the past; forgot about the time. As she felt him growing excited beneath her, she groaned and eased off him. "Mason, I have to get to work."

He trailed a finger across her breasts and down to her damp pubic hair. "The show won't go on without you?"

She sighed. She never wanted him to leave, and here she was, asking him not to love her again. Checking the clock, she said, "We have time for a shower, and that's about it."

"Okay." Grinning like a boy justifiably accused of playing hooky, he led her by the hand through the closet to the bathroom. They spotted the *Playboy* at the same time.

"Did you even check out the centerfold?"

Mason shook his head. "I knew who I wanted." He bent to start the shower. When he turned back around, Taylor saw he was fully erect. Dropping to her knees, she took him in her mouth and kissed him, thrilling to the sensations the intimacy created in her own body.

Mason sighed his pleasure and ruffled her already mussed hair. Taylor kissed her way to the tip of his penis, and blew softly on his navel. He pulled her up and nuzzled against her. "I don't know how I've lived without you. You're so alive and loving. So wonderfully loving."

"When did you know, Mason?"

He looked at her and lifted his shoulders, puzzling out the answer to her question. "It's been gradual, like waking from a dream and not quite remembering when the dream ended and the morning began." He pointed to the sink. "But the truth hit me right here, standing in front of this sink, realizing full well Miss January was the last woman I wanted, and suddenly I knew that you were the only one for me."

She buried her head against his shoulder and spread her hair over his back.

He luxuriated in the feel of the heavy strands caressing his skin. "I realize now I never could have offered to father your child unless I was already in love with you. When I first decided to make my offer, I simply thought I was coming up with a clever solution designed to give us both a child." Stroking her hair, he added, "Except, of course, for how Jillian might feel."

Taylor froze. *Jillian.* She'd managed not to think about her sister since the moment Mason had knocked at her door.

Mason tilted her chin. "Look at me. I promise you we'll work this out." He kissed her again. "We must. And we will."

With him holding her, she believed they would be able to work out their convoluted situation. She smiled and pointed to the water cascading in the tub. "Mason, the water's running."

"So it is." He kissed her again, then reached over to shut off the faucet. "Hold on." He picked her up and, holding her close against him, settled her onto him. "We don't want to waste anything, do we?"

They ended up in the shower eventually, with Taylor laughingly soaping Mason. She forgot about work. She forgot about everything except the two of them, until Mason nudged her out from under the flow of hot water and started to rub the bar of soap over her breasts. When he lathered up, the gold band on his left hand sparked in sharp contrast to the white bar of soap.

She waited until they were drying each other. "Mason, please don't tell Jillian about me."

Mason wrapped his towel around her and drew her close. "I think you must know we haven't had a real marriage for some time."

She pulled away. "I don't want to talk about that." The joy of the afternoon started to dim as the reality of her situation returned. "But no matter what you have to do, please don't tell her you've been with me. She's my sister, and I don't want to hurt her. I've loved you for so long, Mason, and I honestly never would have—"

"Slipped up and let me know?" Mason put his arms around her. "Thank you for telling me the truth, Taylor. You've given me a present I didn't know existed. I'll need some time to handle things with Jillian. I'll move out, work out a separation." He kissed her and said, "I promise I'll be back for you. We should have been together all these years. We'd have a home full of babies now."

Taylor buried her face against his shoulder, still damp from their shower. She wanted to believe him. But as she held on to him, she had the frightening vision that this time together had been their last. Discussing the cold facts of their situation would only spoil the moments they had left. Grabbing the towel away from him, she flicked his leg with it and chased him into the bedroom.

Recovering her suit from the floor, she attempted to brush the wrinkles from it. Mason, wearing his briefs and one sock, searched for the rest of his clothes in the pile on the floor. Watching him, Taylor thought how natural it was to be getting dressed again with Mason. Loving Mason. She picked up her panty hose and pulled them on her right foot as Mason, on his hands and knees, still looking for his sock, burrowed under her purple comforter.

"Ooogha. Ooogha." Muffled roars came from under the

comforter as Mason moved toward her. She thought she heard, "Purple people panty hose eater," then felt Mason kissing his way up her legs.

"Down, boy," she called.

Mason's face appeared from under the fabric. Her breath caught when she saw the love and laughter in his expression. "Taylor, I feel like a new man." Yanking the comforter over both of them, he tipped her back onto the bed. "A crazy man. Crazy in love."

Taylor felt pleasure move across her body like a summer rain as Mason slipped his tongue between her lips. Even one of his simple kisses turned her to jelly, but when Mason turned his full attention to exploring and caressing every nerve center in her mouth, she felt herself slip quickly over the edge. She moved against him, responding to the lure of his kiss, then stilled as he slowed, then pulled free. She thrust the comforter off them and looked at Mason.

Gone was the laughing purple panty hose eater. The late afternoon shadows, darkening the bed, had eclipsed his mood as well. "I'm sorry, Taylor. Reality just hit me." He sat up, then extracted his other sock from the bed. "Come on. Last one dressed is a rotten egg."

"You first. I'll watch." She wanted to pretend, if only for a moment, that it was any morning of the week and her man was dressing for work.

Mason grinned, and obliged her. He stepped into his pants first, which pleased her. She thought men walking around only in dress shirts looked silly. But she loved the sight of a broad, hairy chest rising above unbelted pants. When he shrugged into his wrinkled white shirt, she rose and walked on her knees to the edge of the bed.

While she buttoned his shirt, he stroked her naked body. "I bet your ratings would go through the ceiling if your viewers ever saw you like this."

Taylor laughed. "Don't suggest that to Sid, whatever you do. He'd do almost anything for another ratings point." She did the last button. "Anyway, I think I'll save this outfit for you."

"Thank you." He picked up his tie and knotted it. "It's more than I have the right to ask, but—" he lifted her chin "—wear it for any other guy, and I'll kill him."

"Caveman."

He nodded, tucked his shirt in, and picked up one of his black leather shoes. Holding it in his hand, he paused. "Taylor, love is all or nothing for me. A few minutes ago, when I said reality had hit, I meant I realized what I had to do to Jillian. Marriage has always meant forever to me, but no matter how many times I preach that to myself, I can't make myself feel something for her that doesn't exist anymore."

He sat next to her on the bed and took her hand. "And when I think about you, and how you make me feel, I know the simple truth. What Jillian and I had, way back at the beginning, was good in its own way, but somehow, somewhere, it got off track." He looked away, as if seeing the film of his life with Jillian playing against the darkened wall of the room. "I thought I could make myself continue to love her. God knows I've tried. But forcing it doesn't work. And lately I've wondered whether she feels anything at all for me. I should have told you this before, but I didn't even tell her I was going to be your donor."

Taylor started to shush him, unwilling to hear too much about his relationship with her sister or to consider the consequences of his not revealing their plan to Jillian. He placed a finger against her lips, then dropped his hand. "I know I don't have to tell you all this right now, but I want to. Even lately, I've had times when I thought I still loved her, but those moments always . . . fizzled. Yet facing her with these truths is one of the most painful things, if not *the* most painful, that I will ever have to do." Standing up, he drew Taylor to him. "But I'll do it. For you, I'll do it."

Mason drove away from her apartment hugging the gift of Taylor's love to his heart. He'd been granted a second chance at loving, and this time he had to do things right.

After Mason kissed her good-bye, Taylor dressed and wandered around her apartment, hugging her arms across her chest. She needed to get to work, but she hated to break the spell of their loving by rushing out.

Mason loved her! He really loved her. A dim memory of a childhood game, in which boy and girl are matched up and their fortunes told through a series of questions, nudged at her mind. Yes, Mason and Taylor—they'll have seven kids, and get married on a boat, and live in a pink house, and the first child's name will be Pony. She smiled at the memory and then forced herself back to the present. Time, way past time, to get to work.

Even Burke couldn't spoil Taylor's mood that evening. Not after the incredible events of the afternoon. Her heart still beat to the rhythm of Mason's loving. In the back of her mind, she knew she would have to face her conscience soon, but she wanted to enjoy the bliss as long as possible.

Burke raised one smoothly combed eyebrow when she slid into her seat at the anchor desk. "My, my, the paragon of virtue is running a bit late today. We missed you at the lineup meeting this afternoon."

She smiled, and studied her opening.

Burke leaned over to her. "Christmas come early this year, Taylor? Judging by the light in your eyes, which I must say does you some good, I'd wager Saint Nick came down your chimney today."

"Say whatever you like, Burke." She smiled again, ready in the afterglow of lovemaking to forgive even The Jerk. Of course Burke would assume she'd spent the afternoon in bed. He didn't think; he rutted. "How's your wife? And the baby?"

"They're both fine, thank you." He straightened his tie. "Do I detect something of the hypocrite in you, dear Ms. Drummond? I spend an afternoon caught up in the various pleasures of life, and you read me the riot act. You, however, have obviously spent your day in precisely the same fashion, and you manage to look like one of those fourteenth-century paintings of the Madonna." He leered at her. "Without child, I hope."

That crack threatened her mood, but the stage manager saved her from further discussion with a countdown to air.

Fortunately for Taylor, the news producers had taken into account that they were two days away from Christmas, and stressed the softer news stories. She wanted to smile and sparkle and shout to the world that Mason loved her. The professional in her would have squelched the goodwill had she been doing a story on an apartment house fire, or a fifty-two-car pileup on the Grapevine. Tonight she relayed stories that suited her buoyant spirits. She especially enjoyed the story of an elderly woman, who had adopted twenty-five strays, being saved from eviction from her apartment by a rich eccentric who bought a farm for her and the cats.

While reading the cat story, Taylor felt a prick of guilt. A black and white cat had been hanging around her door for a week, and she had been ignoring it. She assumed it belonged to a neighbor, but now she promised herself to find out. As she was collecting her briefcase, Sid caught up with her.

"Babe, I gotta tell you. You were hot tonight. I sat in my office, watching you, and wanted to crawl through the monitor and throw myself at your feet." He took a step back and studied her face. "Whatever you did to make yourself come alive like that, do it every day."

Taylor laughed, then grew quiet. "Sid, I wish I could."

"Make me a happy guy, Taylor. Keep turning on those viewers, and keep those viewers turning us on." He walked with her to the outer door, opened it for her, and slapped her on the rear. "Now go home to whoever he is."

The high she had experienced started to droop on Thursday when Mason didn't call. He hadn't said he would call, but she expected him to. She waited at home till later than usual and checked for messages at the station. Twice she picked up the phone to dial his office, then dropped it. He would call.

She summoned her best Christmas cheer for the evening broadcast. As soon as she finished, she slipped out of the building before Sid or any of the others could draw her into the festivities taking place in Sid's office. The guy must never go home, Taylor thought as she drove back to her own quiet apartment. But how different was his life from her own? Had Christmas Eve been three days earlier, she would have joined in Sid's merrymaking, rather than go home alone. But now all had changed. What if Mason tried to call her? She wanted to be close to the phone.

When Taylor rounded the landing of her stairs, she spotted the black cat waiting for her at the top. "You must have heard my conscience, kitty," she said as she approached. He held his ground, and as Taylor fit her key into the lock, the cat rubbed against her legs. Once, then back again, as if it enjoyed the contact. When the door opened, the cat bounded in ahead of Taylor.

She closed the door and followed the cat. He jumped onto her stereo cabinet and pointed his nose in the air, then sprang to the ground and began exploring the living room. Taylor smiled and went to the kitchen to check her cupboards for a can of tuna.

The flashing message light on her answering machine caught her attention. For the tiniest moment, while watching the cat, she hadn't thought about Mason. She felt almost guilty for that as she pressed the Play button. Background sounds of music and other people talking filled the room, then came Jillian's throaty voice. Taylor started, surprised and uncomfortable as her sister's words reminded her of the gulf of loneliness she must still face before she and Mason could be united.

"We just called to say Merry Christmas and sorry you had to work on Christmas Eve. Mason says we should turn on the news so you can be here in spirit. Don't forget dinner tomorrow at one o'clock."

Taylor switched off the machine and went in search of a saucer. *Mason says we should turn on the news so you can be here in spirit.* Was that his way of sending her a message? His way of telling her he missed her? She dumped half a can of Chicken of the Sea onto the saucer. The cat materialized beside her, watching her every move. He didn't beg, though. Stroking him on the head, she said, "You're so well behaved. You must have a home." She placed the saucer on the kitchen floor. "I hope your people don't mind if I borrow you for Christmas."

Curling up on her sofa, Taylor thought of what she had to meet head-on the next day. Christmas dinner at Jillian and Mason's home. When her sister had invited her, Taylor had been pleased, except for the news that Claudia, their mother, would be present. Once she had moved to the East Coast, she had started a tradition of visiting a local orphanage on Christmas Day. The station collected toys, and Taylor and some of the other unattached co-workers played Santa Claus to the children. This year, despite the friction with her sister, she had been looking forward to what would at least be a semblance of a family Christmas.

The cat strolled over and settled beside her. Taylor stroked him. Put in its worst light, the situation stank. She had slept with her sister's husband. Tomorrow she had to face Jillian and act normal. Worse, she had to watch Jillian and Mason together. Mason would put his arm around his wife, and Taylor would remember how she felt when Mason had taken her in his arms. Mason would kiss Jillian, ever so gently, and Taylor would want to close her eyes against the memory of his warm lips, his tongue claiming hers.

She sighed and considered not going. But she wanted to see Mason. She wanted to sit in the same room with him, watch his expressive eyes, share his quick humor, and sense him near her, even though she couldn't reach out and touch him. If this pain was the price she had to pay, she would bear it.

Not that she intended to make love to him again until he and Jillian had separated. He had to make a break with Jillian, or he and Taylor had no future together. For seven years she had been true to her love for him, and respected his wedding vows. What had happened the other day had occurred under extraordinary circumstances. Adultery, affairs, sneaking around—none of those were for Taylor.

They hadn't exactly discussed these points the other day; they had been too engrossed in the wonder of loving each other. But Taylor was positive Mason would agree with her.

If only he had called. She wanted to speak with him, to connect with him, before having to face him on his home ground. She needed reassurance, to damp down the insecurity, the fear that he might not love her the way she loved him. All her life, her parents had compared her unfavorably to her sister. Those comparisons echoed in her mind now as she contemplated the reality of Mason leaving Jillian for her. Who would relinquish the graceful, popular Jillian, hostess cum laude, for a woman who had never taken the time to learn how to make an omelet? For a woman whose idea of giving a dinner party was to ask her secretary to make a reservation? For a woman who would leap at a job offer from a network—even if it meant pulling up roots and moving across the country?

Taylor jumped up from the sofa, sending the cat into an irritated sprawl. She had to stop these thoughts. Why shouldn't Mason love her? Yes, it was difficult to change, and yes, it was easier for him to stay with Jillian because it is always easier to keep on doing the same thing you're used to, no matter how painful or stifling it may be. But he loved her. He would come to her.

She settled back onto the sofa and patted the spot next to her. "It's okay, kitty. It's safe to come back now." The cat gave her a look that said he didn't quite trust her mood, but he'd seen worse abuse in his past, and accepted her invitation.

What if she was pregnant? Taylor placed her hand over her abdomen and wondered whether she had conceived. The timing had been optimal, but there were so many variables. If she hadn't conceived, she would have to be patient and wait until Mason was free. Inviting Mason over next month for another try by their original plan was pointless. They would never adhere to the jelly-jar routine.

Taylor reached for an old box of chocolates hidden under a stack of magazines on the coffee table. At the same time, she spotted two packages lying on the table. Her Christmas presents for Jillian and Mason. Unwrapped.

Why hadn't she had the clerk at Neiman-Marcus gift wrap them? No, a week ago, in keeping with her family Christmas concept, Taylor had purchased green and red paper and ribbons, so she could give the presents an old-fashioned do-it-yourself gift wrap job. Grumbling, she slipped out from under the afghan and went in search of a pair of scissors.

Folding tissue around the Judith Lieber evening bag for Jillian, Taylor hoped that Mason honored her request to leave her out of his divorce. Jillian had every right to hate her, but despite all their differences, she didn't want her to. She was her only family. Except for Claudia, who Taylor was loath to count. But even if Jillian didn't know about her now, how would she react when Mason remarried, and she discovered that Taylor was wife number two? Not well. She trimmed the paper to fit the box. Not well at all.

She wrapped Mason's simple present, three conservative, lawyerlike silk ties, thinking of all the future Christmases they would share. And of all the fun presents. Never again would she give him a present so stuffy and sisterly.

Chapter 11

MASON WOKE UP EARLY ON CHRISTMAS MORN-
ing. Jillian still slept. He listened for sounds of his mother-
in-law, installed down the hall in the guest room. Claudia
Drummond had never made a more ill-timed visit. When
he had arrived home from work two days ago, after spending the afternoon with Taylor, his mother-in-law had
greeted him.

His shock showed on his face. Claudia, never one to
mince words, had tipped her martini glass to him and said,
"Don't have a coronary. I'm leaving the day after Christmas." Of course, he had recovered and welcomed her
properly, but her presence had ruined his immediate plans
to ask Jillian for a separation. Claudia would find out soon
enough and doubtless begin tormenting Jillian over the
"failure" of her marriage. Mason couldn't bring himself to
inflict that humiliation on her with her mother in the
house. The least he could do was give Jillian time to adjust
to the idea of their separation before Claudia found out.

And today was Christmas Day. Christmas had always
been his favorite holiday. At home in Iowa the tree in the
living room had scraped the ceiling, and presents had
crowded the floor. His mother had involved all six kids in
every task, from cookie baking to tree trimming to filling
the special feeders they kept for the winter birds. And here
he was this Christmas Day, practicing the words to ask his
wife for a divorce.

Jillian stirred and rolled toward him. "Merry Christmas,
Mason." She kissed him on the tip of his nose.

"Merry Christmas," he mumbled, not returning her kiss.

She fit herself against him. "The guests aren't coming for hours."

He lay still. He listened to the beating of his heart and the rustle of the comforter as Jillian wrapped an arm around his waist. Her breasts rubbed against his chest, the hardened nipples an invitation.

With a yawn and a stretch, he shifted from her grasp. He should have made his mother-in-law stay in a hotel so he could sleep in the guest room. Or slept on the sofa. But again, he had been trying to keep Claudia in the dark about their problems. He took in her lowered eyelids, her strumming of his chest chair. Sex with Jillian? Not after making love to Taylor. "It's such a nice morning. I think I'll go for a run."

Jillian didn't take the hint. She ran her hand down his abdomen to his groin, to the unmistakable evidence of his lack of interest. Even that didn't deter her. "How about a warm-up before you run?" she said, beginning to stroke him.

"Not this morning." He hated himself for not telling her right that moment. *Jillian, I do not want to have sex. I want a divorce.*

"I think we should exchange presents now," she said, then scooted down in the bed and took him in her mouth.

His fickle flesh was perking up, voting for her to continue. But what about Taylor? He placed his hands around Jillian's face and drew her up to his chest, intending to kiss her quickly and head for the shower.

She wrapped her legs around his thighs. Her hair swung across her face, not quite covering the stubborn set to her chin. "I want my present now."

He wondered what had gotten into her. Whenever he had wanted to have sex, she had been like a castle with the drawbridge raised and bolted into place. Now, when she wanted it, he was supposed to give on demand. At some point they had ceased to love each other, and sex had become a weapon; he had used their marriage bed as a battleground for childbearing. And Jillian? He no longer knew what she wanted. Instead of addressing and solving their problems, he had let them slide by, piling up, growing beyond his ability to love her.

Jillian laid her face against his chest. In a whisper so low he could barely hear her, she said, "Please, Mason."

To assuage his guilt at his own sense of failure, he decided to give her what she wanted. Closing his eyes, he rolled over and drew Jillian to him. After tomorrow, he would be free from their charade of a marriage.

Jillian smiled. Thank God he had given in. She spread her legs and let her mind drift. He had to make love to her that day, or all was lost. Once, he wouldn't believe, but twice, he might buy. Since yesterday, when she had been collecting items to send for dry cleaning and picked up his suit coat worn the day before, she had been waiting for her chance to trap him. The smell of another woman was unmistakably present in the fabric of that suit. He had been drifting away from her, and she hadn't caught him in time. Mason, who she had always believed would be faithful to her no matter what she said or did, had betrayed her. Mason, who even now was pumping his life into her, no longer wanted her. Accusing him was the fastest way of losing him. But a baby . . .

Mason lay by her side, unmoving. His eyes were closed. Jillian wanted to scratch the image of the other woman from his lids. Stroking his forehead, she said, "Merry Christmas, Mason."

He didn't answer.

Taylor parked her car in front of Mason and Jillian's house. As she sat and composed herself for the trial to come, an elderly couple approached the house. Taylor collected her gifts, left her car, and walked to the front door with them. Each finishing the other's sentences, they introduced themselves as the Jensens, from just down the block. Taylor told them she was Jillian's sister.

As Taylor knocked, Mrs. Jensen said to her, "We've had Christmas with Mr. and Mrs. Reed—"

"Three years running," said her husband.

"Wallace and I never had little ones—"

"Always too busy seeing the world, we were," finished her husband. "Kind of Mrs. Reed to invite—"

"Us to share a family dinner."

Taylor couldn't help but smile, wondering whether she and Mason would be like that years from now. She was thankful that the smile stayed with her when the door opened and revealed her lovely sister, looking better than Taylor had seen her since she had been in California. Jillian threw her a smile, then drew the Jensens into a greeting embrace.

Taylor sensed Mason's approach, but still wasn't prepared for him appearing in front of her. He wore brown cords, loafers, and a roughly woven blue and brown sweater that made the brown in his eyes sing out. He smiled at her, then leaned forward, welcoming her with a brotherly kiss on the cheek. She marveled at how well he played the role. No observer would ever know from Mason that they had ever been anything other than the friendliest of in-laws.

She lacked Mason's control. Taylor knew her face flushed from the contact. The touch of his lips scorched her cheek. She didn't dare return his kiss, not even with a peck on the cheek. Mumbling "Merry Christmas," she handed him the Neiman-Marcus bag containing their presents, then turned to Jillian.

Her sister sparkled. Blue eyes, darker and more alive than usual, illuminated the warm ivory of her skin. Green silk clung to every faultless measurement.

Taylor shivered as a sense of foreboding settled over her. This image of perfection was the woman Mason had to walk away from—if he truly loved Taylor. She responded as best she could to Jillian's hug and managed another weak "Merry Christmas." She accepted Jillian's arm around her waist, wondering at her unusual show of affection, and also feeling like the hypocrite she was.

Mason escorted the Jensens, and Jillian led Taylor into the living room and introduced her to the other guests—two couples from Mason's firm, plus the Jensens, and another of their neighbors, Lawrence Corning, a fortyish gastroenterologist. And their mother.

Claudia Drummond sat in a high-backed chair next to the fireplace. To greet her, Taylor had to cross the length of the room, traveling to offer obeisance like a subject in a queen's throne room. Taylor had tried not to think about her mother's visit. Not that her mother had come to see her; she wondered if Claudia would have bothered to look her up if Taylor hadn't attended the Christmas dinner. Mindful of the other guests, Taylor played the role of dutiful daughter.

"Hello, Taylor." Claudia dipped her chin a fraction, but made no move to rise from her chair.

"Hello, Claudia." Her mother looked as flawlessly coifed and garbed as she always did. No gray marred her ash-blond hair; no strand strayed in the softly permed short cut. Wearing one of her trademark bright green suits, she could easily be on her way to one of her real estate conferences.

"Your sister gave a lovely party last night. She's such a wonderful hostess. It was a pity you had to miss it."

Taylor shifted from foot to foot and decided against sitting down beside her mother. Despite having learned years ago that trying to be friends with her mother was fruitless, she always found herself at the moment of first meeting thinking somehow this time would be different. But it would never change. Claudia continued to take every opportunity to point out Jillian's virtues and Taylor's shortcomings. "I would think you, as a career woman, would understand that I had to work." If it hadn't been for the answering machine message from Jillian, Taylor wouldn't have known her sister had thrown a Christmas Eve party. No wonder Mason hadn't had time to call her; he was probably busy playing host. A twinge of jealousy struck, and she searched the room for him.

He had his back to her. Disappointed, she looked back at her mother.

Claudia busied herself lighting a cigarette. Once the tip glowed, she said, "I don't like being called a career woman. You know quite well I was content being a wife and mother. Only your father's tragic death forced me into the business world."

Taylor had heard this litany before. "Nevertheless, whether you like to admit it or not, you own one of the most lucrative real estate practices in the city of Chicago. And that does make you a career woman."

Leaning around Taylor, Claudia signaled to Jillian. Like an obedient puppy, Jillian excused herself from Dr. Corning and headed in their direction.

"Taylor, you always were a cheeky, outspoken girl. I see you've only gotten snippier with age."

"What's wrong with acknowledging your success?"

Jillian stepped up, ashtray in hand. Claudia stabbed out her cigarette. "Thank you, Jillian. That was very thoughtful of you. I think it's about time to offer drinks, don't you? I'll have my usual." She lit another cigarette. "I did what I had to do after your father died. And I'll thank you not to criticize the way I've managed. You received your fair share of the insurance money, and you ended up flushing it down the toilet."

"I did not waste that money."

"I've told you before and I'll tell you again. That money put you through law school, and you shamed your father's memory when you gave up the law to traipse around in front of a camera. And if that isn't a waste of money, I don't know what is." She made a moue of disgust. "There is nothing quite so vulgar as local news."

Taylor pointedly turned to Jillian. She had had this argument with her mother before. She had always thought Claudia had been shocked and angry to discover upon her husband's death that he had settled far larger insurance sums upon his daughters than upon his wife. The most generous action Ronald Drummond had ever taken toward his elder daughter was the night he crashed his car into a freeway overpass during a blinding rainstorm. "Do you need some help serving drinks?"

Claudia waved her hand. "Go ahead. Run away. One of these days you'll listen to me. When you're old and gray and no station will hire you and no man wants you and it's too late for you to know the beauty of motherhood—you'll wish you had listened to me." Claudia smiled, as only her mother could do after pronouncing such a curse. "Run along and help your sister."

Taylor wanted to scream her eternal question at her mother. *Why do you hate me so?* Instead, she turned and walked with Jillian from the room. For years she had accepted as truth that she was unlovable, despicable, a troublemaker. Seven years ago, when she fell in love with Mason, she had begun to question that judgment; when Mason had chosen Jillian over her, she had fought the voice within her that said, *I told you so.* With her new career in television and the ensuing popularity, she had struggled to overcome the repeated incriminations and to begin to believe in herself. She was getting there, but spending time with her mother sure warped her progress.

Once they were out of earshot, Jillian said, "So what do you think?"

"She'll never change." Taylor forced her hands to relax. Her fingernails had ground into her palms while she spoke to Claudia.

"Not about Mother." Jillian stepped into the kitchen. "About Lawrence."

"Who is Lawrence?"

Reaching for a chef's apron, Jillian said, "The doctor I just introduced you to."

"I said all of five words to him." Taylor looked around for another apron, spotted the maid preparing Bloody Marys, and smiled in greeting. The woman ducked her head and responded with a smile. "Do you have another apron?"

"Don't bother. I know how handy you are in the kitchen." Jillian reached for a half-empty Bloody Mary and drained the glass. "You could do worse than Lawrence. He has an established practice and a lovely home. About four thousand square feet, with maid's quarters. Divorced. Two children. But don't worry, the wife has them. He makes quite a bundle." Waving her celery wand, she added, "Gastroenterology is a lucrative field. Greater stresses in society, more ulcers." She crossed to a double oven and opened the door, revealing a turkey, browned to perfection.

"Are you trying to set me up?"

Jillian lifted her face. Her skin was tinted a rosy hue from the heat of the oven. "Don't be mad at me. I only want you to be as happy as Mason and I are. You don't know what you're missing."

Taylor stared at her sister, taking in the distant look in her eyes, the glow to her face. She didn't understand how her sister could be talking of happiness when Mason had confessed two days ago how miserable their marriage was. "You certainly speak more highly of marriage today than the last time we were together."

Her sister closed the oven door. "I've learned how important my husband is to me. I love him very much." The light in her eyes dimmed, and she took a long sip of her drink. "I'd kill anyone who came between me and Mason."

Jillian's face had taken on a determined, angry look. Taylor glanced at her hands, at the tray of drinks the maid had finished, at the clock on the wall. Was it possible Jillian suspected her? Her throat was dry; she never, ever should have opened her arms to Mason and let him into her bed and into her heart. Not as long as he remained her sister's husband.

Jillian fluttered her hands and smiled. "What am I doing? This is Christmas Day, I've guests waiting for their drinks, and I'm standing around like I'm at a pajama party. Mason and I are totally happy together, and I want the same for you." She finished her drink and lifted the tray for Taylor. "Every woman should have a Christmas present like I had this morning." She smiled. "If you're lucky, you'll find a man who makes love the way Mason does."

Taylor grappled with the weight of the tray. Now she recognized why Jillian seemed softer and happier. She looked, Taylor realized with a sharp knife to her heart, as if she had spent the morning making love. Between now and the afternoon she and Mason had made love, Mason had had sex with Jillian. Jillian hadn't painted that glow on with a cosmetics brush.

"Don't drop the tray," said Jillian. "That's a new Aubusson in the living room."

Taylor steadied the tray and backed from the room, unable to force her gaze from the satisfied smile on her sister's lips. *We haven't had a real marriage in a long time,* Mason had said. Yet he had made love to her.

Jillian watched her sister leave the room, hoping Taylor managed to deliver the drinks without dumping them on the floor. Taylor had zero hostess skills. Which was one of the chief reasons Jillian had eliminated her from her list of suspects. Despite their past, she could never be the kind of doting wife Mason needed. Jillian knew the two of them had been lovers when they worked together seven years ago. But how much could it have really meant to Mason? It had taken Jillian only two months from the day Taylor left for the East Coast to get his diamond on her finger. Of course, it had required a good deal of manipulation to reach that point, but every objective carried its price.

Taylor slumped against the wall in the dining room, steadying the tray against the back of a chair. She couldn't walk straight into the room where Mason stood until she recovered from the impact of what Jillian had revealed. True, Mason hadn't said he was going straight home to ask Jillian for a divorce. But even if he had decided to wait a few days, possibly because of the holidays, surely he could have avoided making love to her. Anger and disappointment swept over her, and she wondered whether she would be ill. All that time she had waited for Mason to call. All that talk about how telling Jillian would be so painful. But for her, for Taylor, he would do it. She swallowed, fighting against a growing nausea. Had he ever intended to leave Jillian?

If Mason had made love to Jillian, he couldn't be plan-

ning on divorcing her. And even if he was, Taylor wasn't
having anything to do with him now. She wanted to cry,
but she held on to the pain, refusing to let any of it out.
Why, oh, why had he raised her expectations? For seven
years she had survived without a crumb of hope. Now she
had less than nothing.

When she walked into the living room, Mason headed
toward her. She avoided his eyes and politely refused his
offer to carry the tray. Instead, she turned to Lawrence and
asked him to help her dispense the drinks. During dinner,
she riveted her attention on the doctor, listening to him describe recent advances in fiber-optic endoscopes as if she
were considering a residency in gastroenterology. She
sensed Mason watching her, and his mood grew more
somber as the meal progressed.

Jillian had seated their mother next to her side at the far
end of the table, so Taylor managed to escape any further
attacks from Claudia. She didn't think she could bear any
more, not while she still reeled from Mason's betrayal. She
couldn't endure to be reminded how much more people
preferred Jillian to her. She had all the proof she needed.

For dessert, Jillian had decorated individual Christmas-
tree cakes with raspberries and marzipan ornaments.
Claudia exclaimed over how clever and talented her
daughter was. Over the course of the meal, Lawrence's
chair had migrated much closer to Taylor's, and she now
detected pressure against her left thigh. It was definitely
time to leave. Taylor prayed for the meal to end so she
could soon make her excuses and leave for the station.
Right now, even Sid looked like a port in a storm.

Jillian picked up her spoon and tapped it lightly against
her wineglass. "Attention, everyone. I have an announcement."

Taylor crossed her left leg over her right to escape the
doctor's encroachment and observed her sister. Her glow
had increased to more of a supercharged excitement. Her
eyes glittered, rather than sparkled. Her restlessness had
returned.

Jillian waved her spoon. "This is a very special Christmas for Mason and me." She looked down the table toward Mason. "I want you all to share with us our happiness." She raised her wineglass. "We've decided to start a family."

Taylor choked on her Christmas tree.

Lawrence patted her on the back.

Claudia said, "I'm going to be a grandmother?" and drained her glass of dessert wine.

The Jensens, chiming in together with their felicitations, were the first to wish them well.

Sipping on water, Taylor dared to glance at Mason. This news had come as a surprise to him. It *had* to. He sat, unsmiling, deaf to the noises of congratulation.

Jillian looked triumphant, as if she had just won the Pillsbury Bake-Off. Taylor felt sick watching the gleam in her sister's eye, even sicker than she had the day Jillian had telephoned her in North Carolina to announce her marriage to Mason. She could still hear her sister's voice over the gritty connection.

"If it hadn't been for you, we never would have met. I think it was Providence that sent me to stay with you."

It hadn't been Providence at all; Claudia had dumped Jillian in Taylor's lap after her latest in a string of expulsions from various schools. Claudia enrolled her in fashion-design school in L.A., then returned to Chicago. Taylor had been working with Mason for months; she knew she was in love with him and had been for ages, but nothing in her personality allowed her to make the first move to confide her love.

"I hope you wish us well," Jillian rattled on that day. "I know you were sweet on him for a while, but I knew once you decided to move to North Carolina, it couldn't have been anything serious."

No, nothing serious. Twelve times they had spent the night together; a dozen times she had known joy she had felt condemned to live without. And now she must live without.

"We've decided on a small wedding in a judge's cham-

bers tomorrow. But we're going on an incredibly extrava-
gant honeymoon."

Tomorrow. Jillian had taken from Taylor the one man
she wanted, and the next day she would formalize her
coup. Taylor had mumbled her best wishes and set the
phone back in its cradle, remembering the one-armed
Barbie doll, the broken curling iron, the cowering Easter
rabbit; all abandoned by Jillian after she had taken them—
whole, functional, and happy—from Taylor.

Chapter 12

MASON'S CHRISTMAS SPIRIT HAD FLOWN THE coop. He wished his guests would do the same. The two women in his life sat at the far end of the living room. At the moment, Taylor had her head turned away. Jillian watched him, a slight smile highlighting her face. He could almost hear her purring. He couldn't wait to get Jillian alone to interrogate her about her immaculate conception. But more important, he needed a few minutes alone with Taylor.

He'd been kicking himself all day for acquiescing to Jillian's demands for sex. He had tarnished the precious bond he and Taylor had begun to forge the other day. He never wanted her to know; yet he wanted to fling himself at her feet and beg her forgiveness. Now he desperately wished he had allowed himself to call her, to go to see her again the past two days. But he had thought he was doing the honorable thing to stay away from her until he had broken with Jillian. Resting an elbow on the mantel of the living room fireplace, he suppressed a groan; he certainly hadn't done the honorable thing that morning.

He pretended to follow Mr. Jensen's theorizing on the collapse of the public school system and dwelt on his own problems instead. Mason considered himself a cross between a Stoic and a Romantic, a blend that he felt had made him emotionally stronger than most men. Perhaps he only fooled himself. Maybe he considered himself strong because nothing adverse had ever happened to him, growing up snug as a bug in that Iowa farmhouse, trotting off to college with seven hundred other studious, pimply-faced boys, then galloping through law school, all expenses paid by scholarship. He squatted, picked up the poker, and stabbed at the remnants of his Christmas fire, seeking a spark to resuscitate the blaze.

He had a feeling he was soon to learn the truth concerning his emotional resilience. If by some chance he had gotten two women pregnant—*two sisters, not simply any two women, Reed*—he would be testing the limits of not only his emotional strength, but his physical and financial. Taylor looked ready to grab the poker from his hand and use it against him, and he had no doubt that if Jillian found out about Taylor before he had a chance to ask her for a divorce, she'd drag him through court and wring his pockets dry. The only woman in the room who looked particularly happy was Claudia, who had warmed to the idea of becoming a grandmother.

With Jillian's talk of motherhood, he had to reconsider asking for a separation the next day. As much as the possibility that she might be pregnant worried him, the fact that she had dropped it like a bomb at the dinner table in front of guests bothered him more. Jillian had been emotionally off lately, like an out-of-tune piano. With Jillian, middle C just wasn't middle C. The other day, lying in Taylor's arms, the situation had seemed so manageable. Smothering a sigh, he wished his chattering guests would go home and play with their Christmas presents.

Despite the private nature of Jillian's announcement—or perhaps because of it?—the dinner guests refused to excuse themselves. The women's talk turned to babies. From across the living room came snatches of the dialect of pregnancy: ". . . dilated only five centimeters and the doctor yelling at the nurse to hurry me up, so he didn't waste his *Phantom of the Opera* tickets" . . . "La Leche" . . . "thirty-eight weeks . . ."

The men's talk veered to the upcoming bowl games. Mason added a log to the fire. He remembered the argument he and Jillian had when he discovered she planned to install a gas fireplace. She had insisted wood and ashes and real smoke made too much of a mess.

Brushing the bits of bark and soot from his hands, he crossed to the women and offered after-dinner drinks. He tried to catch Taylor's eye, but she kept her head inclined toward Mrs. Jensen, who was describing the virtues of midwives over doctors. Finally, afraid Taylor would leave before he had a chance to explain, he said, "Taylor, would you like to help me with the drinks?"

Jillian, sitting on the fringe of the group, and not joining in with the baby talk, said, "I'll do that, sweetheart," and started to rise.

"Why don't you rest? You've been on your feet all day." Mason hated the falseness in his voice. Was this how people managed double lives, secret lives? By saying phony things to force situations to their own devious ends? He wanted Taylor in the kitchen—alone—for at least three minutes. Long enough to tell her Jillian's announcement had come as a bomb to him, too. Long enough to promise to call her and talk things through. Long enough to smell her hair and run his fingers over the soft skin of her cheek.

When Taylor rose to join him, he was sure his relief flew like a banner from his face. Earlier in the day, he had been too afraid to talk to her one on one, afraid that their secret would show on his face and give him away. Truly, he was a terrible liar. Even before, and more so following Jillian's horrifying announcement, Taylor had been shutting down, closing herself off from him. He wanted to break through the barrier before she sealed the final brick with emotional mortar he could never crack.

He maintained a careful distance between the two of them as they walked from the living room. The length of the room seemed endless. For the first time, Mason was thankful they hadn't installed a formal bar closer to the front of the house, or he'd never get a word in private with Taylor. When redoing this house, Jillian had maintained their entertaining would center around the solarium and the pool. But for Christmas, Mason had insisted on using their step-down, wood-beamed living room. Christmas called for coziness, a concept foreign to Jillian.

They crossed the foyer. Christmas with Taylor, with

their children romping through piles of wrapping paper—that's what the rest of his Christmases would be like.

"Was there something you wanted to say to me?" The coldness in her voice pierced him. She hugged her chest, as if her heart might spill out if she let go. He couldn't blame her; for all she knew, he really was the prick she thought him at that moment.

"Jillian's announcement came as a total surprise to me. I had no idea she might be pregnant."

Taylor looked at the floor. *"No* idea?"

"No." He stepped into the kitchen. The sounds of a television show filtered from the back of the house. The maid had evidently taken a break, and they had the kitchen to themselves.

"Are you saying there is no way this baby is yours?" Taylor whispered in a fierce voice.

The image of Jillian leaning over him only that morning flashed in Mason's mind. He knew his face gave him away.

"What do you think I am—blind? Jillian was humming like Scarlett the morning after Rhett lugged her up the staircase. You think I can't tell when my sister just had sex?" Taylor opened the freezer with a jerk and piled ice cubes onto the already stocked ice bucket. The half-moon-shaped cubes spilled over the top and onto the counter. She swiped at her cheek.

When she looked at him, the pain so clear in her eyes, he wished himself dead for hurting her. "Taylor—"

"You could make love with her after what we shared the other day?" She said it out loud, as if in saying it, she could force herself to face the awful truth.

"I didn't make love to her. It was sex. Just sex. There's a difference."

"Only a man would think that." She jammed the lid onto the ice bucket, scattering the cubes. "What is it with you? Love me and leave me? Once, maybe; but twice? Forget it, Mason. You don't love me or you never could have done this to me."

"I do love you. I told you Jillian's been upset lately, not

herself. She wanted sex, and I thought it would make asking for a divorce easier."

"Don't ask her for a divorce on my account." She slammed her hand on the counter. Ice hit the floor. "If I'm forced to see you, socially with Jillian, I will. But don't call me, don't try to explain, don't try to make things better. We're through." She turned and walked into the dining room, her back straight; only her shaking shoulders betrayed her.

He started after her. From the hallway, he heard Jillian. "You two need some help?" Then she appeared in the doorway. "Where's Taylor?"

He nodded toward the other exit to the room.

"I thought she was helping you." The statement was more of a question—a direct and pointed question from a wife suspicious about her husband's actions.

Mason studied the mess they had made of the ice, and considered his answer. He could say, "She's upset because two days ago I made love to her and promised to leave you, and now she thinks I'm not going to." Then she'd say, "But you made love to me this morning. You couldn't have had sex with my sister. That's impossible. That's—that's—incest." And he'd say, "No, it's not. Incest is sexual intercourse between persons so closely related that they are forbidden by law to marry." And she'd say, "Exactly. Incest," and advance on him with the carving blade from the Henckels set.

"Mason." Jillian snapped her fingers in front of his face. "What happened to Taylor?"

"She wasn't feeling well." And neither was he.

Taylor walked in. She wore fresh lipstick, holly red, and a camera-ready smile. "Oh, there you are, Jillian. Thank you for a lovely Christmas dinner, one I'll never forget."

Jillian raised her brows at Mason. "I'm sorry you have to eat and run, but I know how you career women are. Always rushing off to work." She placed a hand on her abdomen and smiled a cream-licking smile.

At that moment, Mason thought it was possible that he

hated his wife. "I'll see you to the door," he said to Taylor, still hoping for a chance to beg her forgiveness.

"Don't bother." Taylor smiled again—which hurt him more than tears would have—waved, and left.

Mason gripped the counter, and met cold water from the melting ice cubes. Ignoring that, he said to Jillian, "So we're starting a family?"

"Aren't you pleased?" He could read nothing in her wide blue eyes beyond their slightly anxious perusal of his reaction. She stroked his arm.

"Just when did this conception take place?"

Jillian rubbed against him, like a cat marking his owner. "If you've forgotten this morning, darling, I'd better—" she stretched to kiss his lips "—refresh your memory."

Taking her by the shoulders, he backed her off him. "This morning?"

She nodded.

"From having sex this morning, you think you're pregnant?"

"It's possible."

He let go of her. He must have gone mad. Taylor had just walked out of his life. He couldn't be hearing Jillian correctly. "Sex—once—and we're starting a family."

"Twice. Don't forget the night you came home and whispered in my ear about reaffirming our marriage." She began loading tiny crystal glasses onto a tray.

Jesus. She was right about that. He had completely forgotten. Taylor had turned down his offer of donor insemination, and he had turned to Jillian, thinking yet again to make things work in their marriage. The joke was on him. "The last time we discussed this subject, you were still on the Pill. Doesn't that make conception difficult—if not impossible?"

"Oh, Mason, I felt so bad after our little tiff—" she traced a finger up and down his chest, "—that I stopped taking it the very next day. I didn't tell you because I wanted to surprise you. Yes—as a Christmas present."

"Jillian, having unprotected sex twice, after being on the

Pill for years, doesn't necessarily mean that you're pregnant. Do you really not understand that?"

"Of course I understand that, but you never can tell about these things." With her little finger, she smoothed the outside corners of her mouth.

"Correction, Jillian. These 'things' are pure science. Where are you in your cycle? Are you close to ovulation?"

"When did you become such an expert?"

Guilt struck him, and probably showed on his face. Reading the book on artificial insemination so he could father Taylor's child had taught him everything he knew about the biology of conception. "This is basic biology."

"There's no need to insult my intelligence." She narrowed her eyes. "For someone who wants a baby so badly, you sure are trying hard to prove I'm not pregnant."

"I'm—"

Lawrence Corning strolled in. "Hey, you sweethearts, sneaking off for a quickie in the kitchen? Give us single types a break. What happened to your sister, Jilly?" He tapped his pipe against the heel of his palm. "I think she likes me."

"She left." Mason wanted to suggest the man do the same. He wondered why on Christmas Day his house was filled with people with whom he had nothing in common. Other people had their children, aunts, uncles, grandparents. Claudia, with her acid tongue, he still could not make himself consider family. He should have insisted on a trip to Iowa. An Iowa Christmas was a holiday, in a way Christmas in Los Angeles could never be.

Also, a trip to Iowa might have saved him from this predicament.

"I say, you don't happen to have her home number?"

Jillian opened her mouth. Mason said, "She has a strict rule about us giving out her number. Sorry."

"Sorry, Lawrence." Slinging a parting glare at Mason, Jillian shepherded the doctor from the room.

Mason stared at the water dripping onto his two-hundred-dollar loafers. He piled a few bottles of after-dinner liqueurs onto a tray, grabbed the mineral waters requested a lifetime ago by his guests, and walked slowly toward the living room. He'd finish with Jillian later.

The Jensens were the last to leave.

For Jillian, this Christmas had been the longest day in her memory. She couldn't wait to be alone with Mason. For the first time in ages, she wanted him. She'd initiated sex with him that morning because she had to implement her plan to keep him. And for once, she'd enjoyed it. He'd been less giving, more, oh, almost punishing. She got hot just thinking about how angry he looked confronting her in the kitchen. It wasn't like their same old boring fights over her refusal to have a baby. A spark of danger had been ignited, and she wanted more of it.

"Thank God they're all gone," said Mason.

"Come sit by the fire. Mother's taking a nap." She held out her hand, but he didn't take it.

"I'd rather go for a walk."

"I'll change my shoes and go with you."

"Alone."

She wanted to snipe at him, but her other needs were greater. "Go ahead," she said, mustering all the sweetness she could. "I'll straighten the house."

He took the stairs two at a time, then she heard him crossing the hall to their bedroom. She stayed in the front hall, idly unbuttoning the top buttons of her dress. He didn't need a walk. He needed a good fuck. She curved one hand around the shaft of the mahogany coat rack, wondering why she had ignored Mason sexually for so many months. She picked up one bore after another, and right here at home was her own steamroller.

Upstairs in their bathroom, Mason yanked open the bathroom cupboard where Jillian kept her birth control pills. They weren't there. He tried to remember when he had last seen her take a pill. Since the night she "changed her mind," he had barely paid attention to her, usually rising in the morning before she awoke. He should be with Taylor, not here in his bathroom pawing through his wife's belongings, searching for an orderly pill container with the appropriate foil circles popped out. If Jillian was pregnant, he couldn't leave her. Any child was his responsibility.

He checked the rest of the drawers and the medicine cabinet. Nothing. Giving up, he changed his clothes, then slumped on the edge of the water bed. The wave motion of the water bed set up an uneasy rhythm in his gut. He thought of Taylor, the way she had treated him during dinner, as if he were some distasteful insect. She couldn't mean she never wanted to see him again. He loved her; she knew that now. He picked up the bedside phone and dialed the number at the station. A polite voice informed him that Taylor was in a meeting and unavailable. He had to see her and explain. The few minutes alone in the kitchen hadn't been sufficient.

Explain what? Groaning, he moved off the bed. *Yes, I love you and I'm leaving my wife, but I did make love to her and to you, too, and by the way, I can't leave until I make sure she's not pregnant, and are you?* The impact of the situation rolled through his brain, over and over, like an irritating song heard first thing in the morning that refused to clear the mind.

Jillian watched Mason clamber down the staircase. He had changed into jeans, a ragged Stanford rugby shirt, and Nikes. The jeans had long since aged to the texture of baby blue chamois. He landed on the bottom stair and pulled his car keys from his jeans.

"Keys? You said you were going for a walk."

"I thought I'd go for a run at the Rose Bowl." He disappeared momentarily into the coat closet and came back carrying a jacket.

"A run—you'll be gone for ages." She dropped her stance at the coat rack. "You said you were going to take a walk."

He stepped next to her. "I changed my mind."

"Oooh, temper, temper." She wrapped her arms around his neck and flattened her pelvis against his groin. "I'll be waiting for you, so run fast."

He disentangled himself. "I'm not interested in sex right now."

"Well, that's a first." Jillian thought of his constant nagging, pleading, and begging that followed her into dreamland as she floated off on her sleeping pills.

"What do you mean by that?"

"I think you know."

"If you mean I have expected you to fulfill the role of a wife, yes, I guess I do know what you mean."

" 'Role' is right. You treat me like some ornament to show off to your partners and like some inflatable doll in the bedroom. And you always have to talk about babies, except now when I tell you you're going to get what you've been nagging me about for years."

Mason was staring at her with a look she'd never seen before. She caught her breath, suddenly wishing she had kept her mouth shut. She had revealed too much of herself.

"Do you want a divorce?" he asked, still with that blank expression on his face, and with it creeping into his voice, too.

"A d-divorce?" She put her hand to her cheek.

"If you're so unhappy with me, maybe that's what you really want."

"Oh, no." She caught his arm. "I'm not unhappy. It must be hormonal. I'm sure I'm pregnant; positive. Women can tell these things. I'm unhappy because you're going running, but that's because I wanted you to stay here with me."

"For sex?"

She couldn't miss the irony in his voice. "Just to be together. I've felt ever since this morning that we're rediscovering parts of each other that maybe we've been taking for granted."

He didn't answer.

Divorce! How could he even say the word? She certainly wasn't going to ask him if that was what he wanted; she knew better than to offer an option she wasn't prepared to grant. He must be seeing someone else; she had been right about the perfume and woman-scent on his suit. When she found out who it was, she'd kill the bitch. She mustered a smile. "I'm very tired. Why don't you go on and run? I'll try to take a nap while you're gone."

He narrowed his eyes, and Jillian sensed he wanted to move in for the kill and insist on a divorce. Only the thought that she might be pregnant stopped him—and his desire to run off to see his honey on Christmas Day. If she was right and there was another woman, he'd accept her truce and split.

"I should be back in an hour or two."

She wasn't letting him off scot-free. "Why don't you tuck me in for a nap before you go?" She issued the words sweetly, but their challenge was clear.

He followed her to the solarium, where, at her prompting, he tucked an afghan over her legs. "Thanks, sweetheart," she said, closing her eyes. She let him make it to the door, then called, "Please ask the maid to bring me some milk." He nodded curtly and left the room.

As soon as she heard the garage door whir, she threw the afghan to the floor and stomped on it. When the maid walked in, carrying a tray with milk and cookies, Jillian turned around from the bar. "Put it on the table," she snapped. The maid nodded and hurried out.

Jillian tossed the milk down the sink at the wet bar. She watched the white liquid cover the aluminum, then fade in patches. She should follow Mason. Abruptly she decided she had too much pride to do that. Besides, she was confused over her own suspicions of him. A man like Mason, honorable, upright, so goddamn conscientious—how could he be dipping double? But just in case he was, the baby plan would pull him up short. Grabbing the Stolichnaya bottle, she poured herself a double vodka on the rocks.

Red and green tinsel tacked around the newsroom door fluttered in the breeze from the heating vent. Instead of the usual volume, only murmurs floated around the room. The news director believed as many people as possible should enjoy Christmas with their families. Taylor wandered in and dumped her briefcase and coat on the news pod. One of the writers glanced up and said, "Merry Christmas." Nodding, Taylor thought she might very well come to hate that greeting. Christmas just wasn't her day.

August Rivers, the weatherman, walked in. He wore a Santa cap. The peaked end bent double, and the fuzzy white ball on the tip swung across his dark-complected face.

"Hi, Taylor."

"Hey, Santa. What's with the getup?" She liked August. The young man wanted desperately to move from weather to news reporting. He'd have to switch stations to do so; once tagged with "the weatherman" label, the identity stuck. Sometimes switching channels or careers didn't help. Even after weatherman Pat Sajak's move to emcee "Wheel of Fortune," and then on to a brief stint as late night talk-show host, many people still thought of him as that man who used to do the weather.

"Sid's idea. He said it would provide that happy holiday spirit. You know, so when I say, 'Highs in the seventies; in the low fifties at night; sunshine expected into the weekend,' the viewers will want to get out their snow-blowers and pretend it's Christmas."

Taylor smiled, relieved she could find humor in something. "You've got the patter down, but you certainly look silly."

"Gotta do what it takes to get ahead." He went off, whistling, the cap firmly on his head.

She thought of what Sid and Annie wanted to do to her, and knew she couldn't be as compliant as August. Ruffly blouses and pearlescent blue eye shadow. So far she'd held out, but the other day Sid had reminded her that Annie would be in town soon to help her "soften her wardrobe." She'd rather wear August's cap.

Strolling over to the police scanner, she studied the cluttered desks, thankful for the haven the newsroom provided, thankful of all the things she could do to take her mind off Mason and Jillian. Here, she belonged. Here, she was liked and respected. She turned the scanner up a notch, enjoying the sound of the staticky voice issuing intermittently. Anything could come across the box and turn the evening's news topsy-turvy. As anchor, it wasn't her job to monitor the reports, but she missed the good old days in her first reporting job when she was out the door on a moment's notice. Being the queen mother must be a lot like being an anchor: Image counted much more than work product.

"Taylor," called the news director's assistant from across the room, "delivery for you downstairs."

She hadn't ordered anything. She'd been forcing herself not to think about Mason since gaining control over her tears halfway from Pasadena to Hollywood. She couldn't think of him; the pain would overwhelm her. If she went downstairs and found flowers, she knew the tears would come again. And the anger.

"I'm not expecting anything," she called.

The woman shrugged and left.

Taylor sat at her desk and switched on her computer. Calling up the on-line news service, she read the national and international events of the day.

The drifting sweet blend of sausage and cheese came to her nostrils' attention. She sniffed, identifying the smell. Definitely pizza. Swiveling from her terminal, she came face-to-face with the bottom side of a pizza carton. From where she sat, she couldn't see who held the box.

"Mmmm."

The box moved back.

Mason stood behind it, one finger pressed to his lips. That was a good move on his part, because she had to stifle a scream when she saw him. He wore faded jeans, a windbreaker, and a bright red cap. This was not the Mason she knew.

"What are you doing here?" She kept her voice low enough so the others couldn't hear.

He tossed the pizza box onto her desk. "I had to see you."

She kept her eyes fastened on the soggy cardboard.

"Thanks for the pizza, but you and your wife have already fed me once today."

"Taylor, don't." He glanced around. "Is there somewhere we can talk?"

"There's nothing you have to say that I want to hear."

She felt him clasping her hand, tugging at her to rise. If he persisted, someone would notice, and if there was one thing she had learned the value of in television, it was keeping her private life private. From the corner of her eye, she spotted Burke arriving, his Burberry signature scarf draped atop the coat he carried over his arm. She pulled free of Mason's hand and stood. "This way," she said. No one would be in the makeup room this early.

She led the way across the newsroom, well aware that people were wondering what she was doing leaving with the pizza man. "Did you have to come in dressed like that?"

"You try getting past the guard downstairs."

Mason touched the brim of his cap, embroidered with the name of a pizza parlor down the street. "Desperation breeds inventiveness."

She glanced sharply at him. "Don't pat yourself on the back, Mason. I meant what I said about you leaving me alone." Holding the door, she motioned him in. "You have five minutes. And that's more than you deserve."

He took off his cap. "I came to tell you I don't think Jillian is pregnant."

Instead of answering, Taylor lowered herself into Dorothy's barber chair, then selected a makeup brush from the container on the counter in front of her. She stroked her cheek with the furry bristles. "So?"

Mason stared at her. "What do you mean, 'so'? If she was pregnant, I would have to stay with her. But I think it's possible she just got confused. She's only been off the pill a month or so. If she's not pregnant—"

"Only a month? Did you or did you not tell me that you and Jillian hadn't had a 'real marriage' in ages and ages? Continuing to make love to your wife sounds to me like

one of the most important aspects of a 'real marriage.' "
She jammed the brush into its holder.

"I tried to explain why I did what I did. You have to understand what Jillian is like."

"There *is* no explanation for what you did." Taylor climbed out of the chair. "I hope you have a good life."

He followed her to the door. "Taylor, stop. Please don't walk away. I love you."

"You should have thought of that this morning." She refused to look back. When she reached her desk, she dialed security and asked them to escort the pizza man from the building.

"What's the matter? Delivery boy cop a feel?" Burke thought nothing of eavesdropping on other people's telephone calls. He claimed he had scooped his best stories that way, in the distant past when he had put pen to reporter's notebook.

"No."

Burke smoothed his hair, only skimming the glossy surface, a gesture Taylor had come to despise. Real men weren't afraid to run their fingers every which way and leave their hair standing on end. Mason did that all the time. Taylor blinked and shunted her thoughts.

"If he had, I would have come to your aid." He patted her on the shoulder. "This place is dead today. I could have used the excitement."

"Why didn't you come in later?" Taylor had noticed how Burke was a veteran at arriving after any extra assignments had been shopped around. Though his popularity with viewers protected him, it still didn't endear him to any of the other members of the news team.

"Christmas with two kids tearing at my ankles like rat terriers and a third one crying his head off is not my idea of fun."

Taylor thought of all the pleasure she could have had that day with a husband, three children, and a Christmas tree. Well, the right husband. Burke was a jerk, pure and simple. "What is your idea of fun?" Immediately she regretted asking the question.

He grinned, or rather, leered. "I offered to show you once before, but you turned me down cold."

"Forget I asked."

He shrugged. She knew he was thinking it was her loss. Then he said, "You know, something about that pizza man was terribly familiar."

She didn't want Burke, of all people, to figure out Mason had been there. "I eat a lot of pizza. The same guy tends to deliver to this location." Opening the pizza box, cooling on a stack of style and phone books, she tore off a piece and bit into it. "It's even good cold."

"I couldn't possibly eat that. Look at the grease congealed on the surface. Think of my complexion." He moved on.

Taylor threw the pizza into the trash and went in search of the assignment producer. Sid insisted he didn't want his anchors going out on "little" stories, but tonight she needed to write more than her lead-ins to the reports. She needed to work.

Later, when the long day finally drew to a close, Taylor sat back in her anchor chair with a sigh. Everyone else rose quickly, eager to return to whatever holiday celebrations waited for them. Taylor wished she could do another broadcast, maybe a twenty-four-hour telethon—anything to keep her from the loneliness she knew would well up the moment she arrived at her apartment.

On her way out, Taylor noticed Sid's light shone in his office. She thought of stopping to wish him merry Christmas, but he was the scroogiest grinch she had ever met. Yet . . .

She tapped on his door.

"Come in if you must," he yelled.

So much for spreading a little Christmas cheer. Taylor entered. Sid had his shoes off. The big toe of his left foot poked through his sock. On one of the monitors, she recognized the precolorization version of *It's a Wonderful Life*.

She paused a few steps into his office, not sure what to say. This man made her life miserable, with his stupid ideas about Television for the People. Of course television was for people, but what was "the People" supposed to mean? Human beings massed in one clump, indistinguishable as separate thinking, feeling organisms? One block, as defined by the Nielsen rating service? One composite lifeform?

"Cat got your tongue?" Sid rustled open a paper bag on his desk.

"I saw you were in, so I stopped to wish you merry Christmas."

He pulled a container from the sack. "Damn nice of you, but I don't do Christmas. Don't do Hanukkah, either, so don't feel you've made a social, ethnic, or racial faux pas."

"Did anyone ever tell you you're unbelievably rude?"

Sid grinned. "Now, that's more like it. Show some spirit. I hate it when people kiss ass." He held out the container. "Want some ice cream?"

"No, thanks." She made a face.

"Ah, a woman who knows her own mind. Maybe there's some hope for you, Miss Taylor Drummond." He swung his feet off the desk. "You don't want any, go home and leave me and Jimmy alone." He flicked a few spoonfuls into his mouth, splattering his mustache in the process. She turned to go.

"How many times have you watched this movie?" he said, between bites.

"Twice? Three times?"

"You don't know, do you? What are you standing there for, anyway?" He pointed to the monitor across the room. "I've seen this movie seventeen times. Always black-and-white. Can't believe those bastards thought they could improve on the original. Can't do that to a classic. Oh, you could spiffy up some third-rate piece of junk, kind of like a whore might as well wear a lot of rouge and eye shadow, 'cause it just might help hide the sores and bruises, but what the fuck—a true princess don't need no colorization." Sid grinned, as if pleased by his own philosophizing.

Taylor wished she hadn't stopped to see Sid. His ramblings did nothing to improve her spirits. "I take it you don't approve of coloring old films."

Sid glared at her. "I've had it with your finishing-school manners." He mimicked, " 'I take it you don't approve.' Speak fucking English."

She started to say merry Christmas again, just to rub him the wrong way, but he had slumped over his desk and buried his face in his hands. She heard him say, "Merry Christmas and to all a good night."

Taylor closed the door behind her.

Was everyone she knew crazy? Sid, locked in his office with his ice cream and goodness only knew what thoughts and memories. Mason, thinking he could tell her he loved her, then screw his wife, then make everything okay. Jillian, who drank like a marine on furlough, hated the idea of having a baby, then ruined Taylor's life by announcing she was starting a family. Last, there was Claudia. Taylor held her responsible for everything bad in her life not attributable to death and taxes.

Driving away from the studio, she added herself to her roll call of crazies. She had to be to think she could have a baby by her brother-in-law and keep the emotional entanglements to a minimum.

Once inside her door, she dropped her briefcase on the living room floor and switched on her stereo. Christmas carols filled the room from the radio station she had last tuned to, only that morning, when she had whistled along and worried—but in a good way that made her step light and her voice breathless—about seeing Mason again. With a jab, she changed stations. More carols. She powered her compact disc player and popped in a collection of sixties rock and roll. She hadn't known Mason in the sixties.

She hadn't known him in the seventies, either, but she thought the music of that decade had dissipated in strength and quality as the years advanced. Flopping onto the sofa, she wondered if the downhill slide correlated with the end of the Vietnam War. Her reporter's brain corrected "war" to "conflict," and she let the thought pass. Right now she wasn't a reporter, or an anchorwoman, or even a once-damn-good attorney. She was a woman, alone, confused, and possibly—she let herself think about it for the first time in hours—pregnant.

"It's what you wanted," she muttered, over the sounds of the Rolling Stones. The idea had seemed simpler to her when it had been only theory. Plenty of women were single parents. She hadn't factored in the overwhelming feeling of loneliness, though. If she felt this way now, bereft, and as if the whole world rested on her shoulders, how would she feel if she was pregnant? If she had a toddler screaming for attention and there was no one to hand her to? There would be no one else to pick up the physical, let alone the emotional, slack.

Snatching up one of the throw pillows she kept on the sofa, she hit herself over the head with it. Several times. Then she stopped. She simply had to wait and see. Whether she was pregnant or not, she had to purge herself of loving Mason. Right now that should seem easy enough. He had screwed up royally. Yet when she thought of the pain she had seen in his eyes, beneath that ridiculous cap, when he said, "I love you," she knew getting over him wouldn't be easy.

She slapped herself with the pillow again. What point was there in getting weepy again? Any more tears and the puffiness would show through her makeup tomorrow. Hugging the pillow, she snuggled against the couch. The Stones gave way to Judy Collins singing "Both Sides Now."

Chapter 13

JILLIAN CHECKED THE VELCRO STRAPS OF HER aerobics shoes. Automatically she bent her knees and raised her arms shoulder-high as the instructor led the class of ten women into their warm-up.

Studying her body in the floor-to-ceiling mirror, she decided to skip the abdomen crunches for the next few weeks. And wear baggy blouses. She knew Mason well enough to know that as long as he thought she might be pregnant, he wouldn't do anything rash; he certainly wouldn't leave her for another woman. Then, if he believed she had a miscarriage, everything would be simple. The doctor wouldn't let her get pregnant too soon after losing a baby, would he?

She resisted a shudder and concentrated on swinging into a step-kick. Even thinking about babies threw her rhythm off, and after all the years she had been doing aerobics, she knew the drill far better than the instructor.

She turned off her thoughts and tuned in to the rhythm of the music and the joy of feeling her body respond when commanded to perform. "Five times higher," called the instructor, and Jillian kicked her right leg up, sweating, aching, but determined to swing that leg an inch or two higher each time.

By midway through the class, several of the women had wandered off to the drinking fountain, or reduced their moves to mere shuffles. Not Jillian. Even today, despite all that weighed on her, she gave the workout everything she had. At the gym, she was in control. Once in a while, she experienced a similar feeling when a dinner party came together absolutely perfectly, but as soon as her culinary creations were transformed into table scraps, depression set in. What took her days to achieve disappeared down the disposal.

The music slowed and Jillian glanced at the clock. She loved the classes during which she lost all sense of time. That meant her body was in top form. She stretched her arms over her head. Gardening made her feel good, too, but it was more like the cool-down portion of aerobics— gentle, and without the peaks of excitement that she craved.

Reluctantly Jillian left the aerobics floor after the hour ended. She usually stayed for a second hour of toning and firming exercises. But she'd sacrifice a totally flat stomach to keep Mason. And she had to have Mason; she couldn't imagine life without him. No matter how many slimy side streets of life she traveled, she always had a refuge to return to—the shelter of respectability, an identity as Mrs. Reed, the purpose of running her house. She chafed against the pointlessness of it all, yet she did her jobs so well. She didn't know anything else. She had been trying hard to convince herself that her paranoid thoughts of a few days ago—that he was seeing someone else—had been only that. Mason couldn't be begging her to have his child and be having an affair. He was the world's worst liar. Yet he was a successful attorney. That contradiction, she had often wondered about.

As long as she had her pregnancy plan in operation, she had him. Checking her shape again, she concluded a few weeks of less exercise wouldn't wreck her figure completely. She looked over the group of women in the small gym. Most of them were distinctly on the fleshy side, even the regulars who seemed to think working out meant they could eat more. The gym actually served refreshments. Watching the women flock to the snack bar after a workout made her nauseous. Didn't they have any sense of self-denial? Jillian pressed a hand against the ridges of her pelvic bones. The inward curve of her flesh pleased her.

She had joined this pedestrian gym because she wanted

a place to go where nobody knew her. Anonymity satisfied her. Having to smile at the wives of men Mason did business with would hamper her freedom, spoiling the exhilaration of the workout. Choosing a female-only gym had also been a deliberate decision. If there were men, she would be a different person during the class. On would go her male-pleasing persona, up would go her defenses against not being desired, and the next thing she knew, she'd be out behind the building with some brainless hunk. This gym was her refuge from all of the parts of her life she preferred not to think about.

In the shower, Jillian had a sudden thought. Her doctor might be one of Mason's golf partners. She would have to find out. What if Mason happened to mention her pregnancy to the doctor, and the doctor stared blankly at him, and he came home and confronted her with that fact—how would she get around that? Simple. She had switched physicians. It was a natural excuse; the women she knew were always discussing which obstetricians were the best. Jillian shut off the water. One lie did lead to another, but it was all for a good purpose. Skimming the water droplets off her skin, she admired the body she worked so hard to maintain. She intended to be a good wife, and one of these days, she would have a baby for Mason. Just not yet.

"I can't believe you accepted an invitation to the Winstons' party when you knew it would mean we would have to cross the parade route," said Mason. "It could take us an hour to cross Orange Grove."

"I'm sorry. I thought you liked the Winstons," said Jillian, checking her lipstick in the visor mirror.

They inched forward, part of a long line of cars headed toward the street where tomorrow's Rose Parade would begin. The annual party began several days prior to the event, with Pasadena's streets clogged with RVs and countless cars bearing out-of-state license plates.

To Mason, the crowds seemed rowdier every year; less intent on enjoying themselves than proving how obnoxious they could be. Every year Jillian wanted to drive up Colorado Boulevard, where the parade route turned after passing by and paying homage to Orange Grove's more stately surroundings. Colorado was where the real crazies hung out. She liked to sit bumper to bumper, blowing exhaust into the otherwise clear night air, deluged by litter, barraged by streamers of plastic snot, their ears ricocheting from blaring heavy metal—and, of late, rap. Jillian knew his aversion to being out and about in Pasadena on New Year's Eve when she accepted this invitation. It was her means of getting her way. As usual. "Didn't Rosemary invite us to her place tonight?" Rosemary lived in Arcadia, the opposite direction from these street festivities.

"Yes, she did, but it would have been only three or four couples. We're too young for that sort of thing on New Year's Eve. Rosemary's old enough to be your mother. She's sweet, but I thought we should go to a real party tonight." She stroked his hand on the steering wheel. "Next year we may be stuck at home without a baby-sitter. This is the time for us to have a fling. Step out. Live."

Her eyes sparkled and the corners of her mouth turned up. He watched as she added her encouraging, come-on-don't-make-a-scene smile. Other than having accepted this ridiculous invitation, she was trying very hard to please him. Too hard. Talking about babies, for instance. A month ago, she never would have made that remark about a baby-sitter.

None of the flutterings of loving attention rang true. She had denied him for months; denied him sex, denied him basic consideration, denied him a family. The irony of the situation overwhelmed him. Now she was trying to give him everything he had asked for, and it was too late. And after his own stupid, libido-driven behavior, Taylor had slammed the door on their relationship. So he had a wife willing to please him, and the woman he loved wouldn't speak to him. Jillian sat next to him, the picture of suburban beauty out for a night on the town. He might as well make the most of her tempered behavior while waiting to see whether she was pregnant.

Thrumming bass invaded their car from a four-wheel-drive riding on monster-sized tires. Mason frowned and crowded the car a few feet closer to the pickup truck full of teenagers in front of him. "I just wish you had asked me which party I preferred."

"I'm sorry, sweetheart. You're right. I should have."

Jillian shifted toward him. Mason realized he didn't want her to kiss him—or even to touch him. Switching on the compact disc player, he said, "Let's forget about it. Find some decent music to drown out this racket."

She selected one of his favorite Galway flute pieces. Her hair swung forward, shimmering in the interior light she had switched on. Her bare shoulders invited stroking. When she had the music playing, she laid one hand along the back of his seat and toyed with his hair.

That's when Mason realized why her behavior since Christmas seemed so familiar. Favoring his moods, preparing his favorite dinners, not complaining when he stayed at the office until ten or eleven at night—which he had done every day since Christmas—this was the woman Mason had married, not the woman he had been sharing a house with the last few years.

Mason studied Jillian, the lack of expression on her face, her eyes closed, presumably to better appreciate the music. Yet she would rather have the windows lowered, and be screaming along with the music blaring from every side. She was pretending. Maybe she had always pretended. Maybe she didn't know any other way.

A cold sliminess gripped him in the pit of his stomach. He thought of Taylor—often confused about her emotions, but honest. Taylor faced a camera five days a week, but Jillian did more playacting than Taylor ever did.

He fought through the traffic, and let Jillian sit, silent and alone, while he wondered what would happen if he confronted her with these truths. He almost spoke, but the music swelled to a finale, the traffic leapt forward, sweeping them past the worst of the backup, and the moment passed him by.

Five minutes into the Winstons' party, Mason knew he was going to tie one on. He hadn't been drunk in years.

After making partner, and watching several of his peers lose their waistlines and their discretion, he'd decided to quit drinking at business functions.

Now, standing in the steel-and-glass monstrosity the Winstons called home—and they had probably paid a million dollars for that honor, not counting the remodeling costs—and wondering why in the hell the Winstons took their Christmas tree down before New Year's Day, he decided tonight was his night to lose himself. With pregnancy a possibility, Jillian wouldn't be drinking. She could drive home. He asked the bartender for Glenfiddich on the rocks and surveyed the crowd.

When he had last visited Chip and Sissy Winston, who were both securities litigation experts, they had recently purchased this property overlooking the gorge known as the Arroyo. The existing house they had described as a tearer-downer, even though, with five thousand square feet, with some new paint and carpet, it would have been perfectly livable. They had started over from scratch, and from the looks of the living room, with its floor-to-ceiling glass, the Winstons had better not be stone throwers.

Jillian drifted back to him. "Isn't this house lovely? They've done so much to incorporate the out-of-doors. Have you seen the kitchen atrium? Sissy grows herbs there." A woman who looked a lot like Jillian approached and pulled her away to another group. Mason didn't mind. He wanted to observe his wife in action. He wanted to know who she really was.

After a while, he realized he'd downed several more single-malt whiskeys. He was in the midst of a debate over whether contingency fees should be limited as a matter of public policy when he realized how much he hated attorneys' conversations. What did any of them know about contingency-fee arrangements, anyway? None of the five men in the circle, each decked out in a dinner jacket, pleated shirt, and satin-striped trousers, had ever had to survive on collections from auto accidents. They each billed at least three hundred dollars an hour. The starched pleats on the man's shirt next to him rippled, and Mason blinked to clear his vision. Moving his head to the right, he saw a slender woman with long black hair, her back to him. Excusing himself from the debate, he approached the woman, who was standing at one of the three bars Mason had discovered conveniently located on the various levels of the house.

His pulse quickening, he didn't even bother to glance around for Jillian. "Buy you a drink?" he said to the woman.

She looked up at him, a slow smile crossing her face. "Now, here's a big spender."

But she didn't walk away. He took another whiskey and handed her a glass of champagne. He steered her to a sofa, observing the shine of her glossy black hair and the forward thrust of her thighs. She wore a red taffeta dress with a plunging neckline. Rubies hung around her neck, dangling into the valley between her breasts, inviting his eyes to follow.

They did, and he had to repress a desire to lean over and taste with his tongue what his eyes had feasted on.

"See anything you like?" she asked in an amused tone.

He jerked his attention back to her face. "Excuse me. You're very beautiful." Was he slurring his words? He sat up straighter.

"And you're very drunk," she said with a smile. "But you're kind of cute. My name's Deirdre." She held out a hand.

He took it and kissed each fingertip carefully. With a grin, he said, "You're very perceptive. I think my name's Mason, but tonight I'm not sure." Reluctantly he loosed her hand. "You remind me of someone."

She lost her smile. "I really hate that line."

"It's not a line."

Lifting his left hand, she said, "And you're married, too." She stood. "I'm not starting this New Year off wrong. Not again."

He reached for her hand and pulled her back to the sofa. "Please, Deirdre, it's not like that with me. Let me get you another drink, and we'll talk." Her hand felt warm and giving, but it wasn't like Taylor's. Holding Taylor's hand made him feel his circle was completed, made him feel his blood flowed through her heart and back to his.

"Isn't this cozy?" Jillian leaned over the back of the sofa, her blue eyes bluer than he remembered.

She inclined her head toward his lap, and Mason realized he was still holding the woman's hand. He tugged her hand upward to meet Jillian's and joined them together. "Jillian, meet Deirdre. Deirdre, meet Jillian." Then he rose, his one thought to escape outside, and navigated across the Winstons' designer-furniture showroom, giving wide berth to the glass tables and free-standing statuary. At this moment, he couldn't remember why he had set out to get drunk. It was the stupidest thing he'd done in a week.

Jillian found him some time later, sitting on a stone bench carved in the shape of a porpoise, and watching the blinking lights of partygoers on the streets spread out below his view. Shushing sounds from the pool filter blurred the edges of the music coming from the dance band. He felt vaguely sober, but decided that was only a delusion of the fresh air. He hadn't tried to walk since escaping the two women.

Jillian put her arm around him. "Time to go home, Mason."

He buttressed himself against her accusations. None came. Looking at her still-sparkling eyes, he concluded foggily that she was still in a good mood from the party and had decided to wait until they were in the privacy of their car to harass him over Deirdre. Which was ridiculous, come to think of it, since it wasn't Deirdre he'd slept with, it was Taylor. He started to explain that to Jillian as she guided him to say good night to the Winstons, but an interior voice, dead sober, warned him to keep his mouth shut.

When they reached their car, Jillian headed for the passenger side. He followed her. "I think you'd better drive."

She hesitated.

Leaning his elbows on the roof of the car, he said, "You

don't think I would have been holding that woman's hand if I hadn't had too much to drink, do you?"

"You're shouting," she whispered, looking over her shoulder.

"Are you going to drive or do we spend the night here?"

Taking the car keys from him, she said, "You're not very nice when you've been drinking." She crossed to the driver's side. He thought she wobbled a bit on her heels, but decided it was his malfunctioning vision. Settling into the passenger seat, he fell asleep before they cleared the driveway.

Jillian clenched the steering wheel with both hands. Mason always drove home from these functions. She fumed over his inconsideration. To get so shit-faced at a party was embarrassing. It was like fat people eating dessert at a dinner party. Jillian hated excess, and she despised vulgar displays. She, for instance, never showed her alcohol, no matter how drunk she was. That was why Mason, at this very moment, could sleep like a baby and let her take the wheel. If he had any idea how much she had drunk, he would have called a cab. She drove with caution, scrutinizing the speedometer, careful not to go too fast, careful not to go too slow, knowing either extreme aroused the suspicion of the police.

The darkness of the night formed a tunnel through which she guided the car. She hadn't been able to find Mason at midnight, so after the ritual countdown and swigging of champagne, she'd kissed the two men standing next to her. One man was an excellent kisser, almost as good as Mason.

Maybe she should have skipped the last few glasses of champagne, especially after the earlier vodkas she had downed. Jillian slowed the car, confused as to which way to turn. In preparation for the parade, several streets were blocked off, including the one to the Colorado Bridge. She remembered reading that the bridge, known locally as Suicide Bridge, had been closed for renovation. She thought at the time the city probably meant to increase the height of the protective barriers. A car behind her honked, but she sat unmoving, wondering what route Mason had taken to get them there. Then she remembered she had to head south.

She swung the car into a U-turn, went wide, and drove over the right-hand curb before pointing the car forward. Much to her surprise, red and blue lights appeared out of nowhere, advancing on her out of the darkness.

Mason stirred. Jillian groaned and calculated how much she'd had to drink. Mason would kill her, but it was really his fault, for insisting she drive. She stopped the car. "Wake up, Mason."

He sat up, eyes open, instantly alert. "What's going on?"

"All I did was turn around, and bam, here comes the police."

"Keep your hands on the steering wheel and don't say anything." Mason straightened his tie.

A strong light flashed in the window, and the officer tapped on the glass. Jillian lowered the window, then returned her hands to the wheel.

"Evening, ma'am. You usually drive on the sidewalk?" the officer asked, poking his head into the car.

Jillian breathed carefully, certain he was trying to smell her breath. She shook her head and added a confused lift of her shoulders, doing her best to look frail and incompetent, rather than intoxicated. The man wasn't bad-looking; he was Latino, probably in his late thirties. Had she been alone, she would have known how to handle him.

Mason leaned over. "Good evening, Officer. This is my car. Is something wrong?"

"You tell me." He looked at Jillian. "Have you been drinking?"

Jillian shook her head and laid a hand across her stomach. "No, sir," she whispered.

"Let's see your license and registration," he said, flashing the light on Jillian's face once more.

Jillian gave him the papers. While he studied them, Mason leaned toward him again. "The truth is, I'm the one who had too much to drink. I asked my wife to drive my car, which she isn't used to, because she's pregnant and can't drink."

The officer glanced to where Jillian's hand still rested on her abdomen. "Do you know what time it is?"

She knew it was after midnight. "Around one o'clock."

"Just a minute," he said, and walked back to his patrol car.

Jillian shivered. She wanted to raise the window, but was afraid to. What if the officer could tell she had been drinking? What if he made her get out of the car and do all those embarrassing tests? What if someone else from the Winstons' party drove by and saw her standing on one foot or trying to walk some invisible line? Her fear must have shown on her face.

"Don't worry, Jillian. It's only a technicality. You know they come out in full force checking for drunk drivers on New Year's Eve." He dropped his head against the head-rest. "It's a damn good thing I wasn't driving."

That's easy for you to say. Sweat trickled from her arm-pits, tracing its way down the stays of her merry widow. Summoning every ounce of concentration, she considered what a nondrinking pregnant woman would act like in this situation. Probably flustered, because even an innocent person stopped by the police could be frightened. So she let go of some of her icy calm. Too much control might indicate guilt.

In the outside mirror, she saw the officer approaching the car. Blood rushed in her ears. Mason was saying some-thing, but she couldn't hear what it was. If that man told her to get out of the car, she could faint. If she held her breath, she knew she could do it. She had a dim memory of pulling that trick a long, long time ago, but she couldn't place the how or why. Not until the officer rested his el-bows on the side of the Volvo and handed her license and registration to her did she take a breath.

"There you go, Mrs. Reed. Everything's in order, so I'll let you go on. But learn how to handle that car if you're going to drive it. Especially before that baby comes."

Mason thanked him, and the officer returned to his car. Jillian sat there, shaking, unable to move.

"Are you all right?" Mason asked.

She managed a smile. "Being stopped is scary. I'll be okay in a minute."

"He'll sit there until you drive away."

"Oh." She had hoped the patrol car would pull away immediately.

"It's natural to be a little upset, but it's not as if you had anything to worry about." Mason loosened his tie. "Though I think after tonight, I'm swearing off alcohol forever."

"You and me both," mumbled Jillian, edging the car onto the street. A short silence followed, with Jillian holding her breath again, hoping that Mason hadn't heard what she said.

Then Mason shifted in his seat, staring at her as if she were a stranger who had slid behind the wheel of his car. "I don't believe it. You've been drinking, haven't you? That's why you were so nervous."

"It was New Year's. I just had champagne."

"If you think you're pregnant, how can you drink? You know the statistics." Mason slammed a fist against his palm. "What about the child?"

Jillian looked straight ahead. She couldn't explain to Mason that she couldn't not drink. He wouldn't understand; he'd say of course she could. All she had to do was say no. That was the way his mind worked. "It was only one little toast at midnight."

"It isn't good for the baby. If there even *is* a baby."

"I can't believe you said that. And who are you to talk? I had to ring in the New Year by myself. You're the one who was too crocked to drive."

"We're not talking about my behavior, we're talking about an innocent child. Besides, if you only had one drink, why were you so scared about being stopped?"

That question surprised her. Mason always accepted everything she told him. She'd been right to make love to him on Christmas; he was slipping away from her. She couldn't afford to lose him. She had always had a keeper; first her mother, then Mason. When she had found him with that dark-haired woman, he had been feasting on her cleavage. Was she the other woman?

Jillian started to cry. "I had the champagne just before we left, and I was scared and you're right. Of course I won't drink when I'm pregnant. Only, everything is so different. I feel all funny inside, and you know how afraid I am of having a baby."

She heard what sounded like a grunt. He didn't offer to tell her he understood, that he'd been hasty in judging her. The rest of the way home, past the jubilant crowds she loved, he looked out the window, or at the floor, but never at her.

In their garage, he reached for the door handle, then paused. "I don't want you to put off that pregnancy test another day. And if it's positive, you're going to put the baby's health before your pleasure."

Without looking back, he got out of the car and weaved into the house. Jillian slumped over the steering wheel, letting plump tears of self-pity spatter on her dress. He didn't understand. She didn't drink for pleasure.

Chapter 14

FOR SOME, THE NEW YEAR COMMENCES WITH promises of self-improvement, whispered in the shower, or proclaimed boldly to friends, enemies, or anyone who will listen; others start theirs with a hangover, possibly accompanied by promises to quit drinking, or possibly not; Taylor's began with a shopping expedition with Annie the Anachronism.

Taylor dubbed the media consultant that five minutes after she followed Annie into CalMart, a block-long building housing garment industry showrooms. Instead of taking her to Saks or Neiman-Marcus or Bullock's, Annie had driven her downtown to the grimy streets of the garment district. Sid, according to Annie, had some connections with people at CalMart. That in itself would have been okay by Taylor. She had former clients from Harper, Cravens in the rag trade. Her problem with Annie began when the consultant barreled past the showrooms lined with sleek-suited mannequins. Head forward, one hand firmly clutching her shoulder bag, Annie plowed straight for the escalator and led Taylor to "the place that has exactly what we're looking for."

They walked to the end of the long hall. Annie made no effort at small talk; neither did Taylor. Against the pleasant enough hum of conversation created by passing buyers and sellers, twenty-four years dissolved for Taylor. She was back in Chicago, being dragged by her mother from one department store to another, looking for clothing her mother considered suitable for a girl about to enter high school.

"Isn't this lovely?" asked Claudia, holding up a full-skirted green plaid dress with a velvet bow at the waist.

Taylor stubbed the toe of her sneaker against the carpeted floor and refused to acknowledge the question. She'd die rather than wear that dress. She wanted pants, and only pants, for school. Pants were frowned upon; girls were expected to wear dresses. But she and some friends planned to challenge that rule this fall.

Claudia put the dress back on the rack and sighed. "I would have killed to have that dress when I was a child."

"Styles have changed."

"I don't need my daughter telling me about style."

Taylor pulled on one of her long braids. In her opinion, her mother needed exactly that. Claudia continued to imitate Jackie Kennedy, but her hips were too wide for the slim skirts, her chest too chunky for the boxy jackets. And the hats! Taylor hid her head in embarrassment when her mother wore a pillbox hat to the grocery store.

Claudia had moved on. They were in the pants-and-tops section now, so Taylor paid attention. She spotted a pair of purple and white striped jeans with flaring legs. "How about these, Mother?"

Claudia raised her eyebrows. "We're buying school clothes."

"I know."

"Pants aren't allowed at your school."

"They're changing that rule this year." The school just didn't know it yet.

Her mother frowned. "Is this another one of your stories? I won't have you embarrassing me again. Your father and I have worked hard so you don't have to run around like a ragamuffin."

"I want to wear pants. Not dresses. I hate dresses." Taylor addressed the ground, but she made sure her mother heard her.

Claudia yanked the purple pants off the rack. Checking the size, she said, "Wear whatever you want, then. I have tried and tried with you. Your sister wouldn't ask to wear pants. I don't know why you can't be more like Jillian. Pick out three more pairs and wait here for me."

Taylor rubbed the fabric. It felt thick, but soft and velvety. Her mother was always ragging on her to be more like her "perfect" little sister. She'd never be like Jillian, and she would never please her mother. So she had to please herself, and getting the pants pleased her. The rest of her wardrobe didn't matter; she selected several pairs at random. When her mother returned, she was carrying the green plaid dress—in Jillian's size.

"A few dresses, Hesh." Annie's voice, insistent as ever, brought her back to the present. Annie spoke to a thick-nosed man plying his hands as if working hand cream into them, dressed in double-knit beige slacks and a yellow Quiana shirt open to the third button. Flecks of hair and two ropes of gold chain took up the slack.

"For this lovely young woman?" Hesh held his hand out to Taylor. She took it, repressing the urge to glance around for her long-gone purple pants. She had loved those pants. She had worn them the day the principal expelled her for violating the dress code; she had worn them the day she argued her position before the school board; she had worn them the day she returned to school, triumphant.

She greeted Hesh and looked around the display area. Filmy summer dresses, in rayon and polyester, adorned the shop. This was January.

"Hesh sells to every major department store in the South and Midwest," said Annie. "He knows exactly the image we're looking to create."

Hesh smiled, and Taylor saw three gold-capped teeth.

"In the back we have the samples still for this season." Nodding toward the display, he said, "Of course, now we are showing for summer, but we can fit you for winter and spring from our samples. And for Sid, we would run up some more of anything you like."

Taylor wondered what Sid was getting from this deal, other than the pleasure of making her look like a fool. The station didn't run end credits for wardrobe suppliers. The standard deal called for suppliers to advertise in trade magazines that they provided such-and-such for so-and-so. Hesh didn't look savvy enough to press for that deal, but Taylor knew enough about the garment business not to judge a business by the looks of its proprietor. Some of the largest money-making operations functioned out of structures that the fire department should have shut down years ago, their only sign of success the Jags and Lamborghinis parked next to the windowless buildings.

"Nathan, bring out the rack," called Hesh.

A dark-haired boy in his teens wheeled a garment rack through a door at the back of the showroom. The combination of frustration, boredom, and acne on his thin face told Taylor the boy would rather be anywhere than stuck in CalMart during the tag end of Christmas vacation.

"My son Nathan," said Hesh, pointing with pride. "My friends make it big in this business, you know what they do? They send their kids off to those private schools, the ones run by Episcopalians, and try to pretend their kids aren't Jews. Not my kid. He'll learn this business and be able to take it over when I retire."

Nathan kept his eyes downcast and shuffled from foot to foot. Taylor recognized herself in him, and wanted desperately to be able to set the boy free, as she would a bird trapped in a cage. "Hello, Nathan," she said.

He jerked his chin toward her. She figured most people simply ignored him. "Hello," he responded, in a voice still hamstrung by little-boy soprano.

Annie fingered a royal blue polyester number. The sleeves flounced to an end above the elbow. The neckline came to a shallow vee, with bands of fabric crisscrossing under the bust and extending to tie in the back.

Taylor shook her head. Even Vanna White couldn't carry that number off.

"We'll take this one," said Annie, then moved on to a green corduroy jumper and a blouse in a shade lighter. "And this one."

"Excellent color," said Hesh.

Taylor looked at Nathan, and they exchanged shy smiles. She let Annie rummage through the rack, without offering any comments. The battle would be fought between Sid and her. Taylor waved off Annie's suggestion she try them on. "No need. I'm sure everything will fit." She wanted out of Hesh's shop as soon as possible.

While Annie handled the details with Hesh, Taylor turned to Nathan.

"You hate these clothes, don't you?" he said, fixing her with large brown eyes.

She nodded.

He smiled, showing a mouthful of braces for the first time. "So do I. That suit you're wearing has real style. It looks like an Anne Klein."

"It is."

"When I'm in charge, that's what we'll do. Quality. Clothing that says power, without taking away from the woman. None of these *schmattas.*"

Recognizing Yiddish for "rag," Taylor grinned. She handed him her business card. "Call me when you open Nathan's. I'll be your first customer."

When she and Annie reached the studio, with Taylor's new wardrobe in tow, Annie asked Taylor to try on the royal blue dress and meet her in Makeup. Taylor, still holding her fire for Sid, agreed without comment. She found a spare dressing room and slipped out of her wool suit. Holding the blue dress, she thought of all the work she should be doing. She considered her idea for a special report on conditions in the garment district. Though the CalMart building showed a respectable face to the world, she knew how bad the conditions were in some of the sweatshops where much of the manufacturing was contracted out to recent immigrants, some legal, some illegal, slaving long hours, sweltering or freezing in metal-roofed buildings without air-conditioning or heat.

Instead of doing something useful, she was trying on one of the ugliest dresses she had ever seen. The royal blue fabric glinted in the light. With every move of her arms, the swirling flounces brushed against her elbow. Her breasts jutted out, framed as they were by the ties of the dress. The dress did accomplish one of Annie's goals—the woman in the mirror looked nothing like Taylor Drummond.

Grady Hutchings waited impatiently for the steps of his private 727 to be lowered. The pilot had flown the jet in record time from Tulsa to the Van Nuys airport, but they had been delayed at least two minutes by other air traffic. The attendant motioned all was ready, and Grady rose to his feet, eager to be on his way. From the runway, he noticed Pia Zadora's husband's plane taxiing in. Right on schedule, his limousine arrived. The man knew how to run his business, even if he did paint his planes to look like flying brassieres.

Grady entered his waiting limousine, his assistant, Roscoe—he had a last name, but at five syllables, it was a waste of resources to commit it to memory—right behind him. The car moved forward. Roscoe handed him his bourbon and water. "Make a note," Grady said, settling into the cushions. "Find another airport to use if I'm going to be kept waiting."

Roscoe pulled his electronic notepad from the inner pocket of his suit coat and recorded his employer's instructions. Satisfied, Grady closed his eyes.

This trip was more of a junket than he usually allowed himself. He had flown to L.A. expressly to visit his latest investment. He valued all his investments. At home in Oklahoma—two thousand of the prettiest acres of land God ever made, and with some of the flushest oil reserves in the old Indian territory—he began every day with a walk to his stables. He would offer apples to his favorite horses, stallions syndicated at several million dollars each, smiling as the juice dripped from the teeth of the most beautiful horses God ever made. He had grown up in the hills of West Virginia, his only toy a corncob pipe a peddler had given him. Now he had all the toys he wanted, and he loved them all.

Channel Six, Los Angeles, was his most recent acquisition, and Taylor Drummond—the prettiest, most talented

anchorwoman God had ever made—his latest investment.
And now he was on his way to meet her, in the flesh.

He had first noticed her on a trip to Boston. After a
twelve-hour bout with a clutch of investment bankers, he
had retired to his room at the Four Seasons, wishing Laurel Ann were there to minister to his needs. She did that
so well. Much better than his two former wives. But she
was home nursing their second child, and he was alone in
Boston.

He switched on the television. Buying his own TV station had cost him plenty. He had put in place the sharpest
management team he had to oversee the station, but he
kept a keen eye on them, and on the competition. He
hadn't made it into *Forbes*'s issue on billionaires without
personally minding the shop every now and then.

The GM in Los Angeles, Sid Pordsky, had his head
screwed on with the eyes facing forward. Oh, he was
crude, regularly offended people, and couldn't keep his
pants zipped, but he had that flame in his eyes that told
Grady all he needed to know. For whatever reason, Sid
wanted his station to be on top, numero uno in the shuffle
of independents in the second largest television market in
the U.S. of A.

The local news came on, with the faces of the news
team flashing—one, then another—on the screen. He
missed the name, but zeroed in on the face. He sat up
straight against the pillows bunched at his back. Grady
preferred blondes. Both his ex-wives were blond. Laurel
Ann was blond. But he didn't let personal opinions cloud
his business judgment.

The brunette behind the anchor desk looked at him as if
she knew him, as if she cared whether his favorite bull
was sick, as if his life depended on knowing about conditions in south Boston. All of that, she managed to
convey—how? Grady studied her, watching the relaxed
but confident posture, the hands so at ease on the desk. No
pen tapping or paper shuffling, no wide fake smile when
delivering the bad news, yet no crocodile tears either. Jesus, she was everything he wanted in an anchor.

He had missed her name. Once, he thought the coanchor addressed her as Taylor, but that sounded like a man's name to him. Dialing the local station, Grady decided the name suited her. On that woman, a masculine name worked. It called attention to the contrast that would drive men wild—an unmistakably sensuous woman wrapped in the tailored packaging of her suit. The perky blonde they had now at Channel Six looked like a high school journalism student next to this pro. Sounded like it, too. The voice at the other end of the line confirmed the anchor's name—Taylor. Taylor Drummond.

Grady smiled and punched the telephone number for KANG, Los Angeles.

Six months passed before she said yes. Grady had given instructions to get her no matter what the cost, with the proviso that they bargain carefully and not throw in the whole wad at once. More time had passed since she had started to work in L.A. Grady kept an eye on her via his satellite dish in Oklahoma. The ratings had been inching upward since her arrival, and he had delayed his gratification long enough. It was time to visit his latest possession.

When the driver brought the car to a halt, Grady opened his eyes and handed his empty glass to Roscoe. The building needed some touch-up work done on the paint job. Pointing that out to Roscoe, he heaved himself from the low seat of the car and headed into the office of Channel Six.

"Mr. Hutchings is here." Sid's secretary's voice sounded on his intercom.

"Out." Sid waved his hands at the sales staff scattered around his office. "Wring every last goddamn dollar you can out of our improved news ratings. Top sales next quarter wins a prize."

The newest salesperson, the only woman in the group, looked expectantly at Sid and said, "Prize?" The guys grinned at one another.

Sid looked her up and down, real slow, and said with a poker face, "All the pussy you can eat."

The men laughed. The woman chuckled weakly. "You're such a card, Sid."

"Put that on my gravestone. Now, get the hell outta here. Make way for Hutch."

They filed out. Two seconds later, the door swung open again.

Grady Hutchings invaded his office. Large bones, amply decked with solid fat, held up a head that always made Sid think of Yogi Bear. Round, with small ears protruding well up on either side. Towering over Sid, he stuck out a slab of a hand and said in his southern drawl, "Good to see you again, Sidney."

"How the hell you been?" Sid rose from behind his desk to shake his boss's hand, then pulled out one of the leather chairs in front of his desk. From a drawer he produced a box of Havana's finest. "Smoke?"

Grady sat and selected a cigar, setting to work cutting the end with a gold tool he pulled from his coat pocket. "You know how to make a man feel right at home." He concentrated in silence until he had puffed out a parade of smoke rings. Pointing toward Sid with the cigar, he said, "I owe you a bonus."

Sid raised his brows. The old fart owed him more than that, but what the hell, the important thing was to figure out what Hutch thought he owed him a bonus for. Sid had found it damn useful to stay one step ahead of this particular employer.

"Yessirree, that Drummond woman is one fine lady. Comes across on my satellite dish like a meteor streaking through the evening sky."

Shifting in his chair to avoid the smoke drifting his way, Sid lavished a shit-eating grin on the billionaire. "She is good, isn't she?" Fuck, the old man hadn't seen nothing yet. Just wait until he and Annie finished fixing her up. If he liked Taylor Drummond now, he'd love their all-American version.

"I figured it was time to meet her. With the ratings increase and all, I think we owe her some special treatment." He jabbed a finger at Sid. "I know you didn't have any doubts, but no matter how dynamite the lady is, we have to consider the bottom line. And the bottom line—" he traced an upward arc with his hand "—is heading straight up."

Sid smiled again, automatically, wondering if any of Hutch's toadies had reported his objections to Taylor. He spared a glance at Roscoe Krezisylynsky, standing at attention behind Hutch's chair. Sid knew a thousand-dollar suit when he saw it; that punk must contribute something to the bottom line.

". . . and that pleases me," Hutch was saying. He turned the cigar between his teeth. "But, Sidney, I didn't buy this station merely to have a plaything. I bought it for a purpose."

Sid nodded, knowing what was coming next. He had been treated to a dose of Hutch's crusade for Christ and family once before. He tended to curb it around Sid, perhaps in deference to Sid's long dormant, if not dead, Judaism. In Hutch's home state, though, he was as well known for his morality platform as for his oil platforms.

"I would rest easier at night knowing this station was setting the right example for the people of Los Angeles. You know I want the news team to be like a family to the viewers here. I'm convinced a large part of Burke's appeal comes from the way his caring and love comes through. Anybody can read the news in front of the camera, but it takes a special combination to make people care."

Hutch paused, and Sid gave him the nod he seemed to want. Sid noticed Roscoe had his note-taking machine ready in hand. He wished the man would make his point. He needed to take a piss, but excusing yourself from the presence of Grady Hutchings was a greater mistake in judgment than wearing a Rolex on the New York subway.

"Part of that responsibility ties in with the way our people live their lives. I've got to tell you I think Taylor Drummond is the perfect anchorwoman, except for that one point."

Sid had been thinking of his bladder and missed the goddamn point. "Offer you a drink?" he asked, hoping

Hutch would repeat at least part of his speech. Sid poured two fingers of bourbon and handed it to Hutch, hoping the man wouldn't ask him to drink along with him. Alcohol did funny things to him these days.

"So I'll be the happiest billionaire in the U.S. of A. as soon as she ties the knot. Maybe we'll air the wedding, let our viewers be a part of it."

"Wedding?" Taylor? He had definitely missed something.

Grady tossed back his bourbon. "Make a note of that, Roscoe," he said.

"How's your wife?" asked Sid, in a blunt attempt to change the subject. He couldn't imagine anyone getting Taylor to the altar unless she decided to walk there herself.

The large man beamed. "Oh, she's fine, just fine. They don't make 'em like Laurel Ann anymore."

The fuck they don't. Hutch's wife had to be a third his age. The first time he'd seen her, Sid had assumed the sanctimonious Hutch was exercising a dark side and helping himself to some stolen honey from a call girl. Then he found out Laurel Ann had a degree in theology from Oral Roberts University and ran a day-care center back in Tulsa. Plus the church, school board, and city council, to hear Hutch go on about her. Those tits, though, just didn't mesh with that bio. He managed a weak "Give her my best, will ya?"

Hutchings pulled back one stiff white cuff, fastened by the gaudiest gold offered by Neiman-Marcus, and checked his watch.

To Sid's amazement, he caught a glimpse of an old steel-encased Timex on the man's hair-speared wrist. Hutchings must have seen his look of surprise, because he held his wrist in front of his potbelly and regarded it proudly. Tapping out his cigar, he said, "This was the first thing I bought for myself, oh, a good many years ago, when I trudged out of the grime of an oil field and into what was to be my start in the cor-por-ate world." He twisted his hand back and forth, catching the light on the cracked crystal of the watch face. "Reminds me to be humble."

Sid nodded. "Humble" was about the last word he'd use to describe the station owner. Pompous, overbearing, a man even Sid could call sexist—but humble?

"I see it's show time for Miss Drummond." Twisting toward the wall of monitors, he loosened his belt a notch and leaned back a bit more in the chair. "Pour me another bourbon and let's watch the little lady."

Taylor appeared on three of the monitors on Sid's wall. Her blue eyes paled beneath gobs of pastel blue shadow on her eyelids. She kept twitching her elbows, as if the sleeves of the dress were tickling her. And she stumbled over the copy of the lead story.

Hutch shot forward in his chair, an ice cube flying from his mouth onto the carpet. "What in the hell have you done to her?"

If the reactions of the crew were any indication of popular opinion, Taylor figured she would be back in her suits and silk blouses within a week. They gawked. They snickered. Burke said, "I love the way your face cracks when you smile." Annie had insisted that Dorothy apply a heavier foundation, darker eyeliner, and a glittery blue shadow that Annie had pulled from her bag of tricks.

Taylor suffered through the newscast. When she flubbed not only the opening, but the closing, she decided a week was too long. She had made a bargain to try it Annie's way, but once was enough. She could not and would not go back on-air looking like last year's floozy.

Annie was hanging around in the wings, sketching on a pad. Taylor wondered why she hadn't gone to gloat with Sid, and found the answer as soon as the monitors went to black. Annie approached her. "I've drawn some suggestions for hairdos. Let's go see Sid together and discuss them."

Taylor stared at the woman, wishing she could make her disappear. She rose from her seat, a smile fixed in place. "Yes, let's do go see Sid," she said, eager to do battle.

They headed off the set, with Annie cataloging the softness and approachability conveyed by Taylor's "new look."

Without knocking, Annie opened Sid's office door.

"I refuse to participate in this charade," said Taylor, advancing on Sid.

"Isn't this the greatest look?" asked Annie, right behind her.

Without responding, Sid zipped around his desk faster than the crew disappeared from the studio at quitting time. Ignoring Annie, he said, "Taylor, I want you to meet Grady Hutchings. He stopped by to say hello and especially wanted to meet you on his trip out from Tulsa."

Taylor realized the chair in front of Sid's desk was occupied—by none other than the owner of KANG. And here she was, dressed like a housewife from Hot Springs. "Mr. Hutchings, it's an honor to meet you," she said, extending her hand.

He stood. Ignoring her outstretched hand, he gathered her in a hug and smacked a kiss on her right cheek. "The honor is all mine." He handed her into a chair, then rounded on Sid.

"Now, will you please explain to me why the powerhouse I hired is dressed in this . . . this costume?"

Taylor almost kissed the man again. At last, someone with sense, and the power to veto these two. "My question exactly," she said, crossing her arms and staring Sid down.

Annie stepped forward. "Mr. Hutchings, I'm Annie Fleischer, of MediaImage. Mr. Pordsky hired our firm to—"

"That'll do." Sid cut her off, then tugged on his mustache. Addressing Annie, he said, "Your rash experimentation with Ms. Drummond's media image is a gross failure, which may have resulted in the loss of viewers, and therefore, revenue, to this station. In other words, my dear, you fucked up."

Just like that, good old Sid sacrificed Annie. So much for her long lunches and time spent kissing up to him. Sid definitely knew which side his toast was buttered on.

Hutchings jerked his head toward Annie. "Roscoe, fire the strumpet."

"You can't do that," Annie said. "I was merely carrying out his orders—" she pointed at Sid "—to create an image the people could relate to. The whole thing was his idea. I thought it was stupid all along, but the client is never wrong."

"What do you mean, his idea?" Hutchings glowered at Sid, then at Annie. "Even if it was his idea—and it wasn't, because I don't pay this man the money I do so he can ruin the best anchor local news has ever seen—it's your job to catch gross errors in judgment where public image is concerned."

Sid stared Annie down. Now that she knew she had won, Taylor had no need to join in the skirmish. She felt a little bit sorry for Annie for having to take the blame, but the sympathy vanished when she caught sight of herself in a mirror over Sid's bar.

"I have a contract with this station," Annie said.

Hutchings snapped his fingers. Roscoe jumped forward. "Take care of that." Roscoe nodded, made a note, and offered his arm to Annie.

"You can't get out of my contract."

Hutchings smiled. "Fillies are made to be mounted; contracts are made to be broken."

Annie hefted her shoulder bag and shook Roscoe's hand off her arm. "You'll be hearing from my lawyers," she said over her shoulder.

Sid let go of his mustache. "Freshen your bourbon, Grady?"

"Don't mind if I do." He handed over his glass, then patted Taylor's hand with a palm frosty from holding the drink. "Now, Miss Drummond, let's forget all that unpleasantness. You are one fine-looking lady, and it is a pleasure to have you working at our station. I can't tell you how happy I am about our recent ratings, so since my Laurel Ann always says presents speak louder than words, I brought you a little something." Scrabbling in his coat pocket, he fished out a robin's-egg blue box tied with a white satin ribbon. Tiffany.

"Mr. Hutchings, I'm touched. I really am."

He motioned for her to open the box. She did, and gasped when she found a pair of ruby earrings set into a silver backdrop resembling an angel's wings.

She looked into Hutching's beaming face. He said, "Angels. Just like our call letters."

Of course, KANG. She'd always thought the letters were an abbreviation for Los Angeles. Never in a blue moon would she have guessed the owner had angels in mind when he'd chosen the call letters. "They're lovely, but I really don't think—"

"Now, you just enjoy them. Don't worry about the IRS. They never need to know about little gewgaws like these." He winked at her. "You just keep smiling at that camera and telling good stories. And make sure you look like yourself again by tomorrow night's newscast."

She looked at Sid, watching for some sign to indicate whether presents from the owner were commonplace. Sid merely frowned and said, "Why don't you quit staring at them and put 'em on your ears?" Perhaps presents like this were business as usual for a billionaire. She exchanged her simple pearl studs for the ruby angels.

Hutchings beamed at her. "Lovely. Lovely. Sidney, how about a sherry for Miss Drummond?" Sid hustled to the bar before Taylor could decline. She noticed he poured bourbon into a wineglass. She couldn't picture Sid keeping a bottle of amontillado in his office. Whichever he poured, she wasn't drinking—in case she was carrying Mason's child.

She left the glass sitting on the edge of Sid's desk. Grady Hutchings kept staring at her, as if he were seeing the Mona Lisa for the first time. In her heavy makeup and ill-fitting dress, she felt like a fly trapped on a lab slide. Sid was saying something about the improved ratings, and crediting it to her. He certainly knew how to brownnose. Suddenly she couldn't bear it any longer. "Mr. Hutchings, thank you very much for the earrings. It was a pleasure to meet you, but I've got some work to finish." She started to rise.

Hutchings pressed his large hand to her knee. "Don't go." She lowered into the chair, wishing his hand didn't feel quite so warm, heavy, and possessive. A pass from Burke, she could believe, but from Grady Hutchings, Texas oilman turned media magnate—no way. The recent *Business Week* article she had read had mentioned his passion for ponies and his preference for blondes. This had to be simply his style of discussing business with women.

Leaning toward her, he said, "Have you ever thought of tying the knot?"

What kind of question was that? "No, Mr. Hutchings, I haven't."

"Call me Grady." He polished off his drink. "For a pretty woman like you, it seems like a good idea, doesn't it?" He rose. "Pleasure seeing you again, Sidney. Keep that Annie fox away from our henhouse." To Taylor he said, "You might think about marriage. It lends a certain respectability to a woman, especially an older woman."

Taylor's speech on age and sex discrimination died before it raced from her brain to her tongue. The man was joking. Of course—it was probably his way of hinting she was too desirable to be available.

Hutchings walked from the room, his secretary in tow. Taylor thought he looked exactly like a bear leaving hibernation to forage in the woods for sustenance.

The door shut. Taylor looked at Sid, and he looked back at her. She allowed herself a wide grin, cracking the heavy foundation.

Sid said, "What are you sitting there for? You heard the boss. Burn that *schmatta* and go find yourself a wedding ring."

Chapter 15

A MONTH HAD PASSED SINCE GRADY HUTCH-
ings had saved Taylor from Annie and Sid's idea of Anchorwoman of the People. To compensate for losing that
round, Sid had implemented his latest project: sending
Taylor and Burke out as ambassadors to the viewing public. He wanted them out among the citizenry, pressing the
flesh, much like politicians, reminding the people who to
turn to in the maze of choices that was television.

As Sid put it, in a city like L.A., when viewers had
ABC, NBC, CBS, Fox, the other independents, and cable,
not to mention state-of-the-art movie houses, live concerts,
theater, radio, and Dial-A-Porn—they needed a reason to
remember Channel Six.

A station could try filling its prime-time schedule with
hour after hour of news. Then, no matter what time your
viewer arrived home after slogging through gridlock and
freeway marksmen, he could collapse in front of his set,
and watch the mayhem of the city that he'd been
spared—at least for that day. A station could herald itself
as the movie channel, showing more feature films with
fewer interruptions. It made good advertising copy, even if
most of the movies lulled the viewers to sleep in their
Barcaloungers. A station could outbid all others for the
rights to reruns of once hot shows, then hope their staff
didn't quit when the budget didn't allow money for things
like raises and benefits.

Sid snorted at these other ways and means. What he
wanted was a news team the people related to, remem-

bered, revered. So, for the last month, Taylor and Burke had been trotting around town.

This morning Taylor was due to address a journalism class at University High. She stood in her walk-through closet, selecting a more casual outfit than the suits she had fought to retain. She didn't want to look too much like the kids' mothers.

She sighed as she freed an above-the-knee black cashmere skirt from its hanger. She could easily be the mother of a high school sophomore, but as it turned out, it looked as if she wasn't going to be anyone's mother. When she'd gotten her period last month, a bit sketchier and later than usual, she had experienced a pang of relief, followed by a sweet moment of loss.

She fastened the skirt, which seemed snugger than she remembered, blanked the thoughts of Mason that threatened to surface, finished dressing, and checked her image in her full-length mirror. The matching sweater curved softly over her upper body and hugged her hips, ending a few inches above the hem of the skirt. Thank goodness Annie the Anachronism was truly a thing of the past. *Pfft*—like that, Grady Hutchings had made her disappear. For that she had to like him, though his comments about wanting her to be married made her nervous.

So she dismissed them. She had a lot of other more pressing problems to consider. Her period was due again, which made her irritable and reminded her that she had to decide what to do about pursuing artificial insemination. Jillian had called and asked her to meet her for lunch later in the week. Over the phone, her sister had said nothing about being pregnant. Anger diluted by guilt almost led her to say no to Jillian, but the humbly pleading tone to her voice swayed her. She sounded like a woman in need of a friend.

Taylor brushed her hair, humming along with a retro CD of the Rolling Stones. The music of the sixties had eased the agony of her teen years, by embracing her in a subculture where she belonged—and her parents were excluded. When she saw children dragging along with their parents,

Walkman headsets clamped to their ears and bored agony imprinted on their faces—she understood. But the sight, which screamed alienation, always saddened her. She hadn't asked to play the role of outcast.

Taylor dabbed L'Air du Temps, a perfume she had started to wear recently, on her wrists, then reached beneath her sweater to add a touch of scent to her breasts. She switched off her stereo system and left the apartment. She didn't feel like eating breakfast.

She walked down the stairs to the building courtyard. An uncomfortable odor followed her. Wrinkling her nose, she tried to figure out its source. Even in the fresh air of the center patio, the smell persisted. But the smell wasn't one of perspiration; it was almost like flowers that have soured and grown moldy when left in a vase too long.

When she reached her car, she fished in her briefcase for her purse-size atomizer and refreshed her perfume. She buried her nose against the inside of her wrist to inhale the scent.

She jerked away, her stomach lurching. No wonder the smell was following her—the perfume had turned rancid. Taylor drove with her windows down to the high school. Once inside, she found a washroom, empty except for one girl dressed in black lace applying layers of red to her lips, and sucking on a breath mint. Freshly burned tobacco tainted the air. Taylor leaned over the low sink, rubbing her wrists with soap and water. The girl watched her, but with a certain cool reserve that Taylor respected.

"My therapist might be able to help you," the girl offered, putting away her lipstick in a purse that looked a lot like an eggplant covered in sequins.

"Your therapist?" Taylor snagged a paper towel from the dispenser.

"Yeah, with your obsessive-compulsive behavior." The girl pointed to the sink. "Excessive need to wash is a sure sign."

Taylor looked more closely at the girl, guessing her age at fifteen or sixteen. "You're really seeing a therapist?"

The girl lifted a shoulder. The black lace shifted to expose a bony joint. "Everyone does."

Taylor wasn't so sure about that. If "everyone" did it, things had changed a lot since she was in high school. Suddenly she realized she sounded almost like her own mother, reciting, "Things were different when I was a girl."

"Do you tell your therapist about cutting class to smoke in the girls' room?"

"You see anyone smoking?"

Taylor tapped a finger against the side of her nose. For a moment she empathized with the frustration her mother must have gone through during her teen years. That moment evaporated as she remembered that the only time her parents paid attention to her was when she caused trouble. As the memory of her mother's endless lectures swam back into her memory, she repressed the desire to remind the girl of the evils of smoking. "So does your therapist help?" she asked instead.

"With smoking? No way. He doesn't care about anything like cigarettes. That's self-expression. We're working on real problems."

The ghost of cigarette smoke now mingled with the perfume she'd applied between her breasts. The combination made her vaguely light-headed, like the feeling she suffered one time she had been stuck on top of a Ferris wheel. "When I used to cut class and smoke, I didn't have a therapist to tell me it was okay. I only had my—"

As if on cue, the girl coughed.

"—body to listen to." Taylor tossed the paper towel in the trash. She hoped the girl latched on to that comment. Maybe she had; Taylor saw in the long mirror over the row of sinks that the girl watched her all the way to the door.

While she spoke to the journalism class, she studied the faces of the students. They seemed so young and eager, yet in many ways appeared more sophisticated than she had ever felt as a teenager. As she answered their questions, which ranged from the ethics and legalities of revealing sources, and censorship, to who did her makeup and how much money she made, she experienced again the overwhelming desire to have her own child. She felt also the responsibility of giving life, forming character, shaping the future—and knew that despite her misgivings, she would try again for a child of her own. The end result would be worth the difficulties she would face.

Jillian watched her sister reach for a third piece of garlic bread. The bread was a speciality of the Smokehouse in Burbank, but even two pieces were an indulgence. "I thought you said you weren't very hungry."

"I was wrong."

"It's a good thing you told the waiter to leave the bread basket."

Taylor nodded and continued munching.

Jillian brushed a bread crumb from the white cloth and folded her hands on top of the cleared table. She'd been a fool to think she could confide in her sister. They had almost finished with lunch, and Taylor hadn't even asked her about the baby she was supposedly carrying. Of course, Jillian hadn't volunteered any information, either, but she was looking for a sign. Any show of interest and Jillian knew she would have cracked and spilled the whole story. She needed to talk—desperately so—if she was willing to confide in Taylor. Goody Two-shoes Taylor.

Taylor finished the slice and glanced at her watch. "Did you have something you wanted to talk about? If not, I have to run."

I think Mason is seeing someone else, and I'm not really pregnant. I'm only pretending so he won't leave me. And soon I have to fake a miscarriage, and I'm afraid of what he'll do if he ever finds out. Jillian listened to the backdrop of chinking dishes and genial conversation. Her sister didn't want to know. She only wanted to rush back to her important life. "Actually, I . . ." Reaching for her water glass, she winced as she saw the bored and frustrated look that crossed Taylor's face. She had wasted her sister's valuable time.

"Well, hello there," said a male voice.

Jillian looked at the man stopped at their table. She took in his flat blue eyes, slicked-back red hair, glasses on a chain hanging against his chest. And she remembered precisely where she had seen him last.

He extended his hand. "Harold Browne," he said. "You must remember?" Another man, thinner, with a sweater tied in front and dangling over his shoulders, joined Harold.

Ignoring his hand, Jillian said, "I think you're mistaking me for someone else."

"Hal Browne?" Taylor accepted his hand. "Weren't you at Boalt, the year ahead of me?"

He switched his attention to Taylor. Yes, they had been in law school together. Yes, he was in-house counsel with a studio down the street. Jillian heard their polite chatter, but at a distance. None of it touched her. But this man had touched her. They had met at a bar. When was it? A year or so ago. He had been the worst lay she had ever had. Obviously he hadn't thought that poorly of his performance, or he never would have approached her.

Without introducing the other man, and with one lingering glance, Harold Browne and his companion left them.

"Imagine Hal thinking he knew you," Taylor said.

"I can't think why he would."

"Maybe he met you when you visited me."

Jillian waved her hand. She wanted the subject dismissed, over with and forgotten.

"It doesn't look as if his taste in men has improved much since law school."

"Taste in men?"

Taylor gave her one of her older-sister looks. "Men, Jillian. At Boalt he had an older lover. One of those slide-rule professor types from the engineering school, who never seemed to take a bath or cut his hair."

The napkin had made its way back into her nervous fingers. Dabbing her lips, Jillian said, "You're saying he's gay."

Her sister nodded.

Jillian had gone to his house, admired the flair with which it was decorated, drunk his champagne until they were both quite silly, and then tried to arouse him. Tried and tried and tried. Her memory blurred at that point, either from the champagne or the humiliation of it all. She drank water, swallowing rapidly, to keep from losing her lunch.

"Are you okay?"

Taylor was watching her with a look bordering on envy, which puzzled Jillian. But, of course, her sister thought she was pregnant and figured she was feeling queasy. Jesus, how had she gotten her life into this mess? "I'm fine."

"What were you about to tell me when Hal interrupted?"

"Nothing." Jillian slid to the edge of the booth. "Listen, I don't want to make you late for work. I just wanted to get together for lunch. No special reason." Lies, lies, lies. Her entire life was entangled in lies.

Jillian managed to steer her car a few blocks from the Smokehouse before she had to pull over. Her hands shook worse than an off-balance washing machine. She parked, stepped out, and the next thing she knew, she was standing in a card and gift shop, with Charlie Brown's big eyes staring back at her.

She refused to be ill in public. Every time she thought of Hal Browne—of where that limp cock had traveled before entering her mouth—she wanted to retch. The gagging sensation started in her throat, far below her larynx, and chugged upward as images of the hours she had spent with him crept through the barbed wire of repressed memories.

Concentrating on the card display, she reminded herself that the past was behind her. It could be forgotten. She had walked the straight and narrow path since before Christmas, and she had every intention of staying reformed. Besides, nobody—not her sister, her neighbors, her husband—knew about Harold Browne.

Yet the encounter disturbed her. Never had she considered the possibility of bumping into any of the men she'd had sex with. The world of afternoon sex—frantic humping in shabby motel rooms, followed by despair rushing in to abolish the momentary exhilaration—that world had nothing to do with her other reality. For the two to intersect was to violate a law of nature, as implausible as a character walking off a movie screen and into a moviegoer's life.

Jillian plucked a card from the display. Shopping shunted the turmoil, gave her something else to think about. As she browsed in a store, her purse replete with cash and credit cards, her identity as Mason's wife emerged to seal her from her own sins. Her hands had steadied. Even this triple whammy—that Harold approached her, that he knew Taylor, and that he was bisexual—could be forced into the casket-sized box she labeled as "what's past."

The card she had lifted read "Happy Anniversary" on the inside. She returned it to the rack. Sending anniversary cards to other couples, especially to one's parents, seemed such an inappropriate custom; who else other than the two people themselves should acknowledge the event? She had forgotten her own recent anniversary and resented the elaborate card her mother had mailed to them. Forgotten it until Mason had come home early, primed for sex and celebration. And what had she done? Refused him, as she had done so often over the last few months. Though her performance on Christmas Day had been worthy of an Oscar, it had bought her nothing other than time. Mason treated her like a nun now that he thought she might be carrying his precious offspring.

"Can I help you find anything?"

Jillian jerked another card from the rack and turned to the saleswoman. "No, thanks."

The woman glanced at her watch. "I thought you might be having trouble deciding."

Straightening her shoulders, Jillian delivered one of the glares her mother had taught her to bestow on unworthy domestics. The woman took a step back. Jillian had obviously been staring at the cards long enough for the woman to label her a nut case. Well, she was crackers to dwell on her life. She had to forge ahead, act as if everything was okay, and surely it would all fall into place. Mason would still love her and keep her safe. From the world and from herself. And she was going to be good from now on.

Four days after her talk at University High, Taylor and Burke were to participate in a panel discussion at a breakfast meeting sponsored by a group called TV-TV, Traditional Values for Television. According to Sid, Grady Hutchings had phoned and requested their presence.

Taylor met Burke outside the hotel banquet room in the San Fernando Valley. "I have very mixed feelings about this organization," she said to him in lieu of a greeting.

He buttoned his suit jacket and checked his teeth in the mirror posted by the garage entrance off the circular driveway. "Don't worry. Just drink your orange juice and agree with whatever they say. You're not here as a reporter, or a lawyer. You're here as a guest, and, I might remind you, a representative of the owner of Channel Six." Burke patted his hair. "You know, the guy who pays our salaries."

"You have no ethics at all." Taylor walked beside him into the hotel. "What if these people support censoring of news and programs to promote whatever values they hold to be the only 'true values'? Doesn't that bother you?"

"No. I've got my own set of standards." He produced his copyrighted leer. "Good gams is all I ask for."

Taylor didn't bother responding. She excused herself and headed for the ladies'. Surely this time she'd find what she expected. This month her period was almost a week overdue. She decided her body was only playing games with her, to make her think she was pregnant with Mason's child. After all, she'd had her period last month. Surely the blood would flow soon, a bright red stain offering her back the status quo.

Nothing.

By tonight, then. Since her twelfth year, her period had come as regular as the waning of the moon. It was as much a part of her life as breathing, sleeping, or eating. She spritzed on L'Air du Temps from the new purse-size atomizer she had purchased the day before, then rejoined Burke.

They took their places along with another man and woman at the head table. Taylor looked over the group of about thirty men and women, all well dressed and smiling and chatting with one another. Maybe this organization wasn't the flagship of censorship she feared, but each person believed in his or her cause enough to have paid one hundred dollars for this breakfast.

The emcee introduced himself as Keith Carlyle. Taylor learned the other two panelists were from the parent organization of TV-TV, located in Dallas. She reminded herself that these people were probably friends of Grady Hutchings.

People were still arriving, and no one had moved to begin the meeting. During the lull, Burke spoke easily with the other two, and Taylor listened. She wasn't feeling very well. Once or twice her stomach pitched against her ribs in a way that threatened her composure, then settled back to a mild nausea. Her perfume had shed its earlier promise of freshness and rankled against her nostrils.

Taylor toyed with the idea of excusing herself, but before she could act, the waiters delivered plates of chipped corn beef and gravy poured over pastry shells. The sight of the pink and white cream mixture lapping at the edges of the plate, combined with the cloying odor of her perfume, was too much for Taylor's restless stomach.

She gathered her purse, whispered to Burke that he was on his own, and sought out Mr. Carlyle. She made her apologies, pleading an onset of stomach flu. Then she walked calmly back to the ladies' room and threw up.

Some facts were incontrovertible: Something was very off with her body chemistry, chipped corn beef was one of her favorite foods, and she never vomited. Plus, her period was late.

She needed a pregnancy test. She disliked the one gynecologist she had seen, and she distrusted the at-home kits.

Driving along the freeway, she spotted a sign that said
FAMILY PLANNING CLINIC, and swerved off the exit and into
the parking lot of the building. She wanted to know. Now.
And she wanted both certainty and anonymity.

Two hours later, thumbing through a tattered *People*
magazine, she waited for the nurse to call her name—or
rather, the name she had given them, Mrs. Taylor Smith.
The clinic worked on a first-come, first-served basis. Five
impossibly young girls were already in line when Taylor
walked in. One held a baby like a sack of potatoes against
her outthrust hip. Another was accompanied by an acne-
scarred boy who never lifted his eyes from the floor.

Wondering about the stories they could tell distracted
her from her own situation. She would return and profile
some of these children having, or aborting, their children.
Yet, as time passed, she forgot the problems of the others
and returned to her own situation. The doctor could still
tell her she wasn't pregnant; just nerves, he'd say, clapping
her on the back and telling her to go home and not work
so hard.

But what if she was? What would she do about Mason?

"Mrs. Smith?"

Taylor looked around at the others in the cramped waiting room. When no one rose, the nurse repeated the name.

Hearing the name again jogged her memory. She rose,
self-conscious as she stepped toward the nurse. Taylor supplied the requested urine and blood samples, then changed
into the paper robe handed her, and settled on the edge of
the examination table to wait for the doctor.

The question returned: what to tell Mason. She wanted
nothing to do with him. Yet, if she was pregnant, the baby
was definitely his. As the father, surely he had the right to
know.

He forfeited that right when he made love to Jillian, argued the part of her still wounded by his inconstancy—the
greater part of her. Stuck there, waiting for the doctor,
studying the plastic model of a fetus in utero, she ached to
share the experience with Mason. Had he gone to the doctor with Jillian, held her hand while the nurse drew her

blood and the doctor pried inside of her? She tried to stifle that line of thought by reminding herself that Jillian hadn't confirmed she was pregnant. That thought didn't help; Jillian still had Mason, and she, Taylor, was here alone. She wrapped her arms across the flimsy paper gown, offering herself comfort, and wondered why things couldn't have worked out differently. She pictured the pimply-faced boy in the Raiders T-shirt slumped next to the girl in the waiting room. That girl had someone to hold her hand.

But most of them were alone.

And probably not by choice. She had chosen this path, not stumbled over it after a few minutes of groping following a basketball game or a friend's party. She had been prepared to travel the route to parenthood before Mason reentered her life.

Taylor lifted her shoulders. The paper robe crinkled and she wished the doctor would come soon.

Just then the door opened and a gray-haired woman in a white coat hurried in. She stopped when she saw Taylor, and studied her a few seconds before extending her hand. "I'm Dr. Richmond."

Taylor figured the doctor was analyzing her appearance. She didn't exactly fit the profile of the rest of the patients. Accepting her hand, she said, "Taylor Dru—Smith."

The doctor nodded briskly. "Up on the table and let's do a physical exam."

Taylor lay back and poked her feet into the sheepskin-covered stirrups. The doctor didn't seem inclined to talk. Taylor studied the tattered posters taped to the ceiling. Pictures of Rob Lowe, Billy Idol, and Spike Lee had been edited with black circles with a diagonal slash drawn across the circumference. Someone here had a strange sense of humor.

The doctor withdrew her probing hand and stripped off her glove. "You can get up now. What was the date of your last period?"

Sitting upright, Taylor gave her the mid-January date,

and the date of the one and only time she could have conceived.

The doctor nodded. "Positive, according to both your preliminary lab tests and my exam."

"But I had my period."

"That sometimes happens."

"So you're saying I'm pregnant."

The doctor gave her a sad half smile. "Yes." She scribbled on a clipboard. "The nurse will be in to discuss the options we offer."

Taylor wished she didn't feel so naked. Hugging the paper wrap to her knees, she said, "Options?"

"You've caught this at an early stage. That leaves you several avenues."

"Are you talking about abortion?"

The doctor nodded and slipped her pen into her coat pocket.

"Dr. Richmond, any decisions I had to make were made when I chose to become a parent. I'm having this baby."

The doctor glanced at Taylor's ringless left hand. "I'm sorry I assumed as I did. Most women who come in here only have to decide whether or not they want general anesthesia when the abortion is performed." She gave Taylor another sad smile. Pushing back a lock of hair with the heel of her palm, she said, "Maybe I've been in this business too long. Find a good obstetrician and make an appointment soon. I wish you and your baby the best."

Before Taylor could thank her, the doctor handed her a card. "My private practice. Where I deliver babies." Then she swept out, as briskly as she had entered.

Taylor stepped off the exam table onto the cold linoleum. Her gown fell open and she touched a hand to her abdomen. She looked exactly the same on the outside. Could there really be another life inside her? She shivered and reached for her clothing. As she pulled on her panty hose, she started to cry. Wiping her cheeks with the back of her hand, she smiled. She was really going to be a mother.

More women were crowded into the waiting room. Taylor looked at the blank and lonely faces, and worried for them. As she left, she wished for all the girls a time when their babies would be just as welcome and wanted as hers.

It was possible, Taylor thought later, that the worst thing about being pregnant was not being able to share her news with anyone. She intended to keep her pregnancy a secret at work until her body betrayed her. She couldn't tell Jillian until she decided what to say to Mason. She couldn't tell her mother because she had no desire to, and because she, in turn, would discuss the news—and the scandal—with Jillian. Friends in TV news talked to other friends, and sooner or later, word would drift back to Sid. And she could just imagine what he would say. She wanted that speech postponed as long as possible.

So she had to hug her secret to herself. Every morning, in the shower, she said hello to her baby. She felt a little bit silly doing so, but she decided that babies understood such things. While she brushed her teeth, she explained about fluoride and flossing, and promised her baby the best schools and braces—but most important, she promised her love.

All in all, she acted quite the fool alone. But when she went out into the world, she was the same Taylor Drummond everyone was used to seeing. Once in a while she'd find whatever she had eaten for breakfast, or lunch, threatening to reemerge and embarrass her, but she'd close her eyes briefly, count to three, and fight back the sensation. She was sure no one noticed that slight aberration.

She called Dr. Richmond's office, gave her real name, and went to her first appointment within a week of her visit to the clinic. She liked the older woman, and found her much more relaxed at her Santa Monica office than at the family planning clinic. After that visit, she raided a bookstore and purchased twenty books on pregnancy and child development. The details, she had under control.

What she didn't know was how, when, and what to tell Mason.

* * *

Jillian thought of herself as someone who lied only when the situation called for it. She tended to tell whatever version of events best suited the listener, but to her, that wasn't actually lying. Now, for once, she admitted to herself, she had constructed a situation that called for active storytelling.

Her hand poised over the telephone in her kitchen, she gathered her wits. She couldn't call until she knew her voice would sound true and convincing. Swigging a mouthful of vodka, Jillian acknowledged how tired she was of the whole silly charade.

On Christmas Day she had felt so gloriously whole after that morning's sex with Mason that she was able for the tiniest window in time to envision herself giving him the child he wanted. When she made her dinner announcement about them starting a family, she almost believed her own words. When he pressed her to go for a pregnancy test, she put him off, telling him it was too early to know for sure. When he demanded an answer, she lied about her visit to the doctor and told him she was pregnant. Then she had been very, very careful to hide the telltale signs to the contrary. With Mason staying so late at the office and making no moves to cross an invisible line in the middle of their bed, the pretense had been simple. She was sure he didn't know she had already had one period.

But now it was time to act. With a sigh, she punched the automatic dialing code for Mason's office. The secretary asked her to hold. At the moment, Jillian considered telling Mason the truth: I'm not pregnant and never have been. Why drag him through the emotional upheaval?

Mason answered. Upon hearing his voice, so constant, so deep and reassuring, her desire to keep him hers won out.

"I'm sorry to bother you at work." She let her voice quaver.

"Is something wrong?"

"No. Yes." She sniffed, feeling truly miserable. "I wasn't feeling too well this morning."

"Jillian, what's wrong?"

She took a deep breath. "I was bleeding when I woke up, after you left for work. I called the doctor, went in, and he told me I was having a miscarriage."

She heard his quick intake of breath. She caught the condensation on the outside of her vodka glass and rubbed a cool drop across her forehead.

"Are you all right? Are you at the hospital?"

"I'm at home. The doctor said this early there'd be no complications."

"I'll reschedule some clients and come right home."

"You don't have to do that. I'm just going to sleep for a while."

"Of course I'll come home."

She couldn't face him right now; she would have to be asleep. "The doctor did say one thing . . ."

"Yes?" She heard the anxiety in his voice. He still loved her.

"He said I shouldn't try to get pregnant again for at least six months."

A longer silence than before followed, then Mason said, "We'll worry about that later. The important thing is that you're okay."

She said good-bye and replaced the receiver. Draining her glass, she told herself what she'd done was for the best. If she was going to be a dutiful wife from now on, she needed a husband content to stick by her side. She should call her mother next; Mason would expect that action of her. Instead, she swallowed a sleeping pill with the melted ice in the bottom of her drink and climbed the steps to her bedroom.

The clock on her bedside table read 3:45 as she passed into blessed sleep.

Mason put the phone back in its cradle. He motioned to Fielding, who had discreetly removed himself to the far end of the office when Mason had taken Jillian's call.

Concern on his features, his friend crossed the room, but said nothing.

Mason rubbed his eyes. "I am an utter and complete failure as a husband."

Fielding cocked his head, and Mason knew he would have to explain himself.

"That was Jillian. For months, as you well know, I've badgered her to start a family. After I had given up on her, she became pregnant. Now she's lost the baby." Mason stared at a spot over his friend's shoulder.

"I'm sorry."

"Oh, that's not the worst part." Mason paced behind his desk and gazed out the window, imagining Taylor's face reflected in every window of the building across the street. "The worst part is that I'm relieved."

Fielding shifted in his chair.

Mason cursed his guilt that led him to blurt his problems out like tabloid headlines. He had been the one who wanted a child; he knew damn well she had gotten pregnant to please him. Now, because of his needs, Jillian was at home alone, suffering after losing a child that might have helped them salvage their marriage. And here he stood, thinking that perhaps, after a suitable recovery time, he and Jillian could separate amicably and he could persuade Taylor to forgive him. He had no right to think of Taylor. He could no more leave Jillian now than if she were pregnant. As her husband, he owed her his allegiance.

"Did you realize you weren't quite as ready for parenthood as you thought?"

Mason grimaced. "It's not that simple. It seems I've gone and fallen in love with someone else."

Fielding whistled.

Mason knew his embarrassment showed on his face. "Yes, I stand condemned. I'm the louse who asked you to check up on Jillian."

A flicker of guilt crossed Fielding's face. He said nothing.

Mason assumed he must have misread the expression. Or perhaps his friend was still uncomfortable at having done the task. "Look, I'm sorry about dumping on you like this."

"That's okay. That's what friends are for. And shrinks." With a trace of anxiety, he asked, "How is Jillian feeling?"

"She sounded a little teary and said she was going to sleep, but otherwise she said she was fine."

"Good." Fielding stood and placed a hand on Mason's shoulder. "Don't be too hard on yourself. If I can help in any way, call me. And please tell Jillian she's in my thoughts. I'm sorry to rush off, but I have a meeting with Rosemary."

After thanking Fielding for his support, Mason had his secretary clear his calendar and then he gathered a contract he needed to review. He could do that while Jillian rested—if she was able to rest. Maybe he should check with her doctor. He played golf once a month with Donald Bassinger. Mason stopped on his way out the door and dialed the doctor's office. According to the receptionist, Mason had caught Donald on his way to surgery.

"Mason. Calling to set a game?"

After the events of the day, Mason found that an odd greeting. Weren't doctors supposed to reassure patients and their families at times of illness and loss? "No, I'm calling about Jillian."

"How is she?"

"That's what I'm calling you to find out."

"She was fine the last time I saw her."

"Fine?"

"Sure. Let's see, that would have been December, before the holidays, when she came in for her annual and renewed her birth control pills."

Mason caught his breath and felt a red-hot surge of anger wash through him. Steadying his voice, he asked, "You haven't seen her since December?"

"No."

"Were you in the office this morning?"

"All morning. It was a slow day for the stork. Why?"

"Nothing."

"Anything else, Mason? Next Saturday at Annandale?"

"I'll get back to you on that."

Chapter 16

MASON WASN'T INCLINED TO LOSE HIS TEMper easily, nor was he of a nature to jump to conclusions. The practice of law had reinforced his tendency to seek rational explanations for even the most bizarre of events. As he headed home through the clogged traffic—schools were back in session after the Christmas holidays, and the reprieve granted commuters during those off times had ended—he distilled two possibilities to explain the apparent situation. Either she had changed doctors and not mentioned the fact to him, or, unbelievable as the idea was, she had faked the miscarriage.

Either explanation left him with the feeling that he was living a bad dream that was going to get worse before a ringing alarm set him free. He vacillated between worrying over Jillian and contemplating his worst suspicions. He thought of calling on his car phone to check on her, but didn't want to wake her if she had fallen asleep.

She could have renewed the birth control prescription before deciding to "surprise" him, and after that, switched doctors without telling him. Donald played a decent eighteen holes, but maybe Jillian had found a better obstetrician. Why wouldn't she have mentioned the switch to him? He had simply assumed Donald had been the doctor she had seen when she came home and said the rabbit had died. She knew he played golf with Donald, and Jillian wasn't one to allow him to stumble into a social faux pas. She would have mentioned any change of physician.

By the time he set his parking brake with a jerk, he had worked himself into a combustible mixture of worry and

simmering anger. He dashed into the house and sprinted
upstairs, halting abruptly in the doorway to their bedroom.
Jillian lay fast asleep, her golden hair spread around her,
the picture of a fairy-tale princess. He tiptoed nearer to the
bed. On closer inspection, the peaceful image shattered.
Her hands twitched, and every so often she half turned and
moaned.

She didn't look well. Maybe he should call Donald, or
try to figure out who she had seen that morning. She might
have a follow-up appointment card in her purse. When he
didn't see her purse in the bedroom, he backed from the
room and retraced his steps to the kitchen, where she often
left her keys and purse on the counter.

The maid puttered in the kitchen, preparing dinner. Nodding at her, he collected Jillian's bag and dumped its contents on the table in the breakfast area. He felt like a thief,
sifting through her personal belongings. Women's purses
were a source of mystery to him, and he couldn't remember ever having rifled through Jillian's. If he wanted something she had, like a tissue or a piece of gum, he would
hand her purse to her for her to retrieve it.

He wasn't surprised at all to see that the interior was as
neatly ordered as their house. A wallet, checkbook, and
makeup bag, all in matching leather, made up the bulk of
the contents. A hairbrush and key ring tumbled out, but no
calendar. He felt like a snoop. Was this how Fielding felt,
lurking about, checking out other people's secrets? He was
reaching for the wallet, to look for an appointment card,
when he spotted an interior zippered compartment.

He sensed the maid had paused in her work. She probably wondered what in the hell he was doing. Shifting his
back to block her view, he opened the zipper. No calendar,
only a flat, rectangular pink case—the flat, rectangular
pink case he had been looking for when he had searched
their bathroom on Christmas Day.

Every morning, for years, she had swallowed her vita-
mins and her pill. Every morning without fail.

He withdrew the container of birth control pills, turning
it over and over. Mason opened the case. All but two pills

were missing. He traced the empty sockets that had bits of foil protruding around the edges, right down to the last empty circle. The days of the week were printed above each slot. Today was Thursday. The next pill to be taken lay in the "Friday" spot. He read the sticker inside the lid. It carried the name of a local pharmacy, Jillian's name, Donald's name as prescribing doctor, and the date the prescription had been filled—January 30.

He had to read the date twice.

January 30—three weeks after Jillian had told him the doctor had confirmed her pregnancy.

He stared at the empty sockets, then dropped the case into his coat pocket. Turning to the maid, he said, "I won't be eating here tonight." He climbed the stairs, slowly this time, to rein in the blinding rush of anger that threatened to consume him.

At first, control failed him. He tore into the bedroom, leaned over the bed, and shook Jillian by the shoulders. "Wake up. We have to talk," he said roughly.

It took him several vigorous shakes before she opened her eyes. In those moments, he had visions of himself strangling her and heaving her body off the balcony. He had wondered in the past what fury of feeling drove someone to murder; for once, he had an inkling of the fierce and uncontainable rage that could thrust a normally calm and measured person over the edge.

"Mason?" Jillian rubbed a hand over her face and blinked her eyelids.

He calmed himself, fighting the temptation to wave the birth control packet under her nose. He had trapped witnesses on the stand enough times to know he should never, ever lose control during questioning. After she opened her eyes, he said, "You were so sound asleep, you frightened me."

She yawned and blinked again. "I was so upset about losing the baby that I took a sleeping pill."

"I understand." He felt like a hypocrite, and worse, a cuckold. To think that if he hadn't looked in her purse, she would have played out this little scene, and he would have been none the wiser—only ripped apart in anguish worrying over her and castigating himself for his own guilt. "Tell me again what Donald said."

She pulled her hair away from her face. She looked so young and vulnerable. "He said I should rest, and that I'd be fine, but that I shouldn't try to get pregnant again for six months." She massaged her abdomen.

He had to hand it to her; she played the role to the hilt. "Doesn't he want you back for another visit?"

"No."

"Did you have any trouble getting in to see him?"

"No. They're always very nice about that sort of thing."

"No trouble at all?"

"No." She pushed herself up against the pillows. "They always take you in when there's an emergency."

"Emergency. Of course." Mason wasn't sure whether he hated her more for lying, or himself more for entrapping her. "By the way, I'm playing golf with Donald next Saturday."

He caught the telltale flicker in her eyes, a flicker he'd seen hundreds of times in the one year he had spent as a public defender, back in the days when he believed every defendant innocent, a victim of the biased justice system. Those days had been cut short when he realized most of his clients were guilty, and sure as hell would lie to get out of any rap coming to them. Sickness rumbled in his gut as he realized Jillian was no different.

"You are?" She swung her feet to the side of the bed, hiding her face from him with her movement.

He wondered how far she would go to cover her tracks. "I called him today; this afternoon, in fact. And you know why I called him?" He stepped in front of her and forced her chin up so she couldn't hide from him. "Because I was worried about you. Funny thing is, Donald said he hadn't seen you since December."

"He's busy. He—he forgot." Her voice quavered.

Mason pulled the packet of birth control pills from his pocket. "Give it up, Jillian." He tossed it onto the bed.

Her eyes riveted to the packet, and for the first time she felt truly frightened.

"Jillian," Mason said in a tone of dead calm, "our marriage is over."

"No!"

"Then look at me and tell me you haven't been taking those pills. Tell me you were truly pregnant and lost our child," he demanded, his questions reinforcing the decision he'd already made.

Tears slipped down her cheeks. She held her hands to the sides of her face. "Oh, Mason. I'm so sorry."

"Sorry? How could you do such a thing?" he asked quietly. Mason walked away, entering their closet, a room larger than the childhood bedroom he had shared with his brother. He found an overnight bag and tossed it onto the bed.

"What are you doing?" she asked between sobs.

"Packing." He followed his statement with the action.

"You can't leave me. I'll die. I can't live by myself. I've never been alone. Please, Mason. I only did what I did because I love you."

Mason shook his head and continued to toss underwear into the suitcase. "No, Jillian, you don't know the meaning of love."

"I do. I do. I'll change. I'll make it up to you. Please don't leave me by myself."

"It's too late for apologies." He zipped the case shut. "What you did was unnatural and cruel. You say you love me, but you never once stopped to consider how I would feel."

She leaned forward, her hands outstretched. "Let me explain. I had a reason for everything I did."

He walked to the door, suitcase in hand. "Save your breath, Jillian. I've finally seen through you. For seven years we've wanted different things from this marriage, and that's not going to change with a few excuses. We're not right for each other, and we never have been." Turning away from her tear-streaked face, he left the room.

As he passed the family photos he had insisted be hung

in the upstairs hall after Jillian had banned them from the downstairs as unstylish, he heard her wailing, "Don't go, Mason. I can't live without you."

Jillian heard the far-off whirring of the garage door. How could Mason do that to her—drive off when he knew how upset she was? He hadn't even cared enough to ask what had forced her to such desperate inventions. It was all his fault. If he hadn't been drifting away from her, she never would have lied about being pregnant. Tonight he'd been so eager to leave, he must have someone else. He must have been planning this for a long, long time. But who was she?

Jillian beat the water bed with her fists. The bed swayed in response, mocking her frustrated hammering. Mason belonged to her. This house and her life, presiding over dinner for twelve, sitting at the end of a table, the crystal sparkling in candlelight—this was her life. What would she do if he left her? She shivered. Before Mason, her life had been controlled by her mother. Once Claudia found out Mason had left her, she would swoop in and rescue her, cart her off to Chicago and introduce her to suitable careers for divorcées.

Life without Mason was unthinkable. She'd rather die.

Despite her fury, the haze of the earlier sleeping pill lay over her mind, tempting her to fall asleep and forget the whole mess. Her head drooped as she thought of sleep. And sleeping pills. And death.

She pulled herself out of bed, forcing her feet to move across the nubby carpet. Their carpet. Their bedroom. Mason couldn't leave her. She had to think. She checked the time. A little after five P.M. Mason did care; he had rushed home early to check on her. There had to be a way to get him back. As she paced the carpet, the ideas gathered, then fell into place.

First, call someone else and establish the miscarriage story. Who?

Taylor. After all, she was her sister, and as a relative, she might be contacted.

Next, find some of her old-fashioned sleeping pills, not these new lightweight ones that meted out their reprieve a few hours at a time.

Then tell the maid to bring her hot milk in a few hours. And change her underwear. Black was too dramatic. White too virginal. She chose pale blue lace.

Her plans laid, she padded downstairs. Once she had a double vodka safe in her hand, she called Taylor at work.

When her phone rang, Taylor grabbed it, happy for an excuse to break off her frustrating discussion with the news director. Reggie was being extremely obstinate about her idea of profiling the young girls who ended up at the type of clinic she had visited last week. He didn't think Grady Hutchings would approve. "Drummond here."

She heard a weak hello in what sounded like an echo of Jillian's voice. "We, that is, Mason and I, have some bad news."

Hearing her sister's words phrased that way, her first thought was, at least nothing bad had happened to Mason. "What's wrong?"

"I suffered a miscarriage this morning."

She spoke so low, Taylor barely heard the words. Then their meaning hit her. "I'm so sorry, Jillian." She clasped a hand over her abdomen. "Is there anything I can do?"

"No. I know how busy you are. Don't worry. I'll be fine. I just wanted you to know."

"How's Mason taking this?" Taylor tortured herself by inquiring.

"He's very concerned about how I'm feeling. He said we'll just have to wait a few months more before starting our family."

"Of course." Taylor had asked. She deserved the pain slashing through her gut on hearing the answer. The miscarriage confirmed the pregnancy; the pregnancy confirmed Mason's choice. He had sex with Jillian after promising to leave her; or if the conception had taken place before Christmas Day, Mason had still lied to her about not having a "real marriage."

"I have to rest now." Jillian's voice sounded even fainter. She hung up.

"Bad news?" asked Reggie, all signs of the argument erased from his genial face.

"My sister lost the baby she was carrying."

"Terribly sorry." He rocked back on his heels. "Perhaps we should shelve our argument for another day."

"Thanks, Reggie."

So he had told Jillian they would try again in a few months. For the briefest moment she had wondered whether Mason would take this opportunity to separate from Jillian. But even now, with no baby, it seemed he didn't intend to, despite what he had said when he had rushed in with the pizza on Christmas Day. She was used to getting by alone; she had her baby, and she had her work. Catching Reggie's arm as he turned away, she said, "Never mind, let's finish the discussion now."

He raised his shaggy gray eyebrows. "If you say so."

"Exactly why would Grady Hutchings object to a timely story on birth control education?" She said the words, but her thoughts remained on her sister. As one expectant mother to another, she empathized with Jillian's loss, but she was surprised at how shaken Jillian seemed, considering Jillian had never had a kind word to say regarding either motherhood or babies. At their lunch last week, Jillian hadn't even discussed—either to confirm or deny—her pregnancy. It was out of character for her sister to call her with such personal news.

"When Hutchings took over, the word came down that he wanted us to establish and maintain a certain image. He likened it to Disney's reputation. A parent can know that his little darling won't see a blow job in a Disney movie, was how Sid put it to us." Reggie grinned. "Sid does have a way of expressing himself."

"So we're supposed to exercise self-censorship in accordance with his standards of morality?" Self-censorship; if she knew her sister, that's exactly what she would practice on her emotions. Jillian always shrugged everything off. Even the death of their father, when Jillian was a young teenager, hadn't seemed to touch her.

"Right."

"Don't you think that stinks?"

He shrugged. "I'm two years from retirement in a business that's been good to me, but could have been better. Hutchings pays more than any station in town. You can call it selling out if you like, but I don't have your looks or talent. I knew damn well, years ago, I wasn't anchor material."

"Reggie, I didn't mean to upset you." She liked the older man and thanked her stars daily that he acted as a buffer between Sid and the rest of the news staff. "I don't want to cause you any problems. But if Sid wants this to be television of, or for—or whatever he calls it—the people, we could do a lot for people—not just air all the news that's nice to know."

"Hutchings wants to preach, Sid wants to win ratings, you want to crusade, and I want to retire." Reggie smiled. "When you think of a way to do all four, call me. In the meantime, I hope your sister is okay." He ambled back to his office.

During the next several hours, in what few moments she had to let her thoughts stray, Taylor found herself dwelling on Mason, instead of on Jillian. The irony of her sister's loss—and Mason's—in contrast to her own pregnancy, weighed on her. He wanted a family so badly, and he could have had that, along with the rightness of belonging with her, the woman he had said he loved, if only he hadn't chosen as he had. She had to force a sparkle into her eyes and a smile onto her face when the floor manager counted down to the ten-o'clock news.

She looked up at the end of the news to see Sid bearing down on her. Just what she didn't need. Walking right to her, he thrust a pink message slip into her hand. He yanked on his abominable mustache and said, "I had the message held until after you finished, so if that's a problem, take it up with me."

Taylor read the contents. Jillian was in a Pasadena hospital, with the address and phone number supplied. She expected to see Mason's name under "Caller," but found Fielding Sanderson instead. The black psychologist at the birthday party. Where was Mason? Then she checked the time. The message had been taken at nine-thirty, half an hour before her newscast.

She pushed her chair back. "Why wasn't I given this earlier?"

Burke, still beside her, leaned over and openly read the note. "You were in Makeup then." He creased his forehead. "What's wrong with Jillian?" He sounded genuinely concerned, as if asking after a friend.

Taylor glared at Sid. "That's what I would have liked to have known an hour and a half ago."

"I didn't want you weeping on-camera. It would have ruined the show."

"You've got your nerve. Anyone could have filled in for me. You'd better hope she's all right." Taylor headed across the set, heedless of the yards of cables layered across the floor like tracks in a railroad siding yard.

"There's nobody like you, baby," Sid called after her.

Taylor kept moving. Had Jillian hemorrhaged? She had no idea of the complications that could come from a miscarriage. Even though her sister drove her crazy—like the scraping of nails down a blackboard—she was still her sister—her family. It wasn't her fault she had married the man Taylor loved.

Mason sighted the red and blue flashing lights as soon as he turned onto San Pasqual Street. Their brightness crowded out all other images, and drew him down the street, a macabre play on the light at the end of the tunnel. Spurred by the natural curiosity to explore the scene of a disaster, he accelerated, wondering which of his elderly neighbors had suffered a heart attack or some other nocturnal disaster.

He had returned for his briefcase. He had checked into a hotel before realizing he had left it behind in his stampede from Jillian. It contained a contract he had to review before the next morning. He had waited to retrieve it until he figured she'd be asleep, zonked out with one of her ever-present sleeping pills.

As the distance between him and the flashing lights narrowed, one fact registered, a bit at a time, until the whole message screamed in his brain. The red and blue lights originated from his driveway. His heart raced, as if he were jumping rope at the gym, twirling faster and faster, his blood keeping pace. He stamped on the accelerator, covered the remaining distance, then skidded to a halt.

Two men in white jackets were loading a stretcher into an ambulance.

For a moment, as he leapt from his car and raced to the men, his first thought was that Jillian had been telling him the truth. She had been pregnant; she had lost the baby; he had left her to bleed to death. Guilt, strong and sturdy as an Iowa cornstalk, pushed all rational thought from his mind.

"What's going on?" he called to the men. Someone gripped his elbow. Turning, he saw Fielding. "What's happened? What are you doing here?"

"Are you Mr. Reed?" asked one of the white-jacketed men.

Mason nodded.

"Your wife was found unconscious, a bottle of sleeping pills next to her side. We're leaving for the hospital. You can ride with us."

Mason nodded again. His neck had turned to Silly Putty, his mouth to a glue pot.

The attendant handed him an envelope. "We found this, too." Mason took it and climbed into the ambulance. He dimly heard Fielding calling that he would follow him. Jillian lay on the stretcher, her face white, her eyelids lowered. One attendant worked over her, but Mason's vision was glazed to the details. He turned the envelope over in his hand; his name, in Jillian's handwriting, staggered across its face. He had to think she had done this accidentally. He couldn't believe his leaving her had triggered this; that made him responsible, as if he had choked the pills down her throat and pressed her lips together until she swallowed them. But the envelope spoke otherwise.

Mason shuddered. Suicide was not the sort of thing he connected with himself or anyone close to him. Suicide was antithetical to every aspect of his being. "She was all right when I left the house. Upset, but definitely not suicidal."

"Why don't you open the envelope?" asked the attendant.

Mason started. He hadn't realized he'd spoken aloud.

With an unsteady hand, he reached for it. Smoothing out the single sheet, he read:

I can't live without you. I only did the things I did to keep us together. I know you're in love with someone else.

The scrawl wavered first downward, then corrected with a jerk, only to rise off the horizon of the lined yellow tablet. She had used one of his legal pads from his study to write the note.

He folded the note over and over, into smaller and smaller and smaller squares, the words she had cried as he had walked out echoing in his mind. *I can't live without you.* He had suspected she was unstable, and out of anger and disgust, he had snapped. Faced with the truth of her actions, he had had no space in his heart or mind to consider what effect his walking out on Jillian might have on her. When he couldn't reduce the square further, he sat, turning it over and over between his fingers, his eyes on her shuttered face.

At the hospital, after Jillian was wheeled inside, someone ushered him to the waiting room, where he filled out forms and took a seat as requested. Fielding appeared shortly. Mason roused himself to ask his friend how he had happened to be at their house.

"I called to see how Jillian was feeling. Your maid was quite hysterical. I couldn't understand a word she said, so I whipped over there. I told her I was a doctor and she let me in. It seems she had no idea where to find you."

Mason wondered whether the maid had mentioned him

leaving with a suitcase in tow. For the moment, he ignored the question in Fielding's voice.

Fielding stretched his legs. "Was Jillian more upset about losing the baby than she let on?"

Mason looked Fielding straight in the eye. "There wasn't any baby."

"Mason, I was in your office when she called."

"She made the whole thing up."

"You're sure of that?"

"Absolutely." Mason grimaced. "We had quite a scene." Rising, he paced the small floor space. He didn't want to talk about this, not with Fielding, not with anyone. If Jillian had tried to kill herself, she had done so because he said their marriage was over. Even though her own despicable deceit was her responsibility, guilt lay heavy on his own shoulders.

Fielding didn't press him. He sat, quietly, waiting with him. Along with a sniffling baby crying in the arms of a woman with pink foam rollers wound in her hair, along with a young man holding his arm and swearing, "I'll get the motherfucker who did this to me," along with an old man standing in a corner knocking his head against the wall, spittle crusting his beard—they waited. Finally someone called Mason's name and ushered him into the back.

He expected a doctor or nurse. Glenda, the young woman who held out her hand and led him past a large, U-shaped desk crowded by medical personnel, introduced herself as a social worker. In their walk, he glimpsed bleary-eyed men and women in long white coats, speaking rapidly into minicassette recorders, women on the phone, and two lab techs laughing together. But no sign of Jillian. He expected quiet; noise rammed him from all sides. Glenda steered him into a room the size of a coat closet and shut the door, sealing off the din. With her clipboard, she gestured toward an orange plastic chair. Mason sat. "How is my wife?"

"She's resting as comfortably as we can expect at the moment. The doctor has treated her, and she's being given intravenous hydration. I'm sorry you were kept waiting so long, but your wife asked that you not be allowed to see her."

"So she's conscious now?" At hearing she was going to be all right, relief overshadowed his surprise that she had asked for him to be kept out.

"Yes. You'll be able to speak to the doctor soon, but as the social worker on the case, I wanted to talk to you about Mrs. Reed, and about any questions you might have about treatment and intervention."

Mason looked at the earnest young woman. She meant well, but he didn't want someone holding his hand. He wanted to know if Jillian was going to be okay. "Is she going to live? Is she going to be hospitalized?"

"She's alive and actually doing very well. That's one of the reasons we need to talk. It seems your wife planned her dosage very carefully."

"How do you know that?"

"From the analysis of the ER physician and from the paramedics, who stated that your wife was found with a bottle of sleeping pills by her side. Only several of them were missing."

Mason felt sick. "You're suggesting she did this as a cry for help or attention?" He knew, instantly, that was true. Any woman who would fake a pregnancy and a miscarriage would risk harming herself by planning a dramatic overdose.

Glenda nodded.

He looked at his shoes.

"Your wife has asked to be transferred to an alcohol-and-drug-dependency treatment facility."

"Jillian?" That was totally out of character for her; other than agreeing to talk to Fielding, she had refused to see a therapist to discuss her fear of having a child. To ask for in-patient treatment was an even bigger step. But perhaps this little stunt had convinced her she needed help.

"I did suggest it, but she responded rather eagerly."

"What do we have to do to make arrangements for treatment?" If Jillian was willing to go, he'd see that she received the best help available. He meant what he said about their marriage being over, but he wasn't going to walk out on her when she was this desperately troubled.

"I've already called the facilities that will accept a patient who needs medical supervision. There is a place here in Pasadena that will take her tonight. It is the most expensive, but Mrs. Reed said that wouldn't be a problem."

He heard the request for confirmation in her voice. "No problem."

"I'll call them and finalize the arrangements." She made a note on her clipboard, then looked back at him. "When someone close to us goes into dependency treatment, this can stir up all sorts of emotions, especially when it follows a trauma like attempted suicide. If you want someone to talk to about this, I'll be happy to give you some names of good people."

He appreciated her efforts to help him. "Thanks, but that won't be necessary. My concern is getting my wife the treatment she needs."

"I understand that concern. Often, though, the situation is a family one, from problems arising within the relationship. Your wife told me she tried to kill herself because you were having an affair—"

"She said *what?*"

Glenda didn't flinch at his shout. "She told me—"

"Don't repeat it. Look, my wife needs help. Serious help that starts with learning to distinguish truth from falsehood." He crossed his arms. "I'd like to talk to her doctor now."

She studied his face, then nodded and left the room.

Mason stared at the wall, the color of limeade mixed with olive oil. He wasn't about to sit there passively waiting for the doctor. He wanted to see Jillian, both to confirm that she was going to be okay, and to shake some sense into her.

Smoothing his suit jacket, he opened the door and stepped into the bustle of men and women. No one gave him any notice. A large chalkboard on his left had room numbers with names next to them, but he didn't stop to figure out the system. Moving by purposefully, he glanced

at his watch, then turned left down the corridor. At the
first room, he peered in. No Jillian. Same thing at the next
doorway. A nurse looked up from checking a thermometer
and smiled. He nodded and passed on.

He found Jillian in the third room, in the end cubicle.
An IV bag draped from a pole, its clear tube snaking
down, across the white sheet, and worming its way into a
pulsing blue vein on her left arm. Her chest lifted and
dropped, lifted and dropped. She didn't open her eyes. A
plastic pan, shaped like a kidney bean, was propped close
to her shoulder. Shiny liquid glazed the bottom of the mustard yellow pan.

His beautiful, desirable wife.

Mason felt a strange tugging at the back of his throat.
He swallowed, to clear the blockage. The woman he had
lived with for seven years had disappeared, little by little,
and he had not noticed, had not seen her dissolving in
front of his eyes.

This body, drained of energy, the face washed free of its
delicate coloring, the blond hair mussed and ravaged by
the fretting movements of her head—this woman, he did
not know at all.

Perhaps he had never known Jillian.

Her lids flicked open, then shut. She whispered something, and he leaned forward to hear. "I didn't want you to
see me this way."

Now, that was the Jillian he knew. That's why she had
told the social worker to keep him out—her pride in her
appearance. He should have figured as much. "Oh, you
don't look so bad." He stepped to her side.

She raised several fingers off the sheet, then dropped
them back to the sheet. He took her hand and held the
clammy fingers. No matter what he had said to her earlier
that evening, she was still his wife. Seven years together
didn't simply evaporate in one evening. He cared what
happened to her, and seeing her like this, he ached for her.

"I'm sorry for what I did. For everything," she whispered.

He squeezed her hand.

"Do you forgive me?"

The lump in his chest hardened. Forgive her for lying about being pregnant and suffering a miscarriage, for preventing him from leaving her, for keeping him from Taylor? No, he couldn't say he forgave her. But he felt sorry for her. "Don't worry about that right now. Rest and get better."

She closed her eyes.

After a few minutes, he said, "Is it true you want to go for alcohol-dependency treatment?"

She tipped her chin downward.

He took that as a yes. He thought of her drinking and lying about it on New Year's Eve. He thought about her constant double vodkas and her passing into sleep sedated almost every night. He had been blind. Very blind.

"Mason?"

"Yes?"

"What you said about our marriage being over . . ." The pace of her breathing increased, and she squinted her eyes as if hit by pain.

He waited.

"You're not leaving me now, are you? I'm going to be so much better. After I get home, I promise I'll be like a new person." She closed her eyes. "What I wrote in my note . . . I meant that. I can't live without you."

He didn't think the great gulf between them could be bridged, whether Jillian never took another drink, whether she bore a child, whether she never lied to him ever again. Her actions had extinguished the small flame of whatever love he had left for her. Once it was snuffed out, nothing could relight it. He might be able to live with her, but his heart would be empty. But right now she was sick, and he had vowed to stand by her in sickness and in health. "I'll be at home when you get out."

A nurse carrying a clipboard entered. She reviewed the discharge instructions with Jillian. Glenda poked in, looked surprised to see Mason, but didn't chastise him. Two ambulance attendants followed her.

Mason walked beside Jillian as they wheeled her out of the room.

"Don't come with me," said Jillian. "I want to do this on my own."

He squeezed her hand again and then she was gone, through the wide doors and into her second ambulance of the evening.

Before he could escape the vocal swarm of the emergency room, a doctor with a heavy five-o'clock shadow approached him and rattled off a medical diagnosis, which Mason tried to absorb. It was lucky for her, concluded the doctor, that her maid found her when she did.

Fielding wasn't in the waiting room.

Taylor was, looking exactly like she had just stepped from behind the camera, except for the little girl she held on her lap. She was reading to her from a tattered copy of *Where the Wild Things Are,* her long hair falling forward over her shoulders, hiding from his view the smile that he knew would be curving on her lips.

He couldn't bear to see her now—not knowing that he had pledged to be there for Jillian to help her recover. He could only do that as long as Taylor didn't exist for him. She had made it easier, in a way, by kicking him out of her life. But right now he wished he could trade places with that little girl. He'd give almost anything to be held in Taylor's arms again.

She looked up and saw him. Turning to the woman sitting beside her, she said something, and settled the little girl on the woman's lap. The woman smiled her thanks, and Taylor rushed to where Mason remained standing.

"What happened? How's Jillian? Can I see her now?"

He looked at her, saw and heard her concern, and wanted to offer comfort. He thought of touching her, but knew he could not. "She's going to be okay."

"Thank God. Fielding Sanderson called, but I wasn't given the message until after the newscast, which is why I got here so late. By the way, he said he'd be outside walking around. He seemed very concerned about Jillian, but he said I should ask you about what happened to her."

She looked at her feet, then bit her lip. In a low voice, she said, "I was sorry to hear about the baby."

"Baby?"

"Jillian's miscarriage. She called me earlier today and told me she had lost the baby."

"She did?"

She raised her eyebrows. "I *am* her sister."

"You don't understand." He took her elbow. "Let's go outside."

"I want to see Jillian."

Mason sighed. "She's been transferred. Come on. I'll explain everything outside." Eyes wide, she went with him through the double doors, past the harshly lit hallway, out to the fresh nighttime air. He gulped in several breaths and loosened his tie. Looking around, he found a bench by a bus stop, and they sat down. He couldn't think of his own emotional needs right now. A streetlamp cast Taylor's face partially into shadow. He thought of her, holding the child in the waiting room. She was so giving, so loving; why couldn't he be the one to receive that love?

"Mason?"

"Forgive me." Taylor was Jillian's sister and had a right to know. If Taylor were a client, he'd know how to handle the situation. "Your sister tried to—"

He heard Taylor's quick inrush of breath.

"Tried to—" Then the impact of the whole situation hit him at once. He heard the sob in his voice as he finished with "Kill herself."

"My God. I don't believe it." Taylor opened her arms, and Mason slid into her embrace. It was for her own comfort as much as his.

"It's not something that's easy to believe." He rubbed his cheek against her hair. "I'm sorry to tell you like this—just blurting it out."

"She must have been very upset about the baby." Holding him, rocking him against her, next to the life growing within her, she understood how such a loss could unhinge.

Mason righted himself, seemed to realize where he was, and shifted from her hold. "There was no baby. She knew how much I wanted a child, so she pretended—made the whole thing up—then to get out of it, called me at work this morning and said she'd had a miscarriage." He spoke like a man recording into a tape machine. Slowly. Precisely. Not at all as if he believed his own words.

Taylor sat very still. She couldn't imagine any woman doing such a thing. "How do you know there's no baby?"

Mason uttered a strangled laugh. "Let's just say any DA would take a case with this much circumstantial evidence."

"So you found out, confronted her, and she tried to kill herself?"

"Right." He rubbed his eyes. "To be precise, I found her stash of birth control pills, told her our marriage was over, and stormed out. Then she overdosed on sleeping pills, probably washing them down with vodka. God, I can't even believe this myself."

Taylor wasn't sure she had heard him correctly. *Told her our marriage was over* resounded in her brain. No baby, no marriage; Mason was free. Correction; he had been free, up until Jillian tried to kill herself. Knowing Mason, she knew he wouldn't walk out on her now. "If you'd left the house, how did you find out about the overdose?"

"I went back to collect my briefcase and found the ambulance in the driveway."

Taylor shivered. "How awful."

"The entire situation is awful. My life is so screwed up." Mason groaned, then smiled apologetically. "Sorry. Self-pity is quite out of place."

"It's Jillian we have to think of right now. You said she'd been transferred. Where?"

"By ambulance to a drug and alcohol treatment center."

"Oh." Taylor clasped her hands between her knees. The chill of the night and Mason's news had started them shaking.

"She chose to do that. In case you're wondering, I did not have her incarcerated or anything medieval like that."

"How long will she be there?"

"I have no idea. She wanted to go alone." Turning to

her, he studied her. He seemed to be absorbing her into his memory. "This isn't the time or place to talk about what happened between us, but I want you to know, again, how sorry I am for everything."

"Mason—"

"No, please don't interrupt. I'm not going to burden you with any declarations of love. But there are two things I need to tell you, and one question I need to ask. First, Jillian left a note in which she said she knew I was in love with someone else."

"Are you saying she knows about me?"

"I'm positive she doesn't. I'm not even sure she knew what she was saying at the time. The handwriting is so loopy, she must have been almost out when she wrote it."

"You think she took a shot in the dark, based on the assumption that you wouldn't be leaving her if there wasn't someone else?"

"Yes."

She transferred her hands from her knees to the warm pockets of her armpits. "And the second?"

"I told Jillian I'd be there for her, at home, whenever she came out of the clinic. It's the least I can do." He stared across the street, as if the employee parking lot of the hospital held images of great interest.

"I understand." The worst part was—she did understand. Taylor would have hated him taking the opportunity of Jillian's absence to come on to her. He had chosen Jillian, and his duty lay with her. She agreed with that, but she still felt lost, alone, and empty. Despite her hurt at what he had done, she realized she'd been wishing for some miracle to bring him back to her, some miracle to let him share in the secret she carried within her.

"About the question." He shifted. "I hate even to ask this, but I haven't seen you since Christmas Day, and I need to know. Did we . . . I mean . . . are you pregnant?"

His question caught her off guard. How could she tell him now, with Jillian in the state she was, and knowing that he had promised to be there for his wife when she came home? "I—I got my period." She said the words in a rush, in a hurry to stumble over the half-truth. She couldn't bring herself to say the words *I am not pregnant*. That seemed a jinx that might swing back to haunt her.

"I guess that's good, considering the circumstances. I've wondered, but I decided that if you had any news in the opposite direction, you would have called. No matter what."

No matter what. No matter you made love to your wife when you were supposed to be leaving her for me. Her hurt, suppressed by her concern for Jillian, welled up again. "Right," she said.

"Under the circumstances, I don't think we . . ." Mason trailed off.

She didn't want him to say it. "No. The deal's off."

"I'm sorry I won't be the father," he said quietly.

Taylor felt the chill winter's night surround her as she stared straight ahead.

Chapter 17

SID DIDN'T BELIEVE IN FATE. HE DIDN'T BE-
lieve in God. He didn't believe in Good winning over Evil.
He believed the universe ran on the principle that people
were willing to do whatever it took to get whatever it was
they wanted. He called it the Crown-Me-King, Fuck-You
principle.

His many years in the news business had served to so-
lidify his belief in this precept. Burke Washington, who
had exited Sid's office only moments earlier on what had
been, until his visit, a fine April morning, had once again
proved the rule.

"Sid," Burke had said in a casual voice upon entering
his office, "Sid, I have something on my mind."

"Sit down and unload."

Burke sat, somewhat more delicately than Sid cared for.
He liked a man to fucking act like man. Not that he
doubted Burke's manhood; he'd heard too many complaints about Burke's roaming hands. Then Sid realized
why the careful settling in, the attentive verification of the
crease in his trousers, the downcast direction of Burke's
baby blues: Burke had some shit to pass on and didn't
want any of the odor blowing back in his face.

"Get you a drink?" he asked, without bothering to
move.

Burke waved off the offer. "I want you to know that I
like working with Taylor. At first, I was concerned. She
didn't exactly fit the image of what I expected in my co-
anchor. But we've grown into a certain workable pattern
over the last several months."

"You got a problem or are you writing a letter of reference?" Their ten-o'clock news ratings had never been better, and Sid knew Burke chafed at Taylor getting the credit for that increase.

Burke looked insulted, and took a moment to pat his hair. "I've noticed Taylor's condition, and I wonder what plans you have to replace her." Burke glanced at Sid to see the effect of his statement.

"Condition." Sid didn't make it a question; he knew better than to be caught off guard.

Burke widened his eyes. "I'd say she's around four months pregnant, and after three children of my own, I've learned to estimate these things pretty closely. Surely you've discussed this with her," he said, his voice oozing with concern.

Burke's words hit Sid like brass knuckles, but the expression on his face never changed. "Hey, what kind of GM do you think I am?" he asked brusquely, as he jumped up, rounded the desk, and ushered Burke toward the door. "Of course we've worked out the matter. If you're concerned about who her replacement will be, don't give it another thought. I've got that well under control."

Burke paused at the door and withdrew a slip of paper from his breast pocket. "I'd appreciate it if you'd give this person a long look. She's a special friend of mine." Then he winked and left, whistling.

Sid slammed the door after him, then retreated to his desk to think.

Crown-Me-King, Fuck-You. Burke, in exchange for his information, wanted his friend hired. That much was clear. He toyed with the right side of his mustache, tapping the bristly hairs with the tip of his tongue. A sudden onslaught of pain attacked his gut, and he clutched his side. Why the fuck couldn't the woman have waited a few more months to get knocked up? He reached into his desk for the pain pills that were the only friend he had left. He couldn't afford to lose Taylor. Not now.

* * *

"I don't bring just anybody here," said Fielding to Mason, pushing open the door to The Huntsman, a bar far off Mason's usual pathways.

Giving his eyes a minute to adjust to the sudden darkness, Mason searched for sources of light in the cave of a room. One by one, he made them out—the glow from the television, harsh green and red neon beer signs, flickering candles stuck in bowls of orange, netted glass, the back-lighting set to flatter the liquor bottles across the back of the bar. Three men sat at the bar; several others lounged around a table across the room.

"Oh, yeah," Fielding added, "better buy a Bud for the big guy in the corner."

Mason nodded and followed Fielding to a seat at the end of the bar under the television.

Fielding called to the bartender, "Orville, my man."

The bartender, a giant black man, made his way over, pausing to pour two drafts on his way. He shoved them across the bar to two other men just walking in.

"Orville," said Fielding, placing a hand on Mason's forearm, "I want you to meet the man here. Name of Mason, but don't hold that against him. His mama—she didn't know no better."

"Hi," said Mason, wondering if Fielding realized he had swung into street lingo.

Orville merely inclined his chin and rubbed the bar with a damp towel.

"My regular, and the man will have . . ."

"A Bud," said Mason. "And one for the guy in the corner." Though he didn't know which guy in which corner Fielding meant.

Orville showed a few teeth then, as if he found Mason's request amusing. Without comment, he served their drinks, then lumbered to the group at the far side of the room, a draft beer almost hidden in his hand.

"So," said Fielding, "you wanted to talk."

Instead of answering, Mason tasted his beer. Even with Fielding, who had been down the alcohol trail, he found it difficult to discuss his feelings over Jillian's treatment and impending return home.

Fielding pointed to the television above their heads. "I sat under here so the pictures wouldn't distract us, and the background noise will keep whatever you say just between the two of us."

He nodded, appreciative of Fielding's attempt to put him at ease. Above his head, he heard the sounds of a make-believe man coming home from work at a shoe store and being greeted by his make-believe wife with a litany of her all-too-real complaints. They should know *his* problems. "Jillian's being released from the treatment center tomorrow."

Fielding scratched his chin. "And you don't know how to handle that."

"No." He pointed to his glass of beer. "What do I do about this? Am I supposed to go home tonight and empty the liquor cabinet? Turn down invitations to parties? What do I say to her—hello, dear, how were your two months in the dry-out tank?"

Fielding chugged a mouthful of mineral water. "What do you feel like saying to her?"

"I don't know what to say."

"I asked what do you *feel* like saying?"

"I'm happy that she has been receiving the help she needed. But I'm angry at her for having put it off for so long. I find myself thinking that if she had turned around sooner, our marriage wouldn't have reached the stage it has." He took a sip of Bud. The noises of the television and the rumble of male voices receded as his concerns took center stage. "Then I feel guilty for thinking that. She's the one who's been suffering and unhappy, and I was absolutely blind to her problem. I kept pushing her to start a family. No wonder she always said no. She knew she shouldn't get pregnant if she couldn't stop drinking."

"You blame yourself for not paying enough attention to her?"

"Yeah. But she never seemed like an alcoholic."

"Only bums on the street swilling Thunderbird out of paper sacks are alkies, right?"

Mason nodded. "Intellectually I know differently, but not in my gut."

Fielding knew what Mason meant. For years he hadn't identified his own problem for much the same reason. However, Jillian's situation was more complicated. "I think it's possible Jillian isn't an alcoholic in the true sense of the word. I think she drinks to cover up feelings, but I believe that doesn't necessarily mean she's an alcoholic. Though, mind you, some people would disagree with me on that statement. The problem is, when you concentrate on the alcohol, the other more fundamental problem can get lost."

Mason was looking at him strangely. "She's in a drug and alcohol treatment center. She tried to kill herself with pills and vodka. What do you mean she's not an alcoholic?"

Fielding hitched his leg up on the barstool. He never should have started a train of thought he wasn't prepared to finish. "I think the root of her unhappiness is something other than alcoholism."

"What's that supposed to mean?"

"Why do you think she's so unhappy?"

Mason looked away and didn't answer.

"I'm only suggesting that not drinking won't solve whatever is bothering her," Fielding said carefully.

"So don't expect miracles tomorrow?"

"No miracles." He wished he could have come right out and explained about her compulsive sexual behavior. But the Sexaholics Anonymous guidebook he had acquired stated that sometimes the worst thing for a relationship was telling the spouse all about the secret life before coming to grips with healing. It was up to Jillian to decide what Mason should know; it wasn't his place to interfere. And if he did, would Mason simply "kill the messenger"? Or would he only hear that he, Fielding, a black man, had wanted his wife and must be making up the rest to cover for himself?

"How long have you been . . ." Mason stopped, looking embarrassed.

"A drunk?"

"Not drinking."

"I've been sober eight years."

"It doesn't bother you to watch other people drink, to come to bars?"

"It bothered me a lot at first. I thought my life was over. But after a while I realized I was just starting to live." He laughed. "That sounds corny as hell, but it's true."

"Do you mind me asking why and when you started to drink?"

"Not if it will help you understand. I grew up with my grandmother, one of those Baptists whose lips never touched liquor. No drugs, no drinking, no dancing. I got to college, and wow—I had to sample everything. And I liked it all. The rituals, the sociability, the blinding release of falling stinking drunk to the floor. For years I liked it, then one day I realized I no longer liked myself."

"What triggered that?"

"Keshia left me, my practice fell off, my friends drifted away—except for my drinking buddies. I was nursing a bourbon at the time, probably my fifth of the evening, when a light bulb went off in my head. I threw the drink down the sink, poured everything else I owned after it, and smashed the bottles in the trash can."

"That must have been difficult."

"Nah. That was the easy part; every drunk loves a melodrama. The hard part was the next day and the next night and the day after that."

"So you just did it on your own."

He grimaced. "Yeah, kind of like a surgeon taking out his own liver. I don't recommend it, but I was too goddamned stubborn to admit I needed help from anyone else." He didn't want to talk about himself anymore. Remembering his own path, dredging up the emotions, reliving the turning point to sobriety—these feelings, he wanted to leave neatly in place. He knew he should read that urge as a warning sign. He ought to get those feelings out and exorcise them, look at what he was hiding from himself. But he kept postponing that housecleaning. "By the way, did you go to any counseling sessions at Jillian's treatment center?"

Mason fiddled with his cocktail napkin. "I made two appointments, but both times something came up at the office and I had to cancel."

Fielding chewed on the ice cube. Classic denial. "I'll offer one suggestion, as a friend, for dealing with Jillian, and please don't brush it off without thinking it over."

"What's that?"

"Tell her the truth."

Heading to the station from Dr. Richmond's office, Taylor thought of the summer months stretching ahead of her, and of her belly, beginning to stretch beyond the limits of secrecy. Soon she had to talk to Sid and work out a deal for eight weeks off. She wanted more, but knew asking for longer would be tantamount to asking for her walking papers. She also wanted to discuss with him having the director shoot the newscast in such a way as to keep her pregnancy undetected for as long as possible. Preferably through gestation. She didn't expect any backlash from viewers in Los Angeles, but she wanted to avoid offense—and keep her job.

She swung off Sunset, to the side street that led to the station's parking lot. Hanging around the guard kiosk at the gate were several reporters, minicams in tow. What story were they after? Something to do with Grady Hutchings? She had skipped the newspapers and trade publications she normally scanned every morning in order to read a book on child development, so she had no idea if some story regarding their station had broken.

Then a chilling thought occurred to her. What if Hutchings had sold the station? That would send reporters sniffing around. The staff was often the last to know of such media deals. Anxious to get inside, she sped into the lot. Instead of opening the gate as soon as he spotted her, the guard left the gate arm down and leaned out of his kiosk. It was Dallas, a young wanna-be actor who specialized in soap opera auditions and macho.

Taylor lowered her window.

He winked. "Afternoon," he said, turning his chin so she could catch his profile.

"Hello, Dallas. What's happening?"

"Why don't you tell me?" He winked again, then waved his arm to someone Taylor couldn't see.

Two of the reporters had their mikes shoved into the car window before Taylor could react.

"Ms. Drummond, is it true you bought the outfit you're wearing at MothersWork?"

"Ms. Drummond, do you have any comment to the story in *The Reporter* this morning?"

"Ms. Drummond, do you have anything to say about Keith Carlyle's call for your resignation?"

Taylor's heart slammed into her chest. Control. She had to stay in control. Keeping her face pleasantly neutral, she pushed their microphones and eager faces from her window. "I have no comment at this time." To Dallas, she said, "Open the gate. Now."

He did so, smirking. Taylor pulled into her parking spot and realized she was shaking. Those men were only doing their job, the same job she had done hundreds of times. Shoving a microphone and a camera into someone's private life, heedless of how many wounds they inflicted in the process. She shivered; it sure felt different on the other end of the stick.

How had they found out about her baby? Looking at her spreading waistline and the flowing suit and jacket, a style she had started wearing as soon as she knew she was pregnant to hide the evolution of her figure, she wondered who had guessed and who had told. So much for keeping her baby her own quiet secret. She had no time for regrets; she had to find the article in the trades and tackle Sid before he ambushed her. Grabbing her briefcase, Taylor moved rapidly into the building.

She didn't have to search for the article. Burke had

taped it to her terminal, with a smiley face squiggled above his signature. She read:

> Sources in the know report that anchor Taylor Drummond, Channel Six, KANG, will give birth independent of husband or fiancé. Some say this miraculous conception is expected to ignite viewers concerned over the example set by men and women on the tube.

Taylor ground her teeth. She hated having her personal life trotted out for others to gawk at. But no one had promised her easy or fair. She realized the usual hum and clatter had wound down. Looking up, she saw everyone else had stopped working to watch her. Wadding the clipping into a ball, she tossed it onto the desk. To the room in general, she said, "The print media. What do they know?" Then she walked out, in search of Sid and an answer to one question: Did she still have a job?

Sid, as usual, had his feet propped on his desk. He was playing idly with the remote, flicking from channel to channel. Without bothering to look her way, he called for her to enter and sit. Then he continued fiddling with the hand control and sighing to himself.

Taylor cleared her throat. If she were more sure what to say, she would have forged ahead. She wasn't simply on unknown turf; she was on quicksand. Sid could go any which way on this, but only he knew. She didn't think he would come right out and fire her for being pregnant, but getting rid of an anchor was relatively simple. Almost any excuse about viewer perception or image of the broadcast would legitimize him. Just ask Christine Craft.

Tossing down the remote, he swiveled his head around, blew his nose, and said, "Can I get you a glass of milk, Mommy?"

She flinched at the sarcasm and waited for his next salvo.

"Now, the first thing I want to say is how sorry I am, how much it hurts me right here—" he thumped his scrawny chest "—that you didn't confide in me in the first place. To have to read some rumor in the trades and then have to ask you if it's true—now, that hurts."

"I can explain—"

"So it is true." He dropped his feet to the floor with a thunk.

"Yes," Taylor said, steeling herself. "I have no idea how it leaked to the press, but yes, I am going to have a baby."

"Mazel tov." He blew his nose again and wiped his forehead with the handkerchief.

"You're pleased?" she asked, a little incredulous.

"You better believe I am, babe. This baby is the best thing that's happened to me this week. This month. This motherfucking year."

Taylor stared at him, confused, as a giddy sense of relief began to spread through her. "Are you being straight with me?"

"When have I ever not been level? Now, when is the bun coming out of the oven?" Sid leaned forward on his desk.

For the sake of tact, she ignored the first question. "Do you mean when is the baby due?"

He nodded impatiently.

"September," Taylor said in her most businesslike tone. "I'll only need a minimum of time off-air, around eight weeks. I'll be back by November sweeps." Taylor shifted in her chair; he was taking this far too well, which made her nervous.

"I'm not worried about November. I'm thinking of now." He jabbed his finger at her. "April, roaring into May sweeps. The present." Sid was positively beaming.

"It's my intention to deny those rumors and ignore the publicity. I'm not showing, and with careful camera work, no one need know about my pregnancy," Taylor said decisively.

"No one need know?" Sid slapped his forehead. "Ignore the publicity? What are you talking about? This is the best thing for ratings you could have done. Controversy is like wet pussy to a station manager." He leaned back in his chair, looking smug.

She really wished he wouldn't be so crass, especially when it was her life he was planning to ruin. "Forget it, Sid. You are not turning my pregnancy into a three-ring circus." Taylor thought of her shaking hands after the two reporters confronted her in the driveway.

"Then you're fired." Sid put his feet back on the desk and reached for the remote.

Taylor felt shocked, although she knew she shouldn't be.

"You're firing me for being pregnant?" she asked carefully.

He flicked the remote so that the bank of monitors displayed identical commercials for incontinence pads. "Would you look at that shit? Leave a man some pride." To Taylor he said, "No, I am not firing you for being pregnant, single, and/or female. Your popularity with the viewing audience has lessened drastically, and you are free to earn out your salary as a reporter on the midnight-to-twelve-thirty-P.M. shift." He turned back to his wall of video.

Taylor knew he could get away with that; it had happened to other anchors who failed to please. With only herself to consider, she would have walked out of the room. But she had to think about the baby. As a single parent, she had to provide for both of them. She had quite a bit of money saved, but if she walked out the door now, she could be out of work for months. Who would hire her with a baby due in September? Once she was off the air, finding another spot could be difficult. She didn't want to go back to law; she and television belonged together. Having this baby meant staying and listening to Sid.

She stared at him as he made a show of watching the monitors. Finally she asked, "What do you want me to do?"

"Just be yourself. Talk to reporters. Mention the kid on-air. Do a few stories on unwed mothers." He turned back to her with a grin. "Go into labor on the ten-o'clock news. A few simple things, that's all I ask."

A few simple things to wreck her life. A few simple references to the baby's due date, and she'd have Mason pounding on her front door. "I don't think—"

"Stop." Sid held up his hand. "Before you say no, ask yourself why I care. Ask yourself why I want you to do these things."

She had figured the hype went along with his scummy personality. "Okay, Sid. Why? Why are you asking me to smear the details of my private life across the screen?"

Hooking his hands over his belt, he said, "The way I figure it, Hutch will fire you the minute he finds out you're pregnant without benefit of clergy."

Taylor knew his pause was designed to let that sink in. Considering Grady Hutchings had hinted he'd be a happier man if she were a married woman, and thus projecting his sort of image, Sid was right. "Go on," she said.

"But he happens to like you. And the viewers like you. The way I see it, Hutch didn't get as rich as he is letting his personal opinions get in the way of the bottom line. So as long as your big belly makes our ratings go up, you've got a job."

"Why do you think advertising my 'condition' will improve our ratings?"

He stared at her. "Are you kidding? This plan works from all angles. It makes you more approachable, without the polyester-dress angle; men and women both love a mother. Wait till you pop out in front. People will be stopping you on the street to ask how junior's coming along. From the other side, if we upset a few people, we get a few protestors claiming you're a bad influence—bam, that's publicity and we have to cover it, and the rest of the media will, too. People will switch stations to see for themselves."

If Sid was right about all those faceless people changing channels, they would be doing so to gawk at her and her unborn baby. On-air, she would feel naked, as if everyone in the Los Angeles basin could tell her bra size. "And what do you get out of all this?"

"What do I get?" He jumped up and paced around his desk. "You know, I think I'm gonna tell you the truth. The honest-to-God truth." He tugged on the mustache and turned to face her. "I didn't like you at first. I guess you knew that. You were all wrong for what I had in mind."

Taylor nodded.

"But you kind of grew on me. Well, at least you did when the ratings started creeping up and we started getting those phone calls and letters about how intelligent you were. So I'm gonna tell you the truth about why I want you to do this for me."

Taylor wasn't sure Sid knew what "truth" meant. She let him ramble on, though, because it gave her time to think about alternatives. Although she had rejected the idea at first, she could force herself to go back to law. She'd brush up, take the necessary continuing legal education courses. She wouldn't walk back in as partner material, but she could survive. She wanted more than survival, though; she wanted to love going to work.

"I'm forty-nine years old. I went to the doctor a year ago, not feeling too well, and you know what he fucking told me? Told me I was gonna die, and soon, too."

She jerked her attention back to Sid.

"Now he tells me I've got six months, give or take. I look at this face in the mirror, and I don't think it's true, but the rest of me says it is. If Hutch swoops in and fires your butt, he'll fire me, too, and I don't intend to spend my last days lying around my house like a rotting cucumber." He slammed his fist on his desk. "You know what I want? I want to be number one worse than I want one more good fuck before they crate me up and trundle me off to Mt. Sinai Mortuary."

Taylor sat very still. Looking at his drawn face, seeing clearly for the first time how his clothes bunched around his wasting frame, and watching his Adam's apple contort as he swallowed hard, she knew he was telling the truth. No wonder he was so cantankerous. "I'm so sorry," she said, hating the inadequacy of the words.

He blew his nose and tossed the silk square into the trash can. "Don't give me any fucking sympathy. Just tell me you'll do what I ask."

"What—what's wrong with you? Have you had a second opinion?"

He glared at her. "I told you, no sympathy." Resuming he seat, he said, "Leukemia."

The wonder in his voice, the deathly still way he held himself when he said the word, the puzzled frown on his face—these confirmed him yet again. Taylor laid a hand across her abdomen. Death. She had too much to live for to begin to comprehend what fears and regrets Sid, given the sentence meted out to him, must be grappling with.

"You don't want sympathy, so I'll hold my tongue. And I'll do what you want, on one condition. No questions or speculations as to the father. And I also want to know who fed the story to the press. Who knew I was pregnant?"

He smiled the smile of a child treated to two Fudgsicles when his brother was given only one. "It must be your lucky day, 'cause I'm gonna tell you the truth twice. Burke told me you were in the family way, and I fed the story to a reporter pal."

"Burke?"

"The man's married to a brood mare. What do you expect? He knows a bun in the oven when he sees one." He rubbed his hands together. "I'll have my secretary set up a few interviews. I'll want you on *Geraldo* and maybe one of those other yakkity-yak shows. Make sure every time you open your mouth, you mention Channel Six. We're in luck, because I happen to know Hutch took Laurel Ann on a month's cruise to the Galápagos Islands."

She nodded, feeling she'd just made a deal with the devil. Her baby would have a working mother with plenty of money to hire a live-in nanny and purchase Baby Guess dresses. And she would have absolutely no peace for the next five months. She rose, then looked at Sid. He had slipped back in his chair. His eyes were closed. As he sat there, so silent and alone, dying, the picture he made tugged at her heart. Before shutting the door behind her, she paused, wondering whether she should make sure he was okay.

Sid opened his eyes, then winked at her. "So who's the daddy, babe?"

Tell her the truth, Fielding had said. Mason looked at Jillian, reading next to him in bed. The television set played, its low volume helping to soak up the silence between the two of them. In the three days she had been home, they had treated each other like seat-mates on an airplane. Please and thank you and excuse me while I climb over you to go to the lavatory. What book are you reading? Are you going to watch the movie? The question they didn't ask—what's your destination?—lay heavily between them.

Jillian lowered her book. "What are you reading?"

He started, thinking she had read his mind. *"The Rise and Fall of the Great Powers."*

"Boring."

"You?"

She shut her book. *"ODAT.* Again. God, talk about boring."

The *Alcoholics Anonymous One Day at a Time* book. "Then why do you read it?"

"It's supposed to make me a better person." She pushed her pillow higher against the headboard. A beer commercial flashed onto the screen. She hit the remote, silencing the mellow voices assuring them the night belonged to Michelob. Glaring at the screen, she switched the volume back on.

"They're everywhere, aren't they?" Mason asked, feeling sympathetic.

"What?"

"The messages, the invitations, the enticements." The last drink he had taken was the Bud at The Huntsman with Fielding. His own abstinence, unintentional though it was, made him more aware.

Rolling onto her side, Jillian shrugged against the bed. The strap of her nightgown drifted downward, exposing the curves of her breasts. "Drink, drink, drink and you'll be happy, happy, happy."

He closed his book. Perhaps the time had come when they could talk about her experience. "Did you feel you did the right thing—going for treatment?"

She rolled her eyes. "I was certainly happier drinking. I feel like—like a loaf of French bread left on the counter for a week. Stiff, creaky." Smoothing her silk gown over her waist, she added, "At least I lost a few pounds."

"You didn't need to lose any weight."

"That's easy for you to say." She flipped onto her back. "I thought everything would be different. Pow, like magic, my life would be fixed. The only thing that's different is now, instead of seeing life in a nice fuzzy blend of shadows and colors, I have to see the harsh black-and-white edges of everything."

He didn't know what to say to that. He didn't want to seem unsympathetic, but life definitely had its harsh moments; most people learned to cope with that fact as part of growing up.

She turned to him. "Mason?"

Her face, thinned along with the rest of her body, looked like a child's. Her wide eyes overwhelmed her face. They glimmered suspiciously, as if she were repressing tears. "Yes?"

"Thank you for being here for me." She touched his chest with a tentative hand.

He rolled over and took her into his arms, carefully. She was fragile, she was a land mine, she was a wounded child, she was a vengeful woman. Cautiously he let her close the inches between them, fitting herself against him until her gown slithered both up and down to her waist, as she spread her legs and gathered him to her.

He moved in slow motion, regarding himself from a distance. He wasn't making love to Jillian as much as he was saying good-bye to her. His body responded—which he couldn't condemn himself for after the long weeks of abstinence—but his spirit hovered somewhere between the water bed and the television. At one point, as, eyes closed, he moved inside Jillian, he imagined he was on television, looking out of the screen, watching this couple on the bed.

When they finished, Jillian rolled onto her stomach, her hair covering her face. He stroked her back, his hand moving over the knobs of each protruding vertebra, wondering if she felt as empty as he did.

As soon as she was well enough, as soon as he thought she could handle the reality, he was leaving. Not for Taylor, but for himself. And for Jillian.

Mason slipped from the bed and went to wash up in the bathroom. Over the sound of the running water, he heard Jillian exclaim and call his name.

"What is it?" he asked, poking his head out of the bathroom.

"Taylor's on the news."

He didn't want to think about Taylor. Not now. "She's usually on the news." He turned back into the bathroom.

"No, Mason. She's one of the news stories."

At that he came out, a towel wrapped around his waist. They had just had sex, but feeling distant and saddened by the event, he wanted to cover himself from her.

On the screen flashed an inset picture of Taylor, followed by a reporter standing outside Channel Six's building. "Word that unmarried anchorwoman Taylor Drummond is expecting a child has raised a flurry of protests from local church and community leaders. Keith Carlyle, of the public interest group TV-TV, is calling for her resignation, claiming that she is setting a bad example for young women in the community."

Mason stared at the screen, one hand gripping the towel around his waist, the other wrapped around his forgotten toothbrush. She had said she wasn't pregnant. She told him so. If this story was true . . .

"Ms. Drummond's only comment to her fellow reporters was, 'No comment.' "

Jillian had stopped in the act of putting her nightgown back on to watch the news report. "Can you believe she went ahead with that crazy plan?"

"What plan?" There had been no plan; there had been

only the two of them, joined at last, loving each other. If that love had created a child, and Taylor had hidden that from him . . .

Jillian was looking at him oddly. "The artificial insemination one. The one she got so upset with me for talking about at your birthday party. Are you all right?" She drew her gown over her head.

"Just surprised," Mason said hastily. Of course. Jillian was right. Taylor had gone immediately to a sperm bank and simply hadn't discussed it with him that night at the hospital. Under the circumstances, she had withheld the information appropriately enough. She had gone ahead with her plan, without Mason, which is how she had intended to do it all along, before he'd come along and screwed things up. By loving her. Jealousy of the unknown man who had fathered her child raged through him. Feigning a calmness he didn't feel, he asked, "Why the protesters?"

"They seem to think she's setting a bad example." Jillian giggled. "They probably think she got knocked up by a married man."

He flinched, thankful Jillian faced the television and not him. "So there's no mention of the artificial insemination on the news?"

"No. But what else could it be? Taylor's not exactly a man-slayer."

It wasn't the moment to tell Jillian he thought precisely the opposite. "I'm not sure I understand the protest, though. What she does is her own business." He said it out loud, trying to convince himself of that fact. But he felt so left out of her life.

"She's got an image to maintain. And frankly, even as her sister, I find this whole thing strange."

Mason resisted the retort that fought to leap from his lips: *You think any woman who wants a baby is strange.* Instead, he said, "Strange isn't reason enough to call for someone's resignation."

"People get upset when you don't do what's expected. Taylor's going against the rules of society, just like always, and she'll have to pay the price." Jillian yawned and said, "You're welcome to stay up worrying about my weird sister, but I'm going to sleep."

He did stay awake, for hours, studying a calendar and sipping Courvoisier in the den. This was mid-April; she couldn't be very far along. She herself had said there was no guarantee artificial insemination would take the first couple of tries. Finally, his head hazy from the cognac and muddled from his sense that his life was very much adrift, he fell asleep on the couch; his last waking thought was a memo to himself to figure out her due date. Just in case.

Chapter 18

MASON SPOTTED THE CHANTING PROTESTERS carrying picket signs near the Sunset Boulevard entrance of the Channel Six building. According to the radio news, they were headed by a group called TV-TV, which stood for Traditional Values for Television, and they had vowed to conduct a vigil until Channel Six cleaned up the airwaves by removing Taylor Drummond from the evening news.

Mason braked. The late afternoon traffic demanded his attention. He didn't need to think; he knew what he had to do. Since the first news story, he had heard no reports of when the child was due. Jillian, who had called Taylor, hadn't even thought to ask the question. He called the studio twice; both times Taylor refused his call. He got the message: The baby was not his. Both relieved and disappointed, he had set about reconciling himself to that fact.

On his way back from lunch today, he stopped to check with his secretary, Hildy, on an important brief. After the business had been taken care of, she brought up the subject of Taylor's public pregnancy and mentioned Taylor's child would be a Virgo.

"How do you know that?" he had asked, pretending to scan the headline of the *Daily Journal* on Hildy's desk.

"I read it in *Los Angeles Magazine,* in a feature on television newswomen. It was mainly about the really famous ones, but they mentioned Taylor's baby, and said it was due in early September. So the baby will be a Virgo."

Mason felt his pulse jump. Carefully he folded the paper and returned it to the recycling bin Hildy kept at the side of her desk. "I just remembered a meeting out of the building," he said, heading to the door. "Cancel my afternoon appointments for me."

Now, less than an hour later, Mason turned onto a side street and edged his Volvo into a spot between a broken-down VW and a Rolls-Royce. If Hildy was right, Taylor's child was his child, not the seed of some unknown donor. And Taylor, pregnant with his child, had denied the truth to him. That possibility hurt like hell, even though he figured he deserved the kick in the head.

He passed through the picketers. Up close, there didn't seem to be so many. He saw honest faces of average citizens, stripped of their individuality and replaced with a mask of communal indignation. They paced and chanted: "Clean up the airwaves. Fire Drummond now. Clean up the airwaves." He fought the urge to pick a fight with them. What did any of these people know of the woman they were publicly deriding? In selecting her as Symbol of the Week, they chose to view her as an object, not another woman, though most of the protesters were female. As angry as he was at Taylor for his own reasons, he wanted to rage at these people for turning her choice to become a mother into a spectacle.

Inside, he told the guard behind the front desk his name and said he had an appointment with Taylor. She conducted a head-to-toe survey of him, nodded, and looked at a clipboard. Glancing up with a frown, she said, "Your name isn't on the clearance sheet."

"She probably forgot. Just ring her up and tell her her attorney is here to see her."

She pursed her lips. "We have our procedures. If you're not on the clearance—"

"I understand." He jerked his head toward the protesters outside. "You can't be too careful with the nuts outside and reporters swarming around." He pulled out his wallet. "See, here's my ID and bar card. Why don't you pick up the phone and tell her I'm here and see what she says. I don't think she'll be too happy when she finds out I've been sent away." Mason almost laughed at the irony of that statement. Obviously he was the last person in the world Taylor wanted to see.

"You do look like a lawyer . . ."

He leaned over the guard desk and pushed the phone toward her. He should have saved the pizza man cap.

The guard punched four numbers and waited. As soon as she said, "Ms. Drummond," Mason snatched the phone.

"Thanks, I'll take it from here."

Into the receiver he said, "I'm downstairs at the guard desk. They seem to think we don't have an appointment, but if you recall, there's the matter of the contract we undertook on December twenty-third."

Taylor said nothing. He could feel her thinking, sense her deciding what to do.

The guard looked at him uncertainly.

"Come out and talk," he said to Taylor.

Finally, when he thought his fingers would dig grooves into the plastic receiver, she said, "Put the guard back on."

He handed the phone back. "Yes. Yes, right away," she said. She hung up. "Ms. Drummond said to send you in." The guard rose.

"Thanks, I know the way," he said, pushing through the double doors at the end of the lobby.

Taylor stood at the end of the long hallway, arms crossed. He hadn't seen her since the night at the hospital in February. Maybe it was the passage of time in which he'd forced himself not to think about her, or maybe it was her pregnancy, but she looked better than ever. He walked toward her, taking her in. Her face had filled out, and with the fullness had come a look of contentment, as strange as that seemed under the circumstances. Her black hair had been pulled around to the front on one side and fastened with a blue velvet bow. He'd expected a bulging basketball of a belly, but her figure had merely chunked out, giving her a squarer profile. Without the hubbub on the news, he could have passed her on the street and not known she was pregnant.

Like two cats on a fence, each waiting for the other to back down, they faced each other. He wondered what she'd do if, instead of confronting her in anger, he reached out, traced her hair as it fell from her forehead to her breast, then took her in his arms. One kiss and he would know the truth. He was fooling himself; he already knew the truth. That Taylor had agreed to see him told him what he had come to find out. He stiffened and kept his hands at his sides. "I believe you have something to say to me."

Taylor realized that he knew. She sensed the hurt and anger emanating from him. She'd been hurt, too, but now wasn't the time to think of her own pain. They had to put the baby first. She reached a hand toward him, but he didn't respond. He kept staring at her, his eyes not at all the soft brown they usually were.

"I'm waiting," he said.

She gestured around the corner. "We can talk in the control room. No one's in yet." Leading him there, she wet her lips nervously. She could deny the baby was his. But faced with an opportunity to tell the truth, she wanted to. For the baby's sake, if not their own, they needed to sort through this mess they had made. Though she told herself she had kept the baby a secret from him because of Jillian, part of the reason had been to punish him for deserting her. For that she felt both guilty and justified. Dim light filtered in from the news studio below the control room. She flicked on the ceiling fluorescents to kill the shadowed intimacy. Settling into the director's chair, she pointed to the chair next to hers.

Mason remained standing. "Taylor?"

She heard the question in his voice, loud and clear. "It's true. You are the father of my child."

"Jesus. When were you going to tell me? On his twenty-first birthday?"

"I wrestled with that question, Mason."

"Wrestled? Why didn't you pick up the phone and call me at the office? You probably still remember the number."

"When? When I thought Jillian was pregnant? When I thought she had miscarried? When she was in an alcohol treatment center? Just when was the right time?" She fought back tears of anger and frustration.

"Any time would have been better than lying to me about our child."

"Don't call this baby 'our child,' Mason. Not after you slept with Jillian after telling me you loved me."

He clenched his jaw, as if fighting back words. When he spoke, he chose his words carefully. "You know I have apologized for that. I won't go over it again; I promise not to mention it if you won't. But we have to think about the baby now. And I apologize for coming here and yelling at you." He moved to her, knelt, and carefully took her hands in his. "You've been alone through this whole thing, and I show up and rant at you."

She held her hands stiffly, refusing his comfort. "I agree with you about putting the baby first, but I don't need your pity. I was perfectly prepared to become a single mother, and that's exactly what I'm going to be."

He rocked back on his heels. "What do you mean by that? That—" he pointed to her abdomen "—is my child you're carrying."

"And that is a wedding ring you're wearing," she said sharply.

He had no response. Taylor ripped the bow from her head and tossed her hair back. "Unless you're no longer married to Jillian, please don't deny my statements about being a single mother."

He twisted the ring around and around on his finger. "You know I'm still married. And you know why—because she's too fragile to leave right now."

"Right."

He sat down. They looked at each other again. Then they looked at the buttons and dials of the control panel. Finally Mason said, "So where do we take it from here?"

Taylor pressed her fingers to her abdomen. "A few months ago I would have told you to take a flying leap, but now I find myself asking, 'What's right for the baby?' That's what matters to me, more than anything else. That's why I stayed in this ridiculous situation and let the station manager orchestrate this publicity siege."

"The protests are setups?"

"Not exactly, but Sid, the GM, lives for controversy. It was either agree or lose my job."

"I hope you didn't do it for the money. You know I'll take care of both you and the baby."

She looked at him; watched him watching her with a hungry gaze that unsettled her. She wanted him away from her, fast, before he broke her reserves of self-defense. "Thank you, but I'm quite able to do that."

"Is everything okay? Are you and the baby feeling all right?"

She nodded. She hadn't upchucked since the day of the chipped corn beef. However, she'd made darn sure she and that concoction never crossed paths again.

"Do you know whether it's a girl or a boy?"

Taylor shook her head, feeling vaguely ill. The question reminded her of how scared and alone she had felt during the amniocentesis procedure a few days before. The doctor had encouraged her to watch the monitor for the ultrasound picture of her baby, but she had caught sight of the needle. She was worried sick it would slip and her baby would die. "I should have the amnio results back next week. But I'm positive she's a she."

"Hey, how do you know that?"

"Women's intuition."

With the first smile she had seen on his face since Christmas, he reached for her hand, and this time she responded to his touch. His warmth felt so good. Rubbing the back of her hand, gently in circles, he said, "I just want you to know how much it means to me that you're having our baby."

"Don't."

"Crazy circumstances aside," he said, clearing his throat, "I'm pleased."

She didn't answer.

"Please don't lock me out. You know how much I want to be a part of this with you."

"What about Jillian?" she asked quietly.

He winced and stood up. "She thinks the baby is from a sperm bank. Just let her think that. Soon, very soon, she'll be healthier, and then I'll explain. I'm just so worried she'll relapse now."

"Are you sure you shouldn't explain now? Or let me?"

"No. When you see her, you'll understand." He added in a lost tone, "I honestly think she was a happier person when she was drinking."

Taylor studied her feet. They looked larger to her, but her whole body seemed that way these days. She needed to check on her sister, and she certainly didn't want to do anything to hurt her recovery. Yet she didn't think she could deal with Mason. It was just too difficult. "Let's leave things the way they are right now." She rose, and he offered her a hand. Closing her eyes briefly, she said, "I'll let you know."

Unable to resist, he smoothed the hair back from her face. "I know you're angry with me. This is an impossible situation. But please don't shut me out from the baby. I want to be there to help you. To think of you going through it alone will kill me." He placed a soft kiss on the part of her hair, then turned and left the room.

During the next week, as she thought about what Mason had said, Taylor admitted she wanted him back in her life. Try as she had to abolish her feelings for him, she knew she still loved him. She had known since the night she sat next to him on the bus bench at the hospital. She admired him for standing by Jillian and promising to be there for her when she returned from treatment. She began to see how the other side of his willingness to give so generously was a tendency to smooth things over, to try to make everything okay, a trait that very well could have prompted him to have sex with Jillian on Christmas. It didn't excuse the behavior, but it helped Taylor place it in context.

She had been forced to subjugate her desire for Mason as lover. But Mason as the father of her unborn child—she could have him back in her life in that role. She imagined conversations with him: explaining how she talked to her baby, how her views of what mattered had altered during the past few months, how she had hated enduring the amnio alone.

Yet she didn't call him.

She had been strong for so long; she had worked so hard to wean her feelings. He was married to Jillian, and nothing he had said gave her any proof that he intended to seek a divorce. Dealing with him would be torture, a constant reminder of the void within her existence.

Seven days after Mason's trip to the station, Dr. Richmond's office telephoned with the amnio results. She was going to have a baby daughter, a healthy baby girl.

As she sat at her pod at work, staring into her monitor and blinking away tears of joy, a rush of emotions overtook her. A little girl. A daughter. She wanted to laugh and cry and run out and buy pink dresses with lace.

Instead, she picked up the phone and called Mason at work. He deserved to share this moment, and all the rest of the times of their daughter's life, no matter the cost to Taylor.

"Thanks for meeting me," said Fielding, rising to greet Jillian. In her pale yellow dress and wide-brimmed hat, she looked like a daffodil against the green backdrop of the lawn. Only the dark glasses obscuring her eyes marred the image. "And for suggesting this place." He gestured to the terrace surrounded by plants rustling in the June breeze.

"I'm glad you like it." She settled into her chair. "I've always been fond of the Huntington. Coming here is like stepping into another world."

He wished she would remove her glasses. Today would more than likely be the last time he was going to see her, and he selfishly wanted to watch the expressions that danced and warred there. "Do you still play make-believe?" He asked it lightly, to cover the seriousness of the question.

"Sometimes."

"What would you like to be today?"

She tossed her sunglasses onto the table. "A fairy princess who isn't craving a vodka rocks."

He saw at once why she had covered her eyes. She'd been crying, and recently. In typical Jillian fashion, the damage had been repaired, but he saw the signs beneath the extra application of powder. "That's why we're meeting for high tea, isn't it? Because there is no vodka here."

She nodded. Leaning forward on her elbows, she said, "Mason told me about you. It made sense to me that you were a fellow drunk."

"And why is that?"

"It explains why I can talk to you so easily. After all, I barely know you."

That hadn't stopped her from raising her skirt to him last winter. "I'm glad you can talk to me, but I hope it's not simply because I'm a—and these are your words— fellow drunk."

She dipped her head, and the hat blocked her face from his view. After a bit, she said, "I'm sorry for what I did that time you came over for coffee."

"Apology accepted."

Raising her head, she smiled briefly. She seemed about to speak, but a waiter interrupted with the delivery of the tea tray. She toyed with a crustless sandwich, then dropped it back to the plate. "Mason thinks I'm crazy."

Fielding waited for her to continue.

She lifted the bit of bread and rolled it between her fingers. Crushed bread crumbs scattered in the light breeze. "I can tell by the way he's so polite to me, the way he speaks, like he's talking to a sick horse that's about to be sent to the dog-food factory." She dropped the last bit of bread with a surprised look on her face. "Sometimes I think he's right."

Was he a friend or a therapist here? Fielding decided to let her talk. He stirred sugar into his tea.

"I was in that place for a long time. A lot of people left before I did, happy, smiling, hugging and crying. They ran around spouting their little sayings and babbling about their higher power." She pushed her plate away. "Every day I say that stupid prayer and read that boring book, and it means nothing to me."

She ended on a whisper, which was far more wrenching than a shout would have been. He covered her hand with his. After a moment, she shook it off and reached for her teacup. "How was that for melodrama?"

"That wasn't melodrama; that was you being honest."

"Ah, the shrink is in."

He'd lost her, which was to be expected. For Jillian, at this point in her recovery, to acknowledge an emotional truth for longer than a few moments was asking too much. Pressing her would yield no results. "What's your favorite part of the garden?"

"The cactus. It's like being on another planet—wait a minute, you changed the subject."

He pointed to his cheeks and continued chewing. He needed an opening to give her the book he had brought with him. Once he gave it to her, he'd have to leave—for two reasons. One, because she'd be furious with him, and two, because, as Robert Frost said, he had "promises to keep" to himself. He swallowed. "About changing the subject . . ."

"Yes?" She shifted in the chair and fiddled with a spoon. Her nervous energy, the force that drove her to drink and pick up men, was building. He felt it like the strength of a tornado, whirling around her.

"I'm selling my trial consulting business and returning to private practice."

"Why?"

He turned the delicate cup in his hands. "I've been running from my own problems for a long time, and I've learned I have to turn and face them. I've been afraid to return to my practice because of its past link with my drinking. But running away isn't the answer."

"You're telling this to me for my own good, aren't you?"

"Yes and no." He remembered the first time he saw her in that siren red dress, and now, the last time, looking like a buttercup. "I'm sharing this with you because you've helped me come to this conclusion."

"I have?"

He nodded, but didn't burden her with the knowledge of how her forays into bars and shops had helped to bring him to his own moment of truth. It was enough for him that watching her and facing the feelings she stirred in him had led him to realize he had to meet his own past head-on.

She leaned toward him. Her breasts strained against the soft fabric of the dress. She brushed her fingertips across the top of his wrist. "Fielding?"

He heard the suggestion, the offer in her voice, and ached for her to learn she had plenty of value without having to offer her body as consideration. "No, Jillian. You don't want *me.*" He lowered his voice. "If I thought you really wanted me, Fielding, the man, the human being, I might find it damn hard to turn you down. But we've been through this before." Reaching for the small shopping bag beside his chair, he said, "I brought something for you. It's a book I think can help you. If you want it to."

"A book."

"Don't sound so disappointed." He handed it to her; its silver and white binding glittered in the sun.

She read the title on the cover, *Sexaholics Anonymous,* and quickly turned the book facedown. Her face had transmuted to a mask of hostility. "And what is the meaning of this?"

"You said the books and prayers in the center didn't touch you. I think there's a reason for that. I think you haven't faced what lies at the root of your problems. It's not only alcohol; it's something else."

"I'll be the judge of that. I've gone without a drink for four months. Four stinking months." She whispered her words, even though no one was sitting close to their table. "I'm just fine and I don't need your stupid book." She shoved it toward him. *"Sexaholics Anonymous.* What do you think I am, anyway?" She scraped her chair back.

Fielding put the book back into the shopping bag. "All

I ask is that you take it with you." He offered the bag to her. It hung between them, suspended from his index finger.

She stared from his face to the bag and back to his face. "Stay the fuck out of my life," she said. Then she snatched the bag and crossed the terrace without looking back.

Fielding let her go.

Jillian stalked to her car. She'd show Fielding. She'd go to an AA meeting right now and prove she belonged there—along with the other alcoholics. How dare he suggest she needed that other book. Holding the shopping bag away from her body, she shuddered. *Sexaholics Anonymous.* The very name sounded dirty to her, conjuring up the image of Peeping Toms meeting in a dark room to talk about their favorite window scenes. She thought Fielding liked her, and all this time he regarded her as some sort of pervert.

Jillian reached her car, tossed the bag onto the passenger seat, and stepped in. Somewhere in her purse was a list of meeting times and places of Alcoholics Anonymous given to her at the treatment center. According to her list, she could find an afternoon meeting in the basement of a church on Colorado Boulevard. She headed north from the Huntington Library, dreading the experience, but determined to go through with it. She had attended AA meetings while in the center, scoffing—and secretly marveling—at the enthusiasm of the men and women and the way they bared their souls so openly and emotionally. She had limited her participation to moving her lips during the serenity prayer. She didn't mingle during the break for coffee or, if the meeting was a nonsmoking one, during the pause to allow the smokers to rush outside for a quick fix. She hugged her secrets to herself.

If she could stand up and say, "Hello, I'm Jillian and I'm an alcoholic," she'd prove to Fielding he was wrong. She'd prove her sowing of wild oats was simply that. She wasn't some out-of-control sex addict. She could say no as easily as anyone else.

* * *

"We've got a problem, babe."

We? Taylor lounged against the wall inside Sid's office door, reluctant to get drawn in. She wasn't in the mood for a fireside chat with Sid. Earlier this morning, Jillian had again refused to set a time to get together, as she had done since her return from the treatment center. She did it obliquely, claiming to be swamped with other commitments. Today she said she was meeting Fielding Sanderson for tea. If she could see him, why not make time for her own sister?

"Are you gonna stand there all day looking like you're totaling up the Third World debt, or are you gonna listen to what I have to say?"

Wandering to his leather sofa, she said, "I'm listening."

"MediaImage conducted a poll, at my request, and now they tell me that the doomsdayers out front are affecting viewer perception of you negatively."

"What did you expect? They're out there trying to brand me with a scarlet *A.*" The women plagued Channel Six from morning till night, many pushing baby strollers. Six weeks after they had first arrived, they showed no signs of giving up their vigil. The other stations—quick to sense that what was good for Channel Six was not necessarily good for them—had tapered off on the story.

"I can't call them off."

"You said you set them up with a few phone calls to a few buddies, so why can't you do the same thing in reverse?" What a relief that would be. Taylor hated driving by them every morning. At first she had wanted to stop and talk to them, thinking that if they saw her as a woman, they'd understand and go away. Yet knowing they were actually there as pawns of whoever ran their organization made her feel sorry for them. It also caused her to think she couldn't possibly respect anything they might have to say about why they were doing what they were doing.

"They've taken on a life of their own."

"You mean they believe in what they're doing."

"As strange as that sounds, yes."

"I've been getting letters of support. Why not play up that side of things? Some people—men and women—think my having a baby is my own business, bless their hearts."

"Nah. I've got a better idea." Sid addressed a point on the wall as he continued. "You produce a husband, and say you had to keep the marriage quiet for some reason."

Taylor laughed. "Sid, you're grabbing at straws. I have no husband, and if I fabricate one, some enterprising reporter is bound to check the records."

He tugged at his mustache. "Are you telling me you can't produce the father or that you won't?"

Taylor smiled as a vision of Sid sending a camera crew to Harper, Cravens popped in her mind. How nice and simple life would be if she could do exactly that. Since her phone call to tell him about the amnio results three weeks ago, she had slipped into the habit of calling Mason at work two or three times a week. She still hadn't agreed to see him, and he hadn't pushed. "Sorry, Sid, but there will be no shotgun wedding for you to televise."

"Hutch isn't gonna like this."

The baby kicked, a sharp demand for attention. Taylor shifted on the sofa. "I think playing up the controversy was a mistake from the beginning." She laid her hands across her kicking baby. "I wanted this to be my own business and nobody else's. Since that option is lost, I think we should steer around the issue and emphasize the positive points."

"Say that in English."

Taylor, with more difficulty than she was used to, pushed her body up from the sofa. "We might as well try the Pauley-Norville approach. Viewers on the *Today* show loved it when Jane Pauley had twins. She didn't hide her bulk behind a desk. Then Deborah Norville followed in her footsteps. The secret is to make the pregnancy an integral part of the show." She cringed when she heard herself call the newscast a show. These people were rubbing off on her.

"All I was asking you to do before was stir up the ruckus, do some interviews."

"Patting my tummy on-air is easier than making a fool of myself on *Geraldo.*"

"Seems fucking personal to me."

"You are strange. You think nothing of asking me to make a fool of myself as the eye of the storm over single motherhood, but you balk at me dwelling on what I like about being pregnant."

He gave her a weak grin. "You're not such a bad chick when you stick up for yourself."

"Thanks. I'll remember that." She saw him pull open a drawer and reach for a bottle of pills. "You're not having a good day, are you?"

"Fuck, yes. I'm having a great day." He gulped two pills without bothering with water. "Forget that story about dying. I only made that up so you'd go along with me. Now that you've made it your idea, I can tell you I was lying all along."

"No shit." She tried giving him a dose of his own language, knowing he was lying, but knowing that he'd hate sympathy. Sid was dying. Now that she knew, she watched him. Every day he seemed weaker. "You're not such a bad guy when you tell the truth."

The door shot open. Grady Hutchings, tanned and looking more massive than Taylor remembered, stepped through, Roscoe trotting behind. Hutchings bore down on Taylor, his hands outstretched. "I wanted to wish you well in person. A baby is a gift from God and a bundle of joy." He snapped his fingers, and Roscoe handed him a Tiffany's box. "For the little one."

Taylor tried to keep her surprise from showing. Sid had prepared her to expect the worst possible reaction from Grady Hutchings. The gift was a silver spoon. "Mr. Hutchings, I'm touched." She glared at Sid, who was looking surprised.

Grady rubbed his hands together and dropped into a chair. Roscoe moved to stand behind him. Sid offered him a bourbon, even though it was early afternoon, and Grady accepted.

Settling in with his glass, Grady turned back to Taylor.

"Now, let's speak frankly here. I always say, 'Let he who is without sin cast the first stone.' I don't mind telling you that Laurel Ann and I had one in the cooker before she ever walked down the aisle." He gave Sid a man-to-man wink. "You get that man of yours to do the honorable thing before the child arrives, and we'll overlook this little indiscretion. And, I might add, this violation of the morals clause in your contract." Raising his glass, he said, "So when's the wedding?"

Sid said, "Yeah, when's the wedding?"

So Sid hadn't been wrong after all about Grady's reaction. "There isn't going to be any wedding," Taylor said calmly. "And if you check with your legal staff, you'll find that I lined out that portion of the contract." She could let them fire her and dispute it in court, or she could walk a very narrow tightrope with the truth and keep her job. "There isn't going to be any wedding, because the baby doesn't have what you think of as a father." Well, that was true. Grady Hutchings wouldn't consider a man married to another woman much of a father.

"This had better be good," Sid muttered.

She was doing this for the baby, Taylor reminded herself. "In order to have a child, because I believe, as you said, Mr. Hutchings, that babies are a gift from God, I used the services of a ... uh ... donor insemination." Phrased that way, it wasn't exactly a lie. She and Mason had had every intention of using that turkey baster.

"What the fuck is that?" asked Sid.

Hutchings stared at her, saying nothing for a very long moment. Then he smiled. "Well, that's a relief. I thought for a moment you were going to tell me the father was a married man. And that kind of scandal, I wouldn't like at all. Roscoe, get me the church teachings of all major denominations on donor insemination." He looked at Taylor. "I thought they only used that for cattle."

"People, too," she said.

"Roscoe, call Keith Carlyle and have him explain the situation to those people out front. I don't like them cluttering up my sidewalk."

"Yes, sir."

Hutchings finished his drink and rose to leave. "Sidney, the latest ratings book showed a dip. I'm not paying you to put us in the basement."

Chapter 19

THE AA MEETING STARTED OUT OKAY. JILLIAN actually said hello to two people, before retreating to a sagging sofa by herself. Just before the meeting began, a silver-haired man, attractive except for the broken capillaries beetling his cheeks, rushed in. He joined her on the sofa. During the meeting, he shared his story and cried. Jillian patted his hand. He clung to it as he spoke of losing his wife, his kids, his business—all because of alcohol. She stroked his hand soothingly, moved by the emotion he was able to pour forth in front of the group. She wasn't ready to speak, but perhaps by reaching out to him, she could help herself.

After the meeting, he invited her to his place for coffee. After the draining emotional experience of listening to this stranger unburden his soul, she felt bonded to him and pleased that she might be able to aid him, one fellow alcoholic to another.

His entire apartment could have fit into her living room. The furniture looked like it had come from a rental company. When he saw her glancing around, he muttered he was starting over, and would soon be back to his former standard of living. Uncomfortable at being caught at her own snobbery, she nodded, and offered to make the coffee.

He put his arm around her and led her to the beige plaid sofa. "Let's talk first."

She let him pull her to his side, wishing he'd remove his arm. She'd come here to help him, not to seduce him or be seduced.

Without preamble, he shoved her onto her back and weighted her body with his own.

"Let me up," she said. "I came here for coffee."

He stared at her. "What's the matter with you? Are you stupid?" He grabbed her mouth with his lips and stuck his tongue inside.

Jillian struggled against him. Why was he doing this to her? Did she give off some signal that invited men like this? She hadn't even tried to attract this man; she wanted nothing to do with sex with strangers anymore. She pushed against his chest and felt a surge of relief when the man lifted himself off her.

Sitting up, she straightened her yellow dress. He had crumpled the delicate linen and knocked her hat off. "I came here to talk, because I thought you wanted someone to listen to you. I thought I could help you."

"Baby, you can help me." He rose, crossed to the kitchen area, and returned carrying a full fifth of Jack Daniel's.

"You mustn't drink. You said you had quit."

He plunked it onto the glass coffee table, then sat beside Jillian. "Only you can keep me from drinking again."

"What do you mean?"

He grabbed her head and pushed it down toward his groin. "Suck me off, baby. If you don't make me feel like a man, I'm going to have to have that drink."

She twisted her head. "Let me go."

He pushed her head against the bulge in his pants. "Come on, what's the problem? It's just sex. It's not like I'm asking you to take a drink. Just do it."

"You don't understand." She didn't even believe he would take that drink if she fought him off, yet she could feel the numbness setting in, the paralysis that told her she was about to do whatever he wanted her to do. She started to cry. Didn't he know what he was asking her to do? *Just do it,* he said. What difference would it make? He'd be happy and she'd feel like shit. But she already felt that way.

"No, you're the one who doesn't understand." He opened his fly and pressed himself into her mouth.

She gagged. He held her head firmly in place. Her reflexes kicked in and she did what she had always done—obeyed his command.

As she had always obeyed. Her father had taught her that. Like a well-trained dog, or more aptly, a servile geisha, she had trotted to fulfill every command of her father. *Sit on my lap. Fetch my slippers. Where's my drink? Nobody makes a bourbon and water like my little Jilly.* His little Jilly had been only seven years old when Ronald Drummond had first uttered those words, words that became a litany as he taunted his wife with her failures to please him. Only Jilly understood what made Daddy happy.

She squeezed her eyes more tightly shut, trying to obliterate the memory of her father, wishing she could close off her sense of smell as well. She shouldn't think of him while she did this thing. But as she licked and sucked this hateful enemy who forced her to do the one thing that could destroy her, she kept seeing her father standing over the couch. It's important to make the man in your life happy, he had said. Semen dribbled into her mouth and she retched. She couldn't think of her father while this man held her face to his groin, grunting and sighing his pleasure taken at her expense. The man came and Jillian jerked aside. Her life was bottoming out. Nothing mattered anymore.

Afterward, the guy wanted to talk. She wanted to throw up. She excused herself and went to the bathroom, where she opened the leaky taps of the sink to hide the sound of her retching from the man in the other room.

What was wrong with her? Why hadn't she said no and walked out? Any other woman would have done exactly that. Taylor, for instance, would never do anything she didn't want to do. But Jillian always had to do what was expected of her, just like her father had programmed her. She rejected the only towel because it smelled of mold, and wiped her face dry with toilet paper. As she looked into the mirror, she saw the man open the bathroom door. For the strangest moment, his reflection in the mirror even reminded her of her father.

"Everything okay in there?" he asked, sounding concerned. Parental.

Jillian shivered. "Just fine. I'll be right out."

He retreated. This man was someone's parent. She was young enough to be his daughter. Simply thinking of him in that light caused her stomach to pitch again. Her father had always been kind, playing horsey with her on his knee, whispering secrets in her ear, coming into the bedroom at night to tuck her in with sleepy-time kisses. The feelings of nausea grew. The sight of the man entering the bathroom metamorphosed into the image of her father, telling her mother he'd take care of bathing her, her father splashing in the tub, the two of them giggling as he rubbed her dry and fashioned a train he said was fit for his princess from the towel that dwarfed her child's body.

Another vision came, unbidden, like a dream flitting into morning consciousness, then disappearing, chased away by breakfast conversation. This image was of her father, the night before he died, stroking her hair and complaining to her fourteen-year-old self that her mother didn't understand his needs.

Why was she thinking these thoughts? Her father's love for her had been good. For whatever reason, he hadn't thought much of Taylor and had lavished love enough for two on Jillian. She rinsed her mouth and tried to force the confusing images of her father from her mind. She felt so miserable; she couldn't bear any more bad thoughts.

She refused the coffee the man had made and escaped to her car. Her hands shook as she turned the key in the ignition. She hated herself for having done what she'd done, especially when she hadn't even wanted to do it. Her glance fell on the shopping bag with the *Sexaholics Anonymous* book inside. Burying her face against the steering wheel, she cried.

* * *

Mason had promised to give Jillian six months to grow stronger and mentally healthier before asking for a divorce. Midway through that period, he realized he was fooling himself. People didn't change on schedule; sometimes people didn't change at all. Also, the phone conversations with Taylor were whetting his appetite; he wanted more. He wanted all that life with her and their child promised.

"Au jus?" Jillian asked, as she filled his dinner plate with thinly sliced roast beef. The plate trembled in her hands, and he quickly took it from her, declining the sauce.

Cutting a piece of meat, he wondered how to bring up a discussion of her mental state and his need to acknowledge their marriage was over. To avoid a situation he had no idea how to handle, he had been working late as many nights as possible, but recently one of his fellow partners had asked him if things were okay at home. That inquiry was enough to send him home in time for dinner. He saw no reason to trouble his professional life simply because his personal life was one colossal unmitigated disaster. After swallowing the tender piece of meat, he asked, "How was your day?"

"Fine."

"What did you do?"

"This and that." She sipped some water from a wineglass. "I had lunch with your friend Fielding."

"Oh?"

"He seems to be trying to save my soul."

"He has been down the same path. Perhaps he can help."

She swung her head from right to left, like a little girl warming up for a temper tantrum. "I want him to stay away from me."

"Why? Did he do something to upset you?"

"Yes."

Surely he hadn't made a pass at her. Fielding wasn't the kind of guy to go after his friend's wife. But then, he'd be willing to bet no one would peg him as the kind of guy who would sleep with his wife's sister, either. "Something personal?"

She fidgeted with her fork and laid it aside without eating. "Yes."

Jesus. Why didn't she get to the point? "What did he do?"

"Oh, he didn't do anything. It was what he said. He thinks I'm crazy."

His relief must have shown on his face, because she immediately said, "Well, you don't have to look as if you agree with him."

"It's not that, Jillian. I was imagining that he had made some overture."

"You mean sexual?"

"Yes."

"Why is it that men always think everything comes down to sex? I'm upset because your friend thinks I'm crazy, and all you can imagine is that he wanted to screw me." She pushed her chair away from the table.

He stared at her, thinking that Fielding was probably right. "Sit down, please, and let's talk about this." He looked at the pinched lines of her face, the bony shoulders that poked above the neckline of her dress. She seemed to have given up food along with alcohol and sleeping pills. He didn't know what to do to get her to eat or to be happy. He was no shrink; he was simply a man who had married a woman he didn't understand.

"You want to leave me, don't you?" she said in a quiet voice.

He started to deny it, but couldn't. He watched her eyes, so large above the markedly defined cheekbones, gazing at him like a stray cat about to be kicked down the alley. "It just isn't working anymore, Jillian."

She huddled into her chair. "Please don't say that. Not tonight."

"We don't make love. We don't talk. You're unhappy and miserable, and I don't see anything I can do to change that."

"I'll get worse if you leave."

He wondered if that was an observation or a threat. "Are you going to your therapy sessions?"

Jillian nodded. She wished she could tell him about her afternoon, about the horrible man who forced himself on her, about how she had read the opening of the *Sexaholics Anonymous* book, then slammed it shut and thrust it into her underwear drawer. But she couldn't say a word. She couldn't show this man that part of herself; he was ready to walk now, and he thought she was only an alcoholic. If he knew the truth, he'd be sickened. And out the door. "I baked cherry pie for dessert. Let me get some for you."

She headed for the kitchen before he could object. In a way, she wanted him to stop her, force her to spill her guts. Once the messiness was behind her, she could imagine herself feeling relieved to have all the pretense over with.

While she was in the kitchen, searching in a utensil drawer for a pie server, she found a bottle of sleeping pills she'd forgotten about, stuck in the back of the drawer. Or maybe she'd hidden them as a last, secret cache. She didn't remember. They were two years old, double strength. She fingered the ridges on the white plastic top and rolled the amber container in her hand. That man had been so nasty, her memories of her father so disturbing. Cutting an extra large piece of pie for Mason, she pictured drifting off into nothingness, floating away on the cloud of not having to remember what she had done that day. She washed two pills down with several swallows of cooking brandy and returned the vial to the drawer.

Mason noticed a change in Jillian as soon as she entered the room carrying his dessert. She had that faraway look that he had long ago decided was simply the normal appearance of her face. He hadn't seen that expression since before she had checked into the treatment center. The look conveyed relief, as if she had taken an action that allowed her to check out from the burdens of her existence; he didn't believe she could have ingested any substance that so quickly produced the effect. He must be witnessing, and

actually recognizing for the first time, the momentary sur-
cease she gained by giving in to her addiction.

He accepted the dessert and thought about not confronting her. He couldn't live her life for her. But if he saw her
stepping in front of a bus, he would call out. Slashing into
his pie, he remembered the social worker at the hospital
explaining to him that addiction was a family disease. If
Jillian was sick, she had gotten that way with his acquies-
cence, his willingness to make believe everything was
okay. It was her choice whether she used and abused, but
he had to admit to some role in it, even if that role was
simply always looking the other way. After all, his immediate reaction had been to accept the pie, clean his plate,
and kiss her good night. If he expected her to do the hard
work of recovery, he could at least dish out some honesty.

He put his fork down, the pie half-eaten.

"Don't you like it?"

"There's nothing wrong with the pie." Mason pushed
the dessert plate away from him and leaned toward Jillian.
"I want to apologize for ignoring your problem for so
long. This is difficult for me to say, and I'm not at all sure
how to say it. You went into the kitchen a keyed-up, irritable woman, and floated back out, as if nothing could
touch you. Do you know what I'm talking about?"

"No." Gathering the dishes from the table, a job the
housekeeper normally performed, she repeated, "No. I
have no idea what you mean."

"I think you do."

She jumped up, dropping the plates with a crash of
china. "Why are people always telling me I mean one
thing, as if anyone else could possibly understand me?"
She screamed the words at him. "And look at this mess
you caused."

"Jillian. I think you're using again. Whether you admit
it to me or not doesn't matter. What I need to do, to help
you and so I can live with myself, is not play along in silence anymore." Realizing his hands were shaking, he
jammed them into his pants pockets and rose from the table. "I don't know what else to say."

She bent over the shattered dishes, tears streaming down her face.

"Jillian . . ." he said helplessly.

She wouldn't look at him as she snatched at pieces of broken china, making a pile in the middle of the floor. Finally he left the room and went in search of his briefcase.

He heard Jillian go into the den. He didn't know whether she was drinking more or not. Within an hour, she went to bed. Mason felt trapped; miserable if he stayed with her and guilty if he walked out. Following a middle course, he finished the work he had brought home with him, then moved his things into the guest bedroom.

Jillian slept, oblivious to his actions, her body at peace in a way she never seemed to achieve while awake.

Taylor was into her seventh month before she heard from her mother. Her day at work had been particularly grueling; the baby kicked restively, and now that she was home, she wanted nothing more than to put her feet up and take a load off. Her first Lamaze class was set for the next day, and she still intended to go there alone. She knew the method was designed to use a coach to assist in the labor and delivery, but Taylor couldn't bring herself to ask Mason to go with her. She didn't want anyone else with her. Certainly not her sister.

Her sister. Glancing at her belly, which seemed to expand daily, Taylor wondered again what she should do about telling Jillian the truth about the child's father. Part of her felt the decision was up to Mason; yet Jillian was *her* sister. She couldn't break such news on the phone, and each time Taylor called her, Jillian evaded setting a time to meet. It had been months since they'd seen each other.

Kicking off her shoes and dropping onto her sofa, Taylor decided to worry about her sister another day. Right now she had Claudia's letter to deal with. She stared at the powder green envelope. For as long as she could remember, Claudia had used that color of stationery. Taylor still hated it. Before opening the envelope, she switched on her stereo, starting the Michael Franks CD she had left in the day before.

Seven months pregnant and she hadn't written or phoned her mother. Taylor knew her mother would disapprove and couldn't force herself to bring the onslaught on herself. Finally she slit open the letter. It was all she expected and more:

> *Taylor—I have put off writing this letter for some time. Only a mother can understand the anguish I have known. I hear from one of my friends—not my own daughter—that you are expecting a child. Can you imagine my embarrassment to have to learn this tidbit of family news from a business associate? It seems when she was in Los Angeles she learned what a public spectacle you are making of yourself.*
>
> *As to your pregnancy, I do hope you at least know who the father is and have some means of persuading him to do the right thing by you. You may think this old-fashioned of me, but to do otherwise would be to ruin your life. A baby needs a father. You just try to find a man who will take on a woman with another man's child.*
>
> *I am surprised that your sister didn't let me know, or are you managing to keep this a secret from her as well? If you had known what was good for you, you would have married a nice man like she did and had a proper family. But no, not Taylor. You always did know better than anyone else.*
>
> *Before you crumple this letter and throw my advice into the trash, please consider what I am saying to you. Believe me, I know what I am talking about.*
>
> *As always, Claudia.*

Taylor felt a kick in her gut she was sure was more than just the baby exercising her limbs. Or perhaps it was the baby, echoing her opinion of Claudia's letter. She tore it, bit by bit, into scraps and wadded the scraps into a ball. What did her mother know? Claudia and her mousy husband, long dead, and her mantle of widowhood she'd worn for so many years. Any woman who could write that letter should be drummed out of the mother corps.

Yet she felt the pain from the truth in her mother's words. She ached with wanting Mason a part of her life, a part of her baby's life. She wanted him with her when their daughter came into the world, when she first tied on toe shoes, first pitched a softball game, first came home starry-eyed, flushed with the rapture of new love. Taylor had lived her life without Ronald Drummond taking any interest in it; she knew the emptiness that left in a child. She wanted more and better for her own daughter. For their daughter.

But she had no right to go crying to Mason now. Plenty of women managed pregnancy alone. After their daughter was born, then they would work out a sharing of responsibilities. Taylor struggled to maneuver another pillow the length of the sofa to tuck under her aching feet. She wished she felt as tough as she talked. She desperately wished Mason could be by her side during her Lamaze class tomorrow.

Which, of course, was impossible. Even if she had given in and agreed to meet Mason, Taylor Drummond, news anchor, could no more show up at a Lamaze class with a man by her side than she could squeeze into a size six pair of Levi's. With her very public pregnancy, that story would lead the six-o'clock news, and Taylor, as soon as Grady Hutchings found out, would find herself bringing up the tail end of the unemployment line.

No, she'd brave the Lamaze class alone. Besides, even if she could ask Mason, she'd only be tormenting herself. His very presence would be torture, having him next to her yet unable to express her love, unable to breach the barrier of their complicated situation.

The next day, as she drove to the Lamaze class, Taylor wondered again about her mother's attitude. All her life, Taylor had felt rejected by, and driven away from, her parents. One of these days, she was going to ask her mother why. Taylor had ceased to believe it was all her fault.

Carrying her own child in her womb had changed that belief. Hating a part of yourself took a reason, and a darn
strong one.

Everyone else at the Lamaze class was one half of a
couple. Taylor told the teacher, a tiny woman in black
Danskins, that she had come by herself. The woman
looked at her as if she had three heads.

Sitting on the floor, watching the woman next to her
lean back against her husband's chest, watching his arms
come around to circle her distended abdomen, Taylor was
swept with the most overwhelming feeling of loneliness
she had ever experienced. After a lifetime of exclusion—
from her family, from the in-group at school, from the jo-
vial companionship of the other associates when she'd
been so intent on working her way to the top—she had
thought she could handle having a baby by herself. But a
baby wasn't an independent-study project; making a baby
was an act of sharing. During the class, while the other
women gave her occasional sidelong glances, she found
herself reviewing and rejecting every reason she'd ever
enumerated for refusing to see Mason. Watching the other
couples, feeling in her gut the shared experience the class
was meant to be, she realized none of that mattered now.
She needed him.

An hour later, Taylor hovered over her phone. She
hadn't called him from her car phone because she didn't
want to appear too eager, as if she had had to ring him up
right that instant. Instead, she'd driven back to her apartment, and while changing for work, paced back and forth
past the phone in her bedroom, then into the kitchen to
stare at the blue telephone mounted on the wall next to the
stove.

She was never this nervous when she rang him at the
office to deliver a brief report of the baby's prenatal development and of her health. But now that she was about to
permit herself the luxury of seeing Mason again in person,
she didn't know what to say to him.

She paused in front of the small mirror hanging in her
entry hall and practiced a few phrases. "Mason, this is

Taylor, and I—" *And I love you and want you and need you.* "Hello, Mason—" *Please drop whatever you're doing and rush over here.*

"Get a grip on yourself, Drummond," she muttered, and advanced on the kitchen phone. Reaching for the receiver, she pictured Mason as he'd looked that day he'd come to offer to father her child, uncomfortable and awkward and, to her eyes, so adorably wonderful.

She dialed the number of the law firm and waited, feeling a blush build on her cheeks, fanning her face with her hand. After answering Hildy's inquiries on her condition, she shifted from foot to foot, wondering just what she'd actually say when Mason came on the line.

"Taylor, is everything okay?"

He sounded so good, so close, so concerned. "Everything is fine, Mason. I'm sorry to bother you, but I need to ask you a favor."

"Anything." His voice was emphatic.

"Would you meet me tomorrow at Denny's on Sunset?" She pushed the words out in a rush, before she could chicken out.

Silence. On the other end of the phone line, Mason stared at the mouthpiece, fighting a desire to jump from his chair and shout, "Yahoo! The woman finally came to her senses!" Two clients sat across from him, probably checking their watches so they could figure out later whether they were billed for his time out to take this call. But none of that mattered to him right now. Taylor wanted to see him.

"Name the time." He grabbed his pen.

"Eleven A.M.," she said softly.

Mason paced the sidewalk in front of the coffee shop, a stuffed panda stuck under his arm. The last three months had been hell. Taylor had refused to see him since the day he'd stormed the studio and demanded the truth from her. The occasional phone calls from her at the office raised, then dashed, his hopes. His days, he spent billing extra hours, to avoid thinking about his life. His evenings, he spent ignoring and being ignored by a very unhappy Jillian, who professed sobriety and didn't seem to think he could tell how often she gargled mouthwash to cover her secret drinking. Day by day, the tension built, increasing the anxiety he experienced waiting for Taylor to reach out to him.

Now his sentence of banishment had been commuted.

She hurried toward him, skipping every other step, pushing her purse strap back onto her shoulder. As she came closer, he saw her eyes fastened on his, the sparkling blue turned dark and intense. He waved a hand and smiled. Her face lighting up, she smiled in return, and closed the distance between them.

She was heavier, in a way Mason found touching, reminding him of a pre-Renaissance Madonna. Used to Jillian's air of emaciation, he reveled in the robust health Taylor projected.

Stopping a few feet away from him, she said, "Hi, Mason," as shyly as a nun released from a convent.

He resisted the temptation to pull her to him and kiss her in front of the coffee shop doorway. "Thank you for asking me to meet you."

She nodded, looking, despite the glow to her face, vaguely embarrassed. Studying that look, Mason wondered whether she was concerned over his reaction to the changes in her body.

"Motherhood suits you, Taylor."

She blushed. "Thank you. I guess."

"You are the most beautiful pregnant woman I've ever seen."

"I don't know. I'm as big as the *Hindenburg.*"

He checked his desire to reach out and smooth the look of dismay from her face. "I say you're beautiful, and anyone who disagrees can take it up with me." He handed her the panda.

She smiled and clutched the stuffed animal to her belly, as if introducing it to her baby. "Thank you, and thanks for coming to meet me. I'm sorry I didn't call you sooner. Things have been hopping at the station, and there was the fire last week in the Santa Monica mountains, and we were short two reporters. Plus I'm working on an idea for a news show with a magazine format. And . . ." She glanced down at her feet.

"And you weren't sure whether you should or not?"

"Yes."

"It's okay." He tipped her chin up, searching her eyes, wanting her to know he would support her in any way she would allow him to. "I'm here for you." Releasing his hand, he added, "And for our baby."

"I know, Mason." Taylor pointed toward the door, and they headed inside. "But I got myself into this and thought I could tough it out. I actually feel a little foolish calling in the guard at this point."

Pointing to her belly, he said, "You didn't do that by yourself."

"We agreed not to talk about certain matters."

He opened the door for her and held his tongue. Weeks ago, during their first phone conversation, she had made him promise not to talk about their past. She said they had no present or future, that any help she asked of him was strictly for the baby's sake. He was willing to take the relationship, as Fielding would say, one day at a time. He'd promised himself not to mention Jillian unless she asked, and not to tell her he had moved into his own section of the house, and a separation was imminent. This time he planned to do things right.

They settled into a booth and accepted the menus the waitress handed them. Food was the last thing Mason was interested in. At long last, being allowed to feast on Taylor's exquisite features, glowing in the bloom of pregnancy, was more than he could ask for. He put aside the laminated photos of hamburgers and said, "I'm very glad you called me. I hate that you have to go through your Lamaze classes alone." He leaned closer and said in a soft voice, "I'm sorrier than words can say that you've been so alone for months." *But you won't be alone much longer,* he vowed silently.

"Mason, I—"

"It's okay. Let's talk about the Lamaze classes." He pulled a paperback copy of *Six Practical Lessons for an Easier Childbirth* from his pocket. "Let's see . . . I reviewed this section last night—body changes during pregnancy, and the three stages of labor."

"I'm impressed. And touched."

"The least I could do was be ready when you called."

Reaching for her water glass, she paused. "How did you know I would call?"

"Father's intuition."

"Fair enough." She loved the way he smiled when he said that. Not once had she given him any reason to think her request to see him was an invitation to pick up with their relationship where they had left off on the day of their child's conception. But looking at him now, sitting across the table, admiration and love showing in his expression, she found it difficult to adhere to her own conditions. She was allowed to spend time with the father of her child; she was not permitted to be in love with him.

The waitress appeared, order pad at the ready.

Taylor glanced at her unopened menu, unable, despite how much she'd been eating lately, to think of food right now. "Will you give me a few more minutes, please?"

Mason turned a page in the book, concentrating on the text. He knew what he wanted to ask her, but feared she might withdraw at the suggestion.

Taylor thought of yesterday's class, how she had lain on her mat, alone, squeezing her eyes shut against the sight of all the other couples, hand in hand, following the instructor's directions. The baby kicked, and Taylor sent her a silent good-morning. She took a deep breath. After all, this was for the baby's sake.

"Mason, when I called, I said I wanted to ask you a favor."

"Yes?" He'd said, "Anything." And meant it.

"Well, the thing is . . ." Taylor knew she was blushing. She traced the picture of the Slam-Dunk breakfast with her fingertip. "I would like to ask you to practice Lamaze with me. As my coach. At my home."

"Taylor—"

"And you must understand this is strictly for the baby's sake. Nothing else." There, she had to say that before she saw any hope or thought of a future for the two of them appear in his eyes.

"For you and our child, I will do whatever you need me to do." He pushed back his sleeve and checked his watch. "I don't know about you, but I couldn't eat a thing. If you want to practice, I say let's start now." *Now, before she changed her mind.*

Taylor moved faster than she had in weeks, urging her body free from the booth. She didn't want to give herself time to argue the wisdom of her actions. She collected the panda, and smiled as Mason thoughtfully left a tip on the table for the waitress's trouble.

Thirty minutes later, they faced each other across the length of her living room. Trying not to think about the last time they had been together in her home, Taylor watched as Mason once again produced the book. He seemed so calm and practical, like a nurse, that she felt silly letting her mind run wild with memories.

"First," he said, "we'll practice neuromuscular control exercises." Mason extended a hand and settled her carefully onto the thick carpeting. She didn't need his assistance, but she accepted it, indulging in the luxury like a woman wallowing in a bubble bath with a huge glass of ice water after running a marathon.

He raided pillows from the sofa, tucking one under her head and another under her knees. Control, he reminded himself, was what this exercise was all about. And it was a damn good thing for him to remember. Being this close to Taylor for the first time in so long, it took every ounce of control he could muster to keep himself in check. He wanted to bury his face in her hair and inhale her precious scent. He wanted— He pulled his unruly thoughts back under control, then knelt beside her.

"Now to relax," he said, amazed at the irony of his words.

Taylor tried to mimic yesterday's commands, urging her

limbs to go completely limp. It was Mason's job, as her partner and coach, to check to see how relaxed she was. She tried to will her muscles to a state of nontension, but with him so close by her side, she found it nearly impossible. When he reached for her right hand, she tensed in anticipation and giggled. "Sorry," she said, stifling a second giggle. "I guess I'm nervous."

He touched the back of her hand, tracing a soothing path lightly from her wrist to the tips of her fingers. "Shhh. Think of some place where you're absolutely safe and happy."

She closed her eyes and concentrated on how nice his touch felt, remembering how secure she was within his arms. Slowly she relaxed the muscles of her arms, then her legs. He lifted her right hand and wiggled it. She didn't resist, and he did the same with her left. Then he placed his hands under her knees to test the tension in her legs. She started to react by tightening the muscles. "Relax," he said, "then open your eyes."

Taylor looked up at him. Her bent knees reached midway up his chest. He hadn't held her since the day they had made love, the day they had conceived their child. More than seven months. She whispered, "I'm glad you're here."

His answer came in the gentle way he assisted with the relax-and-contract commands and in the way his smiling eyes strayed to the bulge of the baby.

When they paused to rest, Taylor remained lying on the floor, and Mason sat cross-legged next to her. Feeling shy, but thinking how he kept watching her swollen abdomen, she said, "Would you like to feel the baby?"

"Could I?"

She guided his hand and held it against her.

"It's so hard." He seemed surprised. "I thought you'd be soft."

"You obviously don't watch my newscasts, with their in-depth coverage on the process of baby making." She moved his hand across, seeking a kicking foot or jabbing hand for him to experience.

"I do watch you."

He spoke lightly, but she felt herself tense. Just then, the baby kicked outward, against Mason's palm. He started. That was his little girl! The thought suddenly made him feel very humble, yet proud, too.

"Does that hurt you?"

She shook her head. "She likes attention, and right now it's her way of getting it."

Mason circled his hand over the spot where the baby stirred and shifted. "She'll get all the attention she ever needs. I promise that." Reluctantly he removed his hand and helped Taylor to her feet.

"Same time tomorrow?"

"Oh, Mason, I don't think so."

"No tricks, Taylor. This is important for your own health, for the delivery, for the baby. I could drive over before you leave for work, help you, and zip back downtown."

She closed her eyes. She couldn't see him every day; her resolve would crack.

"Every other day?" he pressed her, determined not to be pushed out of their lives again.

"Once a week."

"Twice a week. You go to your class on Mondays, and I'll come over on Wednesdays and Fridays."

"Has anyone ever told you what a tough negotiator you are?"

Mason smiled. "Is that a yes?"

"Yes."

"I'll be on my best behavior." Holding out his hand, he said, "See you Wednesday."

She shook it, all business, then closed the door after him. Watching him from the window, she wondered at her disappointment at his propriety. As a prescription for what ailed her, passionate lovemaking sounded far superior to twenty repetitions of the Kegel exercise.

Chapter 20

"YOU DID WHAT?"

Jillian held the receiver away from her ear. Her sister sounded even angrier than Jillian had expected.

"I invited our mother to stay at my house. I don't know why that should be so upsetting to you." Only, Jillian did have a pretty good idea; after listening to Claudia rag on the subject of Taylor's unborn child, she knew.

"Just don't expect me to visit."

"But, Taylor, I haven't seen you in months. Mason and I miss you, and—"

"You haven't seen me because you have chosen not to see me. You've been avoiding me as if you think pregnancy is a contagious disease."

"I'm sorry, all right? My life has been unsettled." Jillian glanced around her bedroom, kicking the covers on Mason's side of the bed. She mussed them every morning so the maid wouldn't know she slept alone. "But I'm turning over a new leaf and I'm inviting you to dinner. Mason was saying just the other night we should have you over."

"I'll come over after Claudia leaves."

"Please come while she's here." Jillian didn't want her mother guessing at any of the yawning cracks in their lives. "For family." Taylor's long pause told Jillian she had scored with that point. "I know you and Mother don't get along, but think of your baby. She deserves to know her grandmother, and if you never bury the hatchet, you're cutting her off from her family, too."

"Jillian, you can stop now. I don't think it's a good idea,

I don't want to come, and I know the entire evening will be a disaster. What day and time?"

"Sunday night, eight o'clock."

"Thanks for the advance notice."

"If I told you too far ahead of time, you'd change your mind."

Taylor hung up. Jillian leaned against her pillows, cradling the phone on her lap. The next thing she had to do before her mother arrived was persuade Mason to move back into their bedroom. Just for the visit, she'd say, and then make sure he wanted to stay by the time Claudia left.

The other problem she had to solve regarding her mother's visit had to do with drinking. Around Mason, Jillian had been careful to hide her drinking. At the few social engagements they had attended during recent months, she had abstained. She allowed herself three drinks a day, and made sure Mason couldn't smell it on her breath. Her mother would expect Jillian to join her in a before-dinner drink and to serve wine with dinner. Jillian had been careful not to mention her stay in the treatment center to her mother. Claudia wouldn't like that at all. When Mason was with them, she could tell Claudia she was on a a diet and stick to mineral water.

Blue jays squawked on the balcony outside her window, doing battle with the resident mockingbirds. They reminded her of Taylor and her, of Taylor and Claudia, of Mason and her. She smiled at her own philosophical thought. Maybe she was beginning to see life a little more clearly.

Throwing off the covers, she leapt from bed. Sleeping naked was such a waste when you had to sleep by yourself. She checked her ribs; yes, they all showed, rigid against her taut flesh. Her breasts had finally started to shrink, too. With less alcohol, more exercise to pass the time, and her lack of appetite for food, she had lost ten pounds. But until now, her breasts had refused to shed any of their fullness. Jillian thought there was something perverse about her body's stubborn refusal; all the fashion magazines said the first place one lost weight was from the breasts. A little more work on losing a few more pounds, and none of those hateful, horrid, ugly, despicable, lecherous men would ever look at her again.

After showering, Jillian opened her underwear drawer. Pawing through it in search of the panties to match the bra she had chosen, she touched the slick surface of the SA book. She jerked her hand back. Standing there naked, she reached for the book, then withdrew her hand. She hadn't opened the book since the day she brought it home and thrust it into the drawer. Since that day, she had exercised rigid control over her behavior. She measured out the portions of alcohol she permitted herself. She kept her eyes off men and didn't even masturbate. Mason, still encamped in the guest room, didn't approach her. So for more than two months, she had gone completely without sex. To her, that proved the afternoon with the man from AA was an aberration. Two months was such a long time.

A bookmark protruded from near the end of the book. She turned to it, cautiously, wondering if Fielding had put it there for a reason. What she found was an address and phone number in Simi Valley, California, to call for information regarding local chapters of SA. She snapped the book shut. The idea of going to a meeting and talking about what she had done with all those men made her ill. Even thinking about it made her queasy, and she couldn't afford to spend the day moping. She stepped into a pair of bikini panties. Claudia hated a messy house; Jillian had a lot of work to do to get the house ready before her mother arrived that afternoon. Slipping on a Wacoal bra, she bent over to adjust the cups. When she did, she spotted the book again, lying there on the stacks of expensive lingerie, lingerie she had purchased to adorn herself as an offering to man after man after man. Jillian touched the cover of the book, lifting the edge slightly. So what if her house was a mess; her life was a far greater disaster. Taking the book, she carried it to her bed and sat down to read.

"Going somewhere?" Mason gestured with the stuffed Roger Rabbit toy he carried to the moving boxes stacked in the entry of Taylor's apartment. He didn't sound particularly pleased and didn't look nearly as happy to see her as he usually did when he arrived for their Lamaze practice sessions.

She opened the door and motioned for him to follow her through the walkway between the boxes. "I'm moving." Taylor wasn't especially happy herself. Her final Lamaze class had taken place on Monday, two days earlier, and she wasn't sure whether to continue with the practice sessions, or do the sensible thing and ask Mason to make himself scarce.

"You didn't tell me you were moving."

"I bought a house."

"You didn't even mention you were house-hunting."

"We don't exactly share our lives with one another." She said it lightly, but she felt a need to jab him with the truth of her words. The intimacy of the exercise-and-breathing practice sessions were grinding on her, stoking both an emotional and sexual tension she felt increasing to a flash point.

He acknowledged her comment with only a nod, dropped the toy on a box, and followed her in silence to the living room.

Taylor took one look at the boxes stacked in there and stopped. "We'll have to use the other room." The only other room with enough uncluttered floor space was her bedroom. After a nervous pause, she led him into the bedroom. Without commenting on the last time they had been in the room together, she sat on the floor, tailor fashion, resting the bulk of the baby slightly in front of her center of gravity.

He took off his suit coat, laid it on the bed, then dropped to the floor beside her. Pulling a stopwatch from his suit coat pocket, he said, in a brisk voice, "Let's get started. Shall we review the stage one breathing first?"

Taylor positioned herself against her futon bed.

"Contraction begins," Mason called.

She took a deep, cleansing breath, as she had practiced many times before. She kept her eyes fixed on a spot

across the room. The instructor had suggested they fix
their attention on their partner's face, but she couldn't concentrate when she centered on Mason. Massaging her abdomen with circular motions, she counted her breaths.

"Fifteen seconds," called Mason, to mark the simulated
length of the contraction.

His calm and distant manner drove her crazy. Each
practice session, he treated her gently, with respect. He ad-
hered to her rule of never talking about "them." He did it
so well, she found herself wanting to talk of nothing else;
but she forced herself to hold back.

"Thirty seconds," he called.

The only time he had shown any crack in his reserve
had been the first time he'd come over to practice and he
asked to feel the baby. Since then, he had kept his interac-
tions strictly impersonal. Not that he wasn't interested in
the baby; every visit, he showed up with stuffed animals
or bootees or books on child development. She couldn't
fault him at all; therein lay her problem.

"Forty-five seconds."

She knew herself well enough to know that if he had
tried to insinuate himself back into her life, as a lover, not
simply as the father, she would have thrust him away. But
this closeness without sharing, this proximity without being able to touch, this nearness of shared purpose without
shared lives, she couldn't abide either.

"Contraction ends."

Trained by now to do so, she finished with a deep,
cleansing breath. Resting her hands on her abdomen, she
let her gaze drop from the point of concentration on the
opposite wall, but carefully didn't look at Mason. He
wasn't going to like what she had to say.

"Do you want to practice the 'stop pushing' command?"

"No." The baby shifted, and Taylor gave her a reassuring pat. Only three more weeks and she would meet her
daughter face-to-face. She was a little bit scared, and a lot
excited. Before that day, though, she and Mason had to
talk about the subjects she had listed as off limits.

"Pushing?"

"Not now. I don't want to do this anymore."

"You told me the teacher said to keep it up. You're only a few weeks from your due date. We don't want to get out of practice."

Lifting her eyes to his face, she said, "I can't go on like this."

He looked puzzled. "It's almost over. You'll be back to your old self in no time."

"I don't mean my waddling around like a platypus. I mean you and me, seeing each other. I can't do it any longer."

He actually lost color under his summer tan. "We're not 'seeing' each other. We're meeting to work together for our baby's welfare."

"We are seeing each other. Right now, this very moment, you're in my bedroom."

"We're not in bed together."

"No. We're not, are we?"

He stared at her. "Don't do this to me."

Realizing her words had sounded like an invitation, she colored. "I hope you don't think—"

"Oh, but I do. I've just lived through five weeks of torture, behaving like a neutered uncle, and this entire time, you wanted me as badly as I wanted you. Not—" he ran a finger under his collar "—that we're going to do anything about these wants."

"I wasn't asking you to do anything," she said stiffly, embarrassed that she had let her defenses slip, and unaccountably pleased at his admission that he wanted her. "It won't work, Mason. You and I, together, sharing the baby, you on your best behavior, me pretending you mean nothing to me. We have to go our separate ways—for the sake of everyone involved. Especially Jillian."

"It's too late to back out now."

"Why?"

He jabbed a finger in the air, pointing it toward her belly. "Because that's my child as much as it is yours."

"That may be technically true, but we did discuss, way back when we undertook the artificial insemination plan,

the possibility that you be considered the baby's uncle."
She knew she sounded stubborn, like a bad negotiator at
the conference table, laying down some totally unaccept-
able offer without really thinking things through.

"And if you remember, I firmly rejected that lousy
idea."

"I don't see why we can't try it that way." Once chosen,
the position had to be maintained.

"I'm the baby's father, not some jerk-off sperm donor."

"I can see it's a good thing we made it through the Lamaze practice without discussing any of this, or I never
would have let you continue." His anger was getting to
her—doubly so because in her heart she agreed with him.
If she hadn't been trying to protect herself from her own
feelings, she would have dropped the argument. Rolling
onto her side, she pushed herself up from the floor. Mason
offered her a hand, and she brushed him away. "Thank
you, no. I can do this by myself. From now on, I will handle everything on my own."

He rose, swift and graceful, the contrast highlighting her
own clumsiness. "You're not shutting me out. I let you
push me away at Christmas because I was in the wrong. If
I let you walk away now, I would be committing a worse
wrong."

"Why?"

"We belong together."

" 'We'?"

"I have absolutely no right to say this, but, Taylor, I still
love you."

Taylor stood unmoving, watching the mix of emotions
play across Mason's face. He regarded her steadily, his
lips twisted as if his words had burned his mouth. He
crushed his hands into his pants pockets.

"Forgive me," he said miserably. "I promised myself I
wouldn't say those words to you until Jillian and I are divorced." He put his suit coat back on.

She wasn't going to let him walk away as if he had just
visited the dentist and scheduled a future appointment. He
loved her, and she loved him. She rested one hand against

her baby. Already her unborn child had taught her about loving. "Mason, I can't let you leave without telling you how I feel."

"We shouldn't—"

"Hush. Jillian is my sister, and no matter how rocky our relationship is, that fact never changes. I worry that she's refused to see me for months. I love you, and despite everything that's happened, I can't stop loving you. But I can prevent myself from betraying her. When I see her on Sunday—"

"Sunday?"

"She invited me over. Don't you know that Claudia is coming to visit you?"

"No." He tightened his lips.

"Well, she is. I don't want to see her, but I want a chance to talk to Jillian. So I said yes. In a way, I'm afraid to go, afraid she'll look at me and somehow figure out the truth about the baby. And it's important to me to feel that I haven't continued to work behind her back to win you away from her."

He caught her hand, thrilling to the warmth of her skin, the feel of her hand once again clasped in his. "I feel just as strongly as you do about Jillian. I'd love you less if you weren't so concerned. Jillian has serious problems, but she is the only one who can face and overcome them. I can't stop drinking or taking pills for her. If I could, I would." Tightening his grip on her hand, he thought of the ghost his wife had become, following him from room to room when he was at home, her head averted so he couldn't smell the liquor on her breath, reciting her breakthroughs in therapy to assure him she'd soon be back to her "normal" self.

He touched each of Taylor's fingers, memorizing the feel of them. To his delight and relief, she didn't pull away. Gazing at her open face and her loving expression, he promised silently to prove himself worthy of her love. With Jillian, he had truly made a mess of things, and it was all for nothing if he didn't learn from the past. For weeks—since he had moved into the guest room—he had fallen asleep dreaming of kissing Taylor, of lying next to her, his arms around her and their daughter. Checking his impulse to devour her with all his bottled-up, zip-locked longing, he kissed her lightly on the forehead and reluctantly released her hand. "We'll be together soon," he said simply.

She took hold of his shoulders. "Mason, I didn't tell you I love you so we could make plans for the future. I don't want any promises." She smoothed his hair away from his forehead and walked him toward the door. "It's much easier to live without them."

He nodded, understanding. After all he had done to hurt her, she was right to say, *no promises*. Actions counted; words piled up, casualties of deeds undone. "I'll see you on Friday, for practice."

He left, and Taylor wandered into the bedroom, knowing she had only a few minutes to change into one of her MothersWork suits and dash to the studio. Mason loved her. She loved him. And he was still married. Nothing had actually changed; yet she felt as if the fabric of her life had been altered. Despite her talk of not wanting promises, she now had hope for their future.

She wanted to feel the same optimism for her sister's future, but she didn't have enough knowledge. At dinner on Sunday, she would finally have a chance to talk to Jillian. Of course, Claudia would be there, but she could find a chance to pull Jillian aside. As Taylor buttoned her blouse, a spasm in her abdomen caught her unprepared. When the pain retreated, she dismissed it as a stronger-than-usual Braxton-Hicks contraction, the technical term for the pains she'd been having lately. She didn't panic, knowing from her Lamaze class it was not a sign of labor. She probably needed to lie down and rest, but she had to go to work. She had arranged for eight weeks off following the birth, and intended to work until the last possible moment. Sid had hinted at her going into labor on the air, or at least faking it, and she had answered him with a chuckle. She drove to work, savoring Mason's touch, massaging her abdomen, and hoping Sid wasn't going to get the last laugh.

What Jillian was about to do was the hardest thing she had ever done; more frightening than the time the tavern cowboy held a knife to her throat, more gut-wrenching than her pitiful attempt to fake a miscarriage, more desperate than her measured overdose.

She sat in her car across the street from a tract house in an unfamiliar area of Los Angeles. The house looked like all the others on the street, California ranch, white stucco, blue trim. A flagpole rose from the dry grass of the front yard.

Yet this house was different.

For an hour she had watched the house. During the past fifteen minutes, three women had driven up, then entered through the front door. Two looked like all the women she knew, could be any one of her luncheon and charity crowd. The third, waddling up the sidewalk in a shapeless floral sack, couldn't have anything in common with her.

Yet she must.

In another minute she would have to walk through the door of that house, too. She'd known since that morning that her only salvation lay in this direction. Curled on her water bed, reading the *Sexaholics Anonymous* handbook, crying, wiping at her eyes with her satin sheets, she knew she had to get in the car and find those other people who were exactly like her. Even though her mother was due in later that day, she'd stumbled off the bed and dialed the number Fielding had marked.

Jillian gripped the seat on either side of her knees. The soft touch of the leather reassured her; her outward world was still in place. Even as she tried to rely on that thought, she knew it to be a lie. Her world had crumbled in front of her eyes, and she had been the one doing the destroying.

Perhaps it was too late to save her marriage. But she could save herself. No more lies. No more pretending. The book had shown her there were others, others with problems more overwhelming than any she had ever faced, and those men and women had sought help and received the aid they needed to change.

Reaching for the door handle, she noticed, for the first time, that another BMW had stopped behind hers. A blond woman, complete with dark glasses, slumped forward over the steering wheel. Her shoulders shook, then the woman seemed to catch herself. She and Jillian stepped from the shelters of their automobiles at the same time. They met on the sidewalk, exchanged shy smiles, and headed into the women-only SA meeting together.

By the time Mason drove into his driveway that evening, eight o'clock had come and gone. He had charged through the day after seeing Taylor, driven by a sense of purpose and buoyed by having found her again. Now he had to sit down with Jillian and have the discussion that had been looming for months. He'd put off the confrontation with her not only because of her instability, but because it was painful to him, too. A year ago he never would have considered a divorce. Now he had come to view a divorce as the inevitable result of the paths their lives had taken. At moments he thought Jillian felt the same way, yet he supposed it was too much to hope for that they would arrive at the conclusion simultaneously. Since her faked pregnancy and miscarriage, he had known this day was inevitable.

Loosening his tie, he left his car and entered the house. He would move to a hotel tonight, then look for an apartment over the weekend. He planned to give Jillian whatever she asked for from their community property, including the house if she wanted it. If all went as well as these matters could possibly go, he would be free to go to Taylor in a matter of months.

Crossing into the kitchen, he practiced his opening line. *Jillian, we need to talk.* The maid looked up from the kitchen table and smiled.

He said hello, realizing he looked forward to living without a domestic underfoot all the time. Of course, Taylor would have a nanny, but somehow that was different. He had never adjusted to Jillian's insistence on live-in help. "Where is Mrs. Reed?"

"They are in the sun-room."

They? He hadn't thought about the possibility of company. He wanted to face the matter without further delay. Stifling a groan of impatience, he straightened his tie and headed for the sun-room.

He heard Claudia's voice before he reached the doorway. If not for Taylor mentioning her visits, this would be the first he had heard of her coming to town. That Jillian hadn't told him irritated him. In the past, he always grinned and bore Claudia's visit, with her constant insinuations that their lives didn't quite come up to snuff, but right now he was in no mood to deal with her. He'd never forgiven her for showing up to visit at Christmas, and now here she was again, as if she sensed when she could wreak the most interfering, meddlesome damage. Well, this time he wasn't waiting for her to leave before he spoke to Jillian.

"Mason, darling," Jillian called from inside the room. "Look who's here. Mother's come for a surprise visit." Jillian waved him in and lifted her cheek for a kiss.

Knowing damn well she had known about the visit, Mason dodged her cheek and offered his hand to Jillian's mother, who obviously hadn't missed his avoidance tactic. He wondered how many other times Jillian had lied and he had been blind and unaware of the facts. "Welcome to L.A.," he said to Claudia.

"Thank you, Mason. I was just telling Jillian how sorry I am that this trip couldn't have been made under happier circumstances."

For the first time, he noticed his mother-in-law wore, instead of her usual bright greens and purples, a black suit. "Did someone pass away?"

Claudia lifted her martini glass. "I'm referring to Taylor's condition."

"I wouldn't call having a baby cause for mourning." As he spoke, he knew he should keep his mouth shut. Claudia clamped on to a verbal challenge like a pit bull to an animal inspector's leg.

"Becoming pregnant with the child of a total stranger is not my idea of giving this family something to be proud of."

"Excuse me," Mason said. "Jillian, may I talk to you in the kitchen for a moment?"

"Anything you have to say, I'm sure you can say in front of Mother." She clasped her hands together in her lap and gave him the remnant of one of her smiles. He noticed her face was puffy, her eyes reddened. At least she didn't seem to be drinking. Given Claudia's half-empty martini glass, he was mildly surprised Jillian had held out. Her mother hated to drink alone. He took Jillian by the hand and tugged her from her seat. "In the kitchen." Claudia or no Claudia, now was the moment for them to face the truth of their marriage.

He made sure the kitchen door shut behind them. Before he could speak, Jillian said, "Thanks for dragging me out. I wanted to let you know I put your things back in our bedroom, so Mother could have her room."

"There is no 'our,' Jillian."

"Don't be silly. Mother is here, and of course you'll sleep with me." She looked frightened.

"When is she leaving?"

"Monday morning."

He wavered, considered telling her he had been called out of town on business. No. They had told enough half-truths. "I won't stay here and pretend our life is normal. We both know it's not. If you can't deal with telling your mother the truth, that our marriage is over, you can tell her I'm on a business trip until then. After she leaves, we'll talk."

"Our marriage is over," she repeated in a whisper.

"Don't tell me this is a surprise. We haven't shared a bed for months. I've been waiting for your health to return before discussing this—"

"It can't be over now. Not now, Mason. Not today of all days. I've finally understood, I know what I've been doing wrong. Please don't say it's over." Her voice rose higher with each begging phrase.

"I'm sorry, Jillian, but it's over."

She covered her face with her hands and swallowed several lungfuls of air. Then she let her arms fall to her sides. In a calm and clinical manner, she said, "Do you think I'll try to kill myself?"

He wished she didn't sound so detached, as if she were asking the question about a character on a soap opera. But he knew only one way to answer her question, which was a simple, heartfelt "I hope not."

"Don't worry. I'm not going to kill myself. And you know why?" she shrieked. "Because you're not worth it!" She grabbed for the counter, picked up the object lying there, and flung it at him.

He had time to duck, but no time to see what it was she had thrown. It wasn't until he heard the thud, then a metallic clank on the floor, that he realized she had hurled a knife at him.

The kitchen door opened and Claudia strode in. "What's going on, children?"

Jillian turned to her mother, the anger that had spurted forth remarkably under control. "Mason was just called away on a business trip, and I'm saying good-bye. Can I make you another martini? I think I'll have one now."

Mason looked at his wife, then at her mother. They stood, shoulder to shoulder, Claudia unflinching, Jillian white-faced, her breath coming in rapid jerks. He turned and went upstairs to pack.

Chapter 21

REUNIONS MADE TAYLOR NERVOUS. SOME-times they were like a first date, with everyone on their best behavior and chatting earnestly about the moments of their lives. Other times, reunions reminded her of married couples together so many years, they no longer minded their manners in front of each other, feeling free to belch without bothering with a "pardon me." The worst kind of reunion, though, was the kind her family specialized in: seething tensions that occasionally fought their way through beauty-parlor manners, only to disappear as quickly as they had erupted, leaving Taylor feeling confused and out of focus.

She had last seen Claudia at Christmas, but with the other guests there to shield her, she had escaped without too much direct conversation. She had last seen her sister seven months ago, prior to Jillian's suicide attempt. The idea of the three of them together with no buffer caused bubbles of tension to rise in her throat. Swinging her car into Jillian's driveway, she wished Mason were going to be at dinner. When he had come to practice Lamaze on Friday, he had reverted to his considerate uncle self, quieter and more withdrawn than usual. Neither one of them referred to their discussion of two days prior. As he left, he had mentioned, without offering an explanation, that he would not be at dinner on Sunday.

The maid opened the door and showed her through the house to the solarium. As they walked, the woman studied Taylor. With a smile, she said, "Your baby is coming soon."

"Two more weeks." Taylor had gotten used to people approaching her with advice, comments, and questions regarding the state of her body. Pregnant women somehow became the communal property of all frustrated caregivers. In Taylor's case, by appearing on-air under Sid's directive of "put that baby to work for Channel Six," the advice came thick and fast. She received letters telling her what to eat, how to exercise, how to breast-feed, why not to breast-feed. She received one letter, illustrated, on how to enjoy sex up until delivery.

The woman cocked her head to one side, as if she were listening to the baby. "No, I think the baby is ready now."

"I wouldn't mind," said Taylor. She had learned to agree with people when they gave her advice, then go ahead with whatever she planned to do.

The maid left her at the door to the sun-room. Jillian and Claudia, their backs to Taylor, lounged in a white wicker seating group at the far left of the room. A few streaks of pink, left behind by the setting sun and the high smog level, lit the room through its glass walls. No lamps had been turned on. In the pleasant half-light, her mother and sister looked amiable enough. Reminding herself how deceiving that appearance was, Taylor entered the room and said a quiet hello.

Jillian turned, hitting a switch on a table as she moved. All around the room, lights flooded on. Taylor felt like an animal caught in the glare of a car's headlights. Her sister moved toward her, her hands outstretched, in a greater show of affection than Taylor could ever remember. "Taylor, I didn't hear you come in. Mother, look who's here." She put an arm around her. "Come sit down. You look ready to drop."

Jillian moved her hands in too many wavy gestures that didn't quite complete the arc of the motion. Her lips formed a smile, but her eyes refused to participate. She wore an embroidered caftan that, despite its flowing fabric, failed to conceal the gauntness of Jillian's frame. The last seven months had not been kind to her.

Taylor crossed the room with her, watching her mother,

who had shifted to face them. Claudia remained seated, a martini glass in her hand. She gazed at Taylor, letting her eyes settle on the bulge formed by the baby. Shaking her head, she said, "Taylor. How nice of you to come."

"Hello, Claudia." Ignoring the message in her mother's voice, Taylor lowered herself onto a wicker settee. Claudia had to know Taylor hadn't appeared willingly; not after receiving that vicious letter. She arranged the cushions for maximum comfort. The pains she had felt earlier in the week had subsided, but her discomfort increased with each passing day. What a relief it would be to have these nine months behind her, though she wouldn't have traded the experience for anything. And if Claudia started in—which she was sure to do—Taylor would tell her so.

"Jillian, my drink needs to be freshened." Claudia held out her glass.

Jillian scampered to her side. Taylor marveled at her sister's dedication to pleasing their mother. At times Jillian seemed to despise Claudia as much as Taylor did; yet she hearkened to her beck and call like a dog trying to please a cantankerous master. "Taylor, can I offer you something?"

She declined. The pressure from the baby on her bladder discouraged satisfying her thirst in a social situation.

From the bar, where she mixed a new batch of martinis, Jillian said, "I'm sorry Mason won't be able to join us tonight. He's out of town on a business trip." She returned with her mother's drink, and one for herself.

Taylor was surprised to see the drink in her sister's hand, but tried to hide her reaction. Seeing her coddling her martini glass as if she had never heard the expression "twelve-step program" was jarring. What surprised her even more was hearing Mason had gone out of town. He hadn't mentioned that to her on Friday, and with the baby's due date so close, surely he would have. Trying to sound uninterested in the answer, she said, "Will he be gone for long?"

"The funny thing about this particular business trip is that it coincides with my visit." Claudia plucked the olive from her drink. "He left Wednesday evening, late, and if I'm not mistaken, he's due back tomorrow night. Odd, isn't it? Not that I mind if my only son-in-law doesn't care to see me. I can handle that more easily than the absence of a second son-in-law."

The challenge had been issued. But Taylor wasn't giving her mother the satisfaction of an immediate argument. For years she had whipped back with a retort as soon as her mother had fired an opening volley. Tonight she would make her work for a reaction. Especially at this moment when she was considering the news about Mason's supposed business trip. He wasn't out of town; he had been at her place only two days ago. With a nervous thrill, Taylor considered the possibility that Mason had moved out, and Jillian was lying to hide the fact from their mother.

Claudia lit a cigarette. "Did you at least think about my advice?"

"What advice is that?" asked Jillian.

"I tried to explain to your sister that she is ruining her life, but she seems to have ignored me." Claudia took a long drag on her cigarette. "As usual, I might add."

The maid came in to say dinner was ready, cutting off Taylor's response. She had almost said the words she had longed to ask for years: *Why do you hate me?*

Jillian and Claudia rose. They stood watching as Taylor struggled to heft herself out of the low-slung settee. Jillian had a scared look on her face, as if she were witnessing the Loch Ness monster coming ashore. Rising finally, Taylor wondered how long it would take for either her sister or mother to acknowledge her pregnancy in any way other than to criticize her life choice. Curious to see how they would react, she patted her tummy and said, "I guess it must be dinnertime. The baby's kicking and demanding to be fed."

All she got from her sister as they walked to the dining room was, "Isn't it uncomfortable being so . . . big?"

"I guess, but it's worth it."

"What's worth it? Having a test-tube child out of wedlock?" Claudia put her drink glass down at the seat Jillian indicated.

"She's not a test-tube baby, and 'wedlock' is a rather old-fashioned phrase."

"I tried to raise you to respect old-fashioned values, not trounce all over them." The words Claudia used indicated anger, but the corresponding emotion did not register on her face. She maintained the same manicured surface look as when she discussed the weather. Her ash-blond hair curled away from her face in a neat bob. Taylor was struck by the resemblance between Claudia and Jillian, especially by how well they prevented their emotions from interfering with their image.

Taylor bit her tongue rather than reply. She had always considered Claudia's concern for virtue to be rooted in her preoccupation with worrying over what the neighbors might say.

The maid served the soup. Jillian said she was thinking of redoing the house. Claudia nodded, commenting that she'd never been fond of the dining room furniture, and Jillian should replace it. Taylor ate her soup and wondered what Mason was doing at that moment and what had possessed her to agree to come to dinner. The maid removed the soup plates and returned with poached salmon, baby potatoes, and strips of courgettes, summer squash, and red pepper. Taylor glanced at her watch, figuring she could escape within the hour. But after another look at her sister, she realized there would be no escape for her until she spoke to Jillian alone. Her sister needed help.

"Have you decided what to do about a name for the baby?" asked Claudia.

"I think so." She and Mason hadn't talked about it yet, and after last Wednesday, Taylor didn't want to decide without consulting him.

"Do you mean the first or last name?" Jillian displayed her innocent troublemaker face. "Do you name the baby Donor Number Three-Oh-One?" She giggled.

Claudia put her fork down. "I simply do not understand why you had to resort to some strange man in some back room performing an unnatural act. If you had tried a little bit harder, or tried at all, you could have found a husband."

"Maybe I didn't want a husband."

"Nonsense. A child requires a father." Claudia tapped a finger against her wineglass, and Jillian refilled it. "A child needs a father to give it a name and a home."

"So that's what a father is for—a name and a home. What about love? What about respect and caring and helping the child learn about life? I had a father, and he never once did any of those things for me. I'll have you know my child does have a father, and she couldn't ask for a better man."

"Well." A light gleamed in her mother's eyes. "So your child wasn't sired through a sperm bank. And this man, this model of virtue, won't marry you . . . because he's already married, isn't he?"

"That is none of your business."

"So that sperm-bank story was just a cover-up? You've been having an affair all along?" Jillian looked shocked.

"I'd rather not discuss it." She had said enough. Too much.

"Well, my dear, you've certainly ruined your life. If this man—whoever he is—has promised to leave his wife for you, I hope you don't believe him for one minute. Men will say that until they're blue in the face, but they very rarely sacrifice the comforts of home. Not for a bloated body and a squalling brat."

Taylor shivered. She hated her mother for saying those things, but part of her feared the truth hidden beneath the venom. She looked at Jillian, golden in the muted light of the chandelier, at the elegant table, the well-prepared food, the competent service. She looked down at her own bloated—to use Claudia's term—belly and pictured the stretch marks on her breasts and thighs and the jungle of boxes in her unfurnished new house. She shivered again when she saw the smug look on Jillian's face. Jillian had every reason to embrace Claudia's sermon on how men never left their wives. "My situation is different."

"Ha." This time Claudia refilled her own wineglass. "It's different, all right. Instead of hiding your condition, you've paraded it in front of a camera for the whole world to see. Do you know what I've had to endure, listening to my friends being so sympathetic when all the time I know they're laughing at me behind my back?"

"If those are the kind of people you call friends, then that's what you deserve."

"Listen to little Miss Morals here."

Taylor pushed back her chair. "I don't have to stay here and be insulted."

"Go ahead. Run away. You've never listened to me. Why should you listen to me now?" Claudia's voice, for the first time in the argument, was going shrill. "Six months from now, when you're sick and tired of carrying the burden alone and go looking for a man, I hope you have better luck finding a father for your bastard than I did."

Taylor stared at her mother. Two dots of pink flaring in Claudia's cheeks were the only physical sign of her agitation. Folding her napkin, Claudia turned to Jillian. "Thank you for dinner."

Jillian was staring at Claudia, too.

"Did you just say what I think you said?" Taylor asked.

"Yes. Your sister is quite an accomplished cook, something you never—"

"Who is my father?"

"Really, Taylor, this is hardly the time—"

"I can't think of a better time to discuss this. You were pregnant with me before you married Ronald, weren't you? Or was I already born?"

In a flat voice, Claudia said, "If you must know, you were six months old when Ronald and I married."

"Six months?" Taylor couldn't take her eyes off her mother's face. "Ronald wasn't my father."

"He was your father. He took us in and provided for you."

" 'Provided'?" Taylor's voice broke on the word. "He

despised me, ignored me, treated me like lint to be flicked off a jacket. Who was my father?"

Claudia looked from Jillian to Taylor, then down at her plate. "I have no idea who your father was," she said tersely.

"How can that be?" Taylor despised her mother, but she couldn't think in terms of her sleeping around. Not her mother.

"You really want to know, don't you? Well, there were a lot of men, a lot of possibilities." Claudia addressed a point on the far wall. "I picked the boy from the best family and pinned it on him. He was all set to do the right thing until he came to the hospital and saw you. You were all red and ugly and hairy, and you screamed and screamed. He ran away and never came back. For six months I put up with you, shrieking day and night, always fussing, never satisfied. My parents threw me out. I had no one. I met Ronald Drummond on the bus on the way home from the welfare office. He stood up and offered me a seat—I was carrying you—during rush hour. I invited him to dinner. We were married a week later." Lighting another cigarette, she added, "So, you see, I know what I'm talking about."

"My God," said Taylor, staring in horror at her mother, her heart thudding.

"It's not pretty, but I'm sure whatever tale you'll be able to share with your daughter will be even more sordid."

No wonder Ronald had treated her as if she were invisible. No wonder he had doted on Jillian. No wonder her mother always acted as if Taylor had ruined her life. Taylor reached out for a sip of water and continued to stare at her mother. The woman was an emotional fortress; nothing infiltrated her defenses. Had that fierce protectiveness of her feelings started when she was a pregnant teenager with nowhere to turn? She remembered the lost looks on the faces of so many of the girls in the family planning clinic. "That's why you always hated me."

Claudia flicked her lighter. " 'Hate' is a strong word."

"But you did hate me. No matter that you went on to

build your life, you married, you had another daughter, you became successful in your own right—and yet you continued to hate me. Why?"

"You wouldn't understand."

"You're right. I don't understand. I was an innocent child." All those years she had thought there was something wrong with her, some fundamental reason she was an unlovable human being, and it was her mother's past that lay behind that rejection. "You were so wrong to take it out on me."

"Wait and see how cozy your own life is before you cast stones at me." Claudia ground out her cigarette with trembling hands. "I simply will not discuss this matter further. What's past is past. I only mentioned it now so you would see I do indeed know what I'm talking about."

"Do you really mean you have no idea at all who Taylor's father is?" Jillian, whiter than the tablecloth, gripped her wineglass.

"I am through with this discussion."

"No, you're not. Not until you answer my question," said Jillian. Looking at the wineglass as if seeing it for the first time, she pushed it away from her.

Taylor studied her sister's face, wondering why the question was so important to her. Jillian certainly knew who her father was. Unless . . .

"It's unlike you to be so waspish. I don't like being interrogated by my daughters—"

"What is your answer?" said Jillian. "Did you have so many boyfriends, you really can't know? Or did you sleep with every Tom, Dick, and Harry you met in the streets? Even after you were married?" Her voice rose as she gripped the tablecloth. "Why don't you know who Taylor's father is?"

Claudia snapped shut her cigarette case. "I think you can draw your own conclusion." Rising from the table, she added, "I'll be leaving tonight. I'm going to pack. You two can sit here and sift through the past if you must." She stalked from the room, her head held high.

Jillian turned to Taylor. "Can you believe that? She

probably did it with the entire football team, and all these years she's acted like such a prude."

"And now we know why. She didn't want us to turn out the way she did."

"She sure failed on that goal." Jillian sounded bitter.

"Thanks for pointing it out."

A shadow seemed to cross Jillian's face. "I wasn't talking about you."

"I'm the one having the baby minus a wedding ring."

Pushing her hair behind her ear, Jillian said, "There are other ways to screw up your life."

Taylor quit thinking of her own problems and looked at her sister. Her mouth was pursed and trembling. "What do you mean?"

Jillian rubbed her temples, then covered her eyes with her hands.

Taylor looked at the scarecrow her sister had become. Softly she said, "Do you want to talk about it?"

Dropping her hands, Jillian said, "I didn't belong in that dry-out clinic. Oh, sure—" her lips twisted as she pushed the crystal wineglass farther from her plate "—not that I don't overdo the booze. God knows I do. But they couldn't fix me in there. They didn't know what the real problem was, and they couldn't know, because I was far too clever to tell them."

Taylor studied her sister's face. "Are you saying you use drugs, not alcohol?"

Jillian gave her one of her what's-your-IQ looks. "For a streetwise reporter, you sure are naive. Alcohol *is* a drug. No, I mean my problem is something else."

This time Taylor waited for Jillian to continue.

"Men," Jillian said, turning her palms upward, a look of wonder on her face. "It's men and sex. Even when I didn't want it, I'd do it. I felt I had to, to live, to feel, to punish. All those crazy emotions, all mixed up, all happening at the same time."

"Men. Plural."

"Oh, yes." Her hair shadowed her face as she shook her head slowly back and forth. "So many men."

Taylor didn't want to hear anymore. All this time she and Mason had been tiptoeing, banking their love, and Jillian had been playing around. Anger rose within her. As she had so many times before, she wanted to shake her sister until that beautiful head popped off her shoulders. Then she saw the tears beginning to drip down Jillian's cheeks, and felt ashamed of her fury. Jillian was sick and needed help. Then she saw, quite clearly, the connection.

"Just like Mother," Taylor said.

Jillian nodded. "'Fraid so."

Pushing back her chair, Taylor started to rise, to go to her sister to offer comfort.

"Stay where you are." Jillian's blue eyes gleamed, the tears gone. "No sympathy. I needed to spill all this out, to keep it from festering inside, and you happened to be here."

Taylor stayed put. "Are you at least getting help?"

Again, her sister nodded. "I went to a meeting today, to a group called—" she choked and whispered the words "—Sexaholics Anonymous. And there were other women exactly like me. One of them told about her father, about him molesting her, over and over and over again; her earliest memories of him are of him rutting over her." Jillian folded her hands on the table. "And I thought I had problems."

"Ronald didn't—"

"Oh, no. It was much more subtle than that." Jillian's face twisted into a grimace. "You were so jealous of my being Daddy's favorite. Well, I would have traded with you in a flash. Fetch Daddy's slippers, mix Daddy's drink, sit on Daddy's lap. I had no life that wasn't pleasing Daddy. It's all I knew. The night before he died, he held me and told me how unhappy he was with Mother and how I was the only one who loved him and understood him."

Jillian was crying again, thick tears making their way unnoticed across her cheeks. Taylor shivered and held her hands over her baby.

"Then he died. Ran smack into a tree and killed himself, leaving me feeling if I'd loved him a little bit more, tried a little bit harder, sat on his lap a few moments longer the night before, he would have lived."

"You had nothing to do with his death. Claudia said it was raining and sleeting. It was an accident."

Jillian shook her head. "All I knew was that I had to try harder to please. And I became so very good at pleasing others. Especially men."

This time Taylor rose and went to her sister. Kneeling, she gathered her in her arms into an awkward sideways hug, allowing for her girth. Jillian offered no resistance, and after a few seconds, returned the hug.

Rocking her sister against her, Taylor said, "All these years I've been so jealous of you and your relationship with Ronald."

Jillian gave a shaky laugh. "And I hated you because Mother always let you do whatever you wanted to do."

Stroking her hair, Taylor said, "We've treated each other so miserably, and so much of that pain could have been prevented." The baby kicked, a swift reminder that although she and Jillian were healing some of the wounds of the past, the truth about her baby cast a shadow of guilt over their reconciliation.

"Well, isn't this touching." Taylor raised her head at the sound of Claudia's voice. Her mother stood in the doorway, now dressed in a bright green pantsuit. "I've called the airline and one of those shuttle services, so you needn't worry about me."

Expecting her sister to see Claudia to the door, Taylor moved back and regained her chair.

Jillian held her mother's gaze for a long moment, but made no move to scurry to her side. "Good-bye, Claudia."

With a sound of disgust, their mother swept from the room.

"That's the first time I've ever heard you call her by her first name," said Taylor.

"My life is changing." Jillian closed her eyes. "It's damn scary to think of moving forward, but I sure can't go backwards. Not anymore." Opening her eyes, she wiped at her smeared eye makeup with the sleeve of her caftan. She sniffed twice; once to clear her nostrils, the second time to identify the foreign perfume on her sleeve.

Foreign, but familiar.

She looked at Taylor, at her blue eyes—the only physical feature they had in common. Right now, those blue eyes brimmed with concern. Jillian sniffed again at her sleeve, the sleeve that covered the arm her sister had hugged only minutes earlier.

The last time she had inhaled that sweet, lingering perfume, it had been mingled with Mason's scent and the musk of an unknown woman.

Taylor was staring at her, a puzzled expression on her face, the concern in her eyes growing by the moment. Jillian let her stare, remembering, counting back. Two days before Christmas she had found Mason's telltale clothing. Almost nine months ago. Her eyes moved to Taylor's protruding stomach.

No longer unknown.

"It's Mason, isn't it?" she whispered.

"What do you mean?"

"Don't lie to me, Taylor. We've lived through too many lies. Tell me the truth. Who is the father of your child?" She spoke much more calmly than she would have believed possible. Her sister had slept with her husband.

Taylor wet her lips with her tongue. "Mason."

Jillian laughed, a wild, whooping laugh that died in a strangled cough. "Oh my God. Oh my God. You really do hate me, don't you? To do that to me. To sleep with him."

"I don't hate you. I wanted you to know when the idea first came up." Taylor struggled to maintain a grasp on a control she didn't feel. For this to come out after she and Jillian had known the first closeness of their lives devastated her. "He offered to be the sperm donor. At first I turned him down, but later I changed my mind."

"Why?" She spat out the word.

"When it came right down to it, I couldn't accept an unknown donor."

"If that's all there was to it, why didn't you tell me?"

"It went beyond that." She glanced away, then back to Jillian. The least she could do was look her in the eyes. "I've been in love with Mason for years. He came over to donate, and we crossed a line we never should have crossed. We were only together once." Taylor wiped at her eyes. "I'm so sorry."

"Once." Jillian let her eyes fall to Taylor's stomach. "No wonder he believed me when I told him I was pregnant. He must be Mr. Fertility."

"I didn't tell him the baby was his until he figured it out, sometime in April. I wasn't going to see him again."

"You mean you weren't going to after I tried to kill myself?" Jillian laughed again. "There's a magical power in suicide. Once you try it, people are afraid of you, afraid you'll do it again. But don't worry. I'm not going to die; I'm going to live."

"My decision had nothing to do with your overdose. I saw that Mason intended to stay with you, and that was the end for me."

"But at one time he told you he was leaving me?"

Taylor nodded, unable to say the *yes* aloud. Her sister's eyes burned in her gaunt face. Jillian's words about choosing life over death hadn't done much to reassure Taylor as to how her sister might react.

"And you believed him?"

Taylor nodded again.

Jillian jumped from her chair and paced next to the table. "Well, you were right to believe him. Because he is leaving me. And right now I want him to." She swiped at her eyes. "I can't hate you for this. I want to, but after tonight, it's impossible for me." She gripped the back of a chair and leaned over the table toward Taylor. "And do you know why I can't hate you? Because I stole him from you in the first place."

"He chose you."

"Oh, no. Don't you remember, after you received that job offer in North Carolina? You told me how desperately you wanted Mason to beg you not to take the job. Yet you wouldn't go to him and tell him how you felt. But I went to him. Oh, yes. I went straight to his office and told him how much you wanted the job and were only waiting for his blessing before jumping at the chance to get into television full-time." Jillian rocked back on her heels. With a look of wonder on her face, she said, "I think he's always loved you. He was just too stupid to know it."

Taylor was still trying to digest what Jillian had confessed. "You did that?"

"I needed him."

"Why Mason? Why not some other man?"

"He was convenient, and stable, and if I hadn't married, Claudia would have dragged me back to Chicago. I had dropped out of design school, and she would have found out. Like I said, I needed him."

"But you didn't love him."

"What we had was good enough for me."

"That's so sad. Did you ever think about me when you were telling him those lies?"

Jillian sat down again. "Did you think about me when you were screwing my husband?"

Taylor let her face fall into her hands. She had no answer to that question. She heard Jillian get up. Then she felt a hand on her shoulder. Lifting her head, she saw that Jillian had come around the table and now stood next to her.

"I shouldn't have done what I did," Jillian said. "And don't think because I'm apologizing that I'm not furious at you for what you've done. I'm hurt and angry and sickened. But I set the chain of events in motion way back when." She dropped her hand and tucked her hair behind her ears. "I haven't been well lately, but I think after tonight I just may have a chance at getting better."

Taylor turned, and for the second time that evening, opened her arms to Jillian.

The next day, Taylor delayed going to work. As she drifted through the sparsely furnished rooms of her new house, her thoughts meandered from Jillian and Claudia to love and manipulation; from Jillian and Ronald to love and guilt; from her unknown father to love and abandonment; from Mason to the beginnings and endings of love.

Last night she had experienced the first moments of love she had ever felt for her sister. And that love had been born of the revelation of her own betrayal, plus that of their parents and of Jillian's husband.

She paused in the baby's room, the only room she had found time to arrange and decorate. Sunlight entered through the opened white shutters, striking the mobile over the crib to send shadow figures dancing across the mattress. Taylor smiled at the cheerful sight and patted her tummy. Only two more weeks. Picking up one of the frilly dresses from the pile of gifts from the shower given for her at work, she thought of how her own baby had been given life out of the demise of another's love. If Mason hadn't been ready to part with Jillian, he never would have offered to father her child.

Beginnings and endings. Endings and beginnings.

When she couldn't put it off any longer, she went to work. She stopped first at Sid's office. His health had been failing rapidly the last few weeks. He wouldn't allow anyone to inquire after him, and the word "death" was never mentioned. Her heart went out to him. As young as she was, and so close to giving birth and sharing a new life, she couldn't imagine what it would be like to be saying good-bye to life. Sid wasn't even fifty.

Several people were clustered outside Sid's office, all wearing the grim yet excited look of spectators of an accident. Taylor pushed her way through. Two paramedics were lifting Sid onto a stretcher. She took his hand and stifled her impulse to cry out words of sympathy. Sid would hate that.

He looked up from the stretcher, his face gray, his thinning mustache drooping over the grooves worn on either side of his mouth. "Babe, take care of that kid, and make that fuckhead of a father marry you."

The attendants lifted the stretcher, and Taylor let go of Sid's hand, holding back the tears she felt tugging at her eyes.

"And cut your hair," he called from the doorway.

Taylor went on air that evening with a heavy heart. Only her strong sense of professionalism allowed her to produce a smile when the floor manager counted down to opening. Sid was profane, rude, vulgar, obstreperous— almost any derogatory adjective fit him. Yet, as the flesh had withered from his fame, he had mellowed, in a Sid sort of way. For her baby shower, he had given her and the baby a twelve-foot gorilla he had flown in from F. A. O. Schwarz.

Burke finished a story on a gang shooting and fed her a line, so she could lead in to the commercial. She opened her mouth, expecting the proper words to come out. A piercing cramp ripped through her abdomen. The words were replaced by a moaning gasp. She clutched her belly. Instead of simply picking up with the missed line, Burke smiled into the camera and said, "Folks, stay tuned as Taylor Drummond goes into labor. And remember, you saw it here first on Channel Six."

Then they went to black for commercial inserts. The floor manager hurried over. Taylor straightened and gave everyone a weak smile. "I don't know what happened. And, Burke, how could you say that? I can't be going into labor. The baby isn't due for two more weeks."

"The stork doesn't always follow the timetable," quipped Burke.

Patty, the floor manager, asked, "Is that the first contraction you've had?"

Taylor nodded, thinking back over the last few weeks. She'd had numerous Braxton-Hicks contractions, which is what this one must be, too. This pain simply caught her unawares, when she was absorbed in the newscast and not expecting it. If she thought she was actually going into labor, she would get Reggie to call in the weekend anchor on the double and leave the newsroom. But time after time the Lamaze instructor had told them about cases of false labor and of women rushing to the hospital at the first cramp.

"I'll be fine," said Taylor.

"Thirty seconds back," called the floor manager, looking with concern at Taylor as she moved out of range of the camera.

As soon as they were rolling again, Burke said, "Many of you have followed with great interest the approaching birth of our very own television baby." He gestured toward Taylor, and camera one framed them in a two-shot. She smiled, reflexively. "It's safe to say, judging by the pain Taylor has been hiding so valiantly, that the little one will be with us before tomorrow night's broadcast."

Taylor couldn't believe he scrapped the next news story to discuss her contraction on-air, but his doing so fit in with the rest of the summer's programming designed to draw ratings by capitalizing on her mommyhood. The poor producer in the booth would be frantically deciding what copy to cut to accommodate Burke's ad-libbing. She kept her calm outward appearance as she made a mental note to make sure she quit working before she actually went into labor. If Burke could make this much fuss over one false labor pain, she hated to think what he would do on her due date.

To reassure the viewers, at the risk of confusing them, she took a moment to mention she was not in labor, then read the next news story.

Her denial didn't stop August Rivers, when he read the weather report, from predicting sunshine and a bouncing baby girl. The sportscaster, reporting baseball scores, quipped, "Taylor, zero; baby, ten."

Fifty minutes passed and no other contraction occurred, confirming her conclusion that the spasm had not been a true labor pain. Taylor began the closing segment. Her body was wracked with another slice of pain, stronger and more intense than the prior one. When she was able to speak, she mustered a wan smile, and said, "Don't try this at home, folks. Take it away, Burke."

Taylor glanced toward Patty, who motioned that the camera was on Burke and that she could slip offstage. In a way, she could hardly believe she was walking away from a newscast still in progress, but with that second pain, she had felt her body's warning. Her daughter wasn't waiting another two weeks before coming into the world. And Taylor wasn't taking any chances.

The next contraction came only fifteen minutes later, en route to the hospital. At the first pain, Patty had shanghaied one of the production assistants, just in case, and had a car waiting for her at the door. Taylor thought it was too early to go to the hospital, and admonished herself for acting exactly the way the Lamaze teacher said so many first-time mothers did, but she couldn't make herself go home and wash out stockings or knit bootees. This baby was on her way.

Mason had spent the day out of the office, signing a six-month lease on an apartment he located over the weekend, checking into rental furniture, and having a far more civil discussion about divorce with Jillian than he had believed possible. In six months the divorce would be final. He had asked Fielding to meet him that evening. He wanted to let him know his plans for a separation. Jillian would need support through the divorce process, and she seemed to respect and like Fielding. He had returned to private practice, so Jillian could meet with him as either friend or therapist.

Mason drove to the Hollywood Bar, another one of Fielding's old haunts, where they had agreed to meet. The television battled with the jukebox; this place lacked the clannish atmosphere of The Huntsman. Mason ordered mineral water, a habit he had acquired from his friend, and waited for Fielding, who was teaching a night-school course in psychology, to arrive.

Fielding entered just before ten o'clock. He looked more at ease with himself now that he had returned to his private practice and to teaching. Ordering a Perrier, he joined Mason at the bar.

The news came on the television, and the bartender started to switch channels. Mason recognized the opening of Taylor's newscast and asked him to leave the set tuned to Channel Six. With a shrug, the man complied.

Mason stirred the lime in his mineral water with a swiz-zle stick. He looked at Fielding and said, "I'm leaving Jillian."

Fielding, looking unsurprised, gestured with his head toward the television, where Taylor was on camera. "You're in love with her, aren't you?"

Mason followed his gaze. At that instant, Taylor clutched her stomach and gasped. He started, spilling his drink. Taylor? In labor? The water ran over the edge of the bar and dripped on his knee as he listened to her co-anchor confirm his question.

The bartender stalked over with a rag. "That's what you get for watching the news. News is too upsetting. It's a lousy way to end a day, watching that claptrap." He mopped the mess and moved off, still muttering.

Mason waited for Taylor to rush off camera, but she remained seated. "Why isn't she leaving?"

"After only one contraction? Mason, she's a professional."

"But that's our baby."

Fielding chuckled. "Relax, Papa. Babies take their time coming out into this world."

"Right. You're right." Mason kept his eyes on the screen. To his relief, Taylor announced she was not in labor, and he was able to pay more attention to Fielding, who didn't seem at all surprised at his confession of fatherhood.

"How is Jillian taking the divorce?"

"She handled it much more calmly than I anticipated. Of course, considering she threw a knife at me only last week, you can see why I wasn't sure what to expect."

"She's a remarkable woman. Confused, but remarkable all the same."

Mason noted the somber look on his friend's face. "I hope she comes to peace with herself. I just know I'm not the man to help her do that." He nervously checked the television, but Taylor seemed normal enough. "She said she might start a landscape and gardening business. I hope she does. That's one thing she's always loved."

Fielding nodded, a smile lightening his solemn mood.

From the television, Taylor shrieked in pain. Mason bolted off the barstool. "She *is* in labor. I've got to go." He was unsure whether he should drive to the station or to the hospital, but decided the hospital would be the best place for him to wait. It was a good thing he had packed their Lamaze bag a month ago and stowed it in the trunk of his car.

"I wish you all the best," said Fielding, tipping his glass to him, and then to himself.

When the nurse finally let Mason join Taylor in the labor room, he thought he had never seen her looking more beautiful. Her hair curled in ringlets, and perspiration beaded her face. She wore a hospital gown and had a sheet draped over her abdomen. When she spotted him, she raised her arms toward him and smiled. He approached her, and another contraction struck. Taking the hand she offered him, he counted with her, as they had practiced together. Only this time, instead of watching the wall as she had done in practice, she gazed into his eyes. When it ended, he leaned to kiss her. She kissed him back, giving him a promise with her lips—a promise that said she loved him, she forgave him, and they would be together as a family with their daughter. Their daughter Sara.

After that, Mason lost track of time. He concentrated on helping Taylor with each increasing contraction. Dr. Richmond stopped by, examined her, looked surprised, and ordered her moved to the delivery room immediately. That was exciting, but after they moved into the room, things slowed down, instead of speeding up. He swabbed her face with a washcloth, cringed when she cried out, handed her tennis balls to squeeze in her palms, massaged her abdomen with talcum powder, and generally felt useless, helpless, and overwhelmed. He almost swore off unprotected sex, watching the agony she was enduring.

But suddenly the doctor said she could push, and she did push, until her pale skin turned purple and crimson, and he feared her blood vessels would pop. After Taylor filled the room with screams that hinted of a primal connection Mason feared no male could ever truly understand, the doctor called, "The baby's head is crowning." Mason pointed to the mirror overhead, and Taylor gripped his hand. "Our little girl has lots of dark hair," he whispered. She gave him a small smile quickly converted to an enormous, face-filling grimace as she pushed again.

Taylor didn't think about the pain. It was too great to quantify, so she let it wash over her in waves of redness that colored the insides of her eyelids as she pushed. At least the pain of pushing was more bearable than the incredible, death-defying act of not pushing when the doctor had insisted it was too soon. She tried to concentrate on Mason. Mason, swabbing her face with cold cloths, rubbing her back, counting the timing of the forces that threatened to rip her body in two. Mason who had loved her enough to give her this child. Mason who loved her and was going to be hers at last.

After Mason told her about the baby's hair, she strained with all the heart-stopping might she could muster. Her abdomen seemed to collapse upon itself, and she knew the baby had come out. A wail, soft and mewling at first, then growing to a pitch that demanded attention, rent the room. From relief, from suffering the pain, from love for her daughter and for Mason, Taylor started to cry.

She stopped as soon as the doctor handed her baby to her. The infant, red and wrinkly and wailing, was the most beautiful sight she'd ever seen. Enraptured by the sight of her daughter resting on her abdomen, Taylor said, "Isn't she the loveliest baby ever?"

Mason touched Sara's tiny fingers and gazed at Taylor's face. As she lay, holding their daughter, a look of ethereal beauty shone from her eyes. Though she had endured pain beyond telling, she radiated serenity and joy he had never before been privileged to witness. In awe of what she had accomplished, Mason smoothed her damp hair from her face. "Next to you," he said, moved to poetry by the miracle of birth, "she's the fairest lady in all the land."

Epilogue
September, One Year Later

SARA LAY FAST ASLEEP ON THE LIVING ROOM floor, surrounded by a nest of brightly colored gift wrap, her new Ariel doll wrapped in her arms. A smudge of birthday frosting crowned the tip of her delicate nose, and Taylor smiled as she knelt beside her daughter.

So many good things had happened, but Sara was the most precious. And by her next birthday, Sara would have a baby brother.

Mason returned from paying the caterer. At the sight of his wife and daughter curled next to each other on the carpet, he was swept with a wave of gratitude for the gifts life had given him. He joined his family. Reaching for Taylor's hand, he said, "The party was wonderful."

She squeezed his hand in response. "I was just thinking about how many wonderful things have happened to us in the last year." Smoothing the tousled locks of Sara's black hair, she said, "We have so much happiness together, I want everyone else to be able to feel the same." With a thoughtful smile, she added softly, "It was good to see Jillian looking so well today."

Mason nodded. He couldn't agree more. "She's finally finding herself." After consenting to the divorce, Jillian had told Taylor she simply couldn't see her until she'd sorted out her feelings, which she was going to try to do with the help of weekly therapy and Sexaholics Anonymous meetings.

Taylor had been worried sick about her sister, but had respected her desire to be left alone. The night of their mother's emotional bombshell, they had both sensed the potential of a fragile rebirth of a relationship, a friendship between the two sisters that had never before been possible.

A week before the divorce was to become final, she asked to meet with Taylor and Mason. She came to their house, pale and scared, yet determined. Taylor opened her arms to her, and Jillian, with a look of wonder, accepted her embrace. When she asked to see Sara and marveled over her miniature and perfect self, Taylor knew her sister had forgiven her.

Mason pulled Taylor close, thrilling to the way the feel of her flooded him with a desire to pleasure, possess, and cherish her. Sunlight, slicing through the smoggy September afternoon, danced a path across the carpet, swathing Sara in a gentle glow. He smiled and tickled Taylor's ear with a kiss. "What do you say we put our birthday angel to bed, then—" he paused to gaze into her eyes and revel in the sight of her love for him "—do the same ourselves?"

With a long and tender kiss, her heart full of happiness, Taylor answered him. Mason cradled their daughter against his chest, careful to include her new doll so she'd see it when she awoke. With a smile, Taylor slipped her arm around Mason's waist and they headed upstairs, a family.